SUCH MIRACLES AND MISCHIEFS

THE CUPIDS TRILOGY
BOOK TWO

Such Miracles and Mischiefs

TRUDY J. MORGAN-COLE

Breakwater Books
P.O. Box 2188, St. John's, NL, Canada, A1C 6E6
www.breakwaterbooks.com

**A CIP catalogue record for this book is available
from Library and Archives Canada.**

ISBN 978-1-55081-902-1 (softcover)

Cover painting: detail of *Astronomer by Candlelight*, oil on panel,
32 x 21.2 cm, 1665, by Gerrit Dou. J. Paul Getty Museum, US.

We acknowledge the support of the Canada Council for the Arts.
We acknowledge the financial support of the Government of Canada through the
Department of Heritage and the Government of Newfoundland and Labrador through
the Department of Tourism, Culture, Arts and Recreation for our publishing activities.

Printed and bound in Canada.

Breakwater Books is committed to choosing papers and materials for our books
that help to protect our environment. To this end, this book is printed on a recycled
paper and other sources that are certified by the Forest Stewardship Council®.

 Canada Council Conseil des Arts
for the Arts du Canada Canadä

Come all you very merry London girls,
that are disposed to travel,
There is a voyage now at hand
will save your feet from gravel.
If you have shoes you need not fear
for wearing out the leather;
For why, you shall on shipboard go,
like loving rogues together.

Peg, Nell, and Sis, Kate, Doll, and Bess,
Sue, Rachel, and sweet Sara,
Joan, Prue, and Grace have took their place,
with Deborah, Jane, and Mary,
Fair Winifred, and Bridget bright,
sweet Rose and pretty Nanny,
With Ursula neat and Alice complete
that had the love of many.

All these brave girls, and others more,
conducted by Apollo,
Have ta'en their leaves and are gone before,
and their Loves will after follow.

—Laurence Price, *The Maidens of
London's Brave Adventures*, 1623?

And it is a wonder to me to see such Miracles and Mischiefs in Men; how greedily they pursue to dispossess the Planters...when so much of the World is unpossessed; yea, and better Land than they so much strive for, murthering so many Christians, burning and spoiling so many Cities, Villages and Countries, and subverting so many Kingdoms, when so much lieth wait, or only possessed by a few poor Savages, that more serve the Devil for fear, than God for love; whose Ignorance we pretend to reform, but Covetousness, Humours, Ambition, Faction, and Pride hath so many Instruments, we perform very little to any purpose.*

—*The True Travels, Adventures and*
Observations of Captain John Smith into
Europe, Asia, Africke, and America, 1630

Author's note: In some places in this book, as in this 1630 text by Captain John Smith, the word "savages" is used for the Indigenous peoples of the Americas. This word is used in dialogue in this novel to convey the historical attitudes and usage of English settlers toward Indigenous peoples. It does not represent the attitudes or opinions of the author or the publisher. For further reflection on the use of language and portrayal of Indigenous people in this novel, please see the Afterword.

Selected List of Characters

THE DIVISION OF CHARACTERS (OTHER THAN THE THREE MAIN characters) based on place is somewhat artificial, as there is much travelling in this story, but for the most part people are grouped according to where we first meet them. Characters marked with an asterisk are historical—that is, their names and the basic facts of their biography are known from historical record.

Main Characters (all from Bristol and living in the New Found Land as of 1613)

Nancy Ellis, servant to Kathryn Guy, later a captive on the pirate ship *Happy Adventure*.

Kathryn Guy, wife of Nicholas Guy, mother of the first English child born in Cupids.

Ned Perry, Cupids colonist, promised to marry Nancy Ellis.

In the New Found Land

*Nicholas Guy, husband of Kathryn. An original Cupids colonist now starting his own plantation.

Jonathan, Alice, Jem: the children of Kathryn and Nicholas Guy.

Bess and Frank Tippet: servants of the Guy family.

Daisy More: servant of the Guy family, sister of Bess Tippet, twice widowed during her first year in the colony.

Tom Taylor: Daisy's second husband, killed in the attack on the Guy family plantation.

Sheila and Gilbert Pike: an English pirate and his Irish wife who have a plantation in Conception Bay; they are the only settlers with no connection to Cupids Cove.

*Philip and Elizabeth Guy: Philip is the brother of Cupids Cove founder John Guy, left as acting governor when John returns to England. They have two young sons.

*John and Anne Mason: later arrivals in Cupids Cove; John Mason becomes governor of the colony in 1615.

George and Nell Whittington: Cupids Cove colonists. George is one of the original colonists, deeply resented by Kathryn, Ned, and Nancy because of his treatment of Nancy in the summer of 1613.

Sam and Sally Butler, Jem and Elsie Holworthy, John Crowder, William Catchmaid: Cupids Cove colonists.

In Bermuda

Omar, a formerly enslaved man taken from a Spanish vessel captured by the *Happy Adventure*.

Master and Mistress Quickly, Hal, Big Willie: English colonists in St. George's.

In Virginia

*Reverend Alexander Whittaker: Minister in the settlement of Henrico.

Hannah and Silas Ridgely, Mary: servants of Reverend Whittaker.

*Pocahontas: daughter of Chief Powhatan, taken captive by English settlers in 1613.

*John Rolfe: English settler who marries Pocahontas.

*Tomocomo: kinsman of Pocahontas; a Powhatan holy man.

*Matachanna: sister of Pocahontas, married to Tomocomo.
Wapuna, Sokanon, Tala: young Powhatan women who are both kinswomen and servants of Pocahontas, also known by the English
names Mary, Betty, and Sally.

In Bristol

Mistress Perry, Ned's mother.
Dickon, Francis, Sal, Betsy, Mary, John: Ned's siblings.
Edward, Rosie, and others: Ned's nephews and nieces.
Master John Gale: Kathryn Guy's father.
Lily Gale: Kathryn's younger sister.
Tibby: Nancy Ellis's aunt, long-time servant of the Gales.
Walter: a former apprentice of Master Gale.
*Thomas Willoughby: a young nobleman who spent 1612–1613 in
Cupids Cove before returning to England.

At Sea

On the *Happy Adventure*

James Sly, captain
Diligence Brown, quartermaster
FitzRichard, bo'sun
Robin, cabin boy
Murphy, a sailor, formerly the cook
Dillon, a sailor

On the *Treasurer*

*Samuel Argall, captain
Collins, quartermaster
Springer, bo'sun
Francis Withycombe and Red Peter, sailors who become friends with
Ned Perry

On the *White Lion*

*Daniel Elfrith, captain
Vines, the quartermaster
Cutty, Davis, Nico, and Sam, sailors

In Lenape territory

*Juan Rodriguez, translator and trader for the Dutch, who remains to
live with the Lenape

PART I

1613–1614

ONE

A Vow Is Sworn

KATHRYN GUY WOULD ALWAYS REMEMBER THE HOURS before the ill tidings came. How strange to think that one could sit in peace, sewing a little smock for a fast-growing infant, enjoying the sunlight and warm breeze off the sea, irritated by nothing more than a few buzzing flies and the haughty tone of the woman who sat sewing beside her.

In those hours she was living in something like a painting or a play; her peace and happiness seemed real but were wholly artificial. Outside the frame, off the stage, tragedy had already struck. Kathryn, seated on the front porch of Sheila Pike's house, was the painted figure, the costumed player, who knew nothing of what was happening outside.

"When I was a girl in Ireland, in my father's great hall, there was a bard used to sing tales," Mistress Pike was saying now. "Have you heard the tale of Dagda's harp, and how it came back to its true owner after being taken in battle? No? You English..." And she launched into the tale, fortunately only saying it and not singing it. Kathryn tried to resist the story, out of her growing dislike for her only neighbour, but she could never stop herself from falling into a tale, no matter who told it.

In the house behind them, Bess Tipton tended to the babies: Kathryn's son and Mistress Pike's. Bess, Kathryn's maid, was a few months from bearing her own child, and Kathryn was glad of her company. She sorely missed her Nancy, dearest friend as well as servant, who with the rest of the Guy family's household was helping Kathryn's husband, Nicholas, at their plantation site down the shore. The Guys had recently moved from Cupids Cove, where the first English settlers had established a small community three years earlier, to their own piece of land, where Nicholas hoped they would make their fortune by fishing and farming. They were hoping to have the new house closed in before winter. On this balmy summer day it was hard to imagine the icy blasts of winter that would strike all too soon. But Kathryn had already survived one New Found Land winter: she knew what lay in store.

Or so she thought, before her husband's shallop pulled up to the Pikes' wharf. Frank Tipton climbed out of it, running towards the house like a man gone mad.

"Mistress! Mistress!" Frank, Bess's husband, was normally a placid fellow; Kathryn could not remember ever seeing him riled. Bess, with a baby on each hip, came out of the house to join the women on the porch.

Frank was breathing hard when he reached them, having run all the way, and it took him a moment to gather his wind to speak. "We was attacked, Mistress. The new house. We think 'twas pirates. They were gone when—but there was a fire and—and—"

Kathryn stood, put aside her sewing, and took her son from Bess's arms, holding him close as if the warmth of his little body were a shield. Pirates? Fire? The warm day grew cold around her.

"Take a moment, Frank. Tell the tale properly. Is anyone—hurt?"

He nodded, his face bleak. "The master is well, Mistress. He sent me to bring you word. Himself and meself and Ned were cutting wood back in the forest when—when they came. Tom was on the place workin' with Daisy and Nancy. We didn't know nothin' of it till we smelt smoke in the air. When we got back—"

He paused again, taking more gasping, ragged breaths.

"Who was hurt, Frank? Was anyone killed?" Fire was one thing: fire could destroy the half-finished house, ravage the land they needed for gardens, strip the trees that should provide their timber. But if all her people were alive, then they could endure such loss.

"We found—Tom, we found him dead. We took Daisy for dead too, for she'd been shot. But she weren't dead yet—I don't know, Mistress, if she'll live or not. We—we lost the house and the storehouse, and a good stand of trees, but in the end we got the fire out. The rain last night—that helped a good bit. When the master sent me up here this morning, Daisy were still breathing—barely. Clinging to life, he said she was."

Bess cried out, sharply, behind her, and Kathryn reached back to draw the maid close to her. Bess had come to the New World with her two sisters, Daisy and Molly—Molly lost to them already, through sickness that first winter in Cupids Cove. "She will live," Kathryn whispered fiercely. "Daisy is so strong—so strong. But—poor Tom..."

Mistress Pike stood up and took her own child from Bess. She fixed Kathryn with a hard look. "So great a loss," she said. "I told you it was wrong, to let your maids go back to the plantation site. They should have stayed here with you." She turned her back and strode away towards where her husband worked with his men turning fish on the flake.

Kathryn had not expected much sympathy from the chilly Irishwoman. And it hardly mattered: she could not take her eyes from Frank's stricken face. The omission in his sad litany, the name he had not said, was as stark as if he had shouted it. The dearest name: dearer by far than even her husband or poor little Daisy.

"What of Nancy?" she managed to say at last.

Frank shook his head. "I'm sorry, Mistress. We found no sign of her. Nowhere about the place. Daisy couldn't talk, to tell us anything of what had happened. Once we had the fire put out, Ned and I searched the woods, thinking likely Nancy had escaped and was hiding."

"She'd not hide. Not once the pirates were gone. She would have come back to help Daisy, or go to find you."

"That's what Ned said, Mistress. Said if she were alive and anywhere on the shore she'd come back as soon as ever she could."

"But you found no—"

"No body, Mistress. Not even amid the fire—the master thought—well, he said we caught the fire soon enough, that if Nancy had been in there when it caught, there'd ha' been—something to find. I'm sorry, Mistress, to put it so blunt. It means she's likely alive somewhere, but—"

Kathryn buried her face in the soft, silken hair atop baby Jonathan's head. Yesterday—all this had happened yesterday, and she knew nothing of it. Had there been a scent of smoke in the air? She thought not; the wind had been blowing the other way. Their plantation house destroyed, faithful Tom Taylor dead, poor Daisy dying. Her husband and Ned and Frank struggling to salvage what they could. And Nancy—her truest friend, her almost-sister since childhood—Nancy was gone. Dead, perhaps. Or captive on a pirate's vessel. Was that a fate worse than death?

"Take me back there," she told Frank.

"Mistress, I—the master would not want that, I'm sure. He told me only to bring you word, and that you and Bess and the babe were safe here for now."

"Are we?" Kathryn looked out over the rolling land of the Pike plantation. She had not felt particularly welcome in the weeks they had stayed here, but she had not thought that the Pikes posed any threat to her family. Yet Master Pike had been a pirate who sailed with the dreaded Peter Easton. There had been little trouble with pirates this year—word from England was that Easton had been taken under the protection of the Duke of Savoy and was now living like a prince—but if there were still pirates marauding these shores, Gilbert Pike would surely know them, might even be in league with them. Was she sheltering in the household of the very folk who were trying to destroy them? The very folk who might, even now, have her dear Nan on board their ship?

"My husband is distraught, no doubt," she said. "I am sure, with more time to think of it, he would agree with me that we must return at once. Bess, pack our things."

"There's not much room in the shallop, Mistress," Frank protested.

"One man, two women, and a babe in arms? Surely you can take us all. 'Tis a calm day."

"I—we might all fit, Mistress. 'Twill be a risk, though."

"Staying here is a risk. Being at the plantation site is a risk as well, it seems. Better we face what risks we can together."

Sheila Pike was approaching the house again, her child in her arms. She must have overhead Kathryn's words, for she said, "Mistress Guy, you cannot think of leaving here."

Kathryn tried to make her own glare as steely as Mistress Pike's. "Our plantation has been attacked and burned. Thank you for your hospitality, but I must be with my husband."

"What will you do? Abandon your plantation and go back to Cupids Cove? I suppose you must." The Irishwoman sounded almost eager.

"We will leave within the hour," Kathryn said, not answering the woman's question. Nicholas Guy's decision to strike out onto his own land, away from the little community of settlers at Cupids Cove, had not been taken lightly, and she knew he would not easily give up the dream of his own plantation. But that was not something she intended to discuss with her neighbour.

The shallop was, indeed, heavily laden, water lapping close to its gunwales. Kathryn, though she wanted to cling to her baby, left him in Bess's care and helped Frank row.

"Were Daisy—did she know you was there, when you saw her? Can she speak? Is she in any pain?" Bess's inquiries came breathlessly, tumbling over one another. Frank's replies were as gentle as he could make them, but it was clear to Kathryn that he expected they would return to find Daisy dead.

Now they could smell the acrid scent in the air, and as they rounded a point of land Kathryn saw evidence of the devastation. Blackened trees fringed the cleared land, and above the stone curve of beach, she saw the remains of the house Nicholas had been building. A few of the timbers still stood, as charred as the trees around them. The walls and roof were gone, the structure gutted by the flames. Their proud new plantation looked like the haunt of ghosts.

She took the baby as Frank helped Bess out of the boat. Nicholas Guy gathered his wife and son in his arms; for a moment, no-one said anything. Ned Perry, another of the family's servants, came down to the shore to join them, and the little group huddled on shore as if at a graveside.

Bess turned to Ned. "Is she still alive?"

"Daisy? Yes, she is—she seems a little better, though she has lost a lot of blood." Ned turned to Frank. "We made a little shelter up there— near where the garden was—take Bess up to see her."

Nicholas Guy was talking now, telling his wife the story she had already heard, how they had come back to find the place burning and a ship putting out to sea. He was talking about the house, about putting out the fire, about the pirates.

When he paused for breath, Kathryn turned to Ned. "What do you think happened to her?"

Nobody had spoken Nancy's name yet, but Kathryn knew that Ned, like herself, would be thinking of little else.

"I believe they took her," Ned said quickly. "We've found no—no trace of her, in the woods around."

"Though we've not had time for a thorough search," Nicholas Guy put in quickly.

"If they'd killed her, or she died in the fire, she'd—her body would be here on the site," Ned said, swallowing hard. "If she took flight into the woods to get away from them, she'd have come back by now. Nothing makes sense but that they captured her." His green eyes stood out stark in his ash-smudged face. "And if they've got her, Mistress Kathryn, we'll get her back. Somehow."

"Of course." Pirates regularly took men for their crews, but they would only hold a woman if she was worth a ransom. A servant girl would not be worth capturing. Nancy would surely have told them that Nicholas Guy would pay well to retrieve his wife's favourite maid.

The baby began to cry. Kathryn felt the milk swell in her aching breasts; it had been hours since she nursed him. "I have to feed him—" She looked at the burned remains of the unfinished house. The men had been sleeping on the ground under sailcloth; Daisy and Nancy, returning to the site to help with the work, had intended to do the same. But it was a different matter for a pregnant woman and one nursing an infant; that was the reason she and Bess had stayed with the Pikes.

"Come up where we've tried to make poor Daisy comfortable—you can sit down there, and nurse the child, and see Daisy. She's sensible, poor maid—she was looking about not an hour ago, asking us where Tom was. She remembers naught of what happened to him, nor to Nancy either." Nicholas led them up from the beach onto the charred grass, past the still-smouldering ruins.

8

"I knew you would want to be here, but in truth, 'twere best you had stayed with the Pikes till I came for you," he added. "'Tis all very rough here, and I know not what we ought to do—my mind is mazed."

A sheet of sailcloth was stretched between several charred tree trunks. Beneath it, cushioned on a few cloaks, lay Daisy, her weeping sister beside her. Frank sat on a fallen log, and Kathryn joined him there. She had to tell her husband, soon, of her suspicions about Gilbert and Sheila Pike, why she could not have stayed there. But right now there were more pressing matters.

Daisy's face was so white. A bloodstained bandage on her side and another on her arm showed where she had been shot. Not in the heart or the guts anyway—in the hands of a skilled surgeon, she might recover. But there was no surgeon, and she was hardly recuperating in rest and comfort.

"Tom—what's become of my Tom?" she murmured. Her lips were almost as pale as her face.

"Now my sweetheart, don't you worry yourself about Tom, all's well, you just need to rest, so you'll get better," Bess said, trying to sound soothing through her own tears. She was crouched, as well as she could with the babe in her belly, at her sister's side, holding Daisy's hand. "Everything is all right, all is well."

Could anything be further from the truth? Kathryn wondered. Frank rose and left the shelter to join Nicholas and Ned outside, pacing the burnt ground, surveying the damage.

Ned Perry ducked into the makeshift tilt and knelt beside Kathryn. "How is she—?" He gestured towards Daisy.

Bess looked up. "She's holding on. I'll have a look at that dressing now, in a little bit. Was it you dressed it for her?"

"No, Frank."

"So you know not—how deep the hurt was?"

"Frank said it seemed she was grazed by a musket ball, but she'd lost a lot of blood before we found her. We don't know, you see, how long—before—at least, their boats were gone and their ship pulling up anchor before we arrived. So she may have been...."

His voice trailed off. Daisy had lain there, bleeding, in pain, after her husband was cut down. What had Nancy been doing while all this happened? Struggling against captivity? Kathryn tried to imagine. It was all, all her fault that Nancy was here, not scrubbing out trenchers in an English kitchen, living the life she'd been bred for.

Ned stepped out of the shelter where Daisy lay. A few minutes later, when the baby was sated, Kathryn tucked her breast back into her kirtle and followed him outside.

"I am so sorry," she said to Ned.

"I was going to say the same, Mistress. I brought her back here—she would ha' been safe with you at the Pikes' plantation."

"She wanted to come back. And what could you have done against a pirate crew? Like as not Tom tried to defend Nancy and Daisy, and paid for it with his life."

"Better I'd have been killed than her captured."

She looked into Ned's face. She had known it for so long as a boy's face, but he was a man now. They had been children together in her father's house in Bristol. Herself and Nancy and Ned. And now here she and Ned were, on the rim of the world, without Nancy.

"I don't know if I ought to tell you," he went on, his voice rough, "but Nancy and me, we were—well. We pledged troth to each other. The night before—on our way back here. I told her what was in my heart, and she promised to marry me." He glanced up, and Kathryn read the unspoken part of the story in his eyes. She felt glad, for a moment, that Nancy had known that brief happiness at least. Glad, then a great fall of sadness, like plunging off a cliff into the sea.

"She is out there somewhere, Ned. If they wanted to ransom her—would they not send word?"

He nodded. "To Cupids Cove, perhaps. They'd not come back here."

"Or they might—" she had not even told her husband, yet, of her suspicions, but it seemed very natural to tell Ned. "The Pikes—you know that Master Pike sailed with Peter Easton. And the mistress is Irish, and Ireland is a hotbed of pirates. Perhaps Pike still has dealings with these pirates. They might send a message through him to demand Nancy's ransom."

Ned frowned. "But why would Pike pretend friendliness to you and the master if he be in league with pirates who would burn us out and drive us from the shore?"

"I—I know not. I might be wrong—all this has come so sudden, and I'm fair mad with worry for Nancy. But I will speak of it to my husband."

Ned reached out and touched one of her hands, cradled around her son's small body. "I mean it, Mistress—what I said. 'Tis a solemn vow to me, as solemn as the vows I made with Nancy. I will find some way to go after her. To the ends of the earth."

A Search Is Begun

H E WENT INTO THE WOODS BEFORE DARKNESS FELL, searching. It was madness—he had told Kathryn all the reasons such a search made no sense—but Ned could not help himself. What if Nancy had hidden in the forest and been attacked by a wild beast? Or fallen over one of the sharp cliffs into a deep ravine? Even if she had died in the forest—at least he would have her body and know there was nothing more to be done.

Every muscle in his own body ached. Two nights ago, he had lain on the moss-covered ground with Nancy in his arms, every dream he'd cherished finally come true. There had been little enough sleep that night. Last night, he and Frank and Master Nicholas had worked through the darkness, aided and soaked by the rain, to put out the fire. Now he could not imagine lying down to sleep, but he supposed at some point he would drop in his tracks with exhaustion.

He stumbled back to the plantation, finally, through the blackened tree stumps and burned-over brush. They had been lucky to catch the fire as soon as they did, lucky for the rain that came down so heavily just a few hours after. The destruction could have been much worse.

Tom Taylor had not been lucky. Daisy More had not been lucky. And Nancy Ellis, the woman he loved, would need more than luck, if indeed she still lived.

They slept on the ground under sailcloth that night, as the men had been doing all along since clearing the land. Kathryn and Bess tended Daisy's wound and soothed her fever. To his own surprise, Ned did manage a few hours' sleep. In the morning Nicholas Guy sat down with Ned and Frank amid the ruins of what was to have been his grand manor house.

"We must return to Cupids Cove, of course," the master said. "Mayhap once there we can find out what they know of these pirates. I still intend to build on this site, but 'tis too late in the season to begin again. Next year, God willing, we will return early in spring. I've no intention of letting pirates drive me away from my land."

"What of Daisy, sir?" Frank said. "Would she survive the trip to Cupids Cove? And my Bess— she'd be best off, I 'low, down there where there's proper shelter and other women about, but she's fair distraught over her sister."

Nicholas Guy shifted uncomfortably on the fallen tree trunk he had taken for a seat. "In truth, I first thought Daisy's hurts were such that she would not live out the day. If there be hope of her recovery, 'tis all the more reason to bring her back to Cupids Cove, where she might rest in greater comfort."

"And what of Nancy?" Ned felt the harsh rasp of his own voice, perhaps because he'd breathed the smoky air here for two nights and a day. "There's no trace of her in the woods about—I searched. They must have taken her—the pirates."

Again, Nicholas Guy looked uneasy. It occurred to Ned that the master had never imagined himself in a situation where he would have to be concerned about the fate of servant girls—whether they lived or died, whether they were captured by pirates. Daisy had lived in his household for a year—Nancy for longer than that, for she had served his wife back in Bristol—and Ned wasn't sure he had ever seen Master Nicholas address a word to either of them that was not a command or an instruction. They were more useful than the chickens and goats—which had also been taken by the pirates or fled before the fire—but certainly not as important as people of his own class or even menservants. Now these facts—Bess's pregnancy, Daisy's injury, Nancy's disappearance— stood squarely in Nicholas Guy's way.

At any rate, Ned knew he had one powerful ally in any plan to find and rescue Nancy. Nicholas Guy might not see the importance of finding Nancy, but his wife did.

It was three days before the move back to Cupids Cove was complete. Ned and Frank had to take turns rowing the women and their remaining supplies back, with Daisy, still clinging to life, the last to leave.

Once they arrived, there was the matter of finding a bed for the sick woman. The number of settlers had dwindled since the spring, but those who remained had spread out among the three houses, so that the dwelling that had once been occupied by Nicholas Guy's household was now ruled over by George Whittington and his wife. Half a dozen single men still slept in the upstairs chamber, and there were empty beds, but Kathryn flatly refused to bring her people into Whittington's household.

Elizabeth Guy made space for them in her house, the original dwelling house and the largest of the three. Her husband, Philip, Master Nicholas's cousin, ruled as acting governor over the few dozen remaining settlers.

The Cupids Cove colony had been tested, it was true, with hunger, with sickness, with strife, and with the loss of those who had returned to England. But it had not been attacked by pirates. Ned and Frank went with Master Nicholas to tell Master Philip Guy the tale of what had happened to the plantation, and Philip Guy listened with grave concern.

"'Tis true enough that pirates have continued to harry the fishing fleet," he said. "But this attack seems to have been not to press men into service or steal anything of value, but to send a message. To discourage settlement along these shores."

"That seems likely to be true," Nicholas Guy assented. "The only member of our party who survived the attack is one of my wife's maids, who was grievously wounded. She has not been able to tell us much, but she did recall that the men who attacked the place repeated 'Tell your master,' over and over. What they meant for her to tell me is not so clear."

Philip Guy clasped his hands behind his back and paced the main room of the house that had been built during that hopeful autumn three years earlier when the first men had arrived and all things seemed possible. "If this were last summer, I would say 'twas Easton's work, for he pillaged all up and down this shore and seemed determined to rule it as his own little fiefdom. But he is now in the service of the Duke of Savoy. Clearly others have taken up where he left off."

"Philip, do you know aught of a man called Gilbert Pike?"

"No. Is he a pirate?"

"He was. He sailed with Easton, then took a wife—an Irish wife—and built a plantation on the coast here, not far from Harbour Grace. He, his wife, and his servants have been settled here near as long as we have. I do not know if your brother John knew of Pike's plantation."

Philip Guy frowned. "If he did, he never spoke to me of it. We were certain no-one had wintered here before we came to Cupids Cove. You have met this man Pike?"

"Not only met him—my wife and her maidservants stayed in his house for a fortnight while we worked on our own." Nicholas Guy glanced at Ned and Frank. "We have all seen it—a substantial house, and outbuildings, fishing boats and stages and livestock. 'Tis not hard to credit he's been there as long as he says."

Ned was impatient that the talk was taking so long to get to what seemed to him the only important matter, but he knew he could not interrupt a conversation between his betters. So he spoke only to agree. "Master Nicholas is right, sir. 'Tis a big place Pike's got up there—he's been here two years or more, for sure."

"And my wife—pardon me for bringing a woman's fancy into it, but there might be something to what she says," Nicholas Guy added. "She is suspicious of Mistress Pike. The woman is Irish, that much is certain, and she claims to be the daughter of one of their chieftains..."

"...And Ireland is a hotbed of piracy," Philip Guy finished.

Ned coughed, as quietly as he could, and Master Nicholas glanced in his direction. "We have another worry, Philip," the master said. "I had three servants on the place at the time—Tom Taylor, who was killed, the girl Daisy, who was wounded and is still recovering, and another woman servant, my wife's maid Nancy. We found no trace of her, and think it likely she was captured."

"Would she not more likely have been killed?"

"We found no body."

Ned thought again of stumbling through the woods, tripping over roots and rocks, the fear he'd find Nancy splayed on the ground at his feet.

"My wife is...is very fond of this serving-girl," Nicholas Guy went on. "They were raised together, almost as sisters, you know. I would pay a ransom if she could be returned alive."

Philip Guy looked up sharply. "Aye, I remember the lass—and the accusation made against her not long ago."

"A false accusation, sir."

Philip Guy nodded. "Petty spite, of course, but it made things awkward. Still, if the maid has been taken alive and they are willing to ransom her, no doubt the pirates will send word."

Ned waited till they were out of Philip Guy's house to say, "So—that is all you intend to do about Nancy, sir? Wait to see if her captors send a message asking for ransom?"

Nicholas Guy raised an eyebrow. "What else can I do? If she is indeed captured alive, she knows that my wife will ransom her. If her captors are willing, they will send word—likely through the Pikes, if 'tis true that they are confederates. 'Tis not as if I have a ship of my own to go chasing pirates along the shore."

"That will not be good enough for Kath—for your mistress, sir. Nor for me. Nancy was pledged to be my wife. You know I cannot rest till she is found."

"You have been a good servant to me, Ned, and we have suffered much together. But you have always known your place. Do not overstep it now."

Later that night, by the hearth fire, Ned spoke to Kathryn. "I swore a vow to find Nancy. But I do not think either your husband or Master Philip Guy will go in pursuit of these pirates. And I do not have command of a ship that can go after them."

"I thought Nicholas would press Master Philip for the use of the *Indeavour*."

"They believe the best course is simply to wait here in Cupids Cove for the pirates to send word to us."

"I cannot wait for that," Kathryn said. "What if they never send word?"

Ned left the conversation as confused and frustrated as he had been after listening to the masters talk. He walked down to the water's edge and stood on the wharf looking out at the ocean. The *Indeavour*, the barque built by the men of Cupids Cove, lay at anchor, as did the smaller shallops used for daily fishing. Further out, he could see the tall masts of other fishing vessels anchored near the fishing stations all up through the bay. If he could see all the way to Harbour Grace, he knew he would be looking at something akin to a town of ships, boats, and fishing stages, bustling with men at work. So many ships, and not one to take Ned Perry out to sea to find the woman he loved.

In all his life, he had never felt so powerless. Of course, an ordinary working man—a stonemason's apprentice who had never even finished his apprenticeship, who had left all behind to become a colonist—was not supposed to be powerful. He would never command a ship or own a plantation. He would serve a master all his life and hope that master would protect him and those he loved. He had bound himself to the Cupids Cove colony and to Nicholas Guy, trusting in their protection.

Now a link in that chain of loyalty was breaking. If Nicholas Guy and the masters of the colony would do nothing to rescue Nancy, then the only two people in the world who cared enough to try to save her were a servant and a woman. Kathryn had other ties—her vows to her husband and the needs of an infant child—and she was, however brave and good-hearted, only a woman, after all. In the end, any real hope of saving Nancy would fall upon Ned.

And he had no idea where to begin.

THREE

The Task at Hand Is Faced

T HEY LEFT HER THERE ON DECK, SOBBING WITH GRIEF and rage, as the ship pulled away from the shore. A sailor was set to guard her. Why? Would it be any loss to these men if she threw herself into the ocean?

Below, the grey waves churned. She imagined the salt water soaking her clothes, her hair, dragging her down. It would be icy, but at least it would be over quickly.

Nancy tore her eyes from the waves and looked at the shore past which they were sailing. It was dotted with fishing stations, ships' masts marking the bays where their crews were working on shore, drying this morning's cod on the stages. Nobody on those ships or in those coves would look up to question or mark the passage of a tidy brigantine, flying not a black pirate flag but English colours.

They were Englishmen—English, and some Irish, she thought, as their voices washed over her. Not loyal subjects of His Majesty, despite flying his colours. Who were these pirates, and what did they want with attacking Master Guy's plantation and taking her alive? Nancy wished she understood. If she knew who they were and what they wanted, she might know how to survive, how to get free of them.

One thing she did know: the only people pirates kept alive were either sailors who could join their crew or wealthy folk who could be ransomed for money. She was neither. They knew by her dress that she was a serving-maid, and so of no value. Likely they had taken her on board as an amusement, a plaything to be ravished till they tired of her and killed her.

She looked down at the water again.

No. No. Life was still better; life was what mattered.

Nancy could not imagine how, but if she could survive, she might escape.

A man came over to where she sat slumped against the rail. He squatted on his heels, his face not far from hers. She had no idea what his rank might be, but he spoke like a man with some authority. He was an Englishman, nothing gentle in his breeding, but not from the dregs of the docks, either.

"Now, maid. You were servant to this Nicholas Guy?"

Nancy raised her head to meet his gaze. Brown eyes in a narrow, tanned face with a close-cropped brown beard. His expression was stern but not cruel.

"I served his wife. I have been in her service since we were children. Her husband would pay well to ransom me."

"That may be. But we've no orders to take prisoners for ransom."

Then why take me at all? But she would not ask questions. She kept her gaze steady and did not speak again until he glanced away briefly.

"Orders or no, if you send word to Master Philip Guy at Cupids Cove, his kinsman will pay to have me delivered safely back to his wife's service."

"I will tell the captain that. But he's like to say we cannot risk it."

Again, silence, save for the shouted commands and orders of the men working the rigging.

"This ship's no place for you," the sailor said, with a delicacy she had not expected. "But having taken you alive, the captain won't countenance killing a woman."

"Then let me go," Nancy said. "Put me off on shore and I'll walk back to Cupids Cove, if need be."

"Nay, you're part of the loot captured from your master's plantation now, whether you like it or not."

Part of the loot, like the chickens and goats. Nancy thought of Petal, the kid goat she had been raising by hand. At least, unlike Petal, she would not be slaughtered for the table. But there were other forms of sacrifice.

"Most of our crew are godless men, and wicked," the sailor went on. "They'll not hesitate to take advantage of you. I will do what I can to prevent that, for I'll not have such immorality going on. Might be the captain will take a fancy to keep you as his own whore. Wicked though it be, might be your safest course. You can cook, I suppose."

"Of course." She assented quickly; it was the only thing he had said that was not horrifying.

He nodded. "We'll put you to work, then—our last cook died, and the man doing it now is worse than useless." He clutched her upper arm with a grip firm as a shackle, and pulled her to her feet as he rose himself. "You're in luck another way: this ship has a cabin with a berth in it, where the cook can sleep beside the cook-fire. It has a door you can bar. I won't have you out on deck where you can stare at the water and think of self-murder. That is a grave sin, also."

"I'd not have thought a man who could burn another man's home, steal his property, and kill two servants would have such concern over sin."

Even as the words were coming out of her mouth, she tried to stop herself saying them. Of all the places in the world where speaking her mind could bring her trouble, surely the deck of a pirate ship was the one place she should have held her tongue. Apparently even losing everything she held dear and being under threat of death was not enough to teach her wisdom.

Nancy thought of that dreadful week in Cupids Cove when she had been falsely accused of a terrible crime. She had managed, with great effort, to hold her tongue then, to give only the answers that would make her appear the demure and obedient servant girl the masters wanted to see. *I must school myself to do so again*, she told herself.

His brows drew down, but he replied rather than chiding her. "'Tis true, there are few men who fear God aboard this ship. But 'tis no sin to kill in self-defence. Your fellow servants took up arms against our men."

Nancy dropped her eyes to the deck, fought back the urge to argue with him. Yes, Tom had had a musket and Daisy an axe. She herself had not been able to get her hands on a weapon, which was, perhaps, why she had been taken alive.

The sailor led her towards the aft deck, where a group of men stood. As she approached they began to call out.

"Aye, there she is, lads!"

"Cap'n's brought us back a fine piece of flesh!"

"Come hither, lass—my bed is cold and I'll take you to warm it!"

"Shut your mouths!" From the way the others hushed to a grumbling silence, Nancy knew the man leading her, though not the captain, must hold some authority. "Murphy, you're relieved of cook's duty—the maid will take over cooking for us. Belike she'll produce something better than the swill you've been dishing out since we left Ireland."

"She can take the work, sir, if I can keep the berth—I'll be glad to share it with her!" laughed a burly fellow with arms the size of small tree trunks.

"Shut your mouth, I'll have none of that. I'll whip any man who lays a hand on her. Pack up your belongings and clear the cabin. The rest of you, to your duties."

"Aye, sir," a few voices muttered as the sailor called Murphy pushed roughly past Nancy, muttering under his breath. He ducked to enter a small cabin on the port side of the deck, and came out a few minutes later with a bundle under his arm. "Bad luck to have a woman on board, you know," he said as he went below. "You'll be wishing you had me back in the cook's cabin soon enough."

"Bad luck to die by poisoning too," one of the sailors said, and another added, "'Twill be good to have a woman cooking our food, even if we can't tup her."

"Not while Brown is watching, we can't."

The officer—Master Brown, she supposed—ignored these comments. He steered Nancy ahead of him into the tiny cabin that Murphy had just vacated. A dozen smells—something pickled in brine, something else that had gone rancid, something sweet, something sour—assaulted her as soon as they were inside the narrow space.

She had been trying to ignore the heaving motion of the ship. The distress of spirit had almost made her forget the discomfort of the body, but now, pushed into this small, dark space with rotting meat and a dozen other ripe-smelling things, she felt her stomach rise and heave. A tin basin sat empty atop a small table, and Nancy turned to it just in time, retching till she was weak. Her legs shook, and she sank onto the filthy floor.

Once again she felt the sailor's iron grip, this time on both her arms, as he dragged her to her feet. "All you've done is made another mess you'll have to clean," he said. "If you can prove your worth to the crew you'll have less trouble with them. Clean this place up and have something ready to feed the men in two hours. There's food below in the cargo hold. And keep the door barred when you're in here, for your own safety."

He turned and was gone, shutting the door behind him. Shutting her into this dark, foul place.

I have survived worse than this, Nancy told herself, though she wasn't sure it was true. Her stomach still felt sick, but there was nothing else to heave up—and that sternly righteous pirate was right: now she had to clean up her own vomit as well as the filthy cabin.

Turn your hand to the task at hand, she thought. Her Aunt Tib's old saying. Tibby had raised Nancy and taught her everything she knew, there in the Gale household where they had both served back in Bristol. Nancy had used that wisdom—turning her hand to the task, doing whatever work was in front of her—when she was thrust into the strange world of the colony, so far from the Bristol streets where she had been raised, and it had served her well. Now, held captive by these sea-thieves, she had feared immediate death, or rape followed by a slower and more brutal death. Instead, for the nonce, she had been given a job to do. And so she would do it.

The cabin was not, of course, completely dark: otherwise it would have been useless to tell her to bar the door. One side of it was taken up by a small bed; on the other was a brick fireplace, set into the floor rather than the wall, with hooks above it for hanging pots. It opened to a hatch above to let smoke escape, and through this light flooded in, so that after a moment she could find her way around her new prison.

It was just tall enough to stand up in, and she could very nearly touch both walls with her arms outstretched. But it had that stout bar on the door, which was a mercy, and though it was filthy, it was well stocked with pots and rags, and a bucket stood ready filled with sea water, so she had the means to clean it.

She cleaned the ashes out of the stove and used them to scrub the rest of the cabin. Then she inspected the food that was stored there, some of it on shelves and some hanging from the rafters in bags. There was plenty of ship's biscuit, at any rate, and some salted pork—more of that below in the hold, no doubt, and of course there would be salt fish as well. No fancy cooking to be done here. She remembered the voyage over from England the year before; by the end of it, she had been heartily sick of boiled salt meat. Such a diet made sense, of course: even protected by firebricks, a ship's oven could not be allowed to get too hot, and boiling was the safest way to cook under those circumstances.

When the cabin was as clean as she could make it, Nancy took down her untidy hair and braided it tightly, then bound the braids around her head. She had been wearing a coif when the plantation was attacked, but that had gone missing. She had the clothes she stood up in: a petticoat and a sturdy kirtle of brown wool. No apron, but she could perhaps fashion one, and a kerchief, out of some sacking. Strong pattens on her feet, and a pair of stockings. There were a couple of sharp knives among the supplies in the cabin; she tucked one inside her stocking and felt comforted by the blade against her thigh.

She thought of the stores the pirates had captured from Nicholas Guy's plantation. The food that should have fed their family over the next few weeks would now feed the pirates—and that included the chickens and the three goats. There would be fresh meat tonight, which might put the men in a tractable mood.

Nancy cautiously pushed the door open. A lad of about fourteen or fifteen stood nearby, and as she emerged, he said, "You're not to go wandering about on deck."

"You must let me get to the stores if you want to eat," she pointed out. "I need the food you stole from my master. There's flour, and turnips and parsnips, and chickens. I want to kill and dress some of the chickens."

"There's goats too."

She heard a bleat as the boy said it. The three goats—the nanny, the billy goat, and little Petal—tied to the ship's rail. There would be no feed to waste on goats, and they took up space. The only value in capturing larger livestock like goats or pigs would be to slaughter them at once.

Nancy remembered carrying Petal about in her arms as a newborn kid, feeding her like a baby with warm milk when the nanny goat who bore her had died and the others would not take to her. Then she steeled herself. What had she imagined: that she would survive aboard a pirate ship and eventually make her escape with a pet goat trailing by her side?

"Can you send word to the captain?" she said. "I suppose I'll need his permission to slaughter any of his booty."

The message was relayed, and returned to her by way of the cabin boy. "Cap'n Sly says yes, go ahead and kill the goats. He says I'm to help you."

She knelt by the cabin boy on the sunny deck. It pitched and rolled beneath them and the goats bleated in terror. When she was a girl back in Bristol, meat had come from the butcher's stall, dressed and ready for the pot. Since moving to Cupids Cove, she had done her fair share of butchering, for everyone helped with every stage of the work so that all might eat. She had never felt squeamish about it before now. She held little Petal still for the cabin boy's knife.

"You're fond of this one," the boy said.

"I raised her from a kid."

"You gave her a name, I 'low. Shouldna done that."

"We didn't eat much goat's meat in the colony. I thought she'd be giving us milk for years to come." Nancy looked up at the boy as his knife sliced across Petal's throat. "I never counted on pirates."

She laid a hand on the kid's side as its life ebbed out with its blood. She thought of Scripture stories, of the Hebrews bringing lambs and kids to slaughter for sacrifices. *You are my sacrifice*, she said silently to the still-warm body on the deck beside her.

"Most folk don't," the cabin boy said. "Don't count on pirates, I mean. Even them of us as is pirates don't, not always."

The other two goats were slaughtered next: the chickens would live another day. Nancy built up the fire in the cook's cabin and stewed some of the goats' meat along with turnips, parsnips, and some ancient-looking carrots from the ship's stores. The cabin boy, whose name was Robin, hung the rest of the goats' meat below in the hold.

The stew was ready by the time the first watch of sailors were lined up with their bowls, and Nancy was ordered to bring the pot down below deck and dish it up to them. She reserved a good-sized bowl for herself, with a little ship's biscuit to dip into it. She had faced nearly every horror she could imagine in the last hours, but she had no plans to starve to death.

She kept her face blank and her eyes downcast as the men took their tin bowls of food and passed comment on the new cook.

"Ah! That smells good—we'll be all right now we got a woman knows how to cook."

"Better than the swill you made for us, Irishman!"

"I 'low you're better than Murphy at a lot of things, ain't you, love?"

"You lot can leave the cabin boy alone now we've a wench aboard."

"What'll you give me along with my supper, cook? I've got a grand piece of fresh meat I know you'll like."

"Shut your mouths, you heathens," said the stern-faced sailor who had taken charge of her earlier in the day. "I warned you to keep your hands off her."

But another voice cut across his. "Words ain't the same as hands, Brown. 'Tis not natural to bring a woman aboard and expect the men not to have a bit of fun." This was a short but powerfully built fellow who, Nancy thought, must be the captain, for he was the only one to contradict Master Brown.

"Keep it to words only, lads," the man added with a warning in his tone. "Quartermaster Brown's itching for an excuse to whip half of ye."

The men spoke among themselves, and she caught snatches of their talk. She strained to pick out the captain and quartermaster's conversation, for they seemed to be arguing: *Never meant it to come to murder* and *Not our orders*—the phrases drifted across to her as the two men ate a little apart from the common sailors. "I don't give a damn who her father is, she can't give us orders!" Master Brown said at one point, and Nancy wondered who they could mean. She remembered Sheila Pike saying "My father is a king in Ireland," and that her husband had sailed with Peter Easton. Was it Mistress Pike who had given them orders?

The captain found her afterwards when she was back in her little cabin preparing a pot of stew for the next watch of men. She had not yet barred the door, for it was growing dark and she needed the light to see by. The captain leaned in, his bulk filling the doorway. "The quartermaster tells me you're a servant to Master Nicholas Guy?"

Nancy nodded. "Yes, sir. To his wife. She'd pay well to ransom me back."

"Aye, she might, but we're going on to St. John's. I daresay we'd get something other than a ransom if we went down to Cupids Cove now. And we've business in St. John's. You'll be kept aboard as long as you're useful to us." He said *kept aboard* but she heard *kept alive*.

"I'll do as I'm told, sir." Then she dared to dart him a quick glance. "As far as my virtue will allow."

He snorted. "You're a maid, then?"

"Yes." Only two days ago, she would have been able to say that honestly. She had given up her maidenhead so gladly and freely to Ned; a pledge of troth was as good as a marriage in most people's eyes. "And I pray to stay a maid, if you are good Christian men."

"Ha. Well, some of us more than others. Master Brown will give you no trouble—he's a Puritan, and tries to keep the men in line, but most of them don't hew to his way of thinking. But the way I see it, a woman on board ship is only like to cause quarrels and trouble among the men. I'd say the same of a boy if he was too pretty, truth be told. So I'll give them the same orders as Brown did—no-one's to lay a hand on you. Bar the door when you're in here alone," he added, repeating Master Brown's instruction. "I'll have young Robin bring you in a few candles."

"Thank you, sir."

Young Robin, who came later with candles, was apparently not pretty enough to cause any trouble among the crew. She thanked him, placed a candle in the lantern and lit it, then barred the door when Robin went out.

When she had served the next group of men, then finished cleaning the pots and the cabin, she took off her kirtle and her shoes and curled up on the bed at last. It smelled of the sailor who had slept here before her. Only one night since she had lain in the woods in Ned's arms, laughing at the discomfort of a tree root poking into her back, laughing at the possibility of the happy years that stretched in front of them.

One night. A lifetime.

She reached down to touch the knife still tucked in her stocking, as the rolling motion of the ship rocked her to an uneasy sleep.

FOUR

A Bold Escape Is Attempted

NANCY WAS ON DECK, PLUCKING CHICKENS JUST OUT-side the cook's cabin, when the sailors in the rigging began to call out. Since her capture, the days and nights had flowed into monotony: every day sailing along the coast, every night dropping anchor in some cove empty of fishing vessels. The cries and the activity above told her that change was coming.

The ship—which, she had learned, was called *Happy Adventure*—had turned towards two steep wooded cliffs with a narrow passage between them. She recalled Captain Sly saying they were heading for St. John's. As the sailors ran about trimming the sails and Sly manned the wheel to guide them through the passage, she stood up, the chickens forgotten at her feet, to see better.

Ahead, in the deep, sheltered harbour, she saw a forest of masts, ships anchored so thickly that they reminded her of the Bristol docks when she had last seen them, more than a year ago. Had all her life at Cupids Cove—the hardship, the toil, the terror, the joy—taken barely more than a year? It was hard to believe. Last spring, she and Kathryn had left Bristol for the colonies; now Nancy was sailing away from Cupids Cove into the unknown. Another adventure, but whereas last year she had been reluctant but hopeful, now she was an unwilling captive.

Unless she could change her fate, here in St. John's.

This would not be a town like Bristol, or even a colony like Cupids Cove—Governor Guy had told them often enough that Cupids Cove was the only settlement in all this country where Englishmen had over-wintered, brought out wives, built permanent homes. This would be a place of men—fishermen, sailors, captains—living aboard ship or in temporary shelters on shore during the summer.

In a bustling fishing station of this size, at the peak of the season, she could surely find someone who could help her. If she were able to get off the misnamed *Happy Adventure*, elude Captain Sly and his men, then she might find a ship's captain who knew Philip or Nicholas Guy and would return her safe to Cupids Cove.

Sailors were all around her, climbing in the rigging. From his position at the wheel, Captain Sly glanced back and saw her looking at the busy harbour. Quickly, Nancy dropped back to her knees and turned her attention to the chickens. She had to pluck and clean them out here in the open air, then put them on to boil in the pot in her cabin and, while they were boiling, swab the blood and feathers and chicken guts off the deck.

She spent as much time in the cook's cabin as she could bear, usually with the door closed and barred, but the place would stink unbearably if she tried to do any butchering in there, not to mention the need for more light and space than her cabin provided. Every time she went in there and barred the door, she felt like an animal being locked in a cage. But a cage could be a safe place if predators were on the prowl outside.

A shadow fell over her work and she looked up to see the cabin boy.

"Captain says you're to get back in the cabin and not to come out while we're at St. John's."

"I have to finish these," Nancy said, gesturing at the half-plucked carcasses.

"I'm to finish them and hand them in to you. You'll do the cooking in there; I'll fetch and carry for you and bring the food out to serve the men."

"So he don't want me on deck at all while we're here." Nancy kept plucking; Robin squatted down to help.

"Seems that way."

"Why is that, I wonder?"

"Perhaps he don't want anyone from another ship to see you?"

"Or me to see anyone from another ship, might be. And you're to be my gaoler?"

"Sorry. Captain's orders."

"Right." Nancy wiped her bloody hands—she had got hold of some empty sacks and sewn herself a couple of aprons for messy work like this—and went into the cook's cabin. She had survived thus far by playing the meek and biddable captive, and this was not the time to cast aside that role. Not yet.

They dropped anchor late in the afternoon: Robin came to the door for the boiled chicken to serve the men and Nancy handed it over with instructions for him to get each man's share of ship's biscuit from the hold to go along with it. She kept a small dish for herself: she was too nervous to be hungry, but she knew that if any part of her plan were to be successful, she would need strength.

At least, confined to her cabin as she was, she would not have the task of cleaning up after the men's meal: likely that duty would fall to Robin and some other low-ranking sailor. Robin brought back the pot and ladle and she scrubbed those out, as well as her own bowl. She folded the blankets on her berth, also. She wanted to leave this place, to never see it again, but it was against her nature to leave a place untidy.

When all was in order she tried to push open the door of her cabin, expecting to see Robin or another man standing guard. Instead, she found the door would not open at all. She had welcomed having a door she could bar from the inside, to keep out sailors who might wish harm on her; she should have realized they could as easily bar it from the outside, making the cabin into a prison.

Her pulse hammered. She reminded herself that she had never truly expected to get out by the cabin door. She had another plan. That, too, had only a slim chance of succeeding, but she would try it. She would never forgive herself if she did not.

When the light coming down through her chimney space had dimmed to a twilight blue, Nancy climbed up onto the brick wall that surrounded the hearth. It was built like a box, about as high as her waist, to keep the fire well insulated from the wooden deck of the ship and the cabin walls. Scrambling up to stand on the edge of the oven wall, she cursed her skirts: if she could get her hands on a pair of breeches she would be able to move about much more freely. She should have planned this better, stolen some sailors' garb from down in the hold. But it was foolish to think what she ought to have done: this was what she had to work with. A hatch in the roof of her cabin, a woman's clothing, a kitchen knife in her stocking.

From her perch on the end of the oven, she could reach the chimney hatch, then, carefully, she climbed onto the iron bar from which the cooking pot hung, using her hands to keep her balance on the chimney walls. Her head was just below the hatch now. No guarantee that the captain, the quartermaster, or some other sailor would not be standing on the quarterdeck watching her emerge. She listened: the ship was quiet now, with most of the men below deck. She could hear wind in the rigging, a murmured conversation, footsteps. The steps were moving away from her, across the quarterdeck, down the ladder to the main deck, towards the hatch that led below.

She raised her head just above the lip of the chimney-hole. What she saw confirmed what she had heard; the quarterdeck was empty, and on the main deck a sailor stood on watch near the forecastle, his back to her. With the ship at anchor, the tiller was unmanned, and she hoped no-one was keeping watch up in the rigging. From up there, a man would have a good view of her clumsily emerging through the hole.

Nancy lay flat on the quarterdeck next to the chimney. A sailor was pacing the main deck, not looking in her direction. He was the only man above deck at the moment. It was the best possible time to try her escape plan, but she would have to move quickly.

Still lying flat, she edged along the deck until she came to the rail. They were anchored close to another, slightly larger ship; beyond that ship was the shore. Looking up a little, she could see masts rising ahead and behind; as she had thought on her first glimpse of St. John's, this was a busy port with scores of ships at anchor.

On the neighbouring ship, a sailor was also pacing the deck. Nancy wished she had any way to know what manner of ship it was. Were the men aboard it honest fishermen, sober merchant sailors, or pirates like those who held her captive? Her plan was to turn herself over to the captain of some other English ship, to tell them she had been kidnapped, and to beg whether there was some way for her to get back to Cupids Cove. It was a desperate chance, but who knew where the *Happy Adventure* might be headed after St. John's? Wherever the pirates went, the next port where they dropped anchor was likely to be one where no-one had heard of Cupids Cove or John Guy, much less of Nicholas Guy and his wife. If she could not escape in St. John's station, she might never find her way back to the place that, against all odds, she had come to think of as home.

The skies were darkening. Should she dare hail the sailor on the other ship's deck? If she could signal silently that she was in need of rescue, it would surely raise an alarm, would catch the attention of the sailor even now on watch at the far end of the *Happy Adventure*'s main deck.

But she had to make the attempt. This was her moment—now, or not at all.

The sailor on the other ship's deck was close enough to meet her eyes if he happened to look her way. She pulled off the kerchief she had wrapped around her hair and waved it in the air, hoping to catch his eye. She dared not shout.

It worked. He saw her, moved closer to the rail. Even in the dim light she could see enough of his face to note his surprise, not only that there was a woman aboard, but that she was hailing him. He opened his mouth to speak, but stopped when Nancy put a finger to her lips.

Now they looked at each other from the rails of the two ships, the small gulf of black water and twilight air between them. He leaned forward a little, his face a question. A smile quirked the corner of his mouth. Did he think she was some ship's doxy, tired of being used by the men on her own ship and trying to attract another?

"Help me," Nancy said. She wanted to shout it, but she kept her voice just above a whisper, praying he could hear.

The man leaned forward, opened his mouth to speak again.

"Help!" she repeated. This time it was almost a shout.

She heard footsteps, no longer walking but bounding across the main deck of the *Happy Adventure*. The other sailor heard it too, looked from her to the man approaching her. "What say you, lass?" the other sailor called.

"Pay her no heed!" It was Master Brown, climbing the ladder to the quarterdeck now, almost close enough to reach out and grasp her. "Get back below, wench!" To the man on the other deck he called, "'Tis but our cook—she is a wanton maid, and will throw herself in the path of any man she sees. A poor lost creature is all she is."

"He's a liar!" No need for caution now that she had been caught; Brown's hands were on the hem of her kirtle, pulling her away from the rail. "They are pirates! I am a captive! They took me from my home and my mistress!"

Brown cuffed her across the mouth with his free hand. "Shut your mouth, girl." To the other man he said, "You hear how she lies. We are honest English sailors, and the girl signed on with us of her own free will. Too long at sea has drove her mad."

"All lies! Have pity on me!" Nancy yelled—the last words she got to say before Brown clamped one huge hand across her mouth. With his other hand he pulled her away from the rail; the man was brutally strong. He could silence her mouth, but not her eyes; she threw one more desperate glance at the other sailor. It was almost too dark to see his face now, but surely in Brown's cruel silencing of her he could read the truth of her tale.

More of the *Happy Adventure*'s crew were coming on deck now, having heard the commotion above. The captain would be here any moment, but Nancy would not see it; Brown was already dragging her back down the ladder, though she struggled against him.

She heard the sailor on the other ship's deck say "Bad luck to have a woman aboard," and knew he had turned away; her plight was of no further interest to him.

Then Brown had pushed open the door of the cook's cabin and shoved her inside, back onto the bed. "You damned impertinent baggage—after I kept you alive, preserved your maidenhead, kept you safe on this ship—this is your thanks? To betray us to the king's men?"

In truth, she had not even seen that the other vessel was a naval ship.

"What do you expect—my thanks?" she spat back as soon as he released his grip on her mouth. "You must know I want to return to my home."

"And *you* know that cannot be. You do not have the choices you seem to think you have."

"What harm would it do you—or your captain—to let me go?"

"The captain, and his partners ashore, are not eager for anyone to know our business."

"So he will never ransom me."

"No. Better for us all if you'd been killed onshore, or drowned getting on board this ship."

"Better for you, then, if you were to throw me overboard."

He paused again. "Not better for our souls. We kill men in combat, but I could not countenance the murder of a defenceless woman."

He left her alone then, but she could hear from the voices outside that he had stationed a man at her door with orders to watch for any attempt to escape. There would be no clever escape, no throwing herself on the mercy of honest English sailors. She would never set foot on the shore of St. John's fishing station.

Nancy lay in her berth, exhausted with the terror of the last hour, waiting for the racing of her heart to slow. It had been mad even to attempt escape—she could never have got away without being discovered. She saw that now. *But I had to try*, she told herself. Meekly submitting to captivity could only be borne if the goal was to make her captors trust her. Trust her enough that she could either escape or convince them to let her go. Her attempt tonight had foiled all that.

She lay tense with fear, wondering what might happen to her next. But the hours went by; voices murmured and shouted out on deck, and Nancy was left alone. She did not sleep, but the night passed.

FIVE

A Fiery Message Is Delivered

S T. JOHN'S HARBOUR WAS BUSIER THAN ANY NED HAD seen since leaving Bristol more than three years ago. When he said so to Master Catchmaid, the master said, "There'd ha' been more than this a few weeks ago. Some of the ships be already on their way back to market, and the rest will leave soon. In a fortnight this harbour will be all but empty."

"Nobody overwinters here?"

"None I've heard of. The fishermen are glad enough to get home out of it once the fish are caught and stored below decks."

William Catchmaid was taking the *Indeavour* down to Renews to visit the handful of Bristol men stationed there over the summer: the Newfoundland Company had not given up its intention to plant a second colony down on the southern shore, but it was unclear if Renews was ready for overwintering yet. After the attack on Nicholas Guy's plantation, the Cupids Cove colonists were eager to know if there had been other attacks, and Ned had asked to join the crew, hoping he could learn something of the ship that had captured Nancy.

On shore, it became clearer that St. John's was a fishing station and not a town. Beyond the wharves, the sloping ground that swept up from the water was filled with the wooden stages for drying fish, and beyond those, the storehouses where fish and supplies were kept. There were some long, low buildings that might have been shelters for the men who slept onshore during the season, but there were no permanent buildings: no houses or churches or shops. Cupids Cove, for all its small size, was more of a town than St. John's.

Catchmaid had business with some of the other ships' captains, including letters he wanted sent back to England; Ned asked to accompany him on his visits, each time asking what the captains knew of pirates in the New Found Land waters.

"Nay, we've had no trouble with pirates here this season at all," one master after another told them, until their search led them to the man most likely to know about pirates along the Newfoundland coast: Richard Whitbourne, the captain who had been held captive by Peter Easton the summer before. The experience had obviously not put Captain Whitbourne off the Newfoundland fishery. He was a thickset, broad-faced man with a booming voice, and he had many opinions on the subject of pirates.

"'Tis not Easton, that's certain: I know full well he's got other business these days and has no more interest in this part of the world. There's a slew of others, though—small operators, most of them, no fleet, only single ships. Some of 'em used to be Easton's men. They rob ships and fishing stations here in the New Found Land, and then all down along the coast as far as Virginia."

"Where's the money coming from? Who's buying from 'em?" Master Catchmaid wanted to know.

Whitbourne stroked his beard. "There's some English merchants willing to trade with pirates, but from what I hear, a lot of them are bringing their goods to Irish ports. Some of the pirates are Irish themselves, or got some kind of connection there."

Some kind of connection. Keenly aware he was a common labourer speaking up in the company of his betters, Ned coughed. When the other men's eyes were on him, he said, "D'ye know who Gilbert Pike is?"

"A captain? Never heard of him." Whitbourne's dismissal was blunt, but Ned pressed on.

"Not a captain. He used to sail with Easton, but he's settled down and built himself a plantation just beyond Harbour Grace. He has a wife—an Irishwoman. She claims her father is a king in Ireland."

Suddenly all the men in the room were interested in what Ned had to say. A former lieutenant of Peter Easton's, living on the Newfoundland coast with a high-born Irish wife—that was someone who might well play a key part in whatever trade the pirates were now plying. Ned went on to explain how Nicholas Guy's womenfolk had stayed at Pike's plantation, how the Pikes had known all Guy's plans and the location of his land before the attack.

Whitbourne nodded throughout the story. "Those pieces all fit together pretty neatly," he said. "There's a ship was in harbour here— oh, 'twas a fortnight ago, more or less—called the *Happy Adventure*. Now that was the name of one of Easton's ships when he was in these waters, and I heard tell the captain of this one was a fellow named Jem Sly, who used to sail under Easton's command. If he's in league with this fellow Pike, he might well have attacked Nicholas Guy's plantation. But knowing all that don't make it likely we'll ever find or punish them," he added. "They'll be gone by now—mayhap back to Ireland, but I heard rumours they was heading further south, might even be going as far as the Caribbean. Belike they'll harry a few fishing stations on the way and then go after Spanish gold before they cross the ocean again."

"Are there any ships in port here now from—down that way?" Ned realized he had only the vaguest knowledge of what lay between the New Found Land and the Spanish lands to the south, though he knew the English settlement at James Fort was somewhere along that coast.

"The *Treasurer* is still here taking on supplies, I think, if she didn't leave this morning. That will be Captain Argall, out of Virginia—he's been attacking French settlements along the coast."

A ship from Virginia? Ned's heart leapt. If he could sign on with this Captain Argall, perhaps down there, in the southern seas, he might find someone who knew of Captain Sly and his *Happy Adventure*.

He spoke to Master Catchmaid as soon as they were back aboard the *Indeavour*. "I mean to find Captain Argall, if his ship's still in port, and see if he'll take me on as a seaman."

Catchmaid looked at him as if he'd sprouted a second head. "You don't even like being at sea, Ned—what madness is this?"

"I need to head south. Might happen I'll find something that will lead me to this Captain Sly."

"And what can you do to bring justice to him, all on your own?"

"Nothing at all. But if Nancy still lives, and she be aboard that ship, I can find her. Maybe find a way to get her home."

Master Catchmaid shook his head. "Well, true love. I'd never have took you for such a romantic, Perry. But you are not bound to the *Indeavour*, nor to Cupids Cove. You're Nicholas Guy's man now, and I suppose 'twould be for him to say if you might go or not."

"He gave me permission before I left to do whatever I needed to do to find Nancy. 'Tis not just a lover's fancy—though 'tis true, we were promised to wed and I'd move heaven and earth to bring her back safely. But Mistress Guy is very fond of her servant girl."

Catchmaid nodded. "Aye, I know she values the maid."

"I promised Mistress Guy if there was any hope of saving Nancy, I'd bring her back. So I've made a vow, you see."

"Well, I'll not be one to stand in the way of a solemn vow, whether 'tis for love or friendship's sake—seeing as how your master has given you leave to go."

So it was that Ned found himself on the deck of the *Treasurer* later that same afternoon, facing Captain Argall's quartermaster, Collins, telling his story.

"This ship's not in the business of chasing English pirates—we're chasing Frenchmen, making it clear to them that this is English land. We're headed for Port Royal, where the French are trying to plant a colony."

"But after that? You'll go back to Virginia?"

"Aye, before winter sets in."

Ned knew that the longer he delayed finding a ship headed south, the colder the trail would go, and the greater harm might come to Nancy. Most of the ships in St. John's station plied their trade back and forth across the ocean, not down the coast to the south. If the pirates had truly headed south, then the only way he might have of getting close to them would be to ship aboard the *Treasurer*.

Fortune favoured Ned. Argall had captured a French caravel and manned it with his own sailors. With the *Treasurer* short a few hands, he agreed to take Ned on for the duration of their voyage to Virginia.

They sailed west along the south coast of the island, past Renews and then past miles and miles of dark, wooded coastline punctuated by occasional fishing stations, most abandoned for the winter. Then the coast vanished, the water grew wider and wilder, and Ned prayed he would not disgrace himself by heaving his guts like a cabin boy on his first voyage.

His prayer was answered: his stomach was more settled than it had been when they made the voyage across from Bristol. Somehow, in those years and in the voyages up and down the coasts of Conception Bay and Trinity Bay, Ned had grown into a better sailor.

He was kept busy, and as he knew less about sailing than any man on board, he was given the most menial tasks. But Ned knew the trick to that: never pretend to know more than he did. When one of the sailors caught him hauling on the wrong line, lowering a sail he was meant to raise, Ned laughed and said, "Sure, all these lines and sails, 'tis as much a mystery to me as lacing up a lady's petticoat—and not half so much fun as unlacing one!" And the sailor, a young man about his own age called Francis Withycombe, laughed and showed Ned the right way to go about it.

Before long Ned was friendly with them all. By the time they were within sight of the narrow channel of water that led to the French colony, he was beginning to feel something of the same bond with the crew as he had done with his fellow colonists in those first weeks at Cupids Cove. He was learning, too, the business of sails and rigging, learning to scrub the deck with holystone and take his turn on watch.

"What is the captain's business with these Frenchmen?" he asked Francis, who had seven years' experience sailing the seas.

Francis shrugged. "He means to let them know the King of England rules all these shores. There was a crew of French popish priests living in among the Indians at the last place we went—Saint-Sauveur, they called it. We burned all their buildings, and the Indians took off into the woods, but we took two of the papists as prisoners. So I allow we'll do the same to this next place."

Ned felt a quiver of fear. He'd not signed onto this ship with any thought of fighting other men, unless it came to a fight with pirates in which he might have a hope of rescuing Nancy. But of course if Captain Argall was going to deliver a message to the French, it would not be in the form of a polite letter on a gilded page.

Another sailor, a stocky fellow with fiery ginger hair and beard, was great friends with young Francis. Red Peter, as all the sailors called him, told the tale of the attack on the French settlement with some relish. The two priests had been taken prisoner with the promise that if they helped Captain Argall to ferret out other nests of Frenchmen along the coast, they would be returned to France unharmed. One priest was aboard the captured French caravel that sailed along with the *Treasurer*, while the other sailed with Argall and told him how to find the colony at Port Royal.

Port Royal, when it came in sight, was a handful of buildings no bigger or more impressive than Cupids Cove. It was surrounded by the same kind of wooden stockade wall, and the same collection of little boats bobbed at anchor by its wharves. The fishing season was ending, and these men were preparing for the long winter.

There was a closed gate in the palisade wall, but when they drew close enough to drop anchor and put down their boats, they saw it was unguarded. "They've fled," Argall said.

"Of course. They have seen you coming a long way off," said the French priest. "Just as we did at Saint-Sauveur. They will have gone into the woods, to their Indian allies."

The fact that the settlement was abandoned seemed not to trouble Captain Argall; he ordered the boats lowered and the men ashore. "'Twas the same at the other place," Francis told Ned. "They get warning and they run off. We burn their storehouses and shelters."

"Are the Frenchmen truly in the woods with the Indians?" Ned asked as they rowed ashore. He thought of the natives of the New Found Land, those elusive men, their skins stained red with ochre, that the Cupids Cove colonists had met and feasted and traded with, one night in Trinity Bay. From that time until he left the New Found Land, Ned had seen and heard nothing more of the natives. Yet it seemed there were places where colonists and natives traded and mingled together to such a degree that the Frenchmen would take shelter with the Indians if they saw an English ship approach. Better trust oneself to the wild men of the woods than to the English—and, no doubt, English colonists would feel the same if they saw a French ship coming into their harbour.

The settlement was entirely empty. "Are there women here?" Ned wondered aloud as Argall's sailors marched from the shore through the unguarded gate of Port Royal.

"The French bring no womenfolk," Red Peter said. "Or so I have heard."

The dread that Ned felt when he thought of what they were about to do had eased at the sight of the empty settlement. He was more at ease, too, knowing it was a settlement of men only. He would not have to kill anyone, nor would he be leaving women or children homeless.

No violence, but still. The place was so like Cupids Cove that it gave him a shock. He thought of all the long hours he'd worked in the colony, helping erect those first houses, the palisade wall, everything they had worked so hard to build. Surely the French had worked as hard at their colony.

"Here," Master Collins said, thrusting a torch into Ned's hands. "Anything that will burn, but the roof is best. The houses go up like kindling once the roofs are fired."

"Take what you can of the furs before we burn the storehouse!" Captain Argall ordered. They looted the buildings, running out with bags of grain and armloads of animal skins. The thatched roofs of most of the houses were burning now, and the grass was alight in several places; smoke billowed in the air.

Faster and faster it spread as the English sailors swarmed the settlement, gathering what they could, until the fire was moving so rapidly that it was no longer safe for them to remain. "Fall back! To the ships!" came the command, and the men dropped their blazing torches in the grass and picked up their loads of booty.

When they were back aboard the *Treasurer*, Ned found himself trembling from the exertion and excitement and fear. Memories came flooding back. The acrid tang of smoke in the air. The sight of the

TRUDY J. MORGAN-COLE

burning buildings. He and Frank and Nicholas Guy coming out of the
woods, lured by that awful smell, seeing flames licking at the frame of
the house. He had been running for the beach, meaning to fill a bucket
with water so they could begin fighting the fire, when he had stumbled
over the prone body of his friend Tom Taylor. Then he understood
men had done this, come ashore to kill and burn. They had killed Tom,
tried to kill Daisy, and—done what? To Nancy. His Nancy, his love.

On that awful, scorched day, the rain had come, quenching the
flames before they had a chance to spread into the surrounding forest.
No rain fell on Port Royal. Nature did nothing to gentle the hand of
man. It must be God's will, as Argall proclaimed, that the French suffer
for daring to plant their flag on English soil.

SIX

A Troubling Realization Dawns

KATHRYN HAD TRIED SO HARD TO BE PREPARED, TO DO everything right. She had failed so many of the people she cared for over these last months: she tallied her guilt in her head as she lay awake nights. She had betrayed her husband. She had left her servants alone on the plantation to be attacked by pirates. Worst of all, she had abandoned Nancy to be killed or captured, her fate unknown. So many failures, so much loss.

She had done what she could to make amends, or at least to lessen the damage. Her husband would never know of her dalliance. She had faithfully nursed Daisy, who was up and about again, at long last. She had persuaded her husband to give Ned money to help him find Nancy—Master Catchmaid had just returned on the *Indeavour* and reported that Ned had taken passage on a Virginia Company ship in hopes of learning more about the pirates. Kathryn prayed every night that Ned would succeed in his quest.

Still, it all seemed so little against the weight of suffering she had failed to prevent. She was mistress of a household, and she had not protected the people under her care. So she was determined to do this one thing right: she would help at the birthing of Bess's child. Daisy would be by her sister's side as well, of course, but Daisy was still frail. Kathryn would be the strong, capable mistress upon whom both her servants could rely.

She and her household were still staying in Philip and Elizabeth Guy's house—the only house in the settlement that did not feel hostile to Kathryn. The other two households were presided over by George and Nell Whittington, and Sam and Sal Butler, none of whom she could ever forgive for their part in the false accusations against Nancy the year before. There were deep divisions within the community itself—Nicholas often found himself arguing with the other men over the colony's future. Back in England, the company's London investors were at odds with the Bristol merchants, and the Newfoundland Company seemed like to rend itself in two. In Cupids Cove, many of the Bristol men spoke of doing as Nicholas had done and leaving to clear their own land further up the shore. Others insisted they must stay where they were, try to build up the settlement in which they had invested such hope and labour.

Kathryn, like most of the women, took little part in these arguments, but the chill carried over into mill and the brewhouse and the chicken coop, all the places where the women worked together and talked—or, when trouble was in the air, avoided talking. There were many times that autumn in Cupids Cove when she walked into a room and others fell silent at her approach.

"I no longer feel welcome here," she told her husband, curled close in bed at night in hopes no-one around would overhear them. "I know 'tis selfish when we suffered such terrible losses, but I had my heart set on being in our own household by now, on our own land, with our own people about us. And now—"

"I know, my little wife, I know." He stroked her hair tenderly. "Nothing can bring back what we have lost—poor Tom and Nancy. But our house—that we can rebuild, and we will. As soon as the weather breaks in spring we will begin work again."

Kathryn fixed her thoughts on Bess's expected child, thinking that if she could help bring forth a healthy babe, she would have done one thing to nourish a little hope for the future. She and Bess would be able to raise their children together. The only other children in Cupids Cove at the moment were Elizabeth Guy's boys, who were growing fast enough that their mother talked of returning to England so that James, the eldest, could be properly schooled.

Bess's pains began one chilly November afternoon. She was sitting by the hearth spinning wool, and Kathryn was attempting to do the same, but spent at least half her time untangling baby Jonathan from the skeins—he was in a basket near her spindle and he kept reaching out to grasp the wool. He was eight months old now, and Kathryn was delighted that he was showing such interest, grabbing and pulling at things, but also frustrated at how little work she was getting done, when Bess cried out. "Oh, Mistress, I've such a pain in me belly! Do you think it could be time?"

It could be, and it was, as they soon discovered. "Should we call Mistress Butler?" Daisy arranged pillows behind Bess to get her into a more comfortable position in bed.

"No!" Kathryn said, and then, feeling she had spoken too sharply, added, "No need to trouble her. Mistress Elizabeth is right handy, and she has borne two of her own. Between us all, I'm sure we can help Bess through this."

She prayed with all her might that this would go easy for Bess. She prayed it as much for Daisy's sake as for Bess's. Poor Daisy had lost so much in this New World already. She had come here little more than a year ago to marry the man she was promised to wed, and only a few months after their marriage, Matt was dead of sickness, as was Daisy's sister Molly. Then Molly's husband, Tom, with whom Daisy had managed to find a bit of comfort, was killed. The poor girl had lost two husbands, a sister, and much of the use of her left arm in less than a year. Losing her other sister would be a fate too cruel to be imagined.

But all seemed to be progressing well. Daisy brought a posset of herbs from the storehouse that was supposed to help ease the pains of childbirth. Kathryn had a vague idea that lots of hot water and clean cloths were required. But when Bess screamed in the grip of the birth-pains, Kathryn felt at a loss. She had never been at any birthing-bed but her own.

Elizabeth Guy took charge. "Have her waters broken yet?" she asked, and Kathryn remembered that warm gush that had preceded Jonathan's birth. "It feels a bit as if you've pissed the bed," she told Bess, who shook her head and then, a few moments later said, "Oh yes—that's it, that's it, the waters are broke!"

After a cursory examination, Elizabeth Guy agreed, and then it was only for all the women to wait together. Daisy comforted Bess through the pains and urged her to push, and when the baby's head actually began to emerge from between Bess's legs, Elizabeth caught it and drew it forward. Kathryn hovered, feeling helpless, until Elizabeth said, "Bring water and cloths to wash the babe."

And then it was over. So quickly. Kathryn thought her own birthings—Jonathan, and the baby back in Bristol who had not lived—had lasted much longer. Perhaps it only seemed that way when you were the one whose body was being torn asunder by pain. She took the slippery, bloody creature—more like handling a codfish fresh out of the boat than a human infant, she thought—and washed it in the warm water, eliciting lusty howls that made the new mother smile. Then she swaddled the babe and placed him in Bess's arms.

Much as the birth of her own child had done back in the spring, the birth of Bess's child brought some spirit and hope to a colony that had been riven by contention and difficulties for months. All the women, even Sal Butler and Nell Whittington, came by to offer good wishes, gifts of food and remedies they had used or heard from their mothers— ale and colewort for getting Bess's milk to flow, and a drink of butter, ale, and half-cooked eggs to purge her. All of them admired the baby and said he was a fine little lad.

The birth must have put thoughts into Nicholas Guy's mind, for he was passionate behind the curtains of their bed at night. "'Twill soon be time, will it not, to think of us giving young Jonathan a brother or a sister?"

"'Twill not happen yet," Kathryn said, "for I am still nursing him four and five times a day, and there's little chance of falling pregnant when you have a child still on the teat. Indeed, my monthly courses have not even begun again. You may have to wait awhile for another babe."

"No harm in trying, is there?" her husband said as his mouth covered hers in a kiss.

She had begun feeding Jonathan a little bit of pottage and letting him put some soft bits of bread in his mouth. Before long he would need the teat less, and she would begin bleeding and be able to bear her husband another child. Pity there was no surer way than suckling to keep from becoming with child again so soon. Kathryn had always pictured herself as the mother of a goodly brood of children, but she did not want to spend every year of her life either bearing or suckling a babe.

A good thing, though, that giving suck to a babe kept a woman from bearing another right away, for she had slept in Thomas Willoughby's arms seven nights running when her son was but a few months old, and hardly thought of the risks. And now, another four months later, her flowers still had not returned, and...

She lay awake, listening to her husband snore in the hearty sleep he always enjoyed after their amorous embraces. Counting the weeks, touching her own breasts and belly, thinking the impossible. Yes, her breasts were sore, but she was still nursing. Yes, her belly was rounded, but few women were as slim after having a child as they had been before. Surely, surely, surely it could not be? Could she have been such a fool as to let Thomas Willoughby get her with child?

A fortnight later, she was certain. The weather had turned chilly, Bess and the baby were doing well, and Kathryn sat in her bed and looked down at her own body and thought *Yes, I am with child.*

She tried to remember how soon after her unfaithfulness she had gone to her husband's bed again. The affair had ended abruptly when Nicholas returned to Cupids Cove. He had almost immediately begun with plans to remove their household to his new plantation, and Kathryn and the maids had been bundled off to stay with the treacherous Sheila Pike.

In all those hurried weeks, had she performed the duties of a wife for Nicholas? Most likely she had. She could not remember for certain, though she remembered with aching precision every detail of the nights she had spent with young Willoughby.

It might—it might be her husband's child. In the eyes of the law it would certainly be her husband's child.

And Thomas Willoughby would never know. He had gone back to England, back to his wealthy father's estate and the life he was born to. Likely he never gave a thought to the tradesman's wife he had tumbled during his brief exile in the colony.

For weeks Kathryn had been consumed by thoughts of Nancy, of what had happened to her dearest friend, whether Nancy was dead or was suffering torments at the hands of wicked men. Now thoughts of Thomas Willoughby rose up as insistently as they had before she had ever given herself to him. She thought that the fever of desire had burned itself out, that she could be a good wife and mother with no wayward desires. Now she saw that that desire had only lain dormant, waiting to rise up again like a dragon after a winter's sleep, ready to burn and ravage her whole life. Only now it was a desire with no object, no possibility of fulfillment.

If Nancy was still here, could I have told her this? Kathryn wondered. She imagined pouring the whole tale out into her friend's listening ear, but the truth was that when Nancy was with her, she had kept the business with Thomas a close secret. She could not have borne Nancy thinking less of her for her faithlessness. Yet she felt desperate for someone to talk to, someone who might share a little of the burden, and so she imagined Nancy there, and whispered to this imagined friend the things she had never told the real one.

SEVEN

A Reckoning Is Required

FOR A FORTNIGHT OR MORE AFTER LEAVING THE PORT OF
St. John's, Nancy was left in peace. The bar outside her door
was removed, there being nowhere for her to escape except into
the chilly grey water. And thus far, things were not so bad that she
would consider that possibility.

She returned to her routine of cooking the men's meals in her cabin
and serving them below decks. If Master Brown was not about when
she served up the food, there was a barrage of lewd comments, as well
as pinches or slaps on her bottom. Once, Nancy would have swatted
away the hand of any man who offered such impertinence—but once,
she had had a secure position as Kathryn Guy's maid. Now she knew
she could not afford to make any of the sailors angry. Master Brown's
decree that she was not to be assaulted must still have held some sway,
but she did not fully understand the balance of power on this ship, why
and how far the captain would allow the quartermaster's word to be law.

Both men worried her for different reasons. The captain, with his
narrow eyes buried almost to slits above the fat apples of his cheeks,
looked merry enough when he jested with the men, but he eyed Nancy
the way she would eye a slab of pork to see what kind of stew she
could make from it. As for Master Diligence Brown—for such, she had
learned, was his very Puritan name—she ought to have looked up to
him as a saviour. He certainly thought so, for it was his stern edict that

had kept her, thus far, from being used as the ship's whore. But she mistrusted Master Brown too: she saw in his eyes something of that same look that had been in Reverend Leat's eyes, back in Cupids Cove, when he had been willing to credit the malicious accusations against her. If Leat had been a greater power in Cupids Cove, Nancy might well have hanged for that bit of slander.

But neither the captain nor the quartermaster was near when a fight broke out on the 'tween deck one night after supper. Murphy—the leering, greasy-haired Irishman who had been cook before she arrived and who was forever slapping Nancy's backside or pinching her breast as he passed her—laid down a pile of dirty bowls next to the basin where she was scrubbing up. He put an arm around her, his hand grasping her breast.

She squirmed away but he held her fast. "I've work to do."

He put his other hand over her mouth. "You, wench, are a damn sight too saucy for what you are."

Nancy held still. She was usually able to let the men's insolence go at a few slaps, pinches, and coarse words. But Murphy held her firm in his grip. He tore the scrubbing rag from her hand and threw it into the water.

"Stop fighting me, cunny. 'Twill go worse for you." He pulled her away from the basin, towards the wall, and pushed her up against it, one hand holding her pinned in place while the other searched inside her shift and squeezed her bosom hard.

The other men on the 'tween deck were finishing their meal, lingering before going to their duties. A couple of them glanced in her direction, and she heard muffled laughter.

"Please," she pleaded as he shoved his knee between her legs to push them apart. His whole weight pinned her to the wall now, leaving the hand that was not on her breast free to hike up her skirts, grope beneath them.

"Shut your mouth. You been treated like a lady too long on this ship." His hand found the soft place between her legs and she felt the hard probe of his calloused fingers.

"Hoy there, Murphy, keeping all the goods to yourself?" That was another Irishman, a blocky fellow with a great scar across his face, whose name Nancy did not remember. "Give us all a taste."

Murphy took his hand from beneath her skirts and turned lazily to the other man, one hand still holding Nancy in place. "Sorry, fellows—I've got the lass, you'll have to take the cabin boy."

"Bugger the cabin boy."

"That's what I said." Hearty guffaws from the sailors now, but they were drawing closer, and Nancy made another attempt to wrest herself from the sailor's grasp.

"And bugger you too," the scarred fellow said. "You've no more right to take her than I do."

Murphy let go of Nancy then, reached to grab the other man. The scarred sailor dodged him, lashed out with a shove that sent the bo'sun stumbling.

"Come on, lads, fight!" the other sailors cheered. "You can take him down, Dillon!" one said.

Murphy and the other man—Dillon, she supposed—circled each other warily. Nancy, the prize, had been forgotten. She edged away from the group of men, into the shadows. They were between her and the ladder that would take her to the upper deck and the safety of her own cabin.

"Hold her, bo'sun," Murphy said to Master FitzRichard as he threw a punch at Dillon's jaw. "I'll want her when I'm done with this fool." FitzRichard, a sturdy, taciturn man, grabbed at Nancy's arm, but she dodged away from him.

"Men!" A hard voice cut across the cheers as Dillon punched back, catching Murphy on the chin. Quartermaster Brown waded into the fray, and the watchers fell back. Murphy, though, took one more swing at Dillon, only to have the quartermaster grab his forearm in mid-air and hold it fast.

Murphy turned his attention from Dillon to Master Brown, struggling with the quartermaster for a moment before stepping back, lowering his head before the other man's authority. "'Twas no business for you to meddle in," he muttered.

"Anything that keeps this ship from running smooth is my business," Master Brown said. "What was this quarrel?"

"The woman, sir," said one of the bystanders. "Murphy was havin' a go at her, and Dillon, he—"

"Shut your mouth, you," Dillon ordered.

Master Brown said, "Shut your mouths, all of ye. You know what my orders are where the cook is concerned. To your posts now, and no more of this."

The men scattered, all save for Murphy, who stood, facing off against the quartermaster, and Master FitzRichard, who hovered nearby, watching with interest. Nancy stood as still as she could in the shadows.

"To your post," Master Brown repeated.

"Your orders?" Murphy said.

"The captain's orders. My job is to make sure they're followed. As you well know."

"But we're sure, are we, that they are the captain's orders? The captain cares that we keep our hands off the cook? The captain wants us all to say our prayers and be good Christian fellows? Or are those your orders?"

"You need make no difference between them."

"I can see what you're at, Brown," Murphy said. "Ain't it right, bo'sun?"

FitzRichard nodded. "Every man on this ship sees you angling for power, setting yourself up to go against the captain. But no-one overthrows a ship's captain unless the men are with him—and they're not with you, Master Diligence Brown, that they are not."

"I'll see you flogged for that tongue of yours, Fitz."

"You try it." FitzRichard was backing away as he spoke, nearly to the foot of the ladder now, Murphy in his wake. Master Brown followed at a distance. He did not look at or speak to Nancy, and a few moments later, when she no longer heard their voices above, she climbed the ladder herself. She was relieved that none of the men stopped or spoke to her on the way to her cabin.

She barred the door and dropped onto the bed, wrapping the blanket around her shoulders, shivering hard. She wished she had some of the men's ration of brandy.

Nancy took off her apron and kirtle at last and lay down, swaddled in the blanket, to try to sleep. Her mind still raced, but she tried to let the rolling of the ship on the waves soothe her to sleep, as it had done these many nights now. She could not tell herself the lie that all would be well, but she could tell herself *All is well for now.* Tomorrow would be another day.

But tonight was not over. She was almost asleep when a heavy fist pounded at the cabin door.

"Open up, girl."

She thought of Murphy at first, of course. She could ignore him, as she often did when the men hammered at her door. But when the second volley of knocking was followed with another "Open the door!" she knew Master Brown's voice.

"I am abed, sir," she called.

There was a pause. "Cover yourself decently. Then let me in."

Nancy pulled the blanket from her berth around her like a shawl. If it had been Captain Sly, she would have taken the time to pull on her kirtle and apron. But knowing the quartermaster's horror at the thought of anything carnal, she felt that her state of undress would likely make him uneasy, and that was to her advantage. And indeed, when she unbarred the door, he looked discomfited. "I would ha' waited for you to dress properly."

She stood in the opening of the doorway, to discourage him from taking a step inside. "I thought it must be some great matter, and I did not want to delay you further, sir."

Master Brown avoided her eyes. "Let me in, Nance. I must have words with you."

"We can have words here."

"No." Now he met her eyes, and his gaze was once again like iron. Perhaps he only faltered when he was looking directly at her blanket-wrapped body. "What I have to say must be said in privacy." He shouldered past her into the tiny cabin, which seemed much smaller once his tall frame was inside. The last of the early evening twilight came in through the chimney-hole. She moved towards the lamp, but Brown caught her wrist.

"No. Darkness is well enough. Let it be."

"I seem to remember, sir, something said in church about deeds done in darkness."

She could barely make out his frown. "Gospel according to Saint John, chapter three. Men loved darkness rather than light, because their deeds were evil. You are like most poor wretches dragged off to church by your masters—remembering only the odd word here and there, bits of stories that might as well be pagan legends, for all you understand them."

"And yet I understood that bit well enough. Evil deeds in the dark." She had backed away from him as far as she could without moving towards the bed: she was standing up against the brick walls surrounding the fire, now banked and smouldering for the night.

"I have not come to do evil, Nance. I need—I must protect you."

"I'm doing well enough for myself, thanks all the same."

"No. No, you are not." He sat down on the edge of her bed, his hands working busily at each other, clasping and unclasping. "That whoreson Murphy had his filthy hands all over you. You've done what I feared—brought trouble among the men, quarrelling over you."

"'Twas no fault of mine, sir. You know I want none of them." She let a little hint of her true feelings creep into her voice as she said, "I want only to go home."

"But you cannot. The captain will see you put off in some port—down in Virginia, or in Ireland, it might be. He'll not bring you back to your own people, for you're not worth a rich enough ransom to be worth the trouble 'twould bring—on himself and on his own masters, if the folks in the colony knew this trade was going on under their noses."

"I'm happy to be put off in another port. I can find honest work there."

"Honest work?" He barked a harsh laugh. "There's no honest work for a woman, save she be an honest man's wife."

I would have been. But she said nothing.

"You make the men restless, with you here. The captain—he is no Puritan, though he agrees with me that raiding papist ships is a righteous act. He is—a simple man, driven by simple urges. Greed and lust. Like most men."

Time for some humility on her part. "I know you have done me a service, sir. A poor maid like myself might have suffered badly at the hands of these rough men, were you not here to protect me."

"Not for your sake. 'Tis my duty to God not to allow vice on this ship. But the captain does not see it my way."

She wondered if there was truth to the bo'sun's accusation, that Brown was setting himself up against the captain. Would that make things better or worse for her? "May you always keep him on the path of right, sir."

"No, no, no. 'Tis not enough, not anymore." He looked down at his busy hands, fingers knotting into and out of one another. "There is only one way—I told you when first we brought you aboard—for a woman to be safe from becoming the whole crew's whore, and that is for her to become one man's..."

"Whore," Nancy echoed, into the silence.

He looked up; she could make out the tilt of his head. "The captain told me plain—if I don't want you, he'll take you himself. You need a protector, Nancy."

"I thought you said you were my protector, sir. Without me needing to give up my—" what word would mean the most to him? "My virtue." That was the kind of word he liked.

"Virtue! A girl such as yourself—you said you'd been promised to marry a man? You'd have done as your sort do—tumble in some hayloft together, make your own handfasting with kisses and promises. What virtue have you left to guard?"

It all came back to Nancy then, but as if it had happened years ago rather than only weeks: a bed of boughs and needles on the cool ground, Ned's cloak between them and the earth, the blue skies and the pine branches above. Surrendering to his arms, to his sweet kisses, letting him take off her clothes so she was bare as Eve in the garden.

"We were pledged to each other."

"You are no innocent virgin. You are a fallen woman." He stood up suddenly, nearly cracking his head on the ceiling beam, and struck out fast as a snake to grab her upper arm. "I can only protect you if you trust me. Do you trust me, Nancy?"

Fear closed up her throat. He loomed over her, this large man so convinced he knew the will of God. Now, instead of remembering that sacred night in the woods with Ned, she was remembering sitting in the

Sunday service at Cupids Cove, hearing the word *witch* from George Whittington's lying lips. The eyes of the congregation upon her. She found herself shaking as violently as if she were out in a chilling wind. This was something far deadlier than Murphy's careless lust.

"I must make you mine, Nancy, so I can tell the captain you are my woman and no other man can touch you."

She forced words past her shaking lips. "Can you not—tell him 'tis true, without—making it true?"

"Tell him a lie, you mean." He was close, close now, pulling her towards him. He smelt of sweat and the salt air but not of brandy as the captain did; Master Brown was sparing in his use of liquor. Temperate in all things.

"'Twould be a sin, but the lesser sin than—than the other."

He put his hand under her chin, forced her face up to look into his, though she could barely see. "To take a woman such as yourself—'tis hardly even a sin. God will forgive me."

He pushed the blanket off her shoulders, thrust his cold fingers into the neckline of her nightdress. His mouth was on hers now, his beard harsh against her face.

She tried to pull away as he pushed her onto the bed—why? There was no place to flee. He forced her legs apart and her skirt up, the same rough motions Murphy had used. Though Master Brown thought he was so different.

Nancy closed her eyes and prayed that the business he had in mind to do would be over quickly. *Turn your hand to the task at hand.* Surely Aunt Tibby had never imagined she would have to do such a task as this to survive. But thousands of women had to do as much, and worse. The price you paid for having a man to protect you. Protect you from other men doing the very same thing.

His heavy body pressing her down; the stink and sweat of him as he forced himself on her, into her. Her mind spun wildly, looking for something else to latch onto. The only other time—no. She could not think of Ned, of their grove in the woods now. That memory would be tarnished forever. She thought instead of George Whittington, trying to force himself on her, back in Cupids Cove. There were men like this the world over, men who—

Suddenly, almost violently, he pushed himself away from her. The thought flashed through her mind that God had struck Master Diligence Brown with an attack of conscience, until she realized there were thundering footsteps and men shouting orders outside and above. As if he'd never had a thought of assaulting a poor maiden, Brown heaved himself off her, off the bed, and moved to the door. "Stay here," he barked, before leaving her alone in the dark.

EIGHT

A Rich Prize Is Taken

NANCY PUT THE BAR BACK ON THE DOOR AND WENT TO her berth, burying herself again in the mound of blankets. Something was amiss outside—she could hear the noise, feel the agitation of the sailors—but it seemed small in comparison to the turmoil within. The pain and terror of Brown's body on top of hers, pressing into her. Possessing her.

The noise outside continued, and the ship moved as if they were sharply changing course. After half an hour, when the racing of Nancy's heart had slowed, she dared unbar her door and open it a crack. At this time of night, the *Happy Adventure* would usually be ploughing quietly and slowly through the waters, or have dropped anchor in a cove if they were near shore. But now they were under full sail, men in the rigging shouting commands to those below, lanterns lit as if they were going at all speed towards a destination—or running from something.

She stayed behind the shelter of her door until she saw Robin cross the deck. He was the only man on board the ship she did not fear: he was such a green stripling she had little doubt she could best him in a wrestling match if need be. And he had never spoken coarsely to her as the other sailors did: likely he was too frightened to do so. Or perhaps he was truly a decent lad, his decency not yet worn away by his time at sea.

"What's the matter, Robin?"

He turned to answer her. "Cap'n sighted a Spanish ship, just past sunset. He set course to pursue her. 'Tis not common to see them this far north."

"He means to attack?"

"If we can overtake them." The boy was nearly bouncing on the balls of his feet with excitement. He had likely been hoping for a sea battle ever since he signed on to the *Happy Adventure*.

A full moon had risen, lighting the whole sea silver. Now that Nancy knew what was happening, she could see the other ship ahead of them, off in the distance. Abandoning caution, she ducked back into her cabin and pulled on her kirtle and shoes, wrapping the blanket around herself again.

As she stepped out onto the deck, she realized she hardly needed the blanket. It had been a fortnight, at least, since she had been outside at night, and the air was far warmer than it had been in St. John's. They must be well to the southward, now, into warmer climes and kinder seas.

Nancy stood at the railing, listening to the shouts and movement of the men above and around her. Nobody paid her any heed: no-one told her to go back to her cabin, nor did anyone offer a coarse jest or an unwelcome touch. With the deadly business of battle and plunder ahead of them, the men no longer had time for the light business of tormenting a woman.

She stood there a long time and finally went back to the cook's cabin and barred the door. Her sleep was uneasy, but she did at least manage a few hours' rest. When she woke in grey pre-dawn light, the ship was still travelling at top speed.

Some of the men must have taken it in turns to sleep, but even those who had been on watch all night were lively when Nancy went below decks to get food from the stores. She added salt pork to the pottage and passed out more ship's biscuit than she commonly did. If they were able to close the distance between themselves and the Spaniards, it would be a busy day: Nancy only hoped she would be alive at the end of it.

"We're gaining on them," Robin told her as he helped ladle out the pottage, "but Captain says 'tis a long chance, all the same, that we could take their ship."

"Then why is he going after it? Seems an awful risk if he's not sure we can beat them in a fight."

"The old hands are saying 'twill be worth any risk if we do take it, for we'll all be rich men. That galleon will be loaded down with gold, silver—all the riches of America."

"All of them, on that one little ship, is it?" Nancy shook her head. "Well, whatever happens, it won't be making me a rich woman, nor a free one neither, so I'll pray to save my own skin. And you should do the same. I never heard tell of no cabin boys getting rich off captured Spanish gold."

She was still on the 'tween deck after they had all eaten, scrubbing out pots and bowls, when she heard the command. The ship was slowing and coming about. Shouts from above. All the men were up top, except those who manned the guns.

Then it came: the first blast, rocking the ship, cracking the air with its boom. Nancy, caught off guard, stumbled and fell, striking her knee hard. She did not try to get to her feet. She stayed on the deck, her back against the wall and her arms braced round her knees.

Another boom, another crack. The Spanish ship would soon fire back. Nancy pictured a cannonball tearing through the ship's hull, straight into the galley. Would she be safer in her cabin?

Noise, chaos, the boat rocking, the report of the guns. Once, the screams were so loud and the rocking so violent she knew they had been hit. Finally, things seemed to calm—there was a long pause with still more shouting and crying but no more gunshots—and Nancy decided it was time to venture above deck to see what had happened.

The scene on deck looked like madness at first, but she could see that it was an organized madness, with Captain Sly shouting orders, Master Brown relaying them to the men, and each man doing as he was told. The Spanish ship was very near now, smoke rising from its decks, and the sailors on the *Happy Adventure* were throwing out grappling hooks to pull the two ships together. In one spot near the foremast, she could see that a Spanish cannonball had struck the *Adventure*'s deck. She understood little of what was happening, but it seemed that their ship had had the best of the encounter, and they were now preparing to board the Spaniards.

"Have they surrendered?" she asked one of the sailors as he went past.

"No, but they will soon enough. We have them outgunned and out-manned." Then he was gone, and Master Brown, standing at the rail, shouted, "Boarding party, to me!"

A dozen or so of the sailors moved on his signal, swords in hand as they leapt from the rails of the *Happy Adventure*, across the narrow gap that now separated the two ships. The Spaniards waited with their own swords drawn, and as Nancy watched the first man from the *Happy Adventure* leap onto the Spanish ship's deck, he was met with a sword to his gut. But behind him came another who slashed the throat of the Spanish sailor, and then the deck of the Spanish ship was swarming with men and swords and cries and blood, and the *Happy Adventure* cut the grappling lines and pulled a little away from the other ship.

The boarding party was left to its own fate now: to capture the Spanish treasure or die in the attempt. Captain Sly must save his ship, and prevent the Spanish from boarding. Even as they drifted apart, one of the Spanish guns fired again, the ball hitting the *Adventure*'s rail with a great splintering, tearing crash of wood. In the chaos, Nancy ran across the deck to her cabin.

She kept the door ajar so she could see what happened on deck. There was little action, now; they were too far from the Spanish ship to shoot or be shot at, and most of the sailors not busy in the rigging lined the rail to watch the action aboard the other vessel. "They're putting up a fierce fight," she heard one of the men say.

"What happens if they capture it?" she dared to ask a man who stood nearby.

"Captain'll put one of the men—likely the quartermaster—in charge of her, to sail her to a port where we can sell the cargo. Whatever of the Spaniards are still alive will be brought back in chains, to be ransomed if they're worth anything. And we'll have captured a dandy little ship, so Cap'n Sly will have the beginnings of his own fleet."

So Master Brown could leave the *Happy Adventure*, if he captured the other ship and was put in charge of it. Nancy wished she had a moment to think about what that might mean for her, but apart from the shudder she still felt when she thought of the man here, in her cabin, she could not spare thought for that. Things were happening too fast.

Someone cried, "Look!" and a moment later a ragged cheer began. Someone was up in the rigging of the Spanish ship, and the flag of Spain was coming down. "They've taken her!" shouted one man, and "God save the King!" shouted another.

The captured ship would fly a black flag soon, but at least some of the men must have shared Master Brown's conviction that they were doing God's will by fighting for Protestant England against papist Spain. Most of them, no doubt, were cheering not so much for the fall of Spain's banner as for the thought of Spanish gold and silver, and the ransom to be won from the Spanish prisoners.

They dropped anchor not far from the Spanish vessel, and put down boats to go between the two ships. Nancy was busy by then cooking salt pork for the men, and wondering what provisions the Spanish ship would have on board. When the crews were divided, would she be left on the *Happy Adventure*, with the rare luxury of a cabin to herself? Or would she be forced to serve Master Brown on the Spanish ship? Which would be worse?

As she brought the stew-pot down to the galley, Robin caught her by the arm. "Captain sent me to ask if you've any skill in binding wounds and the like."

The *Happy Adventure* had no ship's surgeon; Nancy supposed that simply by virtue of being a woman she was expected to have skill in these matters. As if she had ever dealt with sword and gunshot wounds! "I can do as well as anyone, I suppose. I've not had to bind men up after a fight."

"Matters not—he told me to come fetch you over to the *Caballero*. I'll take over serving the men their dinner."

So she went, rowed over by a taciturn sailor in one of the boats, and climbed the ladder to the deck of the Spanish ship. There was blood on the deck, currently being swabbed up, and a good deal of damage done by the *Adventure*'s guns. She saw no Spaniards, only some of the men from the *Adventure*. "The wounded are below—our men and theirs," Captain Sly told her, climbing up the ladder onto the deck. "We tend to our own first, but the Spanish captain and the best of his men, we need to keep them in fit shape as well, or there'll be no ransom."

Below decks, in the gloom, she smelled blood and corruption. The two sailors already at work bandaging wounds looked at her as if she brought some knowledge or skill with her, and, not wanting to show how little she knew, she looked about and said, "Have you found a chest of linens or any such thing, that you can tear up for bandages? No? You, go about and find one—there must be something we can use. We will need a lot more than what you have here, and more water boiled."

Then she looked at the wounded men, reminding herself that she had seen childbirth twice, and nursed a houseful of people through the scurvy. There was nothing so terrible it could not be borne.

"Nancy. Nance..." Master Brown's voice was a groan of pain, and she looked up from the man she was tending to see the quartermaster lying amid his own blood and some of his guts, too. Someone had made a clumsy attempt to staunch the flow of blood from the wound in his stomach, but the wound had found his vital organs and the bandage was soaked through already. From chest to navel he was one great gash; it was a wonder he was still alive.

She finished the bandage on the other man's arm and went to Master Brown. He had seemed so powerful and fearsome the night before, pushing her onto the bed, forcing her to his will. Now he fumbled towards her hand and grasped it even as she tried remove the mess of his bandages. She pulled away, but really there was no work here to do. She could clean it up, but even a skilled surgeon—had they had one—would not be able to sew Master Brown up. His lifeblood gushed from him; he would never command the *Caballero* to port as a victorious prize.

"You must—must forgive me, Nancy. For...for..."

She bent low enough that he would hear her. "For what you did to me? For the sin of fornication?" She had heard the word in church, and now felt she had been saving it all these years for the moment it was needed.

He nodded, every move clearly costing him. "I...I cannot go to God with that sin on my conscience."

"Last night you told me it was no sin, that God would easily forgive you."

"I...was wrong. I confess."

Someone handed her a pile of torn cloths; they had found some linens, then, to use for bandages. She handed them back. "There's men over there in worse need," she told the sailor. "This one's beyond bandaging."

"Is Master Brown going to die? We all feared it when we saw the wound he took from the Spanish captain."

"He is going to die, yes," Nancy said loud and clear. Then, to Brown, with her mouth close to his ear, she added, "And he is going to die without my forgiveness. You may ask for God's mercy, and perhaps he'll give it, but you'll get none from me. You can die knowing the last things you did in this world were murdering Spanish sailors and raping an innocent maid."

Brown's eyes widened, whether from pain or terror she could not tell, but she did not look away, only held his gaze with her own, hard and unyielding, till the sight was gone from his eyes and she knew he had stopped breathing. Only then did she turn her attention to binding the wounds of the other pirates and the Spanish prisoners.

It had been a successful day for the *Happy Adventure*. Many of the Spaniards were dead, but only three of the pirates—Master Brown and two others had been killed in the hand-to-hand fighting with the Spaniards. The Spanish ship was damaged but able to sail, and Captain Sly decreed that he would take charge of her himself, since Master Brown was dead. He would sail her to Ireland with her cargo: the gold, the silver, and the Spanish prisoners.

The *Happy Adventure* itself he put under the command of Master FitzRichard, leaving most of the crew aboard of her, with the unexpected cargo of six Negro slaves, whom they found bound in the hold of the *Caballero* and transferred to the *Adventure*. "Sail down to the Indies, sell them in one of the colonies down there. There's a better market for black servants there than in England or Ireland," Sly told Fitz. "When you've discharged that cargo, make the crossing. We'll meet at Gerrett's port to divide the spoils."

Sly was as good as his name; he had given Master Fitz his own ship, but kept the most valuable of the spoils on the ship he was commanding himself, giving Fitz little reason to want to mutiny and make off with the *Happy Adventure*. Nancy, still aboard the *Caballero* while these orders were being given, waited silently to see what her fate would be. She felt stronger than she had since being taken aboard: watching Master Brown die without the absolution he craved had filled her with a sense of power.

She was, then, in some measure, prepared to face the captain when he finally stood before her. "As for the wench—you'll be staying on the *Caballero*, coming back to Ireland with me. My fine Puritan friend with his lofty ideals is gone, I'm sad to say, and you're left to the mercy of us poor sinners. But never fret, maid, Captain Sly'll take care of you."

"Master Brown was not such a Puritan as you think him," Nancy said. "He made an assault on my virtue, and he was punished for it."

Sly looked startled. "Is't true? The old hypocrite!"

"That he was. He did not finish his evil deed last night, for he went to see what the business was on deck. When I saw we were going into battle I laid a curse upon him."

"You what?"

Nancy paused. Master Fitz and a few sailors standing round had overheard, and were listening, so she pitched her voice to be heard. "Did you not hear rumours, back in the New Found Land, of how a maid at Cupids Cove was tried for a witch, back in the summer?"

Sly shook his head, but one of the men said, "I heard tell of it from a fisherman in Harbour Grace."

"'Tis true," Nancy said, and that bold feeling of power surged through her again. "That was me—I was accused, and found not guilty. But they were fools, those men in Cupids Cove, for I do have powers—old powers, and strong ones. Why do you think you took this ship, though she was faster than your own? Why do you think no man of rank died save the one who raised his hand against me?" She looked Sly in the eyes as boldly as she had done with Brown in his last moments. "You may take the chance of abusing me, but you'll do it at your peril. You'd better far keep me aboard the *Happy Adventure*, and put me off at the first English colony you find, so I can seek a ship back to the New Found Land. Do otherwise, and I'll curse you all as I did Master Brown."

It was the most brazen gamble she had ever taken. They might disbelieve her and laugh, then teach her who was in charge. Or they might believe her too well. She was gambling that these men would be superstitious enough to believe her a witch and not devout enough hang her for it. When she saw the flicker of doubt in Captain Sly's eyes, she feared her gamble had failed.

But it was the bo'sun, FitzRichard, who spoke. "Don't take no chances with her, Cap'n. My granny—she had the old powers. She'd ha' been hung for a witch for sure, if anyone had taken notice of her— but nobody would speak up in the village, for they were all frighted of her. She could curse their cows and pigs, but if you were good to her, she could bless and cure too. You don't want to get on the wrong side of a witch."

"If a witch she is," Sly said. He did not sound convinced. Then he looked at Master Fitz. "If I leave her on the *Happy Adventure*, she's your trouble, not mine. Mayhap her tale is true and she did curse poor Brown to his death. She can be your curse, or your blessing—take her back to the *Adventure* with you."

"Truth be told, I don't know whether 'tis better to have her on board, or off," Fitz said, stroking his beard.

Now Nancy turned the full power of her gaze on him. Perhaps she truly did have magical powers, she thought. "'Tis as you said about your granny—the same was true of mine." Inventing an imaginary witch grandmother was the least of the sins she would have to be forgiven for when, like Master Brown, she went to meet her Maker. "If people were kind, and brought her gifts, and let her be, she'd bring them good luck. Cure sicknesses, and cast love charms, and the like. I can cast a charm to keep the *Adventure* safe in rough waters, and calm storms, till we get to an English port—but only if ye treat me well. I'll keep on cooking for you and the men, but no-one is to lay a hand on me or offer me any impertinence."

Master Fitz—now Captain Fitz—nodded slowly. "I won't say I'm easy in my mind, to have a witch on board, but as you're here 'tis better to make a bargain with you. I'll keep the men away from you, and you bring us what luck you can."

"And you'll bring me to an English settlement or fishing station?"

"The fishermen are all gone home by now, and there's nothing along the shore but Frenchmen and Dutchmen and Indians till we get down to Virginia," he said. "You might find a ship there to take you to the New Found Land."

She nodded. "All will be well enough as long as you keep your part of the bargain, Captain." She did not add, *or as long as a storm does not come up, and you find I'm powerless to charm it.* Or as long as God did not strike her dead for pretending to be a witch.

I will forgive You for not rescuing me, if You forgive me for whatever I've had to do to survive, Nancy told the Almighty, and got into the boat with Captain FitzRichard, to be rowed back to the *Happy Adventure*.

NINE

A New World Is Explored

APTAIN ARGALL'S SHIP SAILED AWAY FROM THE SMOUL-
dering ruins of Port Royal, the message clearly delivered, and
headed south. They were well out of sight of any coast, open
sea all around, when the dark grey clouds and rising wind warned of
bad weather to come. By nightfall the effort to keep the ship afloat consumed all of every man's efforts as the fierce wind blew and towering
waves threatened to swamp the *Treasurer*.

Dawn brought no easing in the storm, only the ability for the men to
see each other as they staggered around the decks, hauling on the lines
to try to trim the sails and keep some measure of control over the ship.
By the time the wind had died down and the driving rain slackened,
late that afternoon, the *Treasurer* was a battered echo of the trim little
vessel she had been. One of the masts had broken off entirely, and the
sails hung in tatters. Of the captured French ship that had accompanied
them, there was no sign.

"We've lost them for now," Argall told the men. "With luck and
God's grace, they may find their way to James Fort, and we will meet
them there. But we will have to make port and do some repairs to the
vessel. 'Tis a great pity Master Harries was aboard the French vessel."
Harries, the ship's carpenter, had transferred to the caravel to carry
out some small repairs. "I am sure you men can all turn your hands to
the work."

Later in the day, after consulting his charts, Argall announced they would make for a harbour where rumour said the Dutch had a trading post. "I had hoped to send to them, as well as to the French, the message that all this land is under our king's rule," he said. "Finding ourselves so near, and in need of a harbour, we will chance if we can find them."

The idea of burning another settlement hardly appealed to Ned, nor to most of his fellow sailors as near as he could tell, but they needed to make port. When at last they did—making slow progress due to the condition of the *Treasurer*—they saw no evidence of any settlement, not even one as humble as Cupids Cove or Port Royal. There were, however, two other ships at anchor in the harbour. Upon sending a boat over to hail them, Argall discovered they were indeed ships of the Dutch East India Company, exploring the area and trading with the natives.

Ned turned his hand, along with the other men, to repairing the damage the storm had wrought upon the *Treasurer*. He was one of the more skilled carpenters aboard: though he had apprenticed as a stonemason in Bristol, he had spent three years in Cupids Cove working on the settlement's buildings, walls and ships, and had become quite adept at working in wood.

"Perry, I've a mind to put you in charge of the new mast," Argall said, stopping by to watch Ned at work alongside Francis and Red Peter. "You know what you are doing with tools: put together a party to go into the woods and find a decent tree to cut down for a mast. I'm off to dine with Captain Mossel aboard the *Jonge Tobias*."

"He's a fair sight friendlier to the Dutch than he was to the French," Ned said, when the captain had gone and the men returned to their work.

"Aye, well, they are not our enemies," Red Peter said.

"Are they not? 'Tis so long since I've been in England I fair lost track of who we're at war with."

"Not with the Dutch. They are reformers, like us, not filthy papists like the French and Spaniards," the quartermaster, Collins, said. He spat over the rail into the water. "'Tis only a matter of competing for trade in these lands, between England and Holland."

"'Tis not as if we could attack them here, even had we the will to do so," said Francis. "We are in need of friends, and too crippled to make a hasty escape."

"There's no settlement to burn here, anyway," Ned said. "They must not mean to overwinter."

"Not this winter perhaps, but they could be clearing ground for next year. Might be their thought is to start small, as you fellows did up there in the New Found Land." Ned had told them a bit about his three years in the Cupids Cove colony, and all the Virginia men agreed that it sounded like a wise way to plant a colony, bringing a small group of men out first to clear and build, rather than dropping a hundred men on the shores of a foreign land with no plan for how to survive the winter, as had been done in the first years of the Virginia colony.

"But we've got a grand settlement there now at James Fort," Francis added, "and new plantations further up the river, with women settled in and babes being born—'twill be a regular town in a few more years."

"If the Indians don't kill us all in our beds," said Springer, the bo'sun, a dour fellow who seemed always to see the worst side of things. "Are they fierce up in the New Found Land, Ned?"

"We hardly saw them, even when we went looking to trade with them," Ned admitted. "We had the one parley, and after that it was as if they'd melted back into the woods. They have never come near the settlement."

"We'd be better off in Virginia if we could say the same," Springer said.

Captain Argall returned to the *Treasurer* that night in good spirits, having had a pleasant visit with the captains of both Dutch ships. They were, indeed, on a voyage of exploration and trade, but there was no plan at present for a permanent settlement. "They've one fellow aboard—quite the character, looks like an African, talks like a Portuguese, speaks a dozen languages. They brought him along as an interpreter, but he's settled down among the natives here and says he's taken himself a wife, so he plans to stay."

"So they are leaving a man here," said Springer. "Might be the start of something."

"I told them that the King of England has a claim over all this land, from Virginia up as far as the New Found Land, and that the Dutch can do nothing here without the permission of England. They agreed to all that—what more can we do? This fellow Rodriguez is no Dutchman, and he's living among the Indians—no fear he'll be planting a Dutch colony."

Over the next two days, while the men worked on the repairs to the ship, they learned more about the Dutchmen's plans. While the two Dutch ships would soon leave and only Rodriguez would stay behind with the Lenape people, Captain Argall learned that there was another trading post not far away, where a small group of Dutch fur traders planned to overwinter.

It was the mysterious Rodriguez who gave them that news: he came to talk with Captain Argall on the shore while Ned directed his work crew of four men in preparing the tree trunk they had felled to become their new mast. "You English are all hard workers, like the Dutch," Ned heard Rodriguez say. "I have never sailed with an English ship."

"Yet you speak our tongue?" Captain Argall said.

"Oh, I speak many tongues. In Santo Domingo, where I grew up, we saw men and ships from all over. And since I was a boy I had a—what do you say? A *talento*. For the languages." He strolled over to where the men were working. "It is good work your men do here."

Ned looked up at the stranger and grinned. "'Tis glad I am to hear that, for we are without a ship's carpenter and I am learning as I go along."

Rodriguez ran his hand along the surface of the wood, which the men were sanding smooth. "It seems good to me. But I am no carpenter. Only a sailor, and a translator, and a trapper and a trader. Enough work for one man!" His laughter was hearty and his face looked as if he laughed often. He was a short, sturdily built fellow, with brown skin darker than a Spaniard's and curly black hair.

"Too much work for me!" Ned agreed with a laugh, and Rodriguez clapped him hard on the back before turning to continue his conversation with Captain Argall, about whether the Dutch intended to plant a colony. "I think they will not," Ned heard him say, "for they do not want to bring their women over here. Better they do what I have done, and mate with the women already here. You must come to the town, meet my wife and her people!" His voice trailed off as he and the captain continued along the shore.

"Some chance of that—Englishmen or Dutchmen settling down with native wives," Francis said.

"There's some in Virginia as do it," Red Peter said, "but the governor don't like it. My brother lives down there—he brought his wife over from London with him, but some of the single men take up with Indian maidens. They don't count them as wives, though."

The talk of women and wives sliced through Ned with a quick pang. He had been in the company of the *Treasurer*'s sailors for several weeks now, slipping back into that camaraderie of men that he remembered from the first two years in Cupids Cove, before the women arrived. He had not forgotten his quest, nor what he had lost, but he kept busy enough not to brood on Nancy's fate.

Aye, well. If work was the cure for sorrow, then work he would. He bent his head again to the mast.

The Dutch ships left the next day—it was growing late in the fall, and soon the journey across the ocean would be too perilous. Rodriguez joined Argall and the men of the *Treasurer* again on shore as they bid farewell to Captain Mossel and the rest of the Dutchmen, with Argall again repeating his message: the Dutch merchants and their king must know that this was English land.

"English land, Dutch land," Rodriguez said with a laugh to a group of men on the shore when Argall's speech was finished. "It is Lenape land, if land is anyone's. Come, tonight you will feast with me in our village!"

And so it was that the men of the *Treasurer*—save a few that Argall left aboard to guard her—followed Juan Rodriguez through the forest, carrying boxes of the weapons and tools the Dutch had left with him as payment for his services over the past year. Ned couldn't help but think, as he followed the others on a well-worn trail through the woods, of the night in Truce Sound back in the New Found Land. A year ago now, at least, when he had gone off adventuring with John Guy and Henry Crout and the others in search of the natives and, for one brief and strange night, found them. They had had a feast of sorts that night, too—sharing food and singing and dancing by a beachside fire, trading small gifts. And then in the morning the wild men of the forest were gone, leaving behind furs to trade.

The natives of this place seemed to have no fear of white men—as

Rodriguez and the crew of the *Treasurer* entered the large clearing where the settlement was, many of the native men came forward to greet him and be introduced to the new arrivals. "They have all met my Dutch friends, now they meet my English friends," Rodriguez said. "All friends here, as long as all come in peace."

He presented Captain Argall to an older man, who Rodriguez said was his wife's father and chief of their people. The sailors stood around a long time as Argall and the chief talked, but after some time a few of the native men motioned them towards a long, low building. There they sat on the ground, and some of the Indian women came in to serve up the meal—venison cooked in a stew with some vegetables Ned did not recognize, but which were very tasty.

After the meal there was dancing and singing, as there had been that other time with the natives in Truce Sound. The Lenape men shared their strong drink with the English sailors—a different taste than any wine or ale Ned had ever drunk, but it was pleasant, and had the desired effect, lifting his spirits along with the music and drumming and dance. There were fires lit throughout the village, and he wandered around with Francis and Red Peter for a time, greeting the Indians and looking at their village, laughing with the small children who ran up and greeted them, first in their own language, then in Spanish and in Dutch. Ned squatted down to eye level with one little fellow and said, "Good day to you," and the boy repeated it back to him, then ran away laughing, calling "Gooday-to-yooouuu!" to all the sailors he passed.

Ned could not have told what it was that turned his spirits—some change in the music, perhaps, or one drink too many. Suddenly he was standing alone, apart from the other sailors, at the edge of a ring of men dancing around a fire, and amid the music and festivity, he felt again as he had felt on the beach a few days earlier.

Nancy.

He had set out to search for her, and instead he had gone to sack a French settlement and ride out a storm and now to treat and dine with Lenape Indians. Not one thing he'd done in all these long weeks had brought him a single step closer to Nancy. He still knew nothing of where she might be, or how he could ever rescue her.

I've been a fool, he thought, and sank down to sit on the chilly ground, holding his head in his hands.

"Come now, I like all my guests to be merry," came a voice from above him, that deep bass flavoured with the accents of every land. Juan Rodriguez stood above him.

"Forgive me, Master Rodriguez," he said, rising to his feet. "You are a good host; I should be merry."

"You should, indeed. Why are you not?"

"'Tis a common tr-trouble," Ned said, his drunken lips stumbling over the words. "'Tis a woman I lost."

Rodriguez chuckled. "Ah, you may find one here as I did—if it would make you merry?"

Ned shook his head. "Thank you, no," he said again. He thought of what Red Peter had said about the settlers in Virginia taking the native women to their beds, and he wondered if Rodriguez was offering the women of his wife's village to the sailors as bed-mates, or perhaps as wives, since he himself had married one. "My woman was taken by pirates, and I do not know where."

Rodriguez nodded. "Ah, yes. Many pirates in these waters. You know the ship?"

It took Ned a moment to remember the name. "I am told 'tis called the *Happy Adventure*. But this adventure has made me sad."

Rodriguez knew enough English to smile at the wordplay. "I have heard the name," he said. "It may be they go south. I heard of a Spanish ship captured by English pirates not long since—if you go on to Virginia you may learn more of that. But until then, you should try to be merry."

Ned tried—at least, he accepted another drink and several more after, and once he had drunk enough, the prospect of being merry did not seem so difficult. It felt wrong, but he could not remember why exactly.

The group was by now well mixed as to nations—English, Lenape, and Rodriguez himself all drinking and dancing together. It was still mostly a group of men; the Lenape women kept to the fringes of the celebration, though they appeared from time to time to refill the sailors' cups. One young woman stopped to fill Ned's drink again and smiled at him in a way that he almost thought might be an invitation. She wore her hair down, in a long black braid over her shoulder, with a fur cape pulled around her for warmth and a simple dress beneath it. She was foreign to him, and yet in her eyes and smile there was warmth and a kind of recognition, almost as if they had just been talking together.

She said something to him in her own tongue, and then spoke again, more slowly, in what he recognized as Dutch. Like the little children he had met, all of these Lenape people had learned enough of the sailors' tongue to be able to trade. Ned still could not understand, of course; he knew only English. He shook his head, feeling like a great daft fool, and she smiled and laid a hand on his arm.

There were more drinks, more music, more drumming. Ned thought that he danced for a while, with the pretty girl who kept disappearing and reappearing. Then she took his hand and led him away from the firelight circles, out of the cold night air and down a path, his drunken feet stumbling. She was still talking to him and he still did not understand the words, but it felt like a conversation nonetheless, and they both laughed when he tripped over the root of a tree.

In the shelter of trees he kissed her. There was a small house like a tilt in the woods nearby, and she took his hand again as they walked toward it. Ned said aloud, "Oh, I'm the worse for drink" as they went inside, but he supposed the words meant nothing to her.

The next clear thought he had was when he awoke beside her—it must have been hours later, for the sky was beginning to lighten towards dawn. His head pounded, and it took him more than a moment to make sense of the scene. He was lying on a low bed, near the ground, covered with blankets of animal skins and furs, his limbs tangled round those of a sleeping brown-skinned young woman.

Oh God, what have I done? Ned had no idea whether getting drunk and sleeping with native women was something so common that half the sailors aboard the *Treasurer* had done the same, or whether it was such a heinous breach of etiquette that he would be flogged for it. Captain Argall had said nothing about consorting with the natives when taking the men to the feast yesterday, and the thought hadn't even crossed Ned's mind until Rodriguez—damn that man!—had told him he should find himself a woman.

Ned had little memory of the night. He had been fair drunk, and he knew from experience that his manhood was hardly at its best at such times. But his breeches lay on the ground beside the bed. He had no idea whether he had to fear the wrath of the Lenape elders, or Rodriguez, or Captain Argall, or the woman herself. Had she a father or a brother who might burst into the room in a rage and cut Ned down while he lay there bare-arsed?

What a fool I am, he thought, and began to untangle himself from the girl, rising from the bed and lacing up his breeches. He paused, looking down at her, wondering what he was meant to do next. Then she opened her eyes—they were beautiful eyes, dark brown and fringed with dark lashes—and smiled sleepily at him, but made no move to rise from the bed or to stop him going.

Ned had swived exactly two women in his twenty-two years, once each. One was the woman he loved and meant to marry. The other, years earlier, had been a doxy in a Bristol whorehouse; he'd paid his pennies and done the business so that he might know what he was about. He had spent the years between them in a colony populated almost entirely by men; his experience of English women was scanty in the extreme. As for this woman—what such an encounter might mean to her, to this woman of the forest, he could not begin to imagine. Was he meant to pay her something or leave a gift? Or would that be an insult? He was far out of his depth here.

He hovered there, not knowing if he should say something in a language she did not know, or offer a kiss or a touch in farewell. She watched as he put his clothes on, then rose with a blanket wrapped around herself and followed him to the door. She laid a hand lightly on his arm, not as if to hold him back but to bid him farewell, or so he thought. When he stepped out of the tilt and into the cold morning, she made no move to follow him.

Ned stood alone in a clearing with several similar small dwellings; nobody else seemed to be stirring in the chilly air of early morning. He followed a well-worn path that led back to the larger clearing with the long building where they had feasted last night. The fires they had danced around had burned out; he saw a few sailors sleeping on the ground. He saw none of the other Lenape people, nor any sign of their host, Juan Rodriguez.

Ned wandered about the sleeping village, still thinking. It might be the way of this place, for the women to choose men as partners for a night and then to part ways. Or perhaps, for all Ned knew, he was married now by their laws and expected to stay here, like Rodriguez. Which he could not do because, faithless sinner though he was, he still had to find Nancy.

As the sky grew lighter, the men around the fire, who must have slept the sleep of the very drunk, began to stir. A few other men, including the dour Springer, came from the woods as Ned himself had done, looking worse for the wear. Finally he found Francis and Red Peter, sleeping beside each other under a cloak near one of the firepits, and he nudged them awake.

As they made their way back to the *Treasurer* Ned felt he was stealing away like a coward. But the Lenape woman had not seemed as if she would compel him to stay—and what would he have done, in any case, if she had?

It was a party of seven or eight men who walked back to the beach where their boat was pulled up on the strand, and they climbed back into it to row out to the *Treasurer*. None of the men had anything to say about how they had spent the night; Ned wondered if any of the others had found themselves in the arms of Indian woman, and whether those women had gone with the sailors willingly or not. The brown-eyed maid whose warm body he could still imagine next to his own had seemed to welcome his embraces, but how could he know, without a shared language to speak of such things?

"Captain came back about midnight, and he's still sound asleep, so he'll not know who spent the night," Master Collins said when the stragglers boarded the ship. He shot a look of disapproval at the sleepy men, and Ned dropped his eyes as he moved past, not wanting to see his own judgment reflected in the other man's gaze.

TEN

A Storm Rages

ANCY HAD WON—FOR THE TIME BEING. SHE WAS STILL aboard the *Happy Adventure*, under the command of a captain who firmly believed her to be a witch. She still had her cook's cabin with the bar across the door. Master Brown was dead; Murphy, the former cook, was aboard the *Caballero* with Captain Sly, and the reduced crew remaining aboard the *Happy Adventure* all eyed her warily now.

"You never said you was tried as a witch," Robin said one day as he helped her clean up after dinner.

"Master Brown would ha' seen me hanged if he'd known."

"So you really are a witch?" There was a mixture of fear and disbelief in the boy's eyes.

"We captured the Spanish ship, did we not? That took a powerful spell."

"If you really was a witch, how'd you get clear without bein' hanged before?"

"Ah, they're only fools back in Cupids Cove—easy enough to deceive. Half the poor women gets hanged for bein' witches are innocent, you know. A true witch could cast a glamour on the judges, to make them set her free."

Robin nodded thoughtfully, but did not linger once the scrubbing was done. She had scared away the one sailor who was halfway friendly to her, but it was a price worth paying.

God forgive me for the lies I've told, and for pretending to be a witch. She reminded herself again that God owed her something for letting her be captured in the first place.

They're only fools back in Cupids Cove. The words echoed in her mind as she lay tucked up under a blanket that night in her narrow berth. There had been some fools there, for certain—George Whittington first and foremost among them, and that girl Nell who'd been fool enough to marry him. Sal Butler with her slandering tongue. The minister, so anxious to catch a witch that he believed their gossip.

But the rest—they were not so bad, and some had been her friends. Daisy and Bess, her fellow serving-girls, merry and kind. Nicholas Guy, the master—not, perhaps, the dashing lover that Kathryn had dreamed of marrying, but he seemed a decent husband and ruled his household well. The other menfolk in their household, Frank and Tom and the rest—except for Whittington, they were all good fellows. Good, decent folk, all working hard together to make the little colony a success.

And then there were the two dearest people in the world to her—her mistress and friend Kathryn, and her—well, she must say her lover, Ned, must she not? He'd not had the chance to become her husband, not in the eyes of the church. If Nancy had one regret that rose above all the others, it was that she'd waited so long to fall in love with Ned, believing that he still held his boyish fancy for Kathryn. When she finally knew that his regard for herself was true, Nancy had gone to his arms gladly. She played those hours over and over in her mind and wondered if that was all she would ever know of love and passion, in what seemed likely to be a short and brutal life.

As for Kathryn—Nancy hardly knew how to think of herself apart from Kathryn Guy. They had always been each other's echo and looking-glass. Dreamy Kat and practical Nan; pretty Kat and plain Nan; mistress Kathryn and maidservant Nan. Nancy had crossed the ocean not because she wanted adventure—she had never dreamed of any such thing—but because she wanted to be with Kathryn. Or could not puzzle out how to be without her.

Now she was without Kathryn, without Ned. Without a protector or friend, a master or mistress, for the first time in her life.

How long had it been, now? Nancy had no clear idea of the time, only that weeks had passed, her hair had grown longer, and her monthly courses had come twice, which was a relief since she knew she was not carrying a child. If God ever granted her a chance to escape these pirates, she must be ready to move light and fast, with nothing and no-one to burden her.

It must be autumn now, the trees turning colour in Cupids Cove. *October gales, November gales*, she thought, remembering things the fishermen used to say.

Her work was lighter now that half the men had gone with Captain Sly on the *Caballero*. Captain FitzRichard talked of finding a settlement along the coast where they might seize some men, as the small crew made his work more difficult. But Nancy was glad of fewer mouths to feed.

To be sure, there were six new souls aboard, but they added little to Nancy's burden of work. Six Negroes—four men and two women—had been held in the quartermaster's empty cabin since they had been transferred from the Spanish ship. Two of the men had tried to fight off their new captors while being transferred to the *Happy Adventure*, but they had been outnumbered by the pirates. The other two men and the women seemed resigned to their fate, their eyes dulled.

Nancy's orders from Captain FitzRichard had been to keep them supplied with ship's biscuit and water, but to waste no other food on them. "They are cheap to feed—they do not need to eat like Englishmen," he told her with great certainty. "We only need to keep them alive till we get to a land where they have slave markets."

Nancy saw the Africans only when she brought in their daily rations. The cabin where they were confined stank, as they were given only a bucket in which to piss and shit, and that was rarely taken away to be emptied—Nancy refused that duty, so it was Robin's task. The smell affected the whole ship, as did some brooding sense of despair that seemed to rise in waves from the bolted cabin. Nancy was frightened of the trapped slaves, but she was also aware that for the first time she was not the only unwilling captive on the *Happy Adventure*. There were, she thought, folks whose lot was even worse than hers.

That night the wind seemed high and the seas heavier than usual. Nancy had become accustomed to the motion of the sea, had even grown to enjoy it. But tonight as she tried to fall asleep the swell was heavy, and the wind howled in the rigging.

In the morning, conditions were no better. The wind blew hard, rain slapped at her face when she looked outside the cabin; the ship pitched and rolled in the heavy waves. No question of cooking and serving pottage to the crew this morning—they would all have to subsist on ship's biscuit. Every man was busy keeping the ship afloat and steering through the waves.

Nancy barred herself in her cabin. She was only content when she was busy with work to occupy her hours. Otherwise her mind drifted, either to the past from which she was severed or to the unknown future. When they made landfall somewhere, could she find a ship going to the New Found Land? How would she pay for passage? She turned these questions over in her mind as the wind and rain battered at the ship.

Sheets of rain came down through the chimney-hole, and Nancy decided to try to protect herself and her oven by rigging up a spare blanket to block the opening. This proved fruitless, in the end—she had nothing to attach it with and it quickly got soaked through and then fell into the oven—but at least it kept her busy and stopped her from thinking for a little while.

The storm raged all day; she heard shouts that rose to screams, and the pounding of running feet outside and overhead. Then there were no sounds at all except for the howling wind. Had the storm grown so loud that she could not hear the sailors, or had they given up trying to save the ship and gone below to take shelter?

The tossing became so violent Nancy thought surely, surely this was the end. The ship pitched over until she thought that it must capsize. And yet, no, it straightened up and plunged into another sea-trough, keeling just as far in the other direction. Not only was water coming down through the chimney-hole now; it was sluicing under her door.

This was it, then. After surviving capture and the sea battle with the Spaniards, this was how she was going to die. And no-one who had ever cared for her—not Kathryn or Ned back in the New Found

Land, nor Aunt Tibby in Bristol—would ever know what had become of Nancy Ellis.

Hush now, don't be making your life out to be some grand tragedy. She said it to herself in Aunt Tibby's voice, the sort of thing Tib would have said to Kathryn when she was a young girl and got herself all into a swivet. *Hundreds of people drown in shipwrecks every year, 'tis no great thing to go to the bottom of the sea.*

Nancy gripped the wooden plank at the edge of her berth and hung on as the ship mounted the crest of another wave and plunged down again, rolling almost sideways as she did.

At least, she thought, it must soon be all over.

But it was not. Hour after hour, the storm went on, and to Nancy's amazement the ship went on too, not driven to the bottom nor swamped by the sea.

A banging fist at her door summoned her. "All hands below! Maid as well as men—we need everyone to bail." As she struggled out onto the sodden deck in the howling wind, the sailor who had called her added, "Can you charm the storm, witch?"

She could not. What she could do was stand up to her knees below decks, passing along a bucket of chilly water from one man to the next, a futile attempt to keep out the sea that was now pouring in from all directions. It was numbing, exhausting work that was also pointless, for they made no headway against fast-rising water. And as the ship pitched and rolled, the sailors lost their footing, spilled the very buckets of water they had just struggled to fill and pass along.

When it grew too dark to see, the captain ordered the men to stop bailing. "'Tis no good, and I fear we'll be driven onto the reefs or rocks of some island, for I think we be near the Isle of Devils. Get up high and find something to hold to."

When the end did come—midway through what she thought must be the second night of the storm, judging by the change in light and darkness through the chimney-hole—it found Nancy huddled in her cabin, clinging to the bed. There was a screech and a shudder, as if the ship were being torn asunder in the jaws of some great beast. A tearing, shearing split tore through the very heart of the ship, so that the splintering of wood was louder even than the howl of the winds. Nancy was hurled against the brick wall of the oven before collapsing onto the sodden floor of her cabin, now tilted at a rakish angle.

She lay huddled there, in the little corner made by the floor and the oven, and marvelled at how still everything suddenly was. The wind still howled, but the noise of the ship itself, the groan of its timbers as it was battered about in the waves, was suddenly and eerily silent. In its place, after a few still moments, came a man's voice.

Someone was calling, somewhere, and receiving no answer. The ship had run aground, and in the darkness someone was calling out for others, trying to see who else was still on board and alive.

Cautiously, Nancy pulled herself to her feet. Her ankle hurt like it was being stabbed, no doubt from being slammed against the brick wall of the oven, but she could stand, and with effort she could make her way to her cabin door, although it was now at an angle. With effort she pushed it open and climbed outside onto what had been the deck of the *Happy Adventure*.

It was too dark to see much, but there was no doubt that the ship was wrecked and run aground. The wind howled; rain blew down in torrents. Nancy realized she was still holding the blanket she had had wrapped around her in bed, and thought about her knife and her shoes. Whatever was going to happen when the dawn came, it certainly would not involve any more time on the *Happy Adventure*. She had best be prepared.

It took some time to get back into the cabin, longer to find her belongings. She still heard voices, though only a few. When she emerged again the sky was lightening towards dawn. Rain still poured down, but the wind had died. She saw no-one.

Picking her way across what remained of the deck, Nancy pulled herself to the ship's rail. The bow of the *Happy Adventure* was resting in what appeared to be shallow water; she could see land not far away, trees beyond a light-coloured strand. The main mast lay fallen into the water, severing the bow of the ship from the stern, which was far more badly damaged. Debris and bodies floated in the water.

Amid the wreckage, three men waded towards the shore; the water was no more than knee-deep. If they could do it, so could she. And if she could do it without being seen, the pirates might never know she had survived the wreck.

Get away to where? she wondered. There was land near, but what land was it? Who, if anyone, lived on those sandy shores? Natives or white men? And if they were white men, were they English or foreigners? Would they help a woman in distress? Nancy knew one thing: she would take her chances with whoever dwelt on the shore before she would trust herself to whoever of the *Happy Adventure*'s crew had survived.

She had staked her survival on convincing FitzRichard and the others that she was a witch. But any powers they might have believed in would not have been credited after last night. Without that illusion of power, she was defenceless. For the first time since St. John's station, she was in sight of land and unguarded; this was her moment.

She waited until the living men were well out of sight. While waiting, she crawled cautiously around the remnants of the deck, looking for anything else that might be of use to her. She cut off a length of rope that hung loose from the ship's lines, found an empty canvas bag, and filled it with the rope and some soggy ship's biscuit. As she crept about, the rain slackened and stopped. It was a warm morning, the clouds parting to reveal blue sky.

Her most sickening discovery was also the most useful. Underneath the fallen mast she saw a pair of legs sticking out, partly hidden by a piece of sail that was lying on deck. She did not want to look further, but she did: beneath the canvas she found a sailor lying, twisted amid the wreck. Most of his body was unharmed, but one of the fallen masts had caught him squarely in the head, crushing his skull. The lower part of his face could still be seen under the mess of blood and—she looked away.

Then she forced herself to look back. The little of his face she could see, the slight build of the body below it, so different from the burly forms of most of the sailors—this must be Robin.

She felt a moment's pang for the dead boy, then steeled herself. It was like the moment she and Robin had butchered Petal: need was greater than any sentiment.

"You were as good a friend to me as you were able to be," Nancy muttered under her breath. "You'll be an even better friend now, if I can manage it."

She took his knife from its sheath; nothing wrong with having two knives. Then she set herself to tug off his breeches. If there was a time she might have been ashamed to look at his naked lower body, such a time had long passed; all that mattered now was what she could get from him. She hoped the survivors would simply abandon the wreck rather than coming back for salvage, but she could not risk lingering long.

The breeches were off; the tunic was a different matter. It was meant to pull off over his head, which clearly could not be done now, but she managed to cut it free enough to tug it down the other way.

She shed her kirtle and shift and put Robin's clothes on instead. She was sorry to leave that poor, feckless lad naked amid the wreckage. What would the men think if they returned and found his ruined body in that condition?

The sea was calmer now, and the wind and rain had died down. She stood up in her new, torn, blood-spattered garments. The tunic was loose and did not show her breasts, even when she belted it. What was in her head? Something she'd seen the players act out one time, back in Bristol—a maid in dire straits, transforming herself with boy's clothing to slip into a new life. Nancy well knew what dangers might await a woman alone in a foreign land—in any land, truly. She took the long, thick braid of her hair, wet from the rain and the salt spray, and hacked it off just above the shoulders.

Hair cut short, breeches pulled up and laced, tunic belted, knife at her waist. She rolled up her own shift and kirtle—one never knew when it might be practical to be a woman again—and shoved them into the satchel along with the rope and hard tack. She slipped the second knife into her bag.

She had survived. She was alive, though God alone knew where. She thought of God, and remembered her grim determination to save herself. Now she shot a quick prayer to the Almighty: *I've done as much as I can. If you've any help to give, I'll take it.*

Next, to get off the ship. There were no living men in sight as she went to the landward side of what remained of the deck, so she did not fear discovery as much as she feared the long drop from the ship's rail into the water. And though she had seen men wading into shore, she could not be certain how shallow it was here.

In the end it was only a little above her knees, and the sandy bottom cushioned the shock of landing, though pain still shot through her ankle. The sea here was much warmer than the waters off Cupids Cove. After a quarter-hour of sloshing through the shallow waves, she was on a shore covered in fine pinkish sand, fringed by a thick forest.

She was tired now, and hot too, as the sun was rising in the sky. Her stolen clothes were wet, and she wanted nothing more than to collapse onto the sand and eat some of the ship's biscuit—although she would need to find fresh water soon.

Men's voices came from the trees. The survivors of the *Happy Adventure*, returning? Or the men who dwelt in this place coming to examine the wreck? Nancy sprinted on aching legs to the cover of the nearest trees to watch the men emerge a league or so away from her.

She knew them; it was FitzRichard and Dillon and one other sailor. Were they the only survivors? They looked as wet and defeated and exhausted as she felt. Their words were drowned out by the cries of seabirds that circled through the air all around. Something in her wanted to go to the sailors—they were men of her own kind, after all. But she turned and began to walk farther into the forest.

The wood she stood in was a strange one; the trees were not like those around Cupids Cove, the only forest she had ever seen till now. They were much taller and had a sweet, unfamiliar scent. They were sparse near the shore but grew closer together as she pushed farther in, through dense shrubs and bushes. This country, whatever it was, was verdant and fertile, and the ground seemed dark and rich. *Are we in Virginia?* she wondered. There was a sultry warmth to the air; they must be much farther south than the New Found Land.

Before she left Bristol, if she had ever imagined being on a ship at sea, being wrecked on a foreign shore—a fantastical enough conceit in itself—she would have been certain that a little walking would bring one to a town or village, for people were everywhere. Now, after a year in the New Found Land, she knew that was true only in England. In the New World, there could be miles and miles of shoreline or forest with no settlement at all. There were the natives, of course, somewhere deep in the woods. But as she had never seen one herself in a whole year in Cupids Cove, they seemed as alien as talking beasts, or the men whose heads grew below their shoulders—the fantastical creatures of sailors' tales.

Even as these thoughts ran through her head, she was walking—along a path that led through the trees, away from the shore. Surely the very fact that there was a path must mean there were men here as well? Though animals might make paths through the bush. Large animals. She chilled at the thought. The light was dim, filtered through the trees, and now she thought she could hear the sounds of someone or something else moving through the forest.

Was it a wild beast? Or one of the pirates coming after her? Or some other person who dwelt on these shores? She wondered, if there were people here, what manner of people they would be. They might be Spaniards, or French, or Dutch, or the natives of the country. If they were English, she would need a name and a story, but anyone else would only see her as a ragged, English-speaking boy, and deal with her accordingly. She hoped they would deal kindly.

She had been walking through the forest now for—could it be about half an hour? It was hard to tell, and she could barely see the sun. She was tired and thirsty, but more pressing than either of those was the fact that she was now sure she could hear someone else. Not behind her on the path, thankfully, but somewhere off to the side—on another path, perhaps.

And then she stumbled through trees into a clearing, and he was waiting for her, a knife in his hand.

Nancy realized she had Robin's knife in her hand too. When had she taken it from her belt?

She faced the stranger, each of them wary. He was tall, and broad-shouldered, and his eyes glittered at her from a dark face. Then, in a flash, she recognized him.

"You," she said, trying to drop her voice to sound less like a woman's. "You were one of the captives aboard the ship."

He lifted his hands slowly and spread them wide. "No chains now. You will not try to make me serve you, will you, Cook?" He laughed.

She hesitated, then put the knife back into the sheath on her belt. "You know me."

"You are trying to look like a sailor?"

"I thought to, yes."

He laughed again. "You look like a maid in breeches. But you might fool a stranger—in the dark." His voice was very deep, and his accent unfamiliar—not quite like those of the Spanish sailors whose cries she remembered from the *Caballero*, but something like them.

"Where are you going?" She wondered how he had got free of his shackles to escape the ship.

He had sheathed his knife too, and his posture was easy now. "As you are, I think—as far from those men as I can get. You were their captive also?"

"Yes. They took me from my home."

He gestured for her to come closer, and she did, standing beside him on the path now. "It may be safer for us to travel together."

"Do you think there is a town about anywhere? Do you know where we are?"

He shook his head. "I lived one time in Cuba, and some time in Santo Domingo. I do not think this is a place I have been before. There are many islands in the southern seas."

"I know nothing of these parts at all," Nancy admitted. "I was born in Bristol, in England, and went straight from there to the New Found Land, to a place called Cupids Cove."

"Ah. Those places are all far in the north, where the sea and air are cold. This is a kinder land—though the men are no kinder." He was silent a moment, looking at her, then said, "It may be you fear a man of my complexion more than you fear pirates."

Nancy had nothing to say to that. Save for this man and his fellow slaves on the ship, she had never been close enough to a black man to speak to him; there had been Africans among the lively mix of men on the Bristol docks, but she knew nothing of them. She thought of saying *I fear no man* and then *I fear every man*. One felt as true as the other.

Any thought of a reply was cut short by a thrashing, squealing noise in the bushes nearby. Both Nancy and the Negro man whirled to face it, knives out, though Nancy doubted hers would do much good, as she'd never used it for anything other than butchering and cooking.

Fast as an arrow, a hairy, four-legged creature shot out of the bush and past them, thundering down the very path they had been headed along. Nancy had a brief impression of tusks and a snout before its tail bobbed away from them.

In the sudden rush of tension, the slave laughed aloud, and Nancy joined in. "Was that—it looked like some sort of pig?" she ventured.

"I believe so." He sheathed his knife. "I think we know who made this path, and it was not a man. And we know there is pork to eat, if we can catch it."

"I can butcher and cook a pig, but you would have to catch it."

"So that is our plan," he said, and began walking again, down the trail the wild pig had just raced along. Nancy fell in behind him; without further discussion, she seemed to have agreed to his plan that they travel together. It would be nice, perhaps, to believe that her thin disguise lent her a modicum of protection, but the protection of an actual man—even one who had so recently been in chains—was likely to do her more good than Robin's tunic and breeches.

They walked on in silence. Birds screeched in the trees overhead, and they heard the scurrying of small creatures in the bushes. "Look out for snakes," her companion said once, and after that she kept her eyes mostly on the ground.

She was parched and kept expecting that their path would soon cross a brook or a stream, but there was none. "Is there no water in this country save for the sea?" she said at last, and the man said, "There may be none. Some of these islands do not have water like that."

"Then how does anyone—or anything—live here?" Her heart fluttered in her chest: had they landed on a place where it was impossible to survive? Surely there were such places in the world—where men and women could not live. Was this such an island?

They were stopped in a small clearing, and the black man turned and squatted low to the ground. He began digging with his hands in the soft soil. "If there is no water on top of the ground, often water is below," he said.

"You couldn't have done that where I came from," Nancy said, thinking of the hard, stony soil of Cupids Cove. But there, fresh water flowed in abundance from the many ponds and lakes, through rivers to the sea. Here, she watched with some doubt as her companion dug into the earth and water seeped in to fill the small hole his hands had made. "Won't it be salt? Is't not seawater?"

Instead of answering, he cupped his hands and drank some of the water, gesturing for her to do the same. When the tiny well had refilled, Nancy, too, drank a handful of the cool, earthy-tasting water. It was fresh and slaked her thirst a little.

She shared her small store of ship's biscuit as he dug deeper and they both drank again. When she put the round, hard cake into his hands, she was struck by the memory of bringing a pail of water and a few cakes of biscuit to the slaves in the hold. Her hands trembled a bit: surely he was thinking of that too?

Sometime after they began walking again, the trail widened. "This one is not made by pigs," her companion said.

"How do you know?"

He chuckled. "Pig does not use an axe."

She had not noticed the cut-marks in the shortened tree stumps, though now that he said it she could see them. "So if we follow the trail, it will lead to...someone."

Perhaps it would, but not before dark began to fall, and her companion said they would have to look for a place to sleep. So many things she had not thought of—needing to sleep in the woods overnight, needing food. What would she do if she were entirely alone? Tibby's motto—*Turn your hand to the task at hand*—seemed useful only in a place populated by human beings. She had no idea how to survive in the wild.

The man seemed to be better prepared. He cleared away branches and brush in a little grove, and Nancy was struck with the sudden memory of the last time—the only time—she had slept in the woods, in Ned's arms. They had thought little, then, about building a fire or finding food, about making a shelter or keeping safe from wild beasts. Nothing had mattered but the chance to be together.

The enormity of what she had lost rose up like a wave ready to engulf her. But she pushed it back. There was no time or energy to mourn. "Can we build a fire? Would it be safe?"

He shrugged. "I can start a fire, might be. And try to hunt something for food."

"Whatever you find, I can cook." She noticed he had not answered the question about safety.

He made a fire and then was gone for some time, while Nancy dug a small well in the ground as he had done earlier, and gathered some fruits—she was not sure what they were, but they looked edible—from the nearby bushes. When her companion came back, he was carrying the limp body of a very small pig.

"You were successful!"

"Yes. A great hunter." He smiled and handed her the carcass, and she set to work to skin and prepare it.

Roast wild pork, some small soft fruits that tasted sweet, and water that seeped in from the earth. All shared by a small fire in warm, unfamiliar woods, with a man whom the day before she had known only as human cargo. Warm as the night was, Nancy shivered. Once again, life had taken a far stranger turn than anything she could have imagined. She wished she could tell Kathryn this tale of adventure. *Someday, perhaps. But I'll not be able to tell it aright.*

As they ate their meagre meal and the darkness deepened around them, she said, "What is your name?"

After a moment he said, "Which one?"

Did he mean Christian name or family name? Did Negroes even have Christian names, if they were not Christians? "The name you want me to call you by," she said.

"My mother named me Omar. But in the mines where I work, the overseer gives names easy for him to remember. He calls me Paolo."

"What do you call yourself?"

He chuckled. "Omar, in my mind. But hard to remember, when someone shouts 'Paolo!' all day long."

"Shall I call you Omar?"

"If you need to call me by a name."

She waited for him to ask her name, but he did not.

For months she had longed to be free from the pirates, to be off their ship and on solid ground so she could begin finding a way to get herself back to the New Found Land, to Ned, and to Kathryn. Now, in the cruellest turn of Fortune's wheel, she had the freedom she wanted, but no idea where she was or how to seek help in getting home.

But at least she was not left entirely to her own resources. She had found Omar; he was a man, and strong, and resourceful. He did not seem to wish her harm. He slept a few feet away from her, his breath coming steady and even, his back towards her. For all she had heard Englishmen say that the black-skinned Africans were devils, he seemed a milder man than the righteous Master Brown, or the lecherous Murphy, or Captain FitzRichard. She did not need him to be friendly, only safe.

Morning came, dawn light filtering through the trees. It had got cooler through the night, but not cold enough to be uncomfortable, and it promised to be another warm day. Nancy felt sore, cramped and weary. She was surprised to find she had slept at all.

Omar appeared a few moments later with some more of the berries they had eaten last night. They shared them, along with what remained of the roast pork. After eating and drinking, they continued to walk. The path was widening, the trees thinning.

"If we come to a village or a plantation," Omar said, and paused.

"Yes?"

"If there are people there—and if they speak English, or Spanish, we will have to tell a story. Tell who we are. I can do best in Spanish, but as you see, I have some English."

"You speak it very well."

"I have been many places."

"I only speak English."

"And what will you say of yourself, if there are English people here?"

"I would give a man's name, but you seem to think my disguise is not good," Nancy said.

He turned round on the path to eye her critically. "It is bad. But being a woman alone is bad. An English woman with an African man— also bad. Say you are a boy. What is your name?"

"Ned Perry." It came to her lips without thought. She would have taken Ned's name in marriage. Now let her take it for her own, as long as she needed it. Ned would hardly begrudge her.

"Very well. I am Omar again, a free man. Many people believe an escaped slave must be returned to slavery."

They had names then, and knew what they were not—a woman, an escaped slave—but not what they were. They still had no story to tell, and Nancy's mind churned frantically, wondering what tale she could concoct to account for their presence in whatever place this was.

This is the sort of thing Kat would be good at, Nancy thought, with another pang of loss. She was used to thinking of her mistress as the weaker of the two of them, the one who needed to be cosseted and cared for. Could Kathryn have survived the pirate ship, the wreck, have gone off alone into the forest? Perhaps not. But with her fondness for tales, plays, and romances, she certainly could have come up with a likely story to explain these two travellers.

"We will tell them we are sailors," Omar said. "On some ships, men from many lands work together. Our ship sank, and we escaped the wreck, came to these shores, and walked to find a town."

"Most of it is true," Nancy pointed out.

"Yes. But if the men from the ship are here before us, it is a story of—" he gestured at a large spiderweb in one of the trees that edged their path—"of weavings."

"Cobwebs," Nancy said.

"I cannot think of a better—can you?"

"No. We will be sailors," she agreed.

"I was a sailor once, and you a ship's cook. You should let me talk, for the most."

"For certain." Her disguise as a young boy would hold up better the less she spoke. "And if they speak Spanish, you will have to do all the talking."

"I also know Portuguese."

"As well as English? How do—how did you learn so many tongues?"

"As I said. I was a sailor."

A sailor who had somehow been forced into bondage. Nancy wondered about Omar's history, but he was no storyteller and did not seem inclined to lighten their path with unnecessary conversation. So she trotted along silently behind him as the blazing sun rose higher in the sky and the day grew hotter. It was autumn—how could it be so hot?

She almost walked straight into the back of him, keeping her eyes on the ground for the snakes he had warned her of. He had stopped in the path, pointing ahead. Through the thinning trees, there was another stretch of beach, and then the sea. And along the shore, several buildings. "There are folk up ahead. And whoever they be, we must go and beg their help."

ELEVEN

A Feast Is Celebrated

A LL AROUND THE BIG DWELLING HOUSE, VOICES RANG
out in merry harmony.

The boar's head in hand bear I
Bedecked with bays and rosemary!

What Elizabeth Guy brought from the hearth was not, in fact, a
boar's head, but a whole roast piglet. Good thing, too; it would have
better eating on it than a head alone. And while it was not bedecked
with bays and rosemary, it was fragrant and well spiced, and the platter
was adorned with preserved berries and apples and sprigs of evergreen.
Everyone joined in the carol as the Twelfth Night feast was laid on the
long table.

Kathryn picked up her son, who was trying to climb from the floor by
her skirts, and put him on her lap so he could see the feast laid out before
them. At nine months he was still far too young to understand about
Christmas or the twelve days. He only knew that he always wanted to be
up, up, up, able to see everyone and everything happening around him.

"Take care, sweeting," said Nicholas, and transferred the baby to his
own lap. "There's scarce room for two there."

Nicholas was peacock-proud of Kathryn's swelling five-month
belly, and was quick to take her share of any burden and spare her

lifting anything heavy, including the child they already had. Kathryn had almost managed to bury that little stab of guilt she felt every time Nicholas gave her a proud smile or said how fine it would be when they had two children to bring to the new plantation.

She resolved in her own mind that she would never know for certain whether the babe was Nicholas's child or Thomas's. What difference would it make, in the end? Nicholas believed the child was his—had no reason to think otherwise—so it would bear his name and he would raise it and love it. He was a kindly father, she knew already; she was a fortunate woman in so many ways.

Which thus bedeck'd with a gay garland
Let us servire cantico.

Everyone sang with great gusto, though a little distance away Kathryn heard Jem Holworthy mutter, "I don't hold with all this Latin, 'tis popish nonsense."

"Peace, man, 'tis only a carol, just a bit of fun," Nicholas said. "Even a Puritan can enjoy his dinner and a song, may he not?"

"Never said I was a Puritan, only that I don't hold with Latin." But Holworthy tucked into his roast pork right heartily, not too greatly troubled by the popish prattle.

The diners at the feast were all the inhabitants of the big house, Philip Guy's house—the acting governor and his family, Nicholas and Kathryn and their servants, and a half-dozen others. Neither the Whittingtons nor the Butlers were here, both presiding over Twelfth Night feasts in their own houses, though there had been talk of everyone coming together later for dancing and games. Kathryn still longed for the peace and privacy of their own house and land, but she did enjoy a gathering such as this one, with music and feasting and laughter.

She imagined next year—celebrating their Christmas and Twelfth Night feast in their own house. Bess and Frank and the baby would be with them, of course, and her two children, and Daisy. But her imagination persisted in peopling the table with those who could not be there. Ned and Nancy ought to be at that table, and poor Tom Taylor by Daisy's side.

Welladay, 'twas folly to imagine Tom would ever sit beside Daisy again; that poor girl had buried two husbands now. But Ned and Nancy—could they return? She had placed such hope in Ned's idea that he could somehow go find Nancy and bring her home—it was like a knight's quest in a romance. But truly, what were the chances of finding one young woman, with all the vast ocean to search? Even Kathryn, much as she loved tales and romances, knew that love alone was not equal to such a task.

When the meal was done, the singing began again, with Frank taking up the fiddle to play some Christmas tunes. Everyone joined in to sing the one about the cherry tree, and Kathryn's mouth watered at the thought of fresh, ripe cherries. So far no-one had found any growing in this land, and they were among the English delicacies she missed. "I wish I had cherries now," she said to her husband.

He laughed, "You and the Virgin Mary! I vow, if we were in a cherry orchard I'd gladly pick you some."

Kathryn's cheeks flushed. She had forgotten that in the carol, Joseph refused to pick cherries for Mary because she was carrying a child that was not his. "I'll make do with a slice of that pudding, if you'll go and fetch me some," she said quickly. *Whoever fathered this child I'm carrying*, she thought, *'twas surely not the Holy Ghost*.

The door opened, and the chilly night wind blew in. Along with a swirl of snow, seven or eight people entered the room, but it was impossible to tell who they were. Every face was covered up with a cloth mask of some kind. Bess clutched her baby closer and let out a little shriek. "'Tis the pirates come again!" she squealed.

A ripple of nervous laughter greeted her cry—no ship could have come into the ice-filled harbour in the dead of winter—but the voice that responded was easy to recognize as George Whittington's. "Aye, 'tis me, the great Captain Easton—not come to burn and steal, but to mummer and sing for you!" Another of the masked figures put a recorder to the cut-out mouth of his mask, and as the piping began, the mummers all burst into a carol. Frank's fiddle joined the tune, and soon everyone was clapping hands and singing together.

Kathryn would always hate Whittington for his false accusation of witchcraft against Nancy. Now he was making the dreaded pirates into figures of fun, which was cruel to those who had suffered so much, especially Daisy. 'Twas a pity this man and his uncouth ways should be at the centre of the mummering, for Twelfth Night, that magical night of merrymaking before Christmas ended and everything turned commonplace again, had always been her favourite part of the season.

As the mummers pulled off their masks and accepted food and drink, and everyone began forming two lines for a dance, Kathryn's disapproval of Whittington fought with her desire to enjoy the celebration. She could not join the dance anyhow, not with one child growing sleepy on her lap and another growing great in her belly, but her feet tapped a lively patter to the music of fiddle and pipe. "You ought to get up and dance," she told her husband, "don't sit by on my account."

"I'd far rather sit by my lovely little wife than dance with any maid here," he assured her. 'Twas easy enough to pronounce, for there were still very few women in the colony, and every woman at the feast, save for poor Daisy, was some man's wife. *They will have to bring out more women from England again, if this place is to thrive*, Kathryn thought. Nonetheless, she enjoyed her husband's flattery. *He is a good man*, she reminded herself. As she often did.

She finally convinced him to get up and join a circle dance—"'Twill give me pleasure to see you enjoy it, since I cannot dance myself," she told him. Little Jonathan had fallen asleep in her arms, a pleasant weight against her breast, and she sat watching the dancers, losing herself in the music and movement, until she heard George Whittington's voice in her ear.

"Good even, Mistress Guy—and a merry Twelfth Night to you."

She stared straight ahead at the dancers, not sparing him a glance or a word as he settled into her husband's place on the bench. "You've no good wishes for me?" he prodded. "Not even in the season of peace and goodwill?"

"What would you know about either of those things?"

He chuckled. "Aha, still frosty toward me, are you, Mistress? Had I only Thomas Willoughby's blue eyes, mayhap you'd give me a warmer welcome."

Now she turned to look at him, trying to make her gaze haughty enough to freeze the ale in his cup. "I know not what you mean—that wastrel lad has long been gone from these shores. But we all know you are a great one for spreading lies."

He clicked his tongue. "Still angry with me over that, then?"

"For trying to have my maid put to death? Do you suppose?"

"Oh, surely not. She might have got a whipping, or a turn in the pillory if we had one. At worst."

"Had we a pillory, I know who ought to be in it."

Whittington laughed again. "Not me. I am the governor's favourite—pardon, the *acting* governor. Even if I expect to soon see his place taken by another." Seeing that Kathryn still steadfastly ignored him, watching the dancers, he leaned closer to her ear. "I have met your neighbours."

She thought he was talking nonsense—were they not all neighbours here, living cheek by jowl as they did?—but then another possibility occurred to her. Though she still did not turn to look at him, she said, "I have no idea who you mean."

"Yes you do. The fine Irish princess, Sheila NaGeira? And her husband, the dread pirate Pike? Ah, I see that shaft has landed."

"Why should it? We all know that the Pikes are living up the coast by Harbour Grace."

"But how many have visited them? I have."

"I cannot imagine why."

The dance ended and the two circles of dancers broke apart with much laughter and clapping of hands. Across the room, Kathryn saw Daisy and Bess, who had both been pulled into the dance—Bess's babe must have settled down to sleep. A moment of lighthearted fun was so rare for both those poor lasses: Kathryn was glad to see the smiles on their faces as they went hand in hand back to the bench to sit down. Nicholas caught her eye on his way to refill his ale cup and gestured to Kathryn: would she like another? She nodded her thanks.

Whittington was still talking. "Good folk to know, the Pikes. They've plans of their own for this shore—plans that might not fit well with those of the Bristol merchants. They know where the real money is to be made in this place."

Nicholas was weaving his way back across the crowded room towards her, two mugs of ale in his hands. She guessed that when her husband returned, Whittington would scarper, and indeed she heard him shift on the bench. But before leaving, he bent close to her once more and said, "One word of warning, good Mistress Kat—you'd best convince your husband to abandon his plan to rebuild his plantation. 'Tis a dangerous place to settle—he must have learned that by now. 'Twould be well for him to stay here in Cupids Cove, if not to go back to England altogether." And then he was gone, back into the throng of merrymakers.

"Was that cur troubling you?" Nicholas asked.

"Nay—I paid him no heed."

Across the room, she heard men's voices raised in anger, and her first thought was that Whittington had gone to sow discord elsewhere. But no, he was standing aside quaffing his ale, watching the altercation with interest as Sam Butler, his mummer's mask cast aside, argued with one of the new colonists, a man named Warford.

"'Twas Bristol men built this colony, Bristol men who sowed the soil—not your rich masters in London!" Butler said, his words slurring a little. More strong drink had been taken here tonight than was common in the colony, and tempers rose along with the temperature in the room.

"And Bristol men will run it into the ground!" Warford shouted back.

"Peace, fellows!" Philip Guy said, separating the two before they could come to blows. Kathryn watched the smirk on George Whittington's face and thought of how he expected Philip Guy to soon be replaced with another governor.

"Whittington only wants to find trouble wherever he can," she told Nicholas in bed that night, "and see what profit there may be for him in it. I fear he'll find a way to deepen the rift between the London and the Bristol men, and that your cousin Philip be not strong enough to stop it."

Nicholas turned to her in the darkness. He had rigged up a curtain around their bed to give them a shred of privacy, since several other people slept nearby in the large chamber at the top of the house. The hangings also provided a little warmth against the cold of these winter months, though the presence of three bodies in the bed—Jonathan snuggled between his parents—helped as well.

"What was he saying to you? I thought he knew to keep clear of you."

"He came only to torment me, I am sure." She did not, of course, repeat his comment about Thomas Willoughby, but said, "He told me that he has been to see Gilbert and Sheila Pike, that he knows all about them."

"In truth, he said that?" Kathryn could not see her husband's face in the darkness of their bed, but she heard the puzzlement in his voice.

"He did. I do not know when or how—"

"Whittington and a few men took the shallop up the coast in the autumn—looking for salvage, they said, from a wreck. He might well have gone to see the Pikes—but why?"

"The one thing you can be sure of with Whittington is that nothing he does is to any good end," Kathryn said. "If he heard of the Pikes and went to seek them out, he must see some advantage to him in it."

"It might be naught. The man likes to talk, to make himself bigger than he is. He was only a servant in John Guy's household when he came over here."

"He has ambitions," Kathryn whispered. "He gave me a warning— told me I should tell you to abandon the plantation, to stay here in Cupids Cove."

Nicholas gave a sound between a grunt and a snort, and Kathryn shushed him with a finger to his lips. "That runs well with what we feared," he said after a moment, "that the Pikes are in league with the pirates and want no-one settling nearby that might challenge their business. But I fail to see where Whittington comes into it all."

"But what of his warning? Will you heed it?"

"Not a chance." He drew his face closer to hers; she still could not see him, but his breath was warm on her mouth. "Fret not, little wife. You are not afeared, are you?"

Not afeared? After Daisy had been shot, Tom killed, and Nancy stolen away from them? What kind of fool would not be afeared? Aloud she said, "I would not have rogues drive us away from our own land."

"That's my fine, spirited lass. In the summer we'll be there again— along with our new little one. And all will be well."

She could not take much comfort from his promise—all had not been well last summer. She thought of Sheila Pike, that imposing woman with her great masses of black hair piled atop her head and her haughty way of looking down her nose. There was no doubt in Kathryn's mind that if they moved back to the plantation, she would meet the Irish princess again. *And now that I know what your true aim is, I will be more than a match for you, my lady,* Kathryn thought as she drifted off to sleep.

TWELVE

A False Identity Is Assumed

NANCY STAGGERED A BIT AS SHE PUSHED THE BARROW of stones uphill. The sun was no longer burning hot, but it was warm enough that she worked up a good sweat by midday, helping to build the fortifications.

Even in Cupids Cove, she had never worked so hard. There, the women had worked in the gardens alongside the men, but constructing walls and buildings was men's work. Wearing breeches and using a man's name meant doing a man's work, and in St. George's on the Bermuda Islands, that meant, for the most part, working on construction. The governor was putting the settlers to work strengthening the island's defences, building stone forts all around the settlement with wooden towers looking out to sea.

It had been more than three months since she and Omar had walked out of the forest and into the settlement with their tale of shipwreck. The bustling colony reminded Nancy, in many ways, of Cupids Cove—though there were more people here than there had been in Cupids Cove during that busy summer when she and the other women had arrived. This was another English colony—similar to Cupids Cove in the sort of people who had settled it, different in the gentle climate and rich soil all around.

Different in another way, too: there was no stockade fence around St. George's; she and Omar had simply walked into the town. This, she now knew, was because there were no natives on the islands, so the settlers had no fear of attack by land. All their fear was focused on the sea: the Bermuda colonists were more afeared of pirates even than the folk in the New Found Land were. *And with good reason*, Nancy thought: the *Happy Adventure*, had it survived the dangerous reefs offshore, could well have attacked this peaceful settlement, though the colonists' main fear was, of course, the Spanish.

At any rate, wrecks were common enough on these shores that no-one questioned the tale Nancy and Omar told. In fact, they learned, the island had only been settled by accident after a group of English settlers bound for Virginia had wrecked there. The two recent castaways had pronounced themselves ready to work. They had been given beds in one of the communal houses and work to do in helping build the fortifications around the new settlement. There had been no sign of the surviving pirates from the *Happy Adventure*.

Their fellow labourers seemed decent fellows. As at Cupids Cove, there were far more men than women. In the communal dwellings they slept twenty under one roof, with a married couple, Master and Mistress Quickly, to oversee them and keep house. Nancy knew it would be a frightening place to close her eyes without her boyish disguise.

Omar slept in the bed next to hers, and worked and ate with her as often as he could; though they never discussed it, she knew he saw himself as her protector. She was always on edge with this game she was playing, careful to busy herself somewhere else when the men went into the sea to bathe or even when they pissed against a wall or into a bush. She made excuses to go off by herself when she needed the privy, and wondered if her monthly courses were to come on her, how she would conceal them. But she had not had them since arriving on the islands; fear, distress and constant changes made a poor field for her flowers.

Her muscles ached all day and every day, but a body grew strong through repeated labour, whether it was a woman's body or a man's. Though she still lagged behind the others, they put that down to the fact that this fellow Ned was young and inexperienced.

"Never mind, your mate there does enough work for the both of you," one of the other men, Hal, said one day when Nancy apologized for not getting a load up the hill to him fast enough. He nodded at Omar. "Those blacks can work like beasts—'tis why the Spaniards keep them as slaves, you know."

"It seems cruel to me, to keep a man the way you'd keep a beast," Nancy ventured.

"'Tis different for them—they do not feel pain or labour as we do," Hal assured her. "You can see it in Omar—he never tires. I've heard the masters say they could get more work done here if they bought Negroes from the Spanish."

Nancy nodded but said nothing, busying herself with something, and Jem soon passed on to another task. The topic of slaves was an uneasy one, for Omar had told her that slavery, as he had known it, was something far harsher than simply being bound to indentured service: he said he would kill or die before being taken again. Since the English did not keep men bonded for life as the Spanish did, he felt safer in an English colony. But when she told him that night what Hal had said, he nodded.

"It will come, of course. The English will not let themselves fall behind the Spaniards. Only a fool would pay men to work when you can get slaves to do the same labour for nothing."

They sat together on a low stone wall overlooking the docks, eating their evening meal—pastries they had taken from the dwelling house to eat outdoors, away from their fellow labourers. The pastries were more meat than crust; flesh was plentiful on the island, though much of it was odd-tasting, coming as it did from tortoises and seabirds, in addition to the wild pigs. Flour was in short supply, however; as in the New Found Land, the grain was shipped from England, and the large population within the narrow bounds of St. George's settlement was running short while awaiting the arrival of more supplies.

The sun, dropping towards the horizon, glinted off the broad expanse of blue water like a handful of gemstones, and Nancy thought how different the sea looked here from how it had in Cupids Cove—a different, warmer shade of blue.

"So you would not be safe, even here?" she said. "Do you truly think Englishmen would keep you in chains?"

"There is no evil men would not do to other men," Omar said.

Or to women, she thought, but said, "Where could you go, where you could be sure of being free? Back to Africa?"

"No." His voice sounded heavy and cold. There was nothing chatty about Omar, nothing that encouraged confidence and conversation, even for her. She felt she knew him a little by now, well enough to know that when he fell silent after saying that "No," it was not because he did not wish to tell her, but because he did not know, himself, where he would go to live as a free man.

After a long silence he said, "I have never been in Africa. I was born in the Indies—my mother was a slave and my father, I think, must have been the owner or the overseer. I was lucky to get away to sea when I was young. The deck of a ship is safer than land, sometimes."

"Yet when I met you, you were chained in the hold of a ship."

He nodded. "Not all ships are safe."

"You could come with me. If I get back to the New Found Land—there are no slaves there."

He chuckled again, that low deep laugh. "Are there any black men at all?"

"No."

"That is why there are no slaves. Some men never think of putting chains on another man until they see him. Then, they have the thought." He paused to take another bite of his pastry, and gestured at the men milling about on the docks, talking and drinking now that their day's work was done. "Are the people in your New Found Land any better than these here?"

Nancy shook her head. "No—no better. There was a man there who tried to have me condemned as a witch, all because I would not go to bed with him. But there are good people. My mistress and her husband would take you in, I'm sure."

"I will not trust to people's kindness." He stood up, brushing his hands on his breeches. "Perhaps a ship will come soon."

Nancy's first thought, once they knew where they had landed, had been to find a ship that could take her back to the New Found Land.

But few ships had put in to St. George's over these winter months, and of those that had, one was going straight back to England and another to the Virginia colony. She had only the vaguest idea of how all these places were dotted about the ocean, but she knew that at this time of year, no ship would be sailing to the New Found Land, for the fishing season there did not begin until late spring or early summer. As long as they saw no sign of the pirates from the *Happy Adventure* in St. George's, she was content to bide here until spring.

Sometimes she enjoyed doing a man's work, the freedom of striding about in breeches, but she was always wary lest her secret be discovered. "No ship will come that is going where I want to go," she said, falling into step with Omar. "But one may come that suits your purposes."

They walked along the path that followed the shore, stretching out the time before they would return to the crowded dwelling house. The settlement was still a bustle of activity, even with the working day done for most folk—the town was crowded, and the governor wanted everyone to stay within the bounds of the settlement rather than spreading out onto the rest of the islands.

"It might be," Omar said. "I look for a place on a trading ship or a privateer, some ship where the captain does not think so much about a man's complexion. But I wish to see you away safe before I find a ship for myself."

"You are not bound to wait for me."

"If I am not here—it may go harder for you."

A man's protection. Even a man that some of the other workers saw as little better than a beast, because of his dark skin, offered some small degree of protection. Anything was better than being a woman alone in a colony, unattached to any man or family.

When they returned to the dwelling house, the men were passing around a jug of liquor they had brewed themselves, and the mood was uneasy. "Might as well drink, seeing we never got enough to eat," a man they all called Big Willie muttered as he passed the jug along.

"When I signed up to come over here in the fall, they told me this place was the land of milk and honey—jewels lying on the sand for anyone to pick up, soil so sweet you'd only to drop a seed on the ground and grow a tree," young Hal added, taking his turn.

"The land is good enough," said a squat, heavily bearded man whose name Nancy still had not learned after months living under the same roof, "if the governor would let us at it. There's other islands, leagues of good land for planting out there, but we're all penned up here on St. George's Island, running low on rations. Makes no sense."

The jug went round the circle. Nancy sat with Omar on a bench against the wall; nobody passed the jug to them. She suspected the men did not want to share a drinking vessel with a Negro, but perhaps it was just that she and Omar had made no real effort to be considered part of the group.

"There's men living on the other islands, though," one man said. "I heard there's fellows came in off a wrecked ship, got their own islands and they lives like kings there."

"How d'you know that's true?" someone challenged.

"I heard that, but 'tis only tales."

"Hey, blackamoor!" Hal called. "Is that the ship you and little Neddy was on, then? Were there more fellows made it to shore besides you?"

"Or did the two of ye knife the lot of 'em? Wouldn't put it past ye," Big Willie said with a laugh as harsh as the cries of the seabirds outside.

Nancy shook her head. "Don't know. We never saw no-one else. I thought they all drowned."

She waited till the others had moved on to another subject before she exchanged glances with Omar. They both knew that if the other survivors of the *Happy Adventure* ever appeared in St. George's, Omar risked losing his freedom—and Nancy might lose hers as well.

That night, she counted the coins she had in a pouch she kept sewn inside her breeches. They seemed few enough for the months she had laboured here, though she was glad to be getting paid any coin at all, over and above her room and board. Would it be enough for passage on a ship, when one finally came that could take her in the right direction?

A ship did indeed come into harbour the following day. As always in St. George's, it was a long, slow process for a ship to get past the reefs and into the sheltered harbour of the settlement, and involved men from the town going out in boats to see what the ship was and if it should be offered shelter. Two Spanish vessels, more than a month ago, had come close to the harbour but had been scared away when the governor had ordered the guns fired from Gurnett's Head. This one, however, must have been a friendly vessel, for after some time out in the bay, she came in and docked. By the time Nancy and Omar had done work for the day, cargo was being unloaded.

"Grain, sacks of grain!" Mistress Quickly told Nancy when they got to the dwelling house. "Thank the Lord, afore long we'll have flour again. 'Tis some English privateer, I heard, captured a Spanish ship and took all their grain. 'Twill be the saving of us."

"An English privateer," Nancy said to Omar later that evening. "Is there a chance—could this be the ship for you? If it is, you must not stay here for my sake alone."

"I do not yet know," Omar said. "But I am listening while this ship is here. The captain is a man named Elfrith. I want to know what kind of man he is before I ask to serve on the ship."

The two were once again sitting on their spot on the wall looking at the now-bustling dock. "And what do you hear about him?" Nancy asked.

"Hard man. He cheated another captain out of that Spanish prize. But that..." Omar paused to collect his words, as he sometimes did, reminding Nancy that English was not his mother tongue. "How he deals with other captains is not the thing that matters to me. How he treats his men. If he trades in slaves."

"No English captain, surely—"

He laughed again, that low chuckle that had little amusement in it. "You will always believe you English are too good to be slavers."

"You two, there! If you're idling, get busy!" shouted one of the governor's men, pointing at Nancy and Omar. "We need more hands to haul this grain to the mill."

Arms and legs still throbbing from her day's work on the fortifications, Nancy fell into the line of men, heaving a sack of grain onto her shoulders. They trudged along the path to the mill, throwing the sacks onto a pile as each one arrived.

"God's bones, watch out for that!" a man ahead of her called as he skipped nimbly back. The sack he had been carrying had broken open and along with the golden grain, a large black rat scurried out.

"I hope the whole lot of it ain't crawling with rats—that'd be a nice mess to deal with," Big Willie said as he threw his sack of grain onto the pile.

"Worth it though, for some good wheaten bread after so long," Hal chimed in.

"I'd roast and eat the rat along with it," another man offered.

Amid the talk and laughter as the men wandered away from the mill, Nancy caught a thread of conversation. "Told you there was fellows living like kings on the other islands. Couple of 'em were down at the docks today, talking to this one Elfrith. I'd say they're pirates themselves—right hard-looking devils."

"Oh aye, I saw one of 'em—name of FitzRichard, that right?" Big Willie put in. "Said his ship had a pile of treasure captured from a Spanish caravel, if they had the men to get it ashore, and he'd be rich if he could only get to meet up with his captain in Ireland."

"Pipe dreams—he'll no more be rich off that than we'll be from working here."

"We'd be rich, all right, if we could get out from under the governor's thumb and start a plantation somewhere else..."

Their grumbling voices continued into the dwelling house. Nancy waited outside until Omar caught up to her, and told him what she had heard.

His brow wrinkled in concern. "This settlement is not so large. If Fitz and the others are here, he will hear soon enough that a black man is working here, and find me out."

"You should get away—maybe with this Elfrith on his ship?"

"No. From what I hear, I do not think well of him."

"Can you afford to be so choosy?"

"What of you? What you think FitzRichard will do if he knows you are here?"

"He might not know who I am—'tis not as if I'm going about in skirts saying I was a ship's cook. You are in the greater danger."

By morning, the word was that Elfrith's ship was leaving already. "Like as not he wants to get well out of the way before we find out how many rats are in that grain," Mistress Quickly said as she dished up the morning pottage. Rumours about the infested grain were spreading quickly through the settlement: last night's single rat had not travelled alone. And the sails on Elfrith's ship were already up.

After the morning meal, Nancy lagged behind a little, bringing the trenchers to Mistress Quickly for scrubbing. "Mistress Quickly," she said, "happen you'd know what it might cost to take passage on a ship to Virginia? If one were to come into port that was going that way?"

The cook looked Nancy up and down. "Why d'ye want to go to Virginia? You came out to join a colony: you are in a colony now, and I can tell you Bermuda is a far better colony than Virginia. We've run low on supplies this winter, but by summer we'll be thriving, while those poor folks in James Fort are starving. There be no natives here to attack us, the climate and soil are better. A ...a young man can forge a good life for himself here."

"True enough, Mistress." Bermuda colonists were touchy on the subject of Virginia, and hasty to convince everyone that their colony was more likely to find success. "But I've—I've family in Virginia. My sister and brother-in-law went out last year, and I was meant to join them."

"Ah. Well, I know not what a passage might cost you, but it must be less than passage back to England, for Virginia is but two week's sail from here, I'm told. Likely you'll have enough, if you've been saving your wages."

"I have, Mistress. I've always meant to go on from here."

"Indeed, if you've family there, 'tis best." She glanced around the room, empty now as the men had gone off to work, but still lowered her voice. "I hope 'tis true, and you find them. Then you can lay off this mummery." She nodded towards Nancy's worn and stained tunic and breeches.

"I...what mean you?"

"Pish, lass! I know what you are, and my husband knows it, and I'd wager half the lads know it as well. We have kept an eye out for you—'tis easy to understand why a maid might not wish to be known as one, in a place like this. And your blackamoor has them affrighted. Some of the fellows were talking of stripping you bare one day, to test the rumour that you be truly a maid. The blackamoor told 'em if anyone laid a hand on you he'd beat them senseless."

Nancy stood open-mouthed. She had thought Omar was protecting her, but had never imagined how far that protection went, nor how flimsy her disguise was. Mistress Quickly went on chattering as she scrubbed the trenchers from their morning meal.

"Then the lads said it must be true you're a maid, and you are the blackamoor's lover, or else he's the kind to take a boy to his bed. Then your Negro, he said he need not be swiving anyone, man or maid, to want to look out for one who was younger, and alone in this hard world. And they shut their mouths after that, for they're afeared of him." This rush of gossip poured out of her like goose feathers from a shaken pillow, while Nancy stared dumbly. The woman smiled, "For certes, you did not think you had us all fooled, did you? It takes more to make a man than putting on a pair of britches."

"I—if all that be so, then I thank you for keeping quiet, and looking out to my welfare," Nancy said.

"Thank your Negro. But 'twould be best if you were both away from here—you to your family, and him to his own kind."

She took her leave of Mistress Quickly and hurried to the work site, arriving only a few moments late to tote yet another barrow of stones up the hill. From their vantage point, they could see Elfrith's ship sailing out of the bay. When they broke for the midday meal, she sought out Omar and told him what Mistress Quickly had said. "It seems I owe you thanks."

"I believe every man should look to his own business, leave other folks alone," Omar said. "Is it so much to ask?"

"I thought I had done a better job of fooling them."

"You knew you did not fool me."

"So—if I do go to Virginia? I know not whether I should try to keep up the farce, or risk going out alone in skirts."

He was silent for a while. "It is easier, I think, to be what you are. When I find a ship that will take me on, I will not any longer lie about being a slave." He paused, then pulled his shirt aside to reveal his chest, where an ugly round of scarred tissue stood out from the smooth brown of his skin. A slave brand. "As long as it is hidden, any man can expose me."

Nancy put out her hand almost as if she were about to trace the brand upon his skin, but drew it back quickly: there was no such intimacy between herself and Omar. She tried not to stare, either, but the scar was so prominent, and the image of him being marked with hot iron, marked as another man's possession, was hard to banish from her mind. "You will let everyone see that you were once a slave?"

"I will, and will fight whoever tries to put me in chains again. I had rather lose my life than my freedom, I believe."

"I hope you'll not have to make that choice," she said, as they both turned back to their tasks.

As Nancy reached the bottom of the hill with an empty barrow, she heard a sound that chilled her like a knife to her spine. A man was talking to two others, his voice loud and confident. "Aye, so with what we have retrieved from the wreck, if I could but get passage to Ireland and find Captain Sly, I could make us all rich men. Elfrith was no good to me—he was bound for the Spanish colonies."

"There's rumours of a ship coming out from England soon, with more colonists. If you took passage to England—"

"Aye, we could all be wealthy men. Most of the ship's gold went on our other vessel, but we had a good cargo of slaves—six Negroes we meant to sell, all of 'em lost in the wreck."

"That's a pity, for they'd have fetched a good price in the Indies."

She hazarded a sidelong glance at the men as she passed, but she knew already from the voice: FitzRichard, sometime captain of the *Happy Adventure*, was talking to two men, both well-dressed. Some of the better class of Bermuda colonists, the ones who had hope of starting their own plantations. The ease between them suggested FitzRichard was known to them, though he could not have been in St. George's long.

"I'll seek passage on the next ship out," she told Omar later, "and you should too, as long as Fitz is not aboard it. Whether it goes to Virginia or back to England—'tis not safe for us to stay in Bermuda as long as those pirates are about."

Omar, too, had caught a glimpse—not of FitzRichard, but of the other pirates from the *Happy Adventure*. "They are making plans," he told her, "to take what they can, and what they have gathered here, back to their captain, to make them wealthy."

"What have they gathered here?"

"There is a treasure in these islands—a thing called ambergris," Omar told her. "They have some of it, or think they can get some, to sell. But that is not my concern, or yours."

"No. Your concern is that Fitz is talking about the slaves that were lost in the wreck."

Nancy knew she herself had no monetary value; FitzRichard had no reason to claim her as part of his spoils. But he could accuse her again of witchcraft, since she had boasted of it freely aboard the ship. Or he could capture and use her for his own ends—nobody in St. George's would be quick to defend a maid who had passed herself off as a man for all these months. Witch or whore, whatever they could brand her with, she was not safe.

"Take the next ship," Omar told her. "Wherever it is going, as long as those men are not aboard. Work your passage if you must. I will not stay here long once you have gone."

In the days that followed the departure of Elfrith's ship, Nancy lived in greater fear than she'd known since the *Happy Adventure* sank. While most of the colonists were diverted by the arrival of both the grain and what turned out to be an enormous swarm of black rats that had come with it, there was plenty of time for other gossip. And one evening, talk around the table in their dwelling house turned in exactly the direction she had feared most.

"Master Quickly, have you met this fellow FitzRichard?" Big Willie asked as they downed bowls of fish stew.

"Nay, but I've heard of him. A pirate, is he not?"

"A privateer."

"Is there a difference?" someone called out, and several of the men laughed.

"'Tis quite the tale FitzRichard tells—me and some of the lads were hearing him talk today. Of a ship that was blown off course in a gale and sank on the reefs somewhere here in the Bermudas. Himself and two other men were spared and they reckoned the rest of the crew drowned—sometime back before Christmas-tide, this would have been."

"Aye, I've heard the tale," Master Quickly said, and several others agreed.

"Funny thing, though, 'twould be about that same time Omar and Ned here said their ship sank. Two wrecks so close together?"

"These waters are treacherous," Mistress Quickly put in, her eyes flickering in Nancy's direction.

"True, that they are, especially that time of year," another man added. "I always heard it called the Isle of Devils, before folks began settling here."

"But still—this FitzRichard, be he pirate or privateer or call it what you will, he says that part of the cargo they lost was six black slaves, taken from the Spanish. And here a black man and a lad out of nowhere walk into the colony sometime in the fall, saying their ship sank but telling us no more about it." Big Willie fixed his eyes, small in his thickset face, on Omar. "Seems we need to know more about you, blackamoor."

"Do you?" Omar said quietly. "And if I do not tell you more?"

"Then 'tis likely someone might want to tell Master FitzRichard that some of his missing cargo might still be recovered."

"Aye! There could be a reward in it!" Hal said, and a few more voices joined in agreement. But there was a murmur of disapproval as well.

"That's pure wickedness," one man protested, and a few of the fellows near him agreed.

"Why is it so bad? All poor men are in bondage to someone—serving a master, or working off an indenture to some company," another put in. "Why should black men be any different?"

"Selling men into bondage to pirates is hardly the business we came here for," Master Quickly said firmly, "and I'll hear no more of it. All the same," he added, turning to Omar, "with rumours such as these going around, it may be well to tell us a little more of your tale."

Again, the murmurs of agreement as Omar sat in stubborn silence, his arms crossed in front of him. Nancy ground her teeth and sat on her hands. "Why should we trust any of ye?" she burst out. "Some of you would sell a man as quick as look at him, it seems!"

"Nay, don't speak hastily, Ned," cautioned Master Quickly.

"What we have to say, we will not say here," Omar said, his deep voice cutting across the babble of the other men's voices. "I will go to the governor and tell him the tale—not to gossiping tongues. Goodnight."

He left the room, and Nancy scrambled to follow, while the other men continued to talk and argue. Outside, she caught up to him. The road and the docks were quiet now. "Will you go to the governor?" she asked. "Surely you can trust him with the truth—he'd not give a man to pirates, to be sold into slavery."

Omar shook his head. "I am sorry," he said. "I meant to watch over you until you were safely away from here. But I am not going to the governor. I am going back into the forest. There are coves and bays on these islands where a man may survive...for a time."

"But for how long?"

"Till a ship comes that I can trust."

"It is a terrible gamble."

"Not as much as staying in St. George's."

She could not disagree. "Will you go tomorrow?"

"No, I am going now." He lifted the small satchel in which he kept a change of clothes and a few other small belongings. Flint and steel, a knife. Little else to keep a man alive in a strange land. She had not noticed that he had it with him when they left the house.

"Tell them I have gone to the governor. It will be tomorrow, perhaps the day after, they find I am not here. Let them think you know as little as they do. By then, perhaps, there will be some new wonder."

What will I do? Nancy wanted to ask, but did not.

"Stay close to Mistress Quickly," he said, though she had not spoken aloud. "Take ship for Virginia as soon as you can."

"I cannot—" Her words stumbled to silence. "Thank you. For everything. I hope you find a place where you can be safe."

"I hope you find a way back to your home, and your people." Briefly, he laid a hand on her shoulder, then turned away from the road and the houses, onto a path that led back from the ocean to the forest.

She watched him go. They had travelled together, worked together, for—what? Three, four months? She had learned so little about him, and told him little about herself. He did not even know why she had called herself Ned Perry. But she owed him her life, and she would never see him again, never know if he had survived or found a place of safety. Or even if there was such a place, for Omar.

Nancy went back alone to the dwelling house, feeling the thinness of her disguise in this room full of men. She told the master that Omar had gone to the governor. Across the room, Mistress Quickly met her eyes.

The next day, the *Blessing* came into port. She was a ship out from England, bringing dozens of new colonists, and she was travelling on to Virginia before returning across the ocean. In the stir of so many new arrivals, the confusion of where they would all shelter, the arguments about whether everyone must stay on St. George's or spread out onto the other islands—Omar was right. There was something new to divert the men, and no more talk of the vanished black man. Nor of young Ned Perry, who went to the captain of the *Blessing*, told his story about having family in Virginia, and offered to pay his few coins for passage to that colony.

THIRTEEN

A New Master Is Found

T HE WHARF AT JAMES FORT WAS A BUSTLE OF ACTIVITY. In the long weeks aboard the *Treasurer*, Ned had near forgot that it was possible to sight a stretch of land full not only of men, but women and even a few children as well. He had become accustomed to the lonely world of a ship at sea.

He said something of the sort to Francis, who laughed. "That's the sailor's life, Ned, boy. I've spent more years at sea since I was a lad than I have with my feet on dry land. Someday 'twill seem strange to you that you ever lived in a town and woke up with your feet on the floor instead of on deck."

"Not I," Ned said. "I'll be at sea only till I find my Nancy, and then I'll take her back to the New Found Land. Build a home on solid ground and go to sea no more—save for the odd bit of fishing."

Francis laughed. "God's teeth, Ned, you ought to be up on stage with the players. You're like something out of a romance."

"Aye, the brave hero travelling the high seas to rescue the fair maid— 'tis poetry, truth be told," Red Peter said, joining in the laughter.

Ned had to join in too, to be a good sport, as he climbed down the ladder and helped the sailors unload the *Treasurer*'s cargo. This was the end of the voyage: Captain Argall was returning triumphant, having carried out his orders to enforce English rule over all the coast. "Tell them all how we burnt the French colony and made the Dutch bend the knee, lads," the captain said as he counted out the men's pay.

"'Twould make a finer show if we still had the French ship we captured," Red Peter muttered, when they were well out of range of the captain's hearing.

"But we've got our share, so what care we? Come along of us, Ned, and get your first taste of Virginia," Francis urged.

"Do you live here?" Ned asked his companions as they strolled along the riverfront. It seemed so sheltered, this harbour on the broad, quiet river, compared to the ocean that lapped at the shores of Cupids Cove. The town was more populous, too, though it had been first settled only a few years before Ned and his companions had come to Cupids Cove. He wondered how Cupids Cove might look in a few years, if it would grow as James Fort was doing.

"Peter's got a brother here, and he gives us a bed while we're in port. We'll be off again as soon as we find another ship to take us on. Raiding the Spanish down in the Indies is good business this time of year."

"You'd turn pirate?"

"'Tis not piracy, 'tis privateering. There's a good few captains in these parts have letters of marque to attack the Spaniards. If you come along, you'll likely find out more about the ship that took your lady love."

Ned wondered where he might find to lay his head until he found another ship to sign on with: though James Fort was more populous than Cupids Cove, it still looked like a colony, not an English town, and there was no place about that appeared to be an inn or tavern where a stranger might seek lodging. When he asked his companions, Peter said, "Come with us to my brother's house—he'll give you space to lay a blanket on the floor for as long as you need. Folk here are used to making room for travellers."

Red Peter's brother—who might well have been named Red Paul, for he had the same fiery colouring—made Ned welcome, and gave him a straw-stuffed mattress and a woollen blanket to lay before the hearth of their small house, where Francis and Peter also slept, along with Paul's two young sons. "Aye, stay with the lads until you all find another ship to sail with," Paul's wife said, "we're well used to their comings and goings, and one more makes little difference."

Captain Argall and the *Treasurer* were to remain in Virginia until spring; the governor had need of both captain and ship for journeys up the James River. Ned had no interest in those voyages, nor in travelling back to England. He was looking for ships heading south into warmer waters, where the *Happy Adventure* might have gone.

In the following days, as they waited for another opportunity to go to sea, Francis and Peter set to work helping Paul about his house and farm. Ned saw that a fourth pair of hands was not needed there. Not one to waste time, he found work helping with the construction of a storehouse: any colony would always have work for a man who could do both a stone-mason's and a carpenter's work. He told his tale of woe far and wide, asked about Captain Sly and the *Happy Adventure*. A few of the older seamen knew of Sly, knew that he had sailed with Peter Easton, but none had heard anything of what ship Sly was sailing now, or where he had been.

"I hear tell there's a ship coming into port soon—'twas down at Cape Comfort a few days ago—that was taken from the Spanish not long since," said one man over a midday meal on the work site. "Like as not, her captain could tell you a fair bit about pirates and privateers, if that's what you look to know."

Sure enough, the next morning as Ned walked to his workplace, the bustle around the docks told him that a ship was coming in.

She was a neat little barque of about a hundred tons, flying an English flag. When he took a rest from his work at midday and all the labouring men went to find refreshment, Ned strolled back down towards the docks. The ship had her gangplank lowered and a single sailor stood on watch.

"Greetings, fellow! Is your captain aboard?"

"What be your business?"

"I might be looking for a berth, if he's in need of hands."

"That's the captain's business, and I doubt he'll take on any riff-raff from the docks."

The fellow was fair reluctant to disturb his captain's privacy, and though Ned hung about until it was time to return to work, he saw no sign of the captain emerging. That evening over supper, he asked Francis and Red Peter what they knew of this new ship.

"Captain's a fellow name of Elfrith," Francis said, "who was serving aboard the *Fair Isle* when she captured this ship from the Spaniards. Seems Elfrith was meant to follow along behind his old captain with the booty, but instead he went off on his own, down to Somers Isle, so they say, and sold his cargo there for his own gain."

"So he's only been a captain a matter of weeks, and made himself a good few enemies," added Red Peter.

"Still, it might be worth asking if he needs hands," said Francis. "We might look to him ourselves, if he's going on to the Indies and the *Treasurer* is staying in port all winter."

"Or ye could both stay ashore, for once in your lives," said Peter's sister-in-law, bringing a loaf of bread to the table. Both the men laughed, and she did as well, as if she had never expected her comment to be taken for anything but a jest. She was a trim, buxom woman, one of the few Englishwomen Ned had seen in James Fort.

There were few enough women in the fort at all, and many of those were young native women from the nearby Powhatan people. The Indian girls sometimes worked as servants, but they were also kept as mistresses by the English settlers. Ned remembered how in those first two years in Cupids Cove, before the women came, the men had jested among themselves about going into the woods to find Indian maidens to take to their beds. It had never happened in Cupids Cove—the natives of the New Found Land kept to themselves, deep in the woods. But here in Virginia, settlers and natives lived nearby and had much truck with each other, as Ned knew from the tales he had heard.

"I'll tell you what we'll do," Red Peter said when their meal was finished. "We'll go to Cooper's house—like as not, 'tis where we'll find this fellow Elfrith."

Cooper's was not a tavern, for, as Ned had already seen, the fort was too rough and too new to have such a thing. But Cooper, who was a barber, kept an open door and plenty of ale, and was not averse to men offering him money in exchange for his ale. Men came in for a shave and lingered to drink and talk. So, very like a tavern, in truth.

"'Tis a favourite place for sailors to gather," Francis explained as they walked there through the pleasant dusk of the early evening, "especially when a new ship has come in. Everyone wants to hear what news they bring."

Sure enough, when they got to the busy yard outside Cooper's house they found a fellow who must be Captain Elfrith holding forth with a tale about his sea battle with the Spanish vessel he had captured. He was very much the sort of man Ned imagined when he thought about a pirate captain—a dashing fellow with a great mane of dark hair and a brightly coloured doublet over a fine silk shirt. He was holding forth like a preacher in church, but with many a jest that no preacher would ever make.

"From all I heard, your captain meant for you to bring that grain after him to England, not sell it on your own account," Captain Argall said, with a sour expression.

"Ah, you know yourself, Argall, a man has his own way to make in this world," Elfrith said, not much troubled by the criticism. He raised his tankard in Captain Argall's direction. "And, truth be told, I was an angel of mercy to those folk in the Bermudas. They were that starving, they fell upon my shipment of grain as if 'twere manna from heaven."

"Are they starving down there, then? To hear folks talk, you'd think Somers Isle was the land of milk and honey," someone said, and a little bickering began back and forth among the men, about whether settlers in Virginia or in the Bermudas had the better time of it. Ned edged nearer to Francis and Red Peter, who were sitting close to Elfrith.

"So you'll be off to the Indies again soon, sir?" Francis asked the captain.

"Have you need of more men?" Red Peter added.

Elfrith took a deep draught of his drink and turned his attention to the sailors. "Aye, within the fortnight I'll be sailing south," he said. "Were you with himself there on the *Treasurer?*"

"We were, Captain, all through the summer and fall. We attacked the French all up and down the coast."

"If Argall gives ye all a good character, I've work for you aboard. My ship's but lately captured from the Spaniards, so I need a full crew of men."

"We'd be glad for the berth," Francis said. "Myself and Peter here, we're seasoned sailors—seven years at sea. Our mate Ned, here, he's not been to sea so much, but he's near as good as a trained ship's carpenter."

Elfrith glanced at Ned, who said, "I apprenticed as a stonemason back in Bristol, and I did a fair bit of carpentry work, even some ship-building, once I settled with Master Guy in Cupids Cove."

"Aye, you're one of Guy's New Found Land colonists, are you? What is it like, up there?"

Elfrith seemed genuinely interested—he had visited the fishing stations in the New Found Land, and wanted to know what success the colonists were having. Ned told him a bit about Cupids Cove, which led naturally into the subject he wanted to talk about.

Elfrith nodded when Ned got to the tale of the attack on Nicholas Guy's plantation. "Aye, I've heard of this one Sly when he was still under Easton's command."

"Do you know men who might know more of him? Other—captains?"

"Other pirates, you mean?" Elfrith laughed. "You can say it, lad. I call myself a privateer, for I don't attack English ships or settlements, but 'tis a fine line indeed. If you take ship with me and we head to the Indies, you may well find some there who know of Sly and his ship—or belike, you might find the man himself." He narrowed his eyes and looked at Ned closely. "But lad, you ought not get your hopes up about the maid. If she be alive, even still, and aboard the vessel, she'll be no maid any longer. You know how a woman would be used on such a ship, do you not? She'll be no good to you if you do find her."

Something hot and sharp as bile rose up in Ned's gorge, and his face flushed. Bad enough for Elfrith to be calling him "lad" as if he were a beardless boy, but to be warning him of Nancy's fate in such crude terms was harsh indeed. He wanted to punch the man square in the jaw, but he balled up his fists tightly. He needed this coarse man's goodwill if he were to have any hope of succeeding in his quest.

"All the same, sir, I'm bound in honour to try to rescue her if I can," was all he said. Elfrith laughed again.

"You're like some fellow out of a storybook, lad," he laughed, "but if you're a good carpenter, like these fellows say, 'tis enough for me—I've need of a carpenter. I can't promise you'll find your lady love, but you can have a berth aboard my ship all the same. She's got no name now save a Spanish one, but I mean to christen her the *White Lion*."

Walking back from Cooper's later that night in company, Ned was still stewing. "You might be a bit grateful," Francis said. "We got you a berth with Elfrith."

"Thanks for it—though if I'd any choice, I'd sail with any other captain before that knave."

"What have you got against him? Sure you only met him tonight."

Bitterly, Ned repeated the gist of what Elfrith had said. Francis and Red Peter were both silent a moment.

"But you must know, Ned, there's truth in it," Red Peter said at last, "though 'twas harsh of Elfrith to put it to you so. Even if she be alive, she'll have been—mistreated."

"Do you think I don't know it?" The words burst from him, bitter as if they had been kept caged since he left Cupids Cove. No-one had said it aloud to him, of all the people he'd told about the purpose of his journey. "Do you think I've not suffered torments, imagining what they might be doing to her? She's no helpless damsel—she'll fight to survive. But she'd be no match for a shipload of men."

"Then why—"

"Why be angry at Elfrith? Because he made it sound as if I'd toss her aside, if I found her and she'd been—ruined. But what man, if he truly loved a woman, would put her aside so? Would either of you?"

Francis glanced at Red Peter, and some look passed between them that Ned did not understand. After a moment Peter said, "I'm not the one to say about that. But a good many men would feel as Elfrith does. They might save her, for honour's sake, if they could. But to take her back and marry her after that? That would touch a man's honour in another way."

"Well, I would," Ned said. But a feather of doubt troubled him as he lay on his mattress that night, listening to the other men snore and the children murmur in their dreams.

He had tried to block from his mind all the pictures that kept crowding into it, of what the pirates might have done to Nancy. Their love had been something fresh and untouched—they had been like children, he thought now, though they were a man and woman grown. Something in himself had been sullied when he went to bed with the Lenape woman in New Amsterdam, certes. But for Nancy to have been taken by force, raped by a pirate—or by many of them, likely—his mind turned away, again, from the thought. If he ever held her in his arms again, could he banish the thought of other men's hands, other men's mouths, other men's bodies upon hers?

"'Tis folly," he said aloud, and he heard Francis stir. "Shut your mouth," Red Peter grumbled in his sleep.

Ned shut his mouth. He could not torture his mind with such thoughts. All that mattered was finding Nancy.

FOURTEEN

An Indenture Is Agreed Upon

N ED PERRY DIED IN A DOCKSIDE PRIVY IN VIRGINIA. Nancy shed the name and identity she had worn for the last several months and rebirthed herself as Nancy Ellis. The parcel of clothing she had carried since the ship sank went back on: shift, kirtle, makeshift coif for her hair. She took the tunic and breeches she had worn all winter in the Bermudas, thinking briefly of Robin, who had died in them. His blood was still on the tunic somewhere, amid the dirt and grime. She dropped the garments into the privy.

How strange, after all these months, to step outside again in the guise of a woman! She remembered those days of trying to learn to move about and conduct herself as a man would, copying Omar and the other men about her, aping their habit of looking up into people's faces rather than down as a virtuous maid ought to do. Now she would have to unlearn all that, stitch herself back into the pattern she had been born to. She felt the loss of that manly stride she had taken so much time to learn.

The *Blessing* had stopped briefly at James Fort, the main English fort in Virginia, but all the passengers were for a new settlement called Henrico, so Nancy stayed aboard with the rest, not wanting to draw attention to herself by being the only one to disembark at James Fort. Sailing up the James River felt like entering yet another alien world. The trees were thick, green and lush; the air was humid and cloying. It smelled swampy, warm for the time of year—there would still be snow on the ground in Cupids Cove—but unlike the warm, clear, salty air of Bermuda.

Amid the bustle of the ship being unloaded, if anyone noticed a boy slip into a privy and young woman emerge, they showed no sign of it.

Once she was out on the docks in skirts again, Nancy was not sure where to go. She had told the captain her tale of "Ned" having family in Virginia. Now that she realized there was more than one English settlement here, she wondered how she might have been expected to find this family, had they been real.

Henrico seemed a very small settlement indeed—a handful of buildings surrounded by a stockade fence, much like Cupids Cove, with some plantations outside the fence along the river. Certainly it would be too small to have such a thing as a tavern or an inn where she might go to find lodging—if a young woman alone would even be granted lodging at an inn.

I am alone, she thought as she walked along, and then tested out another thought: *I am free*. Free, as she had never been in her life. She had been Kathryn's servant, then the pirates' cook and captive, and then, for a few short months, a labourer in the Bermudas, hiding her true identity. Now she was simply Nancy Ellis, alone and beholden to no-one—but also, with no-one to aid her.

She walked about, looking at the settlement and the people she passed, wondering how she would feed herself without a penny in her pocket. But she should have known she could not walk unseen in a colony the way she might have done back in Bristol: here, as in St. George's or in Cupids Cove, there were few enough people that everyone would spot an unfamiliar face, and before long a middle-aged woman carrying a basket stopped her.

"Have you just come off the ship?"

Nancy nodded, without thinking how she would explain that she had been a different person when on the ship.

"Where are your people?"

"I've no people, Mistress—I was hoping to find work as a maid in some household."

"All on your own?" The woman eyed Nancy sharply. Young women arriving in the colony unaccompanied were apparently rare enough to excite comment.

"Yes, Mistress. My—my sister and her husband were supposed to come out with me but—they took sick, before we were to sail."

"Ah, poor lamb. Well, there's plenty work enough for maids who are willing to toil hard, around here. You might go see Reverend Whittaker—he's like to know who is in need of help." Her kindly manner was somewhat altered by the frown she gave Nancy as she added, "And he'll know if you are being honest. There's no place here for maids who are not virtuous. We have stocks, and a whipping-post."

"Yes, Mistress. I am an honest servant girl looking for a place."

"I'm sure you will find one. 'Twill be an indenture, you know—you will have to agree to work for a year or two years. No getting wages week by week as you might do back in England."

We shall see about a year, Nancy thought—she would be gone far quicker if she had the chance, but she would agree to whatever terms were necessary to put food in her belly. "Show me where this minister's house is, if you please, Mistress."

She had no great faith that a clergyman would be any more trustworthy than another man—at least, she would keep it secret that she had once been accused of witchcraft and later bragged of it to save her skin. But she followed the woman's directions to the house of Reverend Whittaker and asked the serving-woman who answered the door if she might speak to the minister.

"And what might you want to be talking to the reverend about?" The servant was a handsome young woman with golden hair and sharp features, and she folded her arms in front of herself and leaned against the doorpost, sizing Nancy up.

"Only to ask if he knows of anyone in these parts hiring a servant girl," Nancy said, remembering to drop her eyes and lower her tone.

"He'll be hiring someone himself before long, for my term of service is up at the end of this month and I'm to marry, and not a minute too soon if you ask me. I don't think 'tis right to ask a good Christian maid to wait hand and foot on a savage, whether she be a princess or no. My Jacob will have his own plot of land and the two of us can work it together without needing any hands, for 'tis only a small plot and we're neither of us afraid of hard work. We'll do fine for ourselves," she finished, in a voice that suggested Nancy was skeptical of her success.

Nancy did not know what to make of this torrent of words, but she latched onto the one part that made sense. "So the reverend may be hiring a servant?"

"He will be, but I doubt he'll want the likes of you, having just come in off a ship with no name or character. Not knowing who your people are or nothing like that."

"I can tell him all that, if only I could speak with him."

"Well. I'll tell him there's a beggar-woman at the door. We'll see what he says to that." The woman turned and shut the door, leaving Nancy standing outside.

Nancy looked around at the settlement, wondering if she ought to try somewhere else. This house hardly seemed welcoming, and there must be other folk here in need of service, even if it were field work rather than housework. She was just about to turn and go when two women approached the house.

One was an older woman with grey hair tucked modestly under a coif. Her clothing was simple and sober in colour, but of good stuff; Nancy wondered if she might be the wife of the minister. Beside her walked a young woman, probably younger than Nancy herself; very slender, dressed in a dark blue gown, simply cut but of finer quality than that of the woman beside her. Her hair was uncovered, long, and very black, braided into thick plaits but not pinned up or covered. By age she might have been the daughter of the other woman, but she looked quite unlike her: her skin was very brown, and her eyes were dark also.

"And what might you be wanting, my girl?" the older woman said to Nancy.

Nancy repeated her plea for work. "I asked the maid who answered the door, and she said she would go speak to the master, and that I should wait."

The older woman sniffed. "You'll be waiting a long time for young Mary to do anything useful. If you ask me, a stranger just off a ship could do no worse than she's done. Come in, girl, and we'll see what we can do for you. I'm Hannah Ridgely; myself and my husband are servants to Reverend Whittaker—the only useful servants he's got, if you ask me." She nodded her head towards the black-haired woman. "This is the lady Pocahontas, daughter of the Indian chief Powhatan."

The foreign names meant nothing to Nancy, but the word "Indian" was clear enough: it was what English folk called the natives of the country all up and down the coast, though Nicholas Guy had told her once that they were not anywhere near India. So the dark woman was a native, then, living here in an English settlement, dressing in an Englishwoman's clothes.

Mistress Ridgely invited Nancy into the house; both of them walked in a few steps behind the Indian woman, who was straight-backed and walked with great dignity. "You must curtsey to her, for she's great among her own people," Mistress Ridgely instructed Nancy, and when they were all inside the house Nancy did so, bobbing awkwardly in the skirts that now felt unfamiliar.

"Are you come to serve here?" the Indian woman asked in clear but accented English.

"I hope to serve, Mistress. Your serving-maid told me at the door that she was leaving to be married."

"Married!" Hannah Ridgely huffed. She had moved to the table and was unwrapping some parcels she had carried. "She thinks of nothing else but that worthless fool Jacob Harper. If you can keep your mind on your work, you'll be an improvement around here. Come, help me get this lot put away—'tis but a few things I brought up from Master Rolfe's farm."

She passed Nancy a wheel of cheese wrapped in cloth and showed her where to store it on the shelves. Mistress Ridgely moved to stir up the fire, while the Indian woman—Nancy had forgotten her name already—sat down on a bench. Nancy opened the rest of the bags and packages, finding a goodly supply of vegetables and other items. "Master Rolfe is one of the planters 'round here," Mistress Ridgely explained as Nancy unwrapped and put away the food. "He is most friendly towards the princess, and likes to visit with her, but of course someone must go along with her, for decency's sake. And it ought to be someone younger, if Mary were doing her duties. I'm too old to be trotting up and down the roads all day long." She nodded approval at Nancy's quick ability to figure out what supplies went where, and when Nancy asked would she want any carrots or parsnips peeled, she nodded again.

"You'll do well here," she said. "That one Mary, now, she'd stand there like someone fairy-led, till you told her exactly what you wanted done. A good maid looks around for what needs to be done and does it before she's told."

"'Tis how I was brought up," Nancy said. "Do you think, then, the reverend will hire me?"

"The reverend will do what I tell him when it comes to hiring a servant. But he'll want a year's indenture at least."

As she worked beside Mistress Ridgely, Nancy's eyes flickered to the native woman, who sat so still, looking out the window or sometimes turning to watch the maids at work. It came to Nancy then that she had never seen another woman sit so still; even Mistress Sheila Pike, back in the New Found Land, who gave herself airs as if she were a princess, had had to do her own housework. After a moment the Indian woman bent to take some needlework from a basket at her feet; she looked more natural then. Every woman, even the kind of high-born woman Nancy had never seen in real life, kept herself busy with a needle rather than sitting idle.

When the Reverend Whittaker entered, he seemed unsurprised to see a new maid helping Mistress Ridgely prepare supper. He spoke first to the Indian woman, and they talked quietly for a few moments. Only after they had finished did he turn his attention to his housekeeper. "Stew for supper, Hannah?"

"Yes, sir, with some good vegetables we got from Master Rolfe, and one of the chickens that I killed and dressed myself this morning. Sir, this is Nancy—she's come looking for work."

Only then did his gaze, not particularly interested, flicker in Nancy's direction. "Has Mary gone off finally?"

"I don't know where she's to, Reverend, though she may be back when she wants her supper. 'Tis a month yet till her wedding day, but her mind's not on the job, and she's ever flitting back and forth between here and young Harper. When I found Nancy here looking for a place, I thought it best to take her on, for you can see yourself she's a fine worker."

Now he eyed her a bit more keenly. "Where have you come from, Nancy? I know you are not from James Fort."

"No, Reverend. I came on a ship from Bermuda. Before that, I was on a ship that was wrecked, and before that—" she took a deep breath and, without knowing why, realized she had already decided on the truth—"I served my master and mistress in Cupids colony, in the New Found Land. I'm Bristol-born; we came out from there a year and a half ago."

"How did you come to leave there?"

"Pirates, sir. Our plantation was attacked, and I was taken captive."

His bushy eyebrows raised, and Nancy hoped he would not ask for more of her tale.

"Are you trying to get back to your master in the New Found Land?"

Nancy hesitated. But again, the truth, or something close to it, was likely best. "I hope to, someday, sir. But I know that may be a long time hence."

"I cannot have you leaving on the next ship. I need a servant who can commit for some time."

"I told her you'd want a year's indenture, sir," Mistress Ridgely put in.

And so it was agreed. Perhaps, Nancy thought, there was a way to get out of an indenture. If not, she would simply have to serve and wait for a year. She had been five months away already. She wondered, not for the first time, if Ned was still alive, and if he would wait for her. He was true as gold, but he was no fool, not one to pine away all his life for a lass who had vanished like dew on the grass.

They all ate at the one table, Hannah and her husband—a heavy-set man named Silas who looked accustomed to hard work—with Nancy at one end. The reverend sat with the Indian princess at the other end of the long table. Pocahontas, her name was—just the one name, no Christian name and surname, Hannah explained quietly to Nancy. Pocahontas was talking to the Reverend Whittaker about a passage of Scripture she had been discussing. She seemed a clever and learned woman; she spoke excellent English and was, it seemed, learning to read as well.

"Master Rolfe asked me what name I would take, if I were to be baptized, for he said that everyone who is baptized into Christ takes a new name," she was saying. "I thought of the tale of Rebecca, how she came from a far country to be married to Isaac. My home is not far from here, but I feel as if I have come from a long way."

"And Master Rolfe, does he fancy himself to be Isaac?"

"He says that he would not dare look so high."

Visitors came after supper to talk to Reverend Whittaker and Lady Pocahontas—that was what Hannah called her, as if she were a noblewoman in England. While they talked, Nancy and Hannah cleaned up from the meal and began preparations for the coming day. Mary had still not returned, and Hannah finally went out to fetch her, leaving Nancy with a pile of stockings to mend.

Half an hour later she reappeared, reporting to Reverend Whittaker that when Mary had learned a new maid was employed, she had given notice that she was not coming back, but would stay in the household where her betrothed worked. "She did say she will come back tomorrow for her few things, and that she hopes there is no hard feeling," Hannah added. "If you ask me, she has been looking for the excuse to make such a move since they announced the betrothal."

"Well, well, 'tis only natural she would want to be nearby to Jacob before they are wedded. They will both be serving in that house till he finishes out his indenture and they can work their own plot of land."

"She is short-changing you," Hannah pointed out.

"True enough, but we make can exceptions when there is a marriage to be made. We will need more women here before long, young maids willing to marry, if we are to settle this land." He gave Nancy an appraising glance as if to judge whether she might be willing to wed a colonist, and Nancy did not trouble to tell him she had already been part of such a shipment of women in Cupids Cove.

When bedtime came, Hannah led Nancy to one of the two rooms up under the roof. The smaller room was where the reverend, an unmarried man, slept alone. The other room had a bed for the Indian princess and a pallet on the floor where, until now, Mary had slept. Hannah and her husband had their bed downstairs near the fire. "You are to be at hand if she needs anything," Hannah said, "though in truth, she don't demand much. You will have to empty her chamber pot and bring water for washing in the morning."

"I am used to that." In truth, she was fair thrilled at the prospect of sleeping on a good straw mattress again, after the narrow wooden berths in which she had slept on the ships and on the Bermuda plantation. *And I will work hard*, she thought, *and do whatever they ask of me.* She was not about to question the stroke of fortune that had granted her a place to stay and to work immediately upon her arrival in Henrico.

She found out more about the household over the following days. Hannah and Silas Ridgely had been maid and man of all work for the reverend a year ago, but the arrival of the lady Pocahontas months before had thrown this arrangement into some disarray. It had been agreed that the minister's house was the most appropriate place for this alien but exalted person, who was both captive and honoured guest, as a hostage might be in a royal court. But as the minister had no wife or daughter, a respectable woman must act as Pocahontas's companion, not only about the house but to accompany her on the many visits she made around Henrico and, sometimes, down to James Fort.

Hannah's new duties as chaperone to the Indian lady often kept her away from the house, so Mary had been taken into service to help. This involved tending the garden and the chickens, as well as cooking, baking, cleaning, and laundering. Nothing about the work was hard or unfamiliar to Nancy—it was much the same as she had done in Cupids Cove, and the weather in Virginia in February was a fair sight more pleasant than in the New Found Land at the same time of year. Folk here seemed to be thriving, not dying of the scurvy, and Nancy wondered if all the tales they had been told of how bad things were in Virginia were only something Governor Guy had invented to make his own colonists feel as if they were doing better.

But no, Hannah assured her—there had been hard times in Virginia a few years ago indeed. "I was not here myself then, having only come over two summers past. But 'tis true that things was desperate during the Starving Time. There was a tale told that some folks even tried to eat the bodies of the dead, but I don't credit it—no Englishman would do such a thing, no matter how hungry."

The lady Pocahontas sat in a chair by the window with a book on her lap while Hannah rolled out pastry dough and Nancy separated a hare's flesh from its bones. They were making pies for a dinner they were serving to a large group of guests that afternoon. "No Powhatan would do such things either," Pocahontas said now. "The English say many things about my father's people that are not true. We do not eat human flesh, any more than you do."

"Of course not, Mistress," Hannah said, in the bland and deferential tone she reserved for the Indian princess.

Nancy could not quite place how Hannah and others in Henrico felt towards the young Indian woman. They were respectful, certainly—her father was a great chief among the natives. But they certainly did not show the deference they would show to a daughter of the English king, if such an exalted being were ever to appear. She thought again of Sheila Pike saying, "My father is a king in Ireland," and of Nicholas Guy telling the women that every petty chieftain in Ireland called himself a king. Perhaps it was the same here—every Indian chief would call himself a king.

Yet there was something else in their manner towards Pocahontas too, as if the reverence the settlers showed her was a cloak for something else. She was, after all, a natural, a wild woman; until coming to Henrico she had not lived or dressed the way an English woman did, and this strangeness coloured all their dealings with her. It was as if they at once admired and despised her.

Nancy was surprised at her own interest in the princess. She had never thought very much about the native folk in the woods around Cupids Cove, perhaps because she had never seen them. She had, of course, listened with interest to the tales that Ned and the other men brought back from their meeting, but she found it hard to imagine such people herself.

But since Bermuda, since her time with Omar, Nancy found herself thinking more of the different sorts of people in the world, of all the shades of skin and accents of speech she had once heard on the quays in Bristol. How different, and how much alike, were all these sorts of folk? Did the natives have souls, as Christian men and women did? She could not think that Omar did not have a soul, yet she did not think he was baptized, and his skin was darker even than Pocahontas's.

And what if an Indian became a Christian? This seemed to be the plan for Pocahontas: she was studying the Scriptures with the Reverend Whittaker and discussing them with this man John Rolfe. "It will be a great thing for us," Reverend Whittaker said to a visitor one day when Pocahontas and Hannah had gone out visiting, "if we can baptize the first of the Virginia natives into the true faith. What a witness she will be to her people!"

"Does she truly understand all that she is studying?" the other man asked. "Or does she only repeat it back, parrot-like? I have heard that that is all they can do, when the Scriptures are read to them."

"Oh no, she understands it well, and has her own thoughts about it all," Reverend Whittaker assured the man. Nancy, who was mending shirts on a bench in the corner as the men talked, thought this was certainly true, if the conversations she heard by the hearth at night were any indication.

That night the conversation around the table was lively: Master Rolfe was there, sitting beside Pocahontas, as well as three married couples who, Hannah said, owned the largest plantations around Henrico. Most of the talk was about tobacco, the crop that the settlers seemed to stake their hope of prosperity on as surely as those in the New Found Land did on codfish. "I have great hopes of this strain," Master Rolfe told the other men, and proceeded to explain in detail how the kind of tobacco he was growing was far superior to what had been grown in the colony before now.

"Think you that the colony's investors will be glad for tobacco in place of gold and gems?" one of the men huffed. "For that was what they paid for...a gateway to the riches of this New World."

"Gold and silver and gems will come in time," another man asserted. "The Indians know where they can be found—they know the waterways that lead inland, where such treasures lie."

A woman turned to Pocahontas. "Do your people know of it? Where gold can be found?"

"I do not know of it myself," the lady said. "My father's people have a great trade with other tribes, but we do not wear or use the stuff you call gold. It is not known to us."

"There, you see!" Master Rolfe said. "The Spanish may be getting gold from the colonies, but the wealth of Virginia is in its soil."

"And if you are right about this new tobacco strain, you will be a wealthy man," the Reverend Whittaker said.

Master Rolfe bowed his head modestly, but as Nancy reached past him to place a platter on the table, she saw the smile he gave to the lady Pocahontas. The Indian princess did not return the smile, but met his eyes and did not turn away.

"He has spoken to the reverend about it—about asking for her hand in marriage," Hannah told Nancy after the guests had gone home. Pocahontas and Whittaker had gone to walk part of the way back with their guests while the two servants cleaned up after the dinner.

"Would they allow that—for a Christian man to marry a native woman?"

"Oh, she would have to be baptized first, of course, but that's well in hand. The greater thing would be, once she does become a Christian, will Master Rolfe be considered high and mighty enough to wed Powhatan's daughter? 'Twill be the most important match made in this colony, and the reverend thinks the governor might wish to marry her to someone of higher rank."

"Are they...fond of each other?" Nancy wondered.

"Indeed they are. At least, he is fond of her, and I think she takes pleasure in his company, though 'tis hard to know. She told the reverend she was married already, to one of her own people, but that her husband was dead now. 'Tis hard to know what she thinks—they are secretive, you know, not like us."

Certainly the lady Pocahontas was reserved and guarded around most people, though she talked quite freely to the Reverend Whittaker. She spoke little to Hannah, who was her designated chaperone and companion, and Hannah reported that even when they walked all the way to Master Rolfe's plantation to visit him there, Pocahontas had little to say. Nor did she speak much to Nancy, even when they were abed in their shared room.

But when Hannah complained of a cough one morning, Pocahontas turned to Nancy. "I will go today to visit Master Rolfe. If Hannah is sick, it is best she stay at home. You must come with me."

Reverend Whittaker nodded. "That would be well, I think. I cannot spare the time from my work to go with you today, my lady, and it is best in any case for another woman to keep you company."

Keep you company and carry your tackle, Nancy thought, for the lady had a good-sized basket of things to bring with her to the Rolfe plantation, and it made for a heavy burden as Nancy followed her down the winding path that led through Henrico. Men lifted their hats and women bobbed their heads in acknowledgement as they passed, but some of the smaller children stared open-mouthed behind their mothers' backs. The Indian princess was apparently still something of a novelty.

When they passed through the stockade gate and out onto a wider road that led down towards Rolfe's plantation, Nancy kept her position behind the other woman. Then Pocahontas slowed her gait a few steps so that they walked beside each other.

"You were born in England, like these others?" Pocahontas asked.

Startled, Nancy said, "Yes. In Bristol."

"But you did not mean to come to this place."

"No. I went with my mistress to another colony, a place called Cupids Cove. Then I was taken captive—by men on a ship." Did she know what pirates were? The Virginia settlers, living inland on the James River, did not talk of pirates as those in the New Found Land or on Bermuda did.

Pocahontas nodded. "I was, also. Tricked into getting on a ship, and taken here."

I want to go home. Do you? Nancy imagined asking. But she was surprised enough to find Pocahontas putting questions to her and was not about to start making inquiries of her own.

The Indian princess asked Nancy a few more questions about the Cupids colony and about Bristol, though nothing about her own life. Which made sense: no lady of high position would be particularly interested in the private affairs of a servant, but Pocahontas seemed eager to learn all she could about the English and their world.

Nancy sat silent, working on a bag of clothes to mend, while Pocahontas visited with Master Rolfe. Her role, as Hannah had explained it, was to be present so that later, no-one could suggest there had been any impropriety. "Sure there are plenty of Englishmen who've got native women living with them, down in James Fort," Hannah has said, "but no man would treat the chief's daughter so—the governor wouldn't allow it. They need someone present all the time, to guard her reputation."

Whatever the duty, in the days that followed Pocahontas more often asked for Nancy than for Hannah to accompany her on visits to the other Henrico planters. Hannah was not put out by this; she was far happier ordering the household than jouncing up and down the muddy paths of Henrico. As they made their rounds of visits, Nancy grew more comfortable in the company of her new mistress, though there was always a wall of reserve. Nancy had no idea whether that was because of the lady Pocahontas's elevated status as the daughter of a chief, or because she was of another race and language. Or perhaps this was the proper distance between maid and mistress, which Nancy had never known because her bond with Kathryn was so close.

The Indian lady did ask Nancy more questions, on their walks through Henrico or in the quiet of the bedroom at night. Pocahontas wanted to know what Bristol was like, and how the English colony at Cupids Cove differed from the one in Virginia. When Nancy revealed that she had spent some time on Somers Isle, Pocahontas asked about that colony too. "Master Rolfe was wrecked on that island," she said. "His wife and child died there. He does not like to speak of it, but I am most eager to learn of other lands and people," she told Nancy.

Nancy permitted herself a small laugh. "I never used to be. Never was curious about anything beyond the street in Bristol where I was brought up—and now I find myself going all over the world."

"I wish I could go on the travels you have gone. I want to know about your people, about the English. How they live, and how they farm, and how they fight. My people need to know all these things."

"You must know a good deal about the English already—the ones here in Virginia, I mean. You speak our tongue very well, Mistress."

They were close now to the home of Master Wallace, whose wife had invited Pocahontas to come sit and sew with her for a while in the afternoon. "The English came here when I was a child," Pocahontas said. "I have known your language almost as long as my own. I used to be sent as messenger to the fort, in those first times. I would play in the streets with the English lads." She paused. "It seems very long ago."

She looked about at the plantation house they were approaching, the fields around it, the other plantations stretching along the river. More to herself than to Nancy, she added, "We did not think there would be so many of you."

FIFTEEN

Unwelcome News Is Delivered

THE SHIP'S CANNONS BOOMED, THE CRACK REVERBER-
ating through every timber of the vessel. For the first time,
there was no answering thunder from the other ship. "We got
'em," said Sam Brennan, through clenched teeth.

Across a little stretch of water, the Spanish vessel smoked and rocked.
She was a smaller ship than the *White Lion*, about eighty tons, but her
crew had put up a brave fight. Now, as Ned and Sam and the other
men on the *Lion*'s deck watched, the Spanish sailors tied a white flag
to their mast, and the *Lion*'s guns ceased firing.

The *White Lion* drew near the crippled ship; Ned hauled up one of
the grappling hooks and threw it with all his might towards the splin-
tered rail of the other vessel which, he now saw, was called the *Maria
Teresa*. The taking of the ship was accomplished without bloodshed,
save for the handful of Spaniards who had been killed during the gun
battle. Once Captain Elfrith's men had boarded her, the Spanish sailors
surrendered quickly. Ned and his shipmates, except for a few left on
the *Maria Teresa* to see her to port, were back on the *White Lion* in time
for their evening meal.

"Never fought in a battle at sea before?" Brennan asked Ned, as they
dipped their ship's biscuit into a watery stew.

"Not at sea, nor on land," Ned said. "I've been a builder, not a soldier."

"If you stay aboard the *Lion*, you'll have your blade bloodied yet.

Nico, remember that fight we had in the north, off New France?" he called to another sailor, a grizzled fellow who looked seventy years old, though likely he was no more than forty.

"Aye, that was a fine bit of fighting. I killed three Frenchmen that day," Nico laughed.

"I was with Captain Argall when we sacked the French colony at Port Royal," Ned said, "but we killed no-one, only burned the place." He hoped his record of destroying French settlements would give him some credit with these men, but he wasn't about to claim battles he hadn't fought.

He'd been on the *White Lion* under Elfrith's command for two months now, sailing about the isles of the Indies, making port a few times. The capture of the *Maria Teresa* was the first action they had seen. Whenever they were ashore, if other English ships were in port, Ned asked about the *Happy Adventure* and Captain Sly. A few sailors had heard of the captain or his ship, but none knew where they might be found at this time of the year. Back to Ireland where he had connections to sell his goods, someone suggested, or off to the Mediterranean to fight the Turks. Down here in the Indies, no-one had seen the *Happy Adventure*.

Ned fit in fairly well with Elfrith's rough-and-tumble crew, though he missed the company of Francis and Red Peter, who he had thought would take ship with him. A week before Elfrith was ready to leave James Fort, Peter had taken ill with a fever. "He'll not be well enough to sail in time," Francis had told Ned over a mug of ale, "so we'll miss this voyage and catch another later, when he's well again."

"Would you not still take a berth with Elfrith, though?" Ned thought it odd that Francis, who had often said how he disliked staying ashore, would refuse a voyage because Peter was sick—after all, Peter was with his brother's family, who were able to care for him.

But Francis only shook his head. "Nay. We ship out together or not at all. That has always been our way."

Ned shrugged. He knew the two men were friends of many years' standing, but had not realized how close their bond was. "Aye then, you'll likely be in Virginia for the winter."

"Who knows? Captain Argall says he'll take the *Treasurer* up the river for a few trips over the winter and spring. Mayhap we'll see you again, should you come back this way."

Ned had said politely that that would be a fine thing, but he privately doubted he would have any reason to return to James Fort. He had learned what he could in Virginia. He counted himself lucky to have a berth aboard the *White Lion* with Captain Elfrith.

The captured ship and the captors sailed to a group of islands called the Bermudas, where Elfrith had his headquarters on an island no-one else lived on. There was an English settlement on one of the islands, but Elfrith avoided it in favour of this isolated spot that was his and his alone. It was a slow journey, for the winds were low and the ships were frequently becalmed. When they made land there at last, it was in a sheltered cove with a sandy beach fringed by tall trees—a beautiful landscape, the weather mild for early spring. There, the *Maria Teresa* was stripped of her cargo. The ship itself would take a good deal of work before she was seaworthy again, and Elfrith gave Ned the task of assessing the damage and judging how much it would take in time, men, and materials before she would be ready to sail.

The *White Lion*'s men slept aboard ship or in shelters on the beach, while the captive Spaniards, disarmed and guarded, were put to work alongside them, stowing away the goods that had once belonged to their ship. The sun was warm, the air clear, and the days almost merry as the work progressed, and Ned could not help but think that these Bermuda Isles were the loveliest places he'd seen in the world yet.

Pleasant though the land was, Ned was frustrated. None of this brought him any closer to finding Nancy, and every day took her further away, both from him and from any kind of safety. He tried to calculate the weeks and months in his head. Half a year, or close to it, it must be since Nicholas Guy's plantation had been attacked. Half a year with Nancy in the hands of those men.

If I think on it, 'twill drive me mad, he repeated—words he said over and over to himself like a prayer in church.

The day his luck changed seemed much like any other. The crew of the *White Lion* made a trading journey to the southwest and, as they had done so often before, put into a harbour where ships of many nations—some whose trade was legal, some less so—gathered to do business. The scattering of buildings on shore was barely a town, but strolling there in the cool of the evening Ned found a group of sailors gathered outside a large building. Like Cooper's in James Fort, where Ned had first met Elfrith, the place served the function of a tavern without having a sign over the door. He joined a circle of men talking as they drank their ale.

Some of the men spoke English, though there were many tongues threaded throughout the conversation, and, as he always did around sailors who spoke any English at all, Ned found his chance to mention Sly and the *Happy Adventure*.

He was braced, by now, for the usual blank stares, for the men who shrugged and said, "Nay, I've not heard of him," or "I know of the ship, but not where it might be now."

But in this little circle of men, the response was different. The first man to whom Ned posed the question frowned, then turned to one sitting a little distance away.

"*Happy Adventure*, Dickon. Weren't that the name of the ship—"

"The one that went aground off Cooper's Island in the Bermudas? Aye, that she was. I remember saying when we heard of it, what an ill-fated name it was, to call a ship *Happy Adventure* and have her come to such an unhappy misadventure."

Ned's heart vibrated like a plucked lute-string. "You say the ship ran aground?"

"Wrecked in a storm, she were. This would be—when? Late last year," said the first man. "I was in St. George's, the colony on the Bermuda Isles, there a few months gone, and we heard talk of it."

"Wrecked in the November gales, is what I heard," said the other man. "Why d'you ask? Did you used to sail on her?"

"No. I knew someone—did the crew survive?"

The first man he'd spoken to shook his head. "There were only three survivors—three fellows that came to St. George's later, telling the tale of their wreck. All the rest on board was lost."

"Three survivors? What became of them?"

The man shrugged. "I never saw 'em myself, you understand—'twas the tale I was told when I was there. I think they took ship for England or Ireland."

"Likely Ireland—'tis crawling with pirates."

Ned cut in to interrupt a lively discussion of piracy in Ireland. "Only three men—are you sure those were the only survivors? No women?"

"She were no passenger ship—there wouldn't be women aboard. Any rate, none survived but those three, from what I heard."

"There was a woman aboard of that ship," Ned said. Briefly, he told the two men the story of Nicholas Guy's plantation, and Nancy's disappearance. The men around him listened with interest, but the two who had heard the tale of the *Happy Adventure* were adamant that they had only heard of three survivors, all of them men.

The man who had spoken first fixed Ned with a kindly eye. "'Tis a hard word to hear, man, but you must face the thing. If this maid lived to be taken aboard that ship, she never made it to Bermuda. Either she died on the way, or she's at the bottom of the sea."

"Harsh words, Flynn," said the second man, seeing Ned's stricken face.

"Harsh words are true words, and 'tis better to know the worst than be strung along with false hope," the older man said. "When I went off on my first sea-voyage I left a lass behind, true and pretty as you might hope for. While I was down in Portugal I heard word from home, that the plague had come to our village and nearly all our folk were dead. I hoped with all my heart that my Susan had lived—prayed for it, even—but when I got home she were in the ground with all the rest of 'em. It near killed me. I'd ha' done better if I'd given up hope and fixed my mind on the worst."

A little silence fell on the men seated in that little circle in the courtyard: it was rare, in the company of men, for anyone to speak so plainly about love and hope and death. Somebody coughed, and another man said, "By the five wounds of Christ!" under his breath.

Ned could think of nothing to say to this. He stood up, nodded curtly at Flynn, ignored the others. He left the circle, and walked out onto the docks, into the mild blue night. He wished he was a woman, so that he could break down into tears, and there would be no shame in it.

SIXTEEN

An Unwelcome Visitor Arrives

KATHRYN LADLED STEW FROM THE IRON POT OVER THE smouldering fire into the earthenware tureen. She stepped carefully from hearth to table, glancing down to make sure no infants were creeping around her skirts. But no, her Jonathan and Bess's little boy, Will, were both playing on a blanket spread out in the sunshine near the door, though Jonathan was well capable of toddling around now and Will of crawling from place to place with terrifying speed. More than once she had tripped over a small body at her feet— though never, thankfully, while carrying a pot warm from the fire. The only one of the three children who caused her no worry on that score was baby Alice, now napping in her cradle.

Next, from the oven built into the hearth, she took the loaves of bread that had been baking there and brought them to the table. By that time, Jonathan was calling "Mama! Mama!" and Alice had begun to whimper. Kathryn sighed: she had truly hoped the baby was settled for a good long rest now. Perhaps she would fall back to sleep, but the two little boys would need to be seen to.

She squatted down to where the boys played, her son's dark head close to the sandy curls of his playmate. An insect was crawling across Jonathan's open palm and both boys were enthralled; Kathryn was relieved to know that the calls of *Mama* were born only of her son's desire to share the wonder, rather than a signal that he had hurt himself.

Children were a great deal more worry once they could move themselves about.

"Welladay, that is a fine little creature indeed, is it not? But I am sure 'twould be happier out in the grass—shall I put out there?" Jonathan surrendered the insect, and she stepped outside to brush it off onto the ground, enjoying the fresh breeze off the water. The warm summer mornings were ending, but some heat still lingered in these last days of August, and it was good to get away from the hearth fire.

"Papa coming?" Jonathan asked, every inch his father's little lad.

Kathryn shaded her eyes from the noonday sun. There was activity all over the plantation: Bess and Daisy were turning the fish on the flake while Frank unloaded that morning's catch. The season would soon be at an end, but as long as the cod were swimming they would catch, salt, and dry all they could. Nicholas was busy inspecting the boat he had just pulled up onto the pebbles of their small beach, but he turned just as she picked Jonathan up in her arms to look. Nicholas caught sight of his wife and child and waved.

She remembered how, back in Bristol, the chiming of the church bells had told the hours so that everyone knew when to go to work and when to come in to dine. But she had learned here in the New World that if the church bells were silenced, people still knew when to come in for dinner: the height of the sun in the sky or the rumbling in their bellies would bring them to the table just in time.

"There's my fine lad!" Nicholas announced as he bounded up to the house, taking Jonathan from Kathryn's arms. Will put up his hands to be picked up, and Bess was there in a moment to claim him. Kathryn turned back to the cradle, where Alice's cries were growing louder. As her household trooped into the house to eat, Kathryn sat down on the bench, put Alice to the breast, and resigned herself to another one-handed meal.

By the time Alice was sated and back in the cradle, everyone had returned to their afternoon work, which in Kathryn's case meant cleaning up from dinner and watching the little boys. When everything was tidy, she put Alice into a sling, picked Will up to ride astride her hip, and gave her hand to Jonathan to trip along beside her as she went up to the garden. Bess and Daisy, finished with the fish for now, were harvesting carrots and turnips, and Kathryn would join them until it was time to prepare the evening meal.

In the garden, the three women spread out a blanket to put all three of the babies on, and took turns watching them as they pulled up the vegetables that were ready. Next year they would clear more ground and expand the garden, but this small patch was all they had had time to plant when they had arrived at the plantation at the beginning of summer.

There were so many echoes of last summer, Kathryn thought—she had another new baby, and they were again building and planting on the new site. This time, though, much was different. The men had left the Cupids Cove settlement and arrived on the plantation site as soon as the snow melted. The walls of the new house were up by the time the women and children arrived, and the roof covered in soon after. It was simple living for now, just a large single room with the hearth, a table and benches, and everyone sleeping around it on straw mattresses laid on the floor. The sleeping chamber, and the beds to go in it, would wait until the fish were in and the weather turned cold.

This year, there had been no tarrying at the home of Mistress Pike. Indeed, they had heard nothing at all from their only neighbours since arriving at the plantation, though Nicholas said that there was much activity further up the shore, more than might be expected from the fishing boats that were there every summer. Later that evening, as he and Kathryn enjoyed a few quiet moments together at day's end, he spoke of his concerns. "'Tis my thought that there's another nest of pirates up there, the same place where Captain Easton made his headquarters two years ago," he told her, "and Philip thought the same. I hope Governor Mason has no truck with pirates."

"Was he not jailed for piracy himself, only last year?" Kathryn asked. She had picked up what information she could about Cupids Cove's new governor when she and Nicholas had visited the colony last month to bid farewell to Philip, Elizabeth, and their children, who were returning to England. Elizabeth was glad to be going "back to civilization," as she put it, where her boys could go to school. But Philip Guy resented the fact that he had never been named governor, and that the Company had replaced him with this Mason, who was not a Bristol man.

"Aye, but 'twas the Scots who imprisoned him—that's a different matter," Nicholas said with a shrug. "He is in good odour with King James, you may be sure, or he'd not have been made governor here. But he'd best be wary of that crowd up at Harbour Grace. There is a captain up there called Mainwaring who claims he was sent out with a commission to stop pirates in these waters, but I've heard he's as often on the wrong side of the law as the right."

"There's a good many you could say that about." Kathryn sighed and pulled her shawl around her shoulders. She and her husband were sitting on a bench Frank had made out in front of the house, overlooking their cove with the fishing boat, waiting for the next morning's journey. The sun was growing low in the sky; the babies were abed in the house. It was the only hour in the day when Kathryn and Nicholas could sit side by side and rest a little. Somewhere, Bess and Frank were no doubt taking the same opportunity to enjoy a few moments together, while faithful Daisy finished her mending and kept an eye to the three sleeping children.

"Are you weary?" Nicholas asked her now, leaving the subject of pirates aside.

"So weary I can scarce get up off this seat to go to bed! But 'tis you have the harder task—you must be up early and out in the boat."

"These are long days with hard labour for all of us." He stood up and took her hand to help her to her feet. "And we must be abed, for you'll be woken before I will—once Mistress Alice demands her nightly meal. Perhaps 'tis you who has the harder lot."

He kept hold of her hand as they walked back towards the house, and Kathryn tightened her fingers in his. She felt closer to her husband since they had left Cupids Cove this time, closer than she ever had while living there, or certainly in those long-ago days back in Bristol when they were first wedded. Always he had seemed a little distant, ever the lord and master, but here they were partners in the task of building their plantation, and she felt the hours of hard work were binding them together. It was nothing like the heedless passion she had felt for

Thomas Willoughby, but even when she looked at her fair-haired baby daughter, the thought of Willoughby seemed as distant as a dream. It had been nearly a year since she had committed her sin; Alice was three months old, and Nicholas had never doubted for a moment that the little girl was his. Why should he? Life went on, and Kathryn's life was with her husband.

She fell asleep beside him, soothed by the sound of the waves against the rocks below. On cold nights she longed for the time when they might be able to purchase window glass imported from England, but on a warm night like this one the sounds of the sea through the shutters lulled her to sleep and whispered through her dreams.

And then, in the morning, the daily round began all over again. One day as much like another as pearls on a string, so that Kathryn was more startled than she ought to have been by the sight of a small boat making its way into their cove the following afternoon. Pirates, of course, would not come rowing a fishing boat, and this came from the north, not from Cupids Cove to the south. Well before it reached their wharf, she had guessed who it must be.

"Mercy, 'tis that terrible woman from up the shore," she said to Daisy. "Watch the little ones, will you?"

"What woman? Not the pirate's wife?"

"Of course, what other neighbour do we have? I don't know how she dares show her face here." Kathryn put down the basket of clothes she had brought freshly washed from the stream, dried her hands on her kirtle, and headed down the hill to greet her unwelcome guests.

Sheila Pike and her husband were already out of the boat, ordering Frank to go find his master and mistress. Catching sight of Kathryn, Mistress Pike said, "Ah, there is Mistress Guy now—how good to see you again, after so long."

After you sheltered us in your house, then set your pirate friends to attack us, Kathryn thought, but hid the bitter words behind a smile. She extended a hand, and as her husband arrived from the storehouse to greet Gilbert Pike, Kathryn led his wife to the house.

"And you have begun on your new house! How very nice. I am sure it will be a proper little English manor," the Irishwoman said. She was a great beauty, with a proud carriage and a tilt to her chin that some might call haughty. Her long hair was coiled atop her head in a manner elaborate enough to make Kathryn wonder if she had somehow acquired a maid in the last year. Last summer, there had been no women servants in the Pike household, a situation that clearly did not please the mistress. But surely she must have had at least one brought out from England or from her home in Ireland, since someone must be caring for her child back at their plantation.

Kathryn sat her down at the table and Daisy brought cups of ale for both women while Master Pike walked around the property with Nicholas. The women made small talk about the house and children until Sheila Pike finally mentioned the unspoken subject.

"You have done well, to rebuild so completely after that terrible fire," she said. "I would never have guessed."

"It is not precisely the same spot," Kathryn said. "The old house, the one that burned, was a little farther to the south of here, though on our same piece of land. There is nothing left there—the ruins were all pulled down, and the site has begun to grow over again. Would that all our losses were so easily covered up."

"Yes—you lost a man, did you not?"

Kathryn nodded towards Daisy, who had herded the little boys outside to play. "Daisy was wounded, though she has recovered well—her bad arm still troubles her, and likely always will. Her husband was killed."

"How very sad. Did it not make you doubt the wisdom of building in such an isolated place?"

Kathryn opened her mouth to speak, then shut it again. Nothing would be gained by confronting the woman now, no matter how much her blood boiled to hear Sheila Pike speak so coolly of a disaster Kathryn was sure she had had a hand in causing. "You and your husband seem to do very well, and your place is as isolated as ours."

"Oh, very true. But 'tis not everyone is cut out for such a life. You are town-bred, used to having people around and everything you need near at hand. Do you not long to be back in Bristol?"

"I would be well contented here, if I thought we were safe."

"Exactly. This is not a land for those who long for safety."

Kathryn fixed her guest with a long stare. "Mistress Pike, you speak as though an unfortunate accident befell our plantation, but you know that is not so. We were attacked. Along with the man who was murdered, my servant Nancy—you will remember her, a woman dear to me since childhood—was kidnapped. To this day I do not know if she is alive or dead."

Not a ripple of emotion showed on the other woman's beautiful, chiselled face. "There is much lawlessness in these waters."

"As you have cause to know, having been captured by pirates yourself."

"Yes. Of course, I was well treated, because my—"

"—your father is a king in Ireland," Kathryn joined in. She had not forgotten Sheila NaGeira Pike's oft-repeated litany of her illustrious lineage.

"He is indeed," said the other woman.

"Perhaps if my husband and I were as familiar with pirates as you are, we would not have had the ill-fortune to be attacked."

"My husband no longer plies that trade—he is a planter and a fisherman now, even as your husband is."

"Yet so much of that trade still goes on in these parts," Kathryn pressed. "We hear of this Captain Mainwaring, who makes Harbour Grace his home port—on your very doorstep! It would be much to your benefit, I imagine, to trade with such men—especially as your husband knows the business so well."

She saw the brief flutter of Mistress Pike's eyelashes as the shaft hit home. Otherwise her lovely white face was as still as marble. *What a player she would make on the stage*, Kathryn thought.

"'Tis not against the law to trade with privateers who attack the French and Spanish," Sheila Pike said.

"True enough. And this Mainwaring—he is different from Captain Easton, no doubt, and would never attack an English ship or settlement."

"I am sure he would not. I am told he was commissioned to put a stop to piracy, not engage in it."

"And the captain who was there last year?" Kathryn asked. "Was he the same?"

"Captain Sly? He was one of Easton's men, I believe, but we had no dealings with him. As I told you, Master Pike has left piracy and privateering, and we want only to establish our plantation here."

Captain Sly. An apt name, if that was the pirate who had attacked them last summer, Kathryn thought. Aloud she said, "And that is all that we want, also."

Mistress Pike inclined her head slightly. "Of course. I only remind you, not all are suited to this life. Especially English women, who are accustomed to more ease and comfort." She turned, took in the large, open room around the hearth, still bare of furniture or interior walls, mattresses and blankets piled around on the floor. "'Tis a fine start you and your people have made here, Mistress Guy, of rebuilding what you lost last year. But I should counsel you not to become too attached to this house, or to this land. You may find you are more content in Cupids Cove, if not back in Bristol."

The baby began to fuss and whimper. Kathryn was glad for the distraction; she swept Alice out of the cradle and buried her head in the baby's soft, fair wisps of curl.

Outside, the men were concluding what appeared to be a friendly tour of the property. Kathryn wondered what reason Gilbert Pike had given Nicholas for their arrival—one neither rowed a boat nor walked overland such a distance merely to say hello. Of course they must be invited to dine, and the household's simple meal must be stretched to feed two more people, and Kathryn must play the polite hostess while smothering her burning rage towards her guests. She would say nothing to her husband until the Pikes had gone, which, after dinner, they did.

"What did they want with us?" she pressed her husband, when she had told him about her conversation with Mistress Pike.

"He said they only came to be friendly, now that the season is well-nigh over and the fish are in. In truth, Master Pike was most helpful in suggesting how I might hire fishing servants for the season next year, should we wish to have more hands—he has done so the past few years."

"Still, I cannot believe that they came only to be neighbourly. Truly, Nicholas, talking with Mistress Pike confirmed my suspicions—I am sure that she and her husband are in league with pirates. She dropped a name—a Captain Sly—who might well have been the one whose ship attacked us last year."

"They will not do so again this year. I think I have a good understanding, now, with Master Pike. We men do not let our emotions run away with us as women do, you know. This Mistress Pike is a choleric creature, I believe, and you will have no satisfaction dealing with her. Leave it between Master Pike and myself."

Kathryn was not satisfied with that—how could she be? On the other hand, what could she do about any of it? Only fear, more than she had all summer, that they would be victims of another attack, and play out over and over terrible scenes of what Nancy's fate might be.

Oh, Ned, Kathryn thought, as if he were some Roman saint she could offer prayers to. *I hope you can find her, and bring her home.*

In the wake of the Pikes' visit, the work of preparing the season's catch of fish continued, and a few days later the *Constant* sailed out of Cupids Cove, stopping at the Guys' plantation to take their salt fish for sale back across the ocean. It was a great pleasure, watching the men load the fish from the storehouse into the hold of the ship, to think of the modest wealth they would earn from this first summer's work on their own plantation. *The first of many*, Kathryn thought, and tried to stifle the quiver of misgiving she felt when she looked about at their piece of land, their half-built house, their boat and stage, their few livestock.

Bad news, when it came, did not arrive in the form of marauders from the sea attacking and burning their house and land, as they had done the previous year. Instead, a week after the fish had been loaded aboard the *Constant*, when Nicholas and Frank were hard at work on the inside of the house, two of the Cupids men, Jem Holworthy and John Crowder, rowed out to give Nicholas the ill tidings.

The *Constant*, along with a half-dozen other ships of the English fishing fleet, had been attacked by pirates not far off the coast. Almost the whole catch of salt fish from that summer's work all along the coast—including the fish caught at Cupids Cove and on the Guys' plantation—had been stolen. Not by Spanish or French privateers—which, while it would have been unlucky and vexing, would at least been part of the order of things.

"'Twas this Captain Mainwaring," Holworthy reported, "him who was stationed up there at Harbour Grace all summer. Supposed to be over here rooting out pirates, he was, with letters from the king. He attacked the French and the Spaniards all summer, right enough—and then when our own fleet was ready to sail back across the waters, he turned on our own English vessels and attacked them too. He's off to Spain and Portugal with almost the whole summer's catch, to sell for his own gain. And we are left with nothing."

SEVENTEEN

A Journey Is Made Upriver

"THE LADY POCAHONTAS SEEMS CONTENT TO HAVE YOU
serve her," Reverend Whittaker said.

He had walked into the room while Nancy was clearing
away the remains of their morning meal. Hannah was outside feeding the
chickens. Nancy was startled; the minister rarely spoke directly to her.

"I am pleased to be of service, sir."

"She is going on a voyage upriver to her father's lands. The governor
is going to treat with Powhatan, and wants Powhatan's daughter on the
ship. I want you to accompany her. You and she will be the only women
on the ship, but you need have no fear for your safety—the governor
himself is going along, and Master Rolfe. They will ensure the safety
of the lady Pocahontas and her servant."

Another ship, another voyage. Was Pocahontas going of her own will
to visit her father and her people, or was she being taken as a hostage?
Nancy did not ask the question aloud—it was no business of hers—but
the answer still was not clear to her when she and Pocahontas, along
with Master Rolfe and a few other Henrico planters, boarded the ship.
Most of the men aboard were either the vessel's crew or men from James
Fort—important ones, judging by their clothing. One of them was the
governor, but Nancy had no idea which.

A sailor directed her to the one cabin below deck and told her she
could store Pocahontas's belongings there. It was about the size of the

cook's cabin Nancy had occupied on the *Happy Adventure*, though of
course without a hearth. It had one small berth for the lady to sleep in;
Nancy wondered if she herself would be expected to sleep on the cabin
floor. But as she tidied the cabin and arranged Pocahontas's things, the
same sailor—a bluff, hearty young man with fair hair and beard and a
ruddy, sunburnt skin—came in with a hammock. "Captain told me to
put this up in here so the Indian princess's servant will have a place to
sleep. That'd be you, then?"

"It would."

"Slept in a hammock aboard ship before?"

"No. I've been on ships, but one time I had a berth and the other time
I was on the floor of the 'tween deck."

"You'll find this different," he said, raising his eyebrows at the news
she had once been afforded the luxury of a berth. He did not explain
how the hammock would be different, turning his hand instead to
stringing up the cloth bed between two hooks that were already driven
into the beams for that purpose. Nancy tried to imagine herself clam-
bering up into it.

"Do you know how long this trip will take?" she asked.

"Up to the Powhatan's town and back would only be a few days—
mayhap two up and two back—but the governor may want to stay some
time, depending on his dealings with the chief. I only obey orders, me."

"The same for me," Nancy said, and they shared a quick grin before
the sailor disappeared.

Nancy was eyeing the hammock, wondering if she should make a
trial of getting into it, when she heard Pocahontas talking to Master
Rolfe outside.

"I do not know how the governor could be so—so unthinking, unless
he is doing it with purpose," the Indian lady was saying, with more
bitterness in her voice than Nancy had ever heard. "The same ship!
The same cabin!"

"I am sure 'tis only that the *Treasurer* was available to go upriver,"
Master Rolfe said. "Surely the governor meant no insult."

"No insult? The same ship where I was taken captive? This is no
accident."

"'Twas some of your own people betrayed your trust—Captain Argall was only following his orders, to bring you to us. The governor wishes to show your father that you are well treated, an honoured guest."

"A guest is free to leave when she desires."

"Do you desire? To leave—us?"

There was a pause. "I desire to be alone now," Pocahontas said.

She came into the cabin, and sat on the bed, looking through the clothing she had brought. After a time she said aloud, "The governor does not know how little my father values me."

Nancy had no idea what to say in response, but Pocahontas appeared to be talking as much to herself as to Nancy. "Among your people, the daughter of a great chief is a great lady, but it is not so with ours. The... the line that matters is the mother's line, and my mother was—not from a chief's line. My father favoured me despite it—but he has not paid the ransom the English demand for me."

By the time evening fell, Pocahontas's mood had lightened somewhat, to the point that she laughed aloud at the undignified sight of Nancy attempting to clamber into the hammock when it was time for bed. "I'd sooner have had a mat on the floor," Nancy grumbled, but she was secretly pleased to see this lighter side of her mistress. The Indian lady had moments when it was possible to catch a glimpse of who she might have been in a more carefree life, among her own people perhaps, and Nancy thought it likely that she was always guarded around the English. That she would allow herself a few moments of fun—even fun at Nancy's expense—suggested that she was, perhaps, becoming a little more comfortable around her English maidservant.

As Nancy had suspected, the hammock did not make for a comfortable sleeping place, though she had heard sailors talk of how they enjoyed the swing of the hammock while the ship swayed on the waves. Perhaps, as with so many things in life, one became accustomed to it.

It might have been worse had the *Treasurer* been at sea, but the motion of the river was far gentler. Nancy thought, drifting to sleep, of her first voyage, how her journey out of Bristol had begun on a river before the Avon flowed into the sea. Had that been only a year and a

half ago? She felt she did not know that young girl, so full of appre-
hension and uncertainty. How many voyages lay between that day
and this!

In the morning, still a little stiff from trying to accommodate her
body to the hammock, Nancy found a spot on deck where she could
lean against the rail and eat her pottage while she watched the riverbank
slip by. It was a warm morning—she still could not credit how warm
Virginia was in March, and how green, already. What a wonder, that
the world held so many places, and all of them so different.

The lady Pocahontas was breaking her fast below decks with Master
Rolfe, the governor and some other men from James Fort. The sailors
worked on the deck and in the rigging but, as Reverend Whittaker had
promised, they paid Nancy no heed. She did not feel that looming sense
of threat that she had felt at every moment on the pirate ship or even in
her men's costume on Somers Isle.

The only sailor who spoke to her was the blond fellow who had
strung up the hammock the day before. He was dangling from the lines
above her head, and when he jumped lightly down to the deck, he said,
"We be coming up to one of the savages' settlements in a little bit. That'll
be something to see, if you've never seen the like before."

"Why, are their towns so different from ours?"

"Aye, their houses are different—more like huts or tilts. They don't
build in stone or brick—'course, we don't build in stone here either,
there's not much of it in this part of the world, but I don't doubt we'll
make bricks here and build proper English houses someday."

Nancy remembered the men at Cupids Cove saying that the natives
in the New Found Land did not build permanent houses at all, only
temporary shelters that they could pick up and move with them. As
the native town came into sight along the riverbank, she guessed that
these Virginia people were very different from the ones in the New
Found Land—and why should they not be? It was another part of the
world, after all.

When she caught her first sight of the natives, she was shocked:
unlike Pocahontas, who dressed and spoke like an Englishwoman, these
men who stood sentry on the riverbank truly looked like an alien race.

Their clothes were not fashioned like Englishmen's clothes; some were stripped to the waist and wore only loincloths, and all had long black hair on one side of their heads only, the other side shaven. "'Tis said they shave it so that it does not tangle in their bowstrings," the sailor told her. Many of them had their faces and upper bodies marked with some kind of dye. Some were armed with bows, while a few, like the Englishmen, carried rifles.

There was a stir of activity among the men on deck: the crew running to their posts, and several of the James Fort men striding about giving orders. The sailor Nancy had been talking to, who had been called away by someone of higher rank, came back to tell her, "You and your mistress are to get to your cabin. Anyone who's not a sailor or a fighting man is to go below."

Fighting? Nancy thought of asking what was about to happen, but she did not waste breath on the question, and went instead straight to the hatch where the ladder led below. Outside the cabin, Pocahontas was talking with John Rolfe again.

"It is a show of strength only," Rolfe was saying.

"It is not needed! Do you think my people do not know by now—"

The report of one of the ship's guns, cracking the air and rocking the vessel, cut off further words. Rolfe almost pushed Pocahontas into the cabin, and Nancy in after her. "Bolt the door," he ordered as he turned to run in the other direction.

"They are attacking the town," Pocahontas said.

Nancy remembered the sound and the feeling vividly from the sea battle between the *Happy Adventure* and the *Caballero*. She remembered, too, the sickening crash and crunch of the ship being hit from the opposing ship's cannon, the ball ripping through the hull.

But here, there was no answering shot, only the screams and shouts she could hear from the shore. There was no other ship, and from the glimpse she had caught of the Indian town, she had seen no big guns mounted for defence.

"They cannot fight back," Pocahontas echoed her thought. "They have rifles traded from the English, but no cannon."

"Why is the ship attacking? Did you know they would do this?"

Pocahontas shook her head. "It is what Rolfe says—a showing of strength. As if the Powhatan do not already know the English guns are bigger."

I'd have been a deal less likely to come along if I'd known there would be fighting, Nancy thought, and then wondered if she'd have been free to refuse. "Does the governor want war, or peace?"

"It has been both war and peace, ever since the English came," Pocahontas said. Outside their cabin, running feet thundered across the deck and they could hear more shouting, more distant rifle shot, but no more crack of the ship's cannon. "My father and the English governor both want peace—as long as the other will bend the knee."

But the English will never bend the knee to natives, Nancy thought. She did not say it aloud. Pocahontas must know this about the English now, after living so close to them for so many years. They might make treaties and trade with the people of the land, but they would not submit to the rule of Powhatan or any other native chief.

She thought of all the talk of the natives she had heard from the men back in Cupids Cove. They meant to treat and trade with the people of the land if they could find them, to be sure, but also to preach to them, to make Christians and civilized men of them. She was quite sure the English, here in Virginia as in Cupids Cove, would not stop till it was the natives who had bent the knee.

She looked at the young woman—younger than Nancy herself, by a good few years—who sat on the bed in the dimly lit cabin, every muscle tensed. Caught between the world of her home and the world of her captors.

"Go up on deck," Pocahontas said. "Tell me what you see."

Above deck, all was quiet now, only the sailors left at their posts. All the action was on shore, where many of the *Treasurer*'s crew and passengers were fighting, mostly hand-to-hand, with the Indians. Occasionally a rifle shot rang out, but most of the battle was between small clutches of men, twos and threes, with swords and knives and short spears. The English seemed to be winning. She heard men cry out, saw them fall. On the muddy ground close to shore, an Englishman and an Indian struggled together, each armed with knives, and then another

Englishman fired a musket towards them. The contest between equals suddenly turned unequal as the shot shattered the Indian's skull and he pitched forward into the water, his blood staining the river.

Nancy went back down the ladder, shaking. She had seen such violence only once before, in the sea battle, and though this did not touch her person as closely, it was still shattering to see the bloodshed. She told Pocahontas what she had seen, and the Indian woman nodded, as though it were no more than she had expected.

Not long afterwards, the Englishmen returned triumphant. None of them had been killed, and only a few wounded in the skirmish. "They paid our tribute and learned their lesson," she heard John Rolfe tell someone as the *Treasurer* lifted anchor and continued its journey upriver.

That evening, while the ship was still noisy with men recounting their tales of the battle, John Rolfe and Pocahontas stood together talking on the deck, their heads close and their voices quiet. Nancy, at her own spot on the rail, watched them and wondered.

"Next day brings us to Powhatan's town—where we're most like to find the chief," a voice said behind her. She turned, and it was the same sailor she had spoken to a few times before.

"Did you fight with the Indians today?" she asked.

"Not I! I'll not fight unless the ship itself is attacked and boarded—I like to keep my feet off solid ground, if I can help it."

"Have you been at sea all your life, then? Born below deck?" She was surprised to hear a note of teasing come back into her voice. It was so long since she had shared a jest with anyone at all.

"Nearly. Shipped out from Portsmouth when I was twelve—worked my way up from cabin boy. I've been on ships out of Virginia this last two years, but I don't count any place on land my home."

She nodded. "I hardly know where home is myself, these days." She had always meant Bristol when she thought of *going home*—but now when she said those words, the shores of the New Found Land came to mind.

"Your mistress there is cozy with that fellow," the sailor went on, nodding towards Pocahontas and John Rolfe.

"I know nothing about that. Not my business," Nancy said.

The sailor laughed, and scrambled up into the rigging again. "Serves me right for passing comment. I'm too curious for my own good."

That night, Pocahontas said, "Tomorrow, dress my hair like an English lady. I will wear the best gown. And you will come with me, to show I have been given an English woman as a servant. When I go to meet my father and uncles, they must see that I have a high station among your people."

With the limited supplies and space available in the ship's cabin, Nancy did her best to comply the following morning, styling Pocahontas to look as grand as possible. Governor Dale himself—Nancy had finally worked out which one of the men he was—called for the lady Pocahontas and brought her up on deck. Nancy followed, standing a little apart from them on the deck as the Indian settlement came into view and the ship dropped anchor.

This town was far larger than the one they had attacked the day before. This time, there was no firing of guns. A group of native warriors did stand guard on the riverbank, as in the other place. To Nancy they looked fierce, with their faces and bare chests painted, but their guns and bows were lowered.

Nancy was the last of the English in the little procession of people making its way up from the riverside to and through the town. There were fields all around, just as in the English settlement at Henrico, and roads that led through a tidy town. What distinguished it most from the English colony was the houses, which were more dome-like than English houses and were covered with grass matting. Indian women and children gathered near their homes, standing by outdoor cooking fires, and watched the English party pass with the same curiosity Nancy had seen in the eyes of Henrico planters when they saw Pocahontas walk down the road. *We are all a novelty to someone*, she thought.

They were led into the largest of the shelters—still dome-like, but as large inside as a church. There were several more native men here—no women, that Nancy could see—and one stepped forward to speak to Pocahontas and to Governor Dale.

A long conversation ensued, partly in English and partly in the natives' tongue, with Pocahontas sometimes translating for both parties. Nancy was too far back to hear much of it, and she felt both uneasy and overwhelmed. It was very warm inside the shelter, and she was suddenly tired and wished there was somewhere to sit down.

Suddenly, the voices at the centre of the room were raised in anger. "He has not paid, and will not pay!" Nancy clearly heard her mistress say. "He has not even come himself to greet me!" Then a torrent of words in what must be her own language, and an answering rush from the Indian men.

Pocahontas turned and strode away from the men, back towards the entrance of the building, gesturing for Nancy to follow. Outside, she stood for a few moments looking out over the town, her face impossible to read. None of the men, English or Indian, came out to speak to her; Nancy could hear their voices continuing, though doubtless it was more difficult for them to talk without the presence of Pocahontas, who spoke both tongues so fluently.

A couple of women approached, and Pocahontas went to talk to them, her manner relaxing at once. There were embraces, and a flurry of conversation in their own tongue, while Nancy stood off to the side trying to take in as much as she could of this new place. At least she could breathe more easily, away from the close air inside the building.

Despite Pocahontas's hasty departure, when the men came out they all seemed to be in good spirits. Master Rolfe drew Pocahontas aside to speak with her while the governor announced to the English party that there was to be a feast. "We will dine with our dear friends the Powhatan and celebrate our peace with them."

Yesterday war, tomorrow peace. The lady Pocahontas stayed close to John Rolfe now, and Nancy was left more or less to her own devices. She was seated some distance from her mistress during the feast, and was given some tasty roasted meat, a kind of flat bread, and some vegetables she did not recognize. When Pocahontas beckoned her over, Nancy went to join her mistress, who was talking to a group of women. Three were girls—no more than fourteen or fifteen, Nancy guessed. The fourth was older, and the beading and feathers adorning her garments hinted that she was someone important.

"These are my kinswomen," Pocahontas explained in English. "My sister, Matachanna." She indicated the older of the four, then turned to the girls. "Wapuna, Sokanon and Tala will return to Henrico with us, and will serve me when I marry Master Rolfe. You will help them to learn the English tongue and the duties of an English servant."

The girls smiled and bobbed their heads at Nancy; one giggled and hid her face behind her hand, as girls of that age seemed given to do no matter what their race or station in life. The other woman, Pocahontas's sister, had a more steady gaze, and she placed her hand over her heart as she said "Nancy," repeating Pocahontas's introduction.

"Matachanna," Nancy said, and then repeated the names of the three young girls, hoping she had said them aright.

Later that night, back aboard the ship, she said to her mistress, "It is decided you will marry Master Rolfe?"

"Yes," said Pocahontas. "That decision was made today." She did not say who had made it. "My father did not come, and sent only my elder brothers to greet me. They agreed to this marriage."

John Rolfe was a fairly handsome man, Nancy thought, and a successful farmer by Virginia's standards, though he was no nobleman. He seemed genuinely fond of Pocahontas. Still it was odd, to think of this young woman being passed among the men like a coin at market, for the value she could bring to either side. But from the little Nancy knew of wealthy people back in England, this was how their marriages were made, too.

"For the marriage, I must become a Christian," Pocahontas added, "but that is nothing—I will have Whittaker do his baptism to me. Everyone must do some—ritual, when they join another tribe. When I was a child, the English came to our people—there was a man named John Smith. A braggart, but he was kind to me. He did a ceremony with my father, to promise loyalty, and my father promised to treat him as a son. These are the things you must do, between nations."

As Pocahontas spoke, Nancy was unpinning the younger woman's long hair and uncoiling it from atop her head. She looked younger with her hair down. Nancy began brushing it out, then plaiting it.

"This marriage will be..." she hesitated again, the pause that Nancy recognized as Pocahontas seeking out the best word in English. "An alliance," she settled on, finally. "It is what I must do, for my father's people. My people. The governor says he may want a Powhatan wife for himself," she added. "He was looking at my sisters today."

"Hasn't the governor a wife already?"

"Do your great men have only one wife? My father has had many."

"Christians are only allowed one wife," Nancy said, but her thoughts had turned back to her own situation. "You said you want me to train the maids—Wapuna, Tala, and..."

"Sokanon."

"Yes, Sokanon. Does that mean you will take me with you?"

"Yes, if Reverend Whittaker is willing to sign over your—service?"

"My indenture."

"I believe he will give you to me," Pocahontas said. "He wants very much for me to do the baptism, and to marry an Englishman."

In the morning, there was a formal leave-taking ceremony, a farewell from Chief Powhatan's brothers to his daughter and her English allies. Wapuna, Sokanon, and Tala joined the party on board.

"You'll have to string up a couple more hammocks," Nancy said to the friendly young sailor when he passed the spot where she stood at the rail.

"Ah, they're not princesses, like your lady. They can sleep two nights on the deck."

"Not without anyone to guard them. I am responsible for them," Nancy said.

"Quite high and mighty, aren't you?" he said with a grin.

"I am serving a princess," she pointed out.

"Ah, shall I call you my lady, then?"

"You should call me Mistress Ellis," she said, putting on a haughty air.

He frowned. "Your name is Nancy, is it not? Nancy Ellis?"

"It is."

"I know that name." He screwed up his ruddy face as if remembering. "Where'd you hail from, Nancy Ellis?"

"I was born in Bristol, but I came out to settle in Cupids Cove in the New Found Land, and from there I was—"

"Taken by pirates?"

Something leaped and twisted in Nancy's chest. Her heart thudded against the bodice of her kirtle. "Yes. On a ship called the *Happy Adventure*."

His face cleared and he turned to another sailor who was nearby, coiling up a long piece of rope. "Peter! The lass young Ned was looking for—what was her name?"

"His fair Nancy? Lord, who'd forget that? He never stopped talking of her, did he, Francis?"

"You've met Ned—Ned Perry from Cupids Cove? Was he here in Virginia?"

Francis laughed. "Here in Virginia? Lass, he was on this ship—we took him on in St. John's station in the autumn. 'Twas only a month, six weeks ago, that he left us in James Fort for a ship bound to the Indies. He heard a rumour that the ship that captured you was headed that way. And to think you were here all along!"

Ned had been there—on the *Treasurer*, in James Fort. Their paths might so easily have crossed, had she landed in James Fort instead of in Henrico.

The red-haired man came over. More gravely than Francis, he added, "In truth, 'tis grand to see you are alive and well. Young Ned spoke of nothing but finding you, but I was afeared he'd have his heart broke, for I thought surely you must be dead."

"I hope you'll be as pleased to see Ned as he will be to see you, when your paths finally cross," Francis said.

"Pleased? 'Tis all I want—to find him, and go home with him." No doubt, now, about what *home* meant—home was where Ned was. "If you see sight of him again in your voyages, on any ship, in any port—tell him I am at Henrico, serving the wife of Master John Rolfe. And tell him I am waiting for him."

PART II

1616–1617

EIGHTEEN

An Attack Is Carried Out

ANOTHER SETTLEMENT; ANOTHER TAVERN; ANOTHER night of men drinking and bragging and telling lies. Many of the tales were told in Spanish, a tongue Ned now understood a little, after working alongside a few captured Spanish sailors who had joined Elfrith's crew. But with so many men speaking at once, it was just a babble to him. Other voices added to the din, in Portuguese and in Dutch, but even had they all been speaking English, it would have been the same familiar noise: the sound of men boasting of their deeds, whether with the sword or with women.

It was always a diversion to stop in a settled place, one that welcomed a crew with money regardless of what country its men hailed from. They were now far out of English territory, far south of Virginia and the Bermudas, into territory colonized by the Spaniards. This island, Elfrith had told the men, was called Hispaniola, and while there were Spanish settlements, there was also a lively trade in goods legal and illegal, from ships of all nations.

In these waters, Elfrith's ship and crew flew not the English flag but a Dutch flag that gave them freedom to plunder and attack Spanish ships and settlements. Yet their coin, when they had a chance to spend it, was as good as anyone's. And this was a settlement with women in it—more particularly, a town with whores. A rare opportunity for men who spent weeks at sea.

Ned had visited the brothel already with a couple of his shipmates. Some of the women were the natives of the land, and some were Africans brought over to work. None spoke English, which was fine for his purposes. He'd not had the chance to be with many women since he had learned of Nancy's death, but he took every opportunity that presented itself. If the women did not speak his language, so much the better. He wanted to sink into them, to bury his longing in the bodies of women who reminded him in no way of his lost love.

He did not know how long it had been since he had heard of the fate of the *Happy Adventure* one warm night in a port whose name he did not know. He had struggled against that knowledge, but in the end despair crashed over him like a wave. He had travelled leagues and spent months pretending to be some questing knight from a romance, and now his quest was at an end. The *Happy Adventure* was at the bottom of the sea.

He had returned with Elfrith to the sheltered cove in the Bermudas and worked for weeks with a crew of men restoring the *Maria Teresa*, getting her ready to sail again. When that work was done, he had gone back to sea on the *White Lion*, sailing about the Indies, capturing a French ship, giving chase to a Spanish vessel but losing her. When Elfrith made a summer voyage across the ocean, to England and Ireland, Ned went along. It was as good a way to fill his days as any.

In England Ned thought of leaving the *White Lion*, of making his way back to Bristol to see his parents and brothers and sisters, but he could not imagine himself doing it. He had sailed away so bravely all those years ago with John Guy to begin a new life in a new world. Now to return alone, with no fortune in his pocket, having failed at the one task that mattered to him—it was not to be thought of.

There had even been a ship at Portsmouth, where they spent some time ashore, that was making the last voyage of the summer to the New Found Land. Ned had considered asking for passage. Did he not owe it, at least, to Kathryn Guy, to carry what news he had learned of Nancy? Would it bring her any peace to know that her friend was dead?

Perhaps it would; perhaps it would not. But Ned knew he could not be the man to deliver that message. Nor could he ever return to Cupids

Cove, to that place where he had lived with such good heart and hope for the future. It might, after all, be better to leave Kathryn in ignorance. As long as she did not know for certain, she could imagine Nancy alive and well somewhere, miraculously rescued from the pirates.

That was what he let himself imagine, sometimes—that she was someplace inaccessible to him, but safe and well. That was true in its way, if she was dead and in heaven— but it was poor comfort for a man in his position.

If he could not return to either of his old homes—to Bristol nor to the New Found Land—then what was he to do with himself? There was no other place along this shore for an Englishman to settle save in the Bermudas or in Virginia. He thought of binding himself to service there, earning a plot of land. But to what purpose? The great advantage of life in a colony was that a simple working man like Ned Perry might be able to own his own house and farm his own land, a destiny he could never rise to England. But what use of that, when the woman he wished to share it with was gone?

So he stayed on board with Daniel Elfrith and became a fair sailor. He had fallen into the role of ship's carpenter by accident on the *Treasurer*, continued it on the *White Lion*, and could see a place for himself at sea. A good carpenter was valued on any vessel. He could sail the seas, fight when needed, drink and tumble whores on shore. Live aboard ship forever, like Francis and Red Peter.

It was a different life for a different breed of man—one who did not share the common dreams of a roof over his head, a wife by his side, children at his hearth. Those had always been Ned's dreams, and now he found himself like a sword pulled from its sheath: lacking everything that had once surrounded and protected him. Harder, sharper, colder.

Weeks rolled into months, months into a year. Mid-winter came again, and another new year followed.

Sometimes, Elfrith told Ned, he had asked other sailors, other captains, what they knew of the *Happy Adventure*. The few who knew of it all said the same: it had been wrecked off Bermuda with only a few survivors. A Dutch pirate claimed that Captain Sly had been reunited with the few who escaped the wreck and they were back in Ireland now.

Ned only nodded when Elfrith brought him these tidings. What use to go digging up more of the same details?

It was late winter now, though the word "winter" did not have the bite down in these warm southern waters that it did back in Cupids Cove. Ned remembered the snow, the howling winds, like something out of an old tale. Captain Elfrith was frustrated with the results of his winter's privateering and wanted more to show for it. The captain's restless ambition had brought them here, to a coast peppered with Spanish forts, plantations strung between them like beads on a necklace.

It was passing strange to be in a town again; he had almost forgotten what it was like to walk down a street, to hear voices and music coming out of houses, to see women, to sit at a table that did not rock with the waves. But by nightfall Ned was already ill at ease. He slept aboard ship and busied himself with small bits of mending. One day they would pull up anchor, sail off to some other place where Elfrith hoped to capture another enemy ship and win more booty. When that hour came, Ned would still have his tasks to do.

On the morning they set sail, Elfrith told the crew, "We've long known it makes no sense to attack Spanish forts or settlements—they be too well-defended. But all around these islands there are tobacco plantations with African servants that will fetch a good price at market. I mean to attack one of them, then sail further south to sell the blackamoors. We'll come away with a rich prize for ourselves."

The plantation was a few days away, and the *White Lion* hugged the coastline, a strand of lush green trees fringed by white sand. The trees here kept their leaves through the winter, so the land looked fresh even in the cooler months. A beautiful place to put a plantation, Ned thought. He knew now what the soil here was like, and saw how much easier it would be to plant and grow here, rather than trying to hack a garden out of the rocky soil the way they had done at Cupids Cove. The way they would have done on Nicholas Guy's plantation, if the pirates had not come.

Now he saw this work from a new angle. Perched in the rigging of the *White Lion*, Ned saw the sandy shore, the green fields, the planter's large house and the tidy array of outbuildings. He imagined a family there, along with their workers, preparing the ground for planting. He wondered what tobacco was like to grow, compared to the turnips and parsnips they had coaxed from the ground in Cupids Cove. He thought of the mistress overseeing her servants as they cooked and cleaned. Children running about from the house to the fields.

"This is the place. Fellow's supposed to be rich as Croesus, good harvest last year, plenty of gold in store."

"You know he's got gold?" asked Vines, the quartermaster.

"I talked to a man who's been here. Seen it. And he has upwards of twenty Negro servants on the place."

Servants. Sometimes Elfrith called them *slaves*. Ned had been a servant himself—most men were—but he was coming to learn that "Negro servant" meant something different in this part of the world. Not merely to work for a master, but to be owned by him, body and soul. Many Englishmen, Captain Elfrith among them, saw slavery as the natural birthright of the black race, and of the native Indians too, if they could be bound to it. The idea no longer surprised Ned as it once had. "We cannot sell them in English colonies—yet," Elfrith warned. "But there's many a good market that will take them."

The people onshore—black and brown and white, men and women— watched the boats come in, and as Elfrith's boats drew nearer and the folk on shore realized what was coming upon them, they screamed. They ran in terror. As Ned followed the other men out of the boat and pulled it up onto the sand, a broad-shouldered man came running towards them with a musket. He fired at Elfrith's attacking pirates—*no, we are privateers, these Spaniards are the enemy*, Ned had time to think— and a volley of answering shot felled him.

Ned nearly stumbled over the man's body as he ran up the shore. He picked up the weapon and took a moment to gather powder and musket balls from the man's bleeding body. The man was not quite dead—only dying, his glazed eyes fixed on Ned's as his lifeblood gushed out from the wound in his belly. Retrieving the ammunition, Ned got blood all over his hands.

Elfrith's men fanned out, shouting orders in their broken Spanish, promising there would be no more violence if the plantation surrendered.

On the steps of the plantation house, women and children gathered, huddled together with arms around each other.

A tall man—brown-skinned, black-haired—ran from the big house directly towards Ned, pulling a dagger from its sheath. Pulling a dagger on a man with a gun.

But if Ned's aim was bad, the man would be on him long before he could reload. He had one chance. His hands were shaking. He had fired a musket only a handful of times before in his life. He had never fired at a man who was running towards him with a knife. He dropped the ball into the barrel with trembling fingers, braced himself for the recoil of the gun as he squeezed the trigger.

The other man staggered back, blood blooming on his white shirt-front, and fell to the ground. A second shot hit him in the arm. One was Ned's shot and one had been fired by Master Vines, nearby. Ned had no idea which shot was his.

"Hold fire!" commanded Captain Elfrith. A well-dressed man, likely the landowner or his steward, was striding towards them with his empty hands raised. The man shouted a command in Spanish, and the men who remained defending the plantation laid down guns, swords, and knives as Elfrith's men surrounded them.

"Start rounding up the slaves. Men, women and children—all the Negroes you see. Indians too, if they have any," Master Vines ordered Ned and the other men as he ran past. He led another party off, presumably to search for the rumoured gold and any other riches the plantation might conceal.

But the human wealth was Ned's business. Rounding up human beings, like rounding up goats to be milked or sheep to be sheared. They did not come willingly; they saw Ned and the others coming and ran into the green forest all around. "Don't shoot," his shipmate Cutty said, "they're no value to us dead, or even badly wounded."

And so some got away. But most did not. Ned stumbled through a line of trees and found a tiny building that must have been servants' quarters, and a plump young woman sitting on a stone in front of it, a baby clasped to her breast and a small child clinging to her skirts. Terror in her dark eyes as she turned them up to his, and over and over she said words he tried hard not to understand. "*Por favor...por favor...por favor.*" He pulled her up by her arm and towed her and her children along to the ship.

They did not burn the plantation house, as Sly's men had done with Nicholas Guy's. There was no message to send here, only treasure to be gained. There was indeed gold, and they took that along with the good plate, the planter's wife's jewels, and some other treasure. And sixteen slaves. The planter and his people were left alive. They would spread the word to nearby plantations, tell them of the fierce Englishmen they had fought.

"We will teach them to fear us," Elfrith said, addressing his men on deck that night. Brandy and rations were circulated freely. "They'll know the name of the *White Lion* and her men! You've all fought bravely today, my lads! 'Tis a day's work to be proud of!"

Below them, chained in the hold, the slaves kept up a harsh, keening cry of lament.

NINETEEN

A Letter Is Received

"AND SO OUR CHRISTMAS FEASTING IS ENDED—AND WHAT a feast it has been," declared Nicholas Guy, holding a cup of wine aloft. "'Tis grateful I am to have you all here with us, and to have such stores as will see us through the rest of the long winter. To your good health!"

Everyone around the table raised a cup. The children played on the floor, having been let down after finishing their dinners. The pudding was eaten, and everyone, master and mistress and servants, enjoyed the rare treat of French wine to finish off the celebration.

"Mama! Will pushed me—he *pushed!*" came a wail from the floor. Kathryn looked down to see her son, Jonathan, his round face flushed with indignation, as his younger but sturdier playmate stood over him looking innocent.

"Did *not!*" Will insisted, shaking his head.

Little Alice, playing near them with a carved wooden horse, looked over with interest. "Baba?" she said, which was what she called her brother.

Bess moved quickly to scoop up Will, paddling his backside as she did so. "You know better, Will! You must not push or hit."

"Or bite!" added Jonathan.

"Lord-a-mercy, is he biting too?" Bess asked, more to the room in general than to Jonathan. She handed the child to Frank. "Here, take him and teach him his manners, he'll not listen to me."

"I am sure Jonathan was far from blameless," Kathryn said—though she was, in fact, inclined to think her firstborn was blameless most of the time.

Both boys were growing like weeds now, Jonathan close to his third birthday, with Will a half-year behind him. Bess was breeding again, so there would be no shortage of children around the household for many years yet.

As the adults drank their wine and the children settled back to their play, Kathryn looked around the table. It was, indeed, almost everything she had dreamed of, celebrating the twelve days of Christmas in their own house.

This was their second time marking the feast here on their own plantation. The first year had been a poor, hard year indeed: the house still unfinished, the harvest sparse. The pirates' attack on the fishing fleet that autumn had left them all uncertain—while their own supply of salt fish was secure for the winter, the fish they had caught and made would never reach its intended market now, and that would mean they would have no credit for trading when the sack ships came. Not until this year had Kathryn truly felt secure in their home and on their land, able to raise a cup of wine in celebration and feel they could congratulate themselves for their efforts.

Under the roof of their fine new house slept Kathryn and Nicholas and their two children, their two menservants Rafe and Isaac, and Daisy, who was the chief cook and housekeeper. This fall, Frank and Bess had built a small house of their own, where they had some privacy for their little family. The past year had been a good one for fishing, for crops and for livestock. Nicholas had begun to talk of taking on two more men next year, at least for the fishing season. Best of all, there had been no trouble from pirates this year.

When the feasting of the Christmas season was done, the household settled fully into the long tedium of winter. There was still work to be done, but the rhythm of life was different in these colder, darker months. During the summer, most of the time was spent outdoors even in bad weather, and life was driven by the demands of fish and farm. In winter, the men went out only to cut wood and the women to feed the livestock.

They had a barn now, so they did not have to bring the chickens, goats and pigs indoors with them as they had done the first winter. Kathryn appreciated the smell of the house with no bodies other than human ones inside, though even those could get quite strong-smelling after weeks closed up in that tight space together.

Most of the winter's work was done inside—spinning wool, making and mending clothes, building and repairing furniture, mending fishing nets. Winter was also the time when Nicholas pulled out his old shoe-making skills from Bristol—not to fashion new shoes, for as badly as they all needed them, there was, as yet, no steady supply of leather for the work. Instead, he used his hammer and last to mend as many of the old shoes and boots as he could. The fire in the great hearth went full tilt all hours of the day, and often the work was accompanied by songs and storytelling.

The children played mostly in peace, with the rare outbreak of fighting. Kathryn taught them songs and nursery rhymes: in a couple of years, Nicholas had said, he would begin teaching the boys their letters and numbers. And in March, Bess was brought to bed of her second child, another boy. By that time, Kathryn knew that she herself was carrying another little one as well.

"The master would like another boy, but I'd be glad for a girl again—otherwise poor wee Alice will grow up surrounded entirely by lads," Kathryn said to Daisy as they sat side by side sewing squares for a quilt out of worn-out gowns. "A sister would be nice for her."

"If poor Tom were alive, we'd have had a girl for you by now," Daisy said.

"'Tis a great loss to you and to us all," Kathryn agreed, but could not resist going on to say, "All the same, were you minded to, you know that Isaac would—"

"I know very well what Isaac would," Daisy said, "but I do not and will not. I was promised to marry one man when I was seventeen, waited two years for him, came out to this country to wed him, and lost him in less than a twelvemonth. Then I married another and lost him not six months later. There's a curse on me, Mistress—I'll not risk another man."

"That can't be so, Daisy. Men die in this country—from sickness, from drowning, from being killed by pirates—'tis no fault of yours."

"What if I did consent to marry Isaac and he went and fell out of the boat while fishing? Would you believe me then that I was curst?"

Kathryn shuddered. "I would hate to think it, Daisy."

"'Tis not so bad. I am content to be a widow. I have a good place here, and no danger of dying in childbed."

"If we had not been attacked that first summer, Nancy and Ned would likely have a child by now as well, and their own little house, as Bess and Frank do."

"Aye, 'tis true, Mistress. Like my poor Tom, they never had the chance to see the place as it is now."

"But unlike poor Tom, they may yet be alive somewhere."

"That's as may be, Mistress. Surely if Ned were alive, he would have come back by now? I cannot hold out much hope for Nancy, in the hands of such wicked men."

"I refuse to believe it," Kathryn said. "I am sure I would know, in some part of my soul, if Nancy were dead, for I do believe our souls are linked. You may laugh, Daisy, but if I can believe you are under a curse, you can believe me when I say that Nancy is not dead, for I'd know of it if she were."

Kathryn well knew she was the only person in the household who still believed Nancy might be alive somewhere. She put her faith in Ned, believing that if he found Nancy he would bring her back. As long as one month rolled past after another and no word came, good news remained possible.

Spring came, and with it ships from England. Though it was too soon yet to break ground for the garden, and the fish would not strike in for several weeks yet, the men were busy preparing the boats and nets. Meanwhile, the women indulged in an orgy of sewing with the fabrics purchased from the ships, and Kathryn was able to use a little of the coin they had saved from selling last fall's catch to buy a few things for the house. Little by little, piece by piece, they were making it into a proper home. Someday, it would be as fine as the house her husband had in Bristol, and all the better for sitting on their own land.

A ship out of Bristol, the *Comfort*, brought letters to the Guy plantation. There was a letter for Kathryn from her father, bringing her up to date on the news of their household. Hard to believe that her brothers and sisters, who had been children when she left Bristol, were growing up so quickly. John was well into his apprenticeship, and little Phillip would soon begin as apprentice to his father also. Her sister Lily was sixteen and a great help about the house—it would be time, before long, to think of finding a husband for her, "*and twill bee no hard task for she bee as fair a maid as ever you were,*" John Gale added, in a rare moment of sentimentality.

Kathryn wished she could see all their dear faces again, talk to them in person instead of puzzling out her father's handwriting in a letter. But at least it was good to know they were all well. "What news have you from home?" she asked Nicholas when she had finished reading. He had a letter as well, from his sister Joanna.

"Sad news for me, though not unexpected," he said. "My father is dead." The old man had been ailing in the fall, when they last had word from home.

"I am sorry to hear it."

"Aye, he lived a good long life—seventy-four—but I could wish I had seen him once more. And Joanna asks me what I want done with the house and the business, for all is mine now. She thinks I should come back to Bristol to see to it."

"Back...to Bristol?" Kathryn tried out the words as if they were in a foreign tongue.

"Aye. But Rob still manages the cobbler shop, and I will write to him. If he is able to buy it from me, a share of the money shall go to Joanna, to keep her in comfort." He glanced up from the letter to his wife. "Unless you think we should return?"

Kathryn stared at him. Returning to Bristol had not been part of the plan since their first year in Cupids Cove. They had poured so much time and effort into clearing the land, building their house, fishing and farming here. And yet—to be back in Bristol, close to her family, to walk again on cobbled streets, buy from shops and markets, be surrounded by all the life and colour of a town again? Some part of her, she knew, was hungry for that. "Do you mean, to return forever?"

"'Twould be a great expense to go and return in a season, so if I went back, I would plan to stay for some time—perchance to go in the fall and come back here the next summer. Once there, we might decide to stay longer in Bristol. Bess and Frank could manage the land for us here, as well as Rob and his wife can manage the business there." He looked at her more closely. "If I do sell the business in Bristol, we will have no ties there—we will be bound to this place for good. Does that trouble you?"

"I...truly I do not know. Whatever you do, 'twill be a great deal to think on."

"And no need to decide today." He sighed, folding up Joanna's letter. "God rest my father's soul."

The news in his next letter, from a friend in Bristol, was far less personal, but it seemed to make Nicholas angry. "Hark to this! That blackguard Mainwaring who attacked the fleet and stole our catch— he has been pardoned and rewarded by the king, for saving a fleet of Newfoundland ships bound for Spain."

"Rewarded? He should have been hanged!"

"It seems these men do not have to do much to win their way back into the king's good graces," Nicholas said. "'Tis very hard on those of us striving to make an honest living, when those who grow wealthy by robbing us are so easily forgiven."

"Aye, and now a new lot are at it again," said Frank, who had just come into the kitchen with a load of wood for the fire.

"More pirates? What tidings did you hear?"

"From the crew on the *Comfort*. A fishing station up at Red Head Cove was attacked a fortnight ago."

"This time of year? No fish to take—they were looking for men, then."

Frank nodded. "Twenty men they captured, along with all their gear and supplies. And three killed in the fighting."

"Do they know the ship, or the captain?"

"They said 'twas a captain name of Sly."

Kathryn felt her heart jump in her chest. *Sly.* She had heard the name from Sheila Pike; it was etched in her memory. Nicholas's eyes met hers: he was the only one she had shared that name with.

"He is back," she told her husband when they were alone. "For aught we know, he might still have Nancy in his power."

"After so long?" Nicholas said, shaking his head. "I know 'tis hard tidings to hear, my little wife, but I would not have you cling to false hope."

A week passed. Kathryn went about her usual chores, caring for the house and children, cooking and sewing and mending, planting the garden with Bess and Daisy. But her thoughts churned like the waves.

"I cannot rest," she told Nicholas, as they lay in bed together. "There must be a way to get a message to him—to find out what became of Nancy. If she were still alive—hush, I know what you will say, but hear me out—we would pay any ransom we could afford, would we not, to have her back?"

"What do you propose to do—row yourself out in the shallop until you find a pirate ship and demand to board her?"

"Do not laugh at me!" Kathryn protested, though she herself almost laughed at the ludicrous image. She knew her quest seemed like folly to all around her, though she was in deadly earnest.

Can I even think it a quest? she wondered after Nicholas fell asleep and she lay listening to his steady snore, against the background of all the night sounds of the people around them in the house and the wind outside. Ned—poor Ned!—had gone off so bravely, ready to sail the ocean and face down pirates until he found Nancy. Kathryn had given him a few coins and her prayers and good wishes. Oh, the powerlessness of womanhood!

"I promise I will not take the shallop and go out hunting for pirates," she told her husband the next day. "But I know who I can go to, and 'tis only right that a woman should visit her nearest neighbour betimes."

"Mistress Pike, you mean? You have showed no haste to visit her in all this time."

"All the more reason to do so. I can go by the trail through the woods if need be."

"On your own? Even you are not so mad as that. And I cannot spare either myself nor one of the lads to go with you, not when the fish might strike in any day."

"I must go, Nicholas." She turned her face up to his, pleading. She wanted to say *What have I ever asked you for?* She had followed him from Bristol to this New World, followed him from Cupids Cove out into the wilderness not once but twice. She had been the perfect wife— save that she had gone to bed with another man, but that was in the past, and not an error she would repeat. Nor one that Nicholas need ever know of.

She must have put the right look onto her countenance, for his softened and he smiled. "Of a Sunday, perhaps. We cannot fish then, and 'twill be a good day for visiting. Leave the youngsters with Daisy and Bess, and I will row you up to the Pikes' plantation. We shall get to the bottom of the business, find out if they know this Captain Sly and whether he knows aught about Nancy. But—" he shook a warning finger, "you must not raise your hopes too high, my dear. Like as not the Pikes will tell us they know nothing at all."

Indeed, when they visited the Pike plantation on the next fine Sunday, Mistress Pike gave a fair imitation of knowing nothing. Though she had three little ones now and a busy planter's household to run, she still managed to look like the princess she claimed to be as she said, "You had best be clear what you are asking me, Mistress Guy."

Kathryn felt herself poor and dowdy in comparison; though they were both New Found Land planters' wives, she could not help feeling that her own humble origins as a stonemason's daughter were stamped across her brow.

They were on the bench outside Mistress Pike's house while the men were out looking at one of Gilbert Pike's boats. Inside the house, an Irish serving-maid rolled out pastry dough on the table and kept an eye to two small boys and a baby. Kathryn stared out at sea, remembering she had been seated in this very spot when Frank had brought news of the attack on their plantation.

"You wish me to be clear? Very well then. I believe you and your husband know this Captain Sly, most likely that you trade with him. We know he is using Harbour Grace as his headquarters, just as Mainwaring and Easton did before him. The place is a nest of pirates and you are in league with them."

"My husband is a man of business, as is yours. 'Tis no crime to do business."

"It is, if that business breaks the king's peace. But that's no concern of mine. All I want is to talk to Captain Sly, to see what he knows of my maid Nancy and what became of her."

"Mistress Guy, talk sense for once, will you? James Sly attacked your plantation, burned your house, killed one of your servants, injured another and, in your accounting of it, took yet another servant captive. Whyever would he—"

"For a ransom! You know we would pay well for my maidservant's safe return, so why—"

"There is nothing to be ransomed! The girl is dead."

Kathryn gasped. "Are you saying that to be cruel, or do you know this?"

Sheila Pike stood up abruptly from the bench and walked a few steps away. "It is truth. I made inquiries when last my husband met with Captain Sly."

"When was this?"

"When he first came back to these waters—two months ago now, I suppose it was. He has not been in the New Found Land for some time. When he came to speak to my husband, I asked him—that is, I asked him what he knew about the attack on your plantation, and a maid that was taken from there."

Some lying there, Kathryn thought: Sheila Pike had not needed to ask Captain Sly about the attack, for she had surely known of it at the time. But she was not about to debate that point now.

"He told me it was true—your maid was taken. They kept her aboard as a cook. She was not harmed. Before they made landfall, they took a Spanish ship as a prize. When he divided the crew and took the captured ship back to Ireland with the booty, your maid stayed aboard the *Happy Adventure*, bound for the Indies." Sheila Pike fixed Kathryn with a long stare. "He said she told them some mad tale of being a witch, and swore to put a curse on them if they did not let her have her will. He thought it all folly, but deemed it best not to cross her lest she truly did have powers. So he let her go."

"And she went to the Indies?"

"The ship she was aboard of went that way, sure enough. But a year later, the man he had left in command of that ship returned to Sly in Ireland, and told him that the *Happy Adventure*, and all her crew save for himself and two men, was wrecked in a storm off the Bermudas."

"No! It cannot be!"

"It is, very truly. I do not have a heart of stone, Mistress Guy—I know this lass was your friend as well as your maid, and you would ransom her if you could. So I bestirred myself to ask—and that was the answer. She died at sea. Having made her peace with God, we can trust, unless she truly was a witch."

"She was no witch. It was a cruel slander a man in Cupids Cove made against her."

"Then you must put your mind to rest that she is in heaven now, and free from the sad trials of this world."

"That is cold comfort when you are speaking of a woman of five-and-twenty who ought to be wedded, bearing children, living her life at this very moment."

"And had she stayed here on your plantation, she might have been wedded, and died bearing one of those children. It is in the hands of God—who are we to judge?"

"I did not recall you being so pious when last we met."

"There is a great deal you do not know about me, Mistress Guy."

"And never shall, I hope, if you can be so callous about the death of my dearest friend!"

"I did not wish her death."

"You knew someone might die, if this attack went forward."

"I did not know Sly would attack your plantation."

"That is a lie."

The other woman turned on Kathryn with the hauteur of a queen. "Do you accuse me of lying?"

"I do. I believe you knew of the attack, and that you invited me and my maids to stay with you because you did not want the deaths of women on your conscience."

"If that were true, you would owe me thanks."

"So you admit it."

"I admit nothing, Mistress Guy. But I will tell you what I have told you before: your husband and these other Bristol men should not settle on this shore. This is our land."

"Yours—and your pirate allies'."

"Call it what you will—we call it building our future."

Kathryn turned, unable to muster the civil words that would end the conversation politely. She marched down towards the water, where her husband stood with the pirate Pike, admiring the hull of his new shallop. "Take me home, husband. I've no wish to stay here longer."

Nicholas looked up, startled at her abrupt tone. "Are you finished your visit with Mistress Pike so hastily, my sweeting? They have asked us to stay and dine with them."

"I'll not break bread here. We must go at once."

Master Pike laughed; he did not have a pleasant laugh. "Quite the spitfire you have there, Guy."

Kathryn looked at him. "If you are concerned about keeping men's wives in line, look to your own, Master Pike. As for me, I wish nothing more to do with neighbours who are in league with lawless men." It was no woman's place to speak to a man this way, and likely when they were in the boat alone, Nicholas would have something to say about her brashness. But Kathryn had no mind to hold her tongue. "Do not think that you can break the king's peace along this coast, preying on honest planters and honest fishermen, without consequence!"

Nicholas's grip on her arm was firm as he drew her towards the wharf. "I do believe my wife is right—it is time for us to be going, Pike. Thank you for showing me the work on your boats—'tis of great interest. As, indeed, we are all interested in all that our neighbours do. Fare thee well."

In the boat, rowing back to their plantation, he was silent for a while. At last he said, "I did not rebuke you in front of Master Pike, but you know that you should not have spoken so."

Kathryn wanted to argue that she was in the right, but she kept her mouth shut and fixed her eyes on the choppy waves off the bow of the boat. After a moment her husband said, "I told you I had reached an understanding with Master Pike. Now you have put that at risk. 'Twas my fault, perhaps, for bringing you up here to confront Mistress Pike. I fear we are in more danger from their schemes than we were before."

"I know I spoke rashly," Kathryn said. It was as close as she could come to an apology for something she felt no regret over, though she knew that such an outburst from a woman, especially to another man, would shame any husband, and that Nicholas would be within his rights to chide her far more harshly than he had done. She had been outspoken and wilful, there was no doubt. But she would do it again if she had any hope that her rash words could bring Nancy back or right the wrong that had been done to her.

TWENTY

Another Voyage Is Planned

THE VIRGINIA SUN BEAT DOWN HOTTER THAN ANY SUM-
mer sun Nancy remembered in England, though it was only
March. But then, in England she had been a housemaid, never
expected to work out in the fields. Nancy, Wapuna, Sokanon, Tala, and
even Mistress Rolfe worked alongside Master Rolfe and his menservants
at the busiest times of the tobacco season, for tobacco, as the master
was fond of telling them, was a crop that required a great deal of labour.

After two years in the Virginia colony, she was becoming accustomed to the sultry climate, to the way the air often felt damp and heavy.
On the hottest summer days, even the breeze was swampy, wafting the
odours of the marshes and the thousand flying insects that came with
them. In early spring, the heat could be cheering, but after several hours
in the sun planting tobacco, it grew tiresome.

It was time to go inside to prepare the midday meal: the fact that
women worked the fields alongside the men did not mean that women's
work could be ignored. Leaving the other Indian women in the field to
continue the work, Nancy and Mistress Rolfe returned to the house to
prepare food for the rest of the labourers.

"A good morning's work," the mistress said, putting down baby
Thomas, who had been riding on her hip on the way in from the field.
The child had recently begun toddling about, making him a good deal
harder to keep an eye on during the day's work, but he was tired now

from the hot sun and willingly lay down for a nap as his mother and Nancy busied themselves with kitchen tasks.

"Indeed," Nancy agreed. "'Twill be harder by midsummer to keep the young master from running away. It seems no time since he was in swaddling bands." She calculated quickly, as she often did when looking at little Tom Rolfe, how old Jonathan Guy would be now. He had been a babe in Kathryn's arms when she had last seen him; he must now be three years old, running all about the place. She had thought she would care for him while he grew up, that her face would be as familiar to the child as his mother's own. Instead, it was this half-English, half-Indian baby, who had learned to say "Nanny" as one of his first words, who reached his arms for her to take him up if his mother was not nearby. Nancy's throat tightened a little, and then she pushed the thought away and began cutting slices of the bread she had baked when she got out of bed that morning.

"By midsummer, or before then, I think I will have to worry that he does not tumble off the deck of a ship," Mistress Rolfe said, stirring a simmering pot of stewed vegetables over the fire. "My husband has talked to the governor, and they are ever more determined that the voyage to England will be made before summer comes. How long did it take to cross the ocean, when you came from England?"

"I hardly remember—weeks and weeks, it was. Maybe months." That voyage seemed to have been made by another woman in another life.

"If you come with us, you may go to your old home, and see your people again," Mistress Rolfe said.

My people. Nancy thought of Bristol, of Aunt Tib. Was she still living, and all the Gale family? It would be good to go back there, if she could not find a way of returning to Cupids Cove. In her two years serving the Indian princess Pocahontas, now called Mistress Rebecca Rolfe, Nancy had not heard tell of any ships going from Virginia to the New Found Land.

That she was seeking such a passage was hardly a secret. Mistress Rolfe went on, "I know your true desire is to go back to your Cupids Cove, but I do not see a way that can be."

"True enough, Mistress," Nancy said with a sigh.

"I wish you to come with us. Master Rolfe is most eager I should take some of my own people with me. We are to be—exhibited to the English," Mistress Rolfe said, with a smile that showed her teeth but little humour. "The maids will come, and my sister and her husband—they want a Powhatan man of high degree to come along as well, and Tomocomo is a holy man, so he will serve that purpose. You will be of use to them all, in helping them to understand English customs, as well as in serving me and caring for Thomas."

Nancy had heard talk that her mistress would be taken to England, but she had not realized that plans were so far advanced. She had time, while clearing the kitchen after the meal, to discuss the matter with the only member of the household she felt truly at ease with: the mistress's sister Matachanna.

Matachanna was perhaps the least likely person for Nancy to befriend. She did not live in her sister's household, but often stayed with them; her husband, a serious, older man, came less often to visit among the English. Unlike the three young maids and Mistress Rolfe, Matachanna had not been baptized as a Christian nor taken an English name; her husband, Tomocomo, was something like a priest in their religion. While Wapuna, Sokanon, and Tala were now known by the Christian names Betty, Sally, and Mary and dressed in the kirtles and petticoats of English maids, Matachanna still wore the clothes of a Powhatan woman. She covered herself more when she was at Henrico, out of respect for the English customs.

Yet Nancy felt a kinship with Matachanna. She was about Nancy's own age, more settled and mature than the three maids, and less reserved than Pocahontas, who always had something guarded about her—as well she might, Nancy thought, considering all the princess had been through. Matachanna, married to a man of her own people and free to come and go from Henrico as she pleased, was more willing to speak freely, and her English had improved markedly as she and Nancy worked side by side about the house and fields. Most importantly, she had a practical manner about her, a sensible way of tackling whatever job needed to be done, the quality Nancy admired most in another person.

"You would like better if it was a ship going to your New Found Land than to England," Matachanna said when Nancy related the conversation to her.

"Even could I find such a ship, I could scarce afford passage."

"But still you save all your coins." Matachanna was the only person in the household who knew that Nancy had a neat little store of savings tucked inside her mattress.

"The day may come," Nancy said. "But if I go with all of you to England, I may be able to take ship from there."

"You would leave my sister's service?"

"You know I have always meant to go home."

Matachanna handed her a stack of clean wooden trenchers, which Nancy, being the taller of the two, put up on the high shelf. "I think if you come with us, Pocahontas will give you money for your passage home," she said. "She wishes very much to have an Englishwoman she can trust in our party, and she does not trust very many."

"I suppose that's a compliment."

"Along with the women from here, my husband will bring two or three Powhatan men with him—young warriors. The English will see that we can be tamed—like you tame your animals," Matachanna said, with a laugh tinged with bitterness.

The household chores done, there was more work for them outside. "I would be glad never to see a tobacco plant again," Nancy admitted. "I cannot keep up with you in the fields."

"It is easier for us than for you Englishwomen. Our women tend the crops while the men hunt and make war."

"Back in England, only the poor women work in the fields with their menfolk," Nancy said, "but out in Cupids Cove, and here in Virginia too, everyone has to turn a hand to the labour—women and men, great and small."

"So you learn from us. Your ways become like our ways."

In bed that night, Nancy lay awake thinking. She had never planned to stay in Virginia. She had found a good position here, for certes, in the Rolfe household. In one way, it was a far loftier position than she could have imagined for herself—serving a woman who was the daughter of a chief among her own people. And yet she had to work like a farm labourer here, harder even than she had done in Cupids Cove—serving Rebecca Rolfe was certainly nothing like being lady's maid to a gentleman's wife back in England.

None of that, of course, was why she had stayed. Since that morning two years ago when she had spoken to the sailors on board the *Treasurer* and learned that Ned was looking for her, she had clung to the hope that her message would find its way to him. *Tell him I'm here, and waiting for him.* She had truly believed—she *had* to believe—that someday he would hear her message.

Having sent that message out into the world, how could she leave? She had told Ned where to find her, and every ship that came upriver to Henrico, every rumour of a stranger in the village, made her heart leap with hope. A hope that was never fulfilled: he did not come. Still, she stayed, waiting like a maiden in a ballad, for the sea to bring her sailor back to her.

There were unattached men aplenty at Henrico, far more men than women, and more than a few who were bold enough to flirt with Nancy, as well as the more modest ones who discreetly inquired of John Rolfe if they might court his wife's servant. Mistress Rolfe had suggested she could not wait forever. "It may never be," she had said, "and this Jack Harley who asks for your hand is a good man, with good prospects. A woman cannot always have the life she dreams of, you know."

Nancy thought that Mistress Rolfe, clad in her English clothes, wearing her English name, bedding with her English husband, likely knew that truth better than anyone. Women of high degree were frequently bartered away in marriage for the sake of men's land or alliances. Poor women like Nancy were freer to say yes or no to marriage, but in Virginia, as in the New Found Land, it was assumed that every woman would eventually say yes to some man.

Nay, I'll not marry a Virginia planter, Nancy promised herself. But neither would she wait forever for Ned. She was offered passage to England; she would take it. Once there, she could leave the Rolfes' service and make her way back to Bristol. Perhaps she would stay there, slip back into the old life that would have been hers if she had not sailed to Cupids Cove. If not, from Bristol she could find a ship going to the New Found Land. It would be hard to go back there without Ned, but she could be reunited with her mistress and dearest friend.

"I will go with you to England," she told Mistress Rolfe the next day.

"I am grateful, and will reward you well if you stay and serve me there," the Indian woman said. "The governor has said I will be introduced to many of the powerful people in England, and will have to talk to the English chieftains and their wives."

"If you seek someone to guide you in fine manners, and how to speak to lords and ladies, I am hardly the one for that! In England I am even less of a person than I am here, Mistress. I am sure they will give you some English maid who is accustomed to fine society."

"It may be so. All the same, I ask you come with us and remain in my service as long as I require you." Mistress Rolfe was nursing her son as she spoke; when he squirmed away and twisted to get off her lap, she handed him to Nancy. "Call...call Sally here to watch the little one, and you will come help me with this new gown."

"Sally?" Master Rolfe and the menservants called the Powhatan maids by their Christian names, but Mistress Rolfe and Matachanna still called them by their Indian names, and Nancy followed their example.

"They must become accustomed to English names, to speaking English, to behaving like English women. If we do not, the English will think we are...what is your word? Savage. More animals than human, is it not so?"

Nancy had no reply for that; she did not know what wealthy people in England would want or expect to see, in bringing the Indian princess and her maidservants into their manors and palaces. She did not know what she might do in such a place. But she had, at least, the ghost of a plan of what she herself might do next. And it was time to take a step forward. She could not wait forever for Ned.

TWENTY-ONE

Surprising News Is Delivered

CAPTAIN ELFRITH HANDED NED A SMALL BAG OF COINS. "'Tis your fair share, I can do no better than that," he said. "Damned shame I spent all that time training you to be a ship's carpenter. Now some other captain will get the benefit of it."

Ned could not be certain whether the man spoke in earnest or in jest, but he did not greatly care which. He took the silver with a shrug. "You were a fair master. 'Tis no fault of yours that privateering is not for me. I may stay ashore for a time."

Elfrith nodded. "Some men have the sea in their blood. I never thought you were one such. Find yourself a good wife and have a few brats, if that's the life you want." And with no more ceremony than that, Ned bade farewell to the man he'd served for two years, walked down the gangplank of the *White Lion*, and set off along the docks of St. George's town.

Though he had been in the Bermuda Islands often with Elfrith, he had not come, before now, to the English settlement on the islands, which Elfrith rarely visited. It was a tidy little place that reminded him, in some ways, of both Cupids Cove and James Fort, though it was more settled and established than either of those, beginning to take on the shape of a proper English town, with a church and an inn and other marks of permanent settlement.

Ned truly had no idea where he would go or what he would do. Finding a room to sleep in and some labouring work would be a first step. He was not against the idea of going to sea again: it might not be in his blood, as Elfrith had said, but he'd learned to like the rhythm of shipboard living these past few years. A ship's carpenter was always in demand.

But the attack on the tobacco plantation in Hispaniola had soured something in the venture for Ned. It was one thing to chase and capture trading ships of other nations, to take them as prizes. It was a fair fight, and every ship on the sea knew the dangers of piracy and privateering. Attacking a plantation brought back too vividly his memories of the New Found Land and the reason he had left there. The rest of the voyage—sailing further south to sell the captives to Spanish slavers—had worsened the bad taste in his mouth. The Negroes were sold; the coin from their sale made up the best part of the booty that Elfrith divided among his crew, but even once they were off the ship Ned could not forget their faces or the sight of the shackles that bound their ankles.

He was not the only one of Elfrith's crew who was uneasy while the slaves were aboard. "Bad luck," was the most Cutty would say, though Sam Brennan called slave-trading "a dirty business." When Elfrith heard that, he only laughed. "Is the money dirty, too, or d'ye all want your share of it?"

Ned wanted his share. He had done the work and he would take the pay. It was one thing to know that men, women, and children were traded like cattle in markets; it was another thing to see it, to have a part in it. "Englishmen are not accustomed to looking the business in the eye," Elfrith said of the slave trade. "But they will become so. You all will."

Ned felt the coins clink in his pocket. He was becoming accustomed to the sound already.

The choices before him tumbled about in his brain like the money in his pocket. But like the silver, his thoughts need not all be spent tonight.

He found the inn, bought a pork pie and some ale, and paid for a bed for a few nights. There were tables in the inn-yard outside, as befitted such a warm climate, and Ned took a seat at an empty one, thinking he'd be left alone. But the inn-yard and the table soon filled up with working men and sailors finishing their day's work. Amid their talk and drinking, the men played a game of pitching small rocks at the many large, black rats that scurried through the yard, brazen as house cats. "Damn those vermin," one said as he missed his shot.

"You owe me a drink," said the man beside him.

"I've never seen a place so overrun with rats," Ned said to the fellow beside him. "Do they breed here on these islands so much?"

"The Devil take 'em—I never seen such a place for rats," the man said.

"There was none here when we first came out from England," another said. "Some privateer sailed into port with a load of grain he'd taken from the Spanish, and we were all glad enough to get it, for 'twas hungry times that winter—this was a few years ago, now. But then didn't the damned sacks of grain turn out to be crawling with rats? Now we can't get rid of them. They crawl up into our beds at night."

"And up the hole of the privy to bite you on the arse," another man said.

As the men laughed, Ned thought of how he'd first met Elfrith in James Fort, how the captain had bragged of the load of stolen Spanish grain he had brought to the starving settlers in St. George's. Perhaps Elfrith had avoided the port ever since for good reason. The thought gave Ned a wry smile, but did little to lighten his mood. As soon as his meal was finished, he left the table and the company, bought a bottle of brandy, and found a quiet spot to drink alone until he could think no more about either the past or the future.

But if strong drink could still his waking thoughts, it could not stifle his dreams. When sleep claimed him, the images that haunted his nightmares came crowding back. He was on the tobacco plantation, firing his musket at the man running towards him. Then the ground shifted; he was on Nicholas Guy's plantation, and the man in front of him was his old friend Tom Taylor, and still Ned fired the musket and watched the blood soak Tom's shirt as he fell. Then he was by the slave quarters, with the woman screaming *Por favor, por favor* as her children cried, and again Ned raised the gun and fired, and then it was Nancy crying *por favor, por favor*...

He woke with a sour stomach and an aching head. Rather than lying abed, he forced himself out onto the streets, eyeing the little town with a view to what sort of work he might find there. Plenty of tasks for a fellow who had both stonemason's and carpenter's skills, in a place where everything was still being built. Yet the thought of settling on shore, earning a daily wage, made him restless. His feet took him down to the docks, where the *White Lion* had sailed away but a new ship had just come in to port.

As he watched the men offloading cargo, he realized this was a ship whose lines were familiar to him: Captain Argall's ship, the *Treasurer*. He had hardly taken in that surprise when a voice called out, "Look you! 'Tis Ned Perry!"

Even before he spotted the man, he had placed the voice in memory, and sure enough, there unloading boxes and crates stood his old shipmate Francis, smiling and waving at him. Which meant that Red Peter must be somewhere nearby as well.

When their work was done, both men joined Ned ashore. They knew St. George's far better than he did, having made port here often in the last few years, and all three headed back to the inn to drink and talk. Francis and Peter had been sailing with Captain Argall since Ned had left the *Treasurer*, making voyages up and down the James River in Virginia and back and forth to the Bermudas. Last year, they had gone with him across to England and back. Ned told them a little of his voyages on the *White Lion*.

"'Twould be a grand bit of fun, fighting the Spaniards," Francis said wistfully. "But Argall doesn't have any of that kind of business on hand at present. We're sailing back to James Fort to take some of the high-and-mighty folks of the colony back to England. There's a crowd of Indians coming along too, to be shown to the king and the lords in England. Relatives of the Indian chief—his daughter's married to an Englishman."

"Is that so?" Ned remembered the long-ago night on the beach at Truce Sound, dancing and singing and trading trinkets and furs with the natives of the New Found Land. Perhaps by now the settlers up in Cupids Cove were doing the same thing—treating and trading with the natives, marrying their women, bringing shiploads of them over to England to see and be seen. He opened his mouth to say something about it, but Francis and Red Peter were giving each other an odd look, and then Francis said, "We've news for you, Ned."

"We'd not forgot it," Peter said. "Just waiting for the right moment, like."

"'Tis old news now, sad to say," Francis said, "but we'll pass it on nonetheless. We saw your Nancy."

"What?" The sounds of talk and laughter in the room suddenly blurred to a buzzing in his ears, and he felt as unsteady in the head as he had when he'd downed that skin of brandy last night. "Don't be saying such a thing—'tis not possible. I've known for two years now that she's dead."

"'Twas almost two years ago we saw her on the deck of the *Treasurer*, and in faith she was far from dead then," Francis insisted.

"Where was this?"

"In Virginia. We were sailing upriver to treat with the Indians, and that Indian woman was aboard, the daughter of the chief. This one Nancy was her servant—tall lass, brown hair with a bit of red to it—would that describe her?"

"It cannot be. In Virginia?"

"Aye, alive and well in Virginia—but again, 'tis two years gone by now. Your news may be fresher, even though 'tis sad."

"No." The tale he had heard had never put Nancy in Virginia at all; he had always believed her to be aboard the *Happy Adventure*, wrecked here on the Bermuda coast. He could not imagine Francis and Peter would make up such a tale only to taunt him when they first saw him again after so long.

"Did you tell her—?"

"Aye, as soon as I found out she was Nancy from Cupids Cove, I told her of you, and didn't her face light up like a torch at night? She seems a rare fine lass, and she said at once that if we saw you again, we were to tell you she was at Henrico, serving in the house of Master—what was his name?"

Red Peter shrugged. "I don't recall, but she was serving the Indian princess, so belike 'tis the same Englishman who married the Indian woman. 'Tis no matter—if you come with us to Virginia, either she will be there, or those folk will know what's become of her."

"She said special, to tell you she was waiting for you," Francis added.

"But she might have tired of waiting."

"You'll not know unless you go to Virginia," Red Peter pointed out. "I thought she was dead," Ned repeated, like a man in a dream. "They told me her ship was gone down."

"Come back to the ship with us, and talk to Argall," Francis urged. "He'll take you on—he knows you're a good hand. 'Twill give you passage at least back to James Fort, so you can find your Nancy." Francis seemed well pleased with this plan, polishing off his tankard of ale with a happy sigh. The romance had almost reached its happy ending: hero and heroine would soon be reunited, and all thanks to his own cleverness in passing on the message.

But Red Peter, ever the older and the steadier of the two, gave Ned a long, keen look. "Francis is right—Argall will take you on if you ask him. And we'd be glad to have you aboard. But that's always supposing, Ned, that going back to Virginia and finding the lass is what *you* want to do."

And to that Ned said nothing at all.

TWENTY-TWO

The Atlantic Is Crossed Again

NANCY HAD NOT BEEN ON A SHIP IN TWO YEARS AND had not missed it. Now they sailed on that same ship, the *Treasurer*, in the opposite direction: down the James River towards the open sea. Their departure from James Fort was full of as much pomp and circumstance as that small settlement could muster, for the journey not just of the acting governor but, more importantly, of the Indian princess and her English husband, was treated as something like an international embassy.

Settling onto her pallet on the 'tween deck that first night as the ship docked at Point Comfort, Nancy thought about the odd double life of the Rolfe family. They were hard-working colonial planters, everyone in the household working long days tending to house, garden, livestock, and tobacco crop. Mistress Rolfe's Sunday gown was of good stuff, but simple and sturdy, as the clothing of any colonist's wife must be. Everyone in the household had hands calloused from work in the fields. But on this ship, Master and Mistress Rolfe had been given one of the two cabins, with Governor Dale having the other: they were to be treated as colonial royalty in England.

"She is to have all new gowns in London, and that will be more work for us," Wapuna said to Nancy, as they settled to sleep. *Sally.* Nancy reminded herself that she must get in the habit of calling the Indian maids by their Christian names.

"No doubt they'll have English seamstresses to make those gowns for her over there, though we may still have to alter and mend them. They will be in the style the women are wearing now in London, whatever that may be. Rich women in England dress different than women do in the colonies—you will laugh to see some of their styles, I am sure."

Sally was silent for a moment. "It will all be so very strange."

Yes, it would be. Strange for Nancy, to be back in England in such a different style from her former life, but how much stranger for the natives in the party. The three maids, Matachanna and her husband Tomocomo, and two young warriors. Eight Powhatan Indians, counting Mistress Rolfe herself, all travelling to England to be shown to the king and queen.

"Think of everything you will see," she said to Sally now. "I have never been to London myself, but they say it is a great city. And you will see the palace where our king lives." The biggest and finest house she herself had ever seen was Sir John Young's house in Bristol, which stood out dimly in her memory as a grand pile of stone perched a little above the rest of the town. She knew there were bigger manors out in the countryside, but she herself had never seen them; her girlhood had been confined to Bristol's streets.

She thought of Kathryn, who loved to hear stories of kings and queens, palaces and balls, even though she had never seen such things with her own eyes either. Kathryn loved tales of romance and adventure, yet it was Nancy who had ended up living through events dramatic enough for any player's stage: accused as a witch, captured by pirates, wrecked at sea, separated from her lover who had gone to try to rescue her, and now serving a native princess who was off to meet the king. *If ever I see you again, my Kat, what a tale I will have to tell you!*

Nancy allowed herself that one wistful thought—imagined herself sitting by a hearth with Kathryn, telling the tale of her adventures, Kat's hands clasped and her eyes wide as she listened. *But it does not feel like an adventure when you are living through it*, Nancy thought.

She had not, of course, forgotten her previous voyage on the *Treasurer*, and looked among the crew for the two sailors who had told her that they knew Ned, but she did not see them in those first days of the voyage. She hoped one or both was aboard so that she might ask if they had more news of Ned. Even if the news was that Ned was dead, she would rather know the truth than go on in ignorance.

Soon they were on the open sea, out of sight of land. The Indians in the party were intrigued by the ship and the ocean; they had not seen the like before, having lived most of their lives inland and having seen the sea only from occasional views of the coast. Powhatan's people, Matachanna had told Nancy, travelled widely on the inland river in their long canoes, but they did not go out upon the ocean. Much as Nancy had done on the voyage over from England to Cupids Cove, they marvelled that any body of water could be so vast.

About a week after their departure, a commotion lured the passengers up on deck one afternoon. All eyes were on the grisly sight of a man being strung up from the yardarm. "'Tis a Spanish spy who was found among the crew," Master Rolfe told the women, "and having been discovered, he will be punished in the eyes of all."

"Oh, I cannot bear to watch," Mary said, putting her fingers over her eyes. But Matachanna gave her a sharp jab in the ribs. "You have seen men punished by our chiefs before. Watch and see how the English punish their enemies."

The gruesome scene was over with surprising speed, the man's lifeless body jerking a few times before it dangled lifeless. All the crew as well as the passengers were up on deck, and among the sailors near the main mast Nancy caught sight of a familiar face. The man was half-turned away, but something about his build and colouring snagged at her memory. Surely this was one of the sailors she had met before?

Then, as the dead spy's body was cut down, the sailors returned to their work and the passengers began to make their way below, the man drew nearer. His eye fell upon Nancy, standing next to Matachanna at the rail, for just the briefest moment before he turned away. Nancy thought it likely that the crew had been ordered not to approach Mistress Rolfe's women.

But she was certain it was the same man she had spoken to more than two years ago. There was no light of recognition in his eyes, though: either she was mistaken, or he did not remember the encounter as vividly as she did.

What confirmed it in her mind, later that same evening, was the sight of the second sailor. She had just settled baby Thomas Rolfe for the night, changed his clouts and given him back to his mother, and come up on deck alone for the first time. The man she had seen at the hanging was blocky and red-haired; this one was the fair-haired fellow. He was swabbing the deck and looked startled at her approach.

Not just startled: not the way a man would be if you came upon him unawares and his nerves were affrighted. No. He looked her in the eyes, as the other man had, and she was certain he knew her. His wariness was not just that of a sailor who had been told to leave the womenfolk alone: he knew her and wanted to avoid speaking with her.

"Forgive me," she said as he looked away, back to his task. "I'm sure I am not mistaken—did we not meet before on this ship? My name is Nancy Ellis."

He looked back her now, his eyes wide and blue in his sunburned face. "God forgive me," he said, "I cannot deny it. We did meet then."

"You told me then you knew a man called Ned Perry. I gave you a message to carry to him. I suppose—is there any chance you ever saw him again?"

The young man gaped, his mouth hanging ajar as if he could not find the words to fill it. "I—that is, I was—we all..."

She did not notice, at first, that a second sailor had joined them: this one also young, taller than the other, and strongly built. He came up almost behind Nancy, but spoke to the fair-haired man.

"Don't trouble to make up lies, Francis—you've no talent for it. You've not broken your promise—she found you." Then he turned to Nancy. "I can ask my friends to keep quiet for me, but not to lie for me. Good day, Nancy."

She thought she would know his voice anywhere, to the ends of the earth—which was, after all, nearly how far she had gone, trying to get back to him. It was Ned's voice, the voice of her girlhood taunter, her Cupids Cove friend, her one-time lover and promised husband. But it was the voice of a stranger too: she had never heard Ned's voice without a note of teasing laughter in it. Not even the first time he'd asked her to marry him and she refused; not even on that one night when she'd lain in his arms on the forest floor and let herself at last be loved. In sadness, in passion, in every hardship, he had kept that lightness that was, for her, who Ned Perry was.

Now there was a hardness to the edge of his voice, and the same in his face, though his green-eyed gaze against the deep tan of his skin was as bright as ever.

"Ned," she said at last. "You are—here. You have been here, all this time?" As if he could have dropped out of the sky just now.

"All this time," he said.

"And you did not—you said nothing?" Worse than that. Not only had he not spoken to her the moment she came aboard, he had tried to hide from her. It was not such a large vessel, though full of passengers and crew; he must have gone out of his way to avoid her, and told his friends to keep out of her way.

"For what—what possible reason?" Her voice almost broke on a sob, but she reined it in. A ship full of pirates had not destroyed her: damn Ned Perry if he would make her cry.

"Forgive me," he said. "I was...waiting, I suppose. I was not ready for—for this meeting."

"Not ready? Not *ready*?" There, that was better; she felt anger rising, so much better than tears. "After all this time, after all I've been through, always trying to get home to you—then sending word by this one—" she threw a glance at the other sailor, who was stepping backwards with his scrubbing bucket as if he could melt into the horizon—"after all that, you find out I am aboard the same ship you are serving on, and you *wait*? Because you are *not ready* to see me? God in heaven, Ned, I always said you were a fool, but I never took you for a knave who would use a woman so!"

"Forgive me," he said again. He spread his hands, but made no move to take her hands in his or do anything she might have expected, in all the dreams she'd had of this moment. "'Tis worse than you think—I knew before we left James Fort. 'Twas the reason I went to Virginia—because Francis told me you were there—and the reason I signed on for this voyage—because I learned you would be in Master Rolfe's party."

She stared, waiting for him to say more, to explain himself, but he stood there as gap-mouthed and silent as a codfish pulled from the water. "And so?" she prompted finally. "You came back to Virginia to find me, you came on this ship because I would be aboard of her, and then—you *hid* from me?"

"I was going to speak," he said. "I have meant to, every day. I told Francis and Peter it were best if you did not see them, so that I could choose my moment."

"What moment were you waiting for? Marry, Ned, what did you think I would do when I saw you? Did you think I would be angry with you? Did you think I'd hold some blame against you, for not being there when I was taken? How petty did you think I was?"

Now it was happening, would she or no—tears brimming to her eyes. She turned away, and hated herself for thinking that at the sight of her tears he would turn her about, take her in his arms. Just the touch of his hand on her shoulder would have unlocked every gate.

"No—no—none of that!" His anguish was as great as hers; she could hear it in his voice though he never reached out to touch her. "I thought none of those things—I never thought you would have changed. 'Tis I who changed, Nancy, and I could not bear—"

"Could not bear what?" She stared out at the ocean; she could not bear to look at him. "It has been nigh on three year since I was taken. I'm no fool. I told myself, Ned might have settled down somewhere else, given up on finding me. Taken a wife, had a child, gone on with his life. I'm not such a shrew as I'd blame you for such a thing—you're a man of flesh and blood, not a knight in a romance! Only I thought if we met you'd tell me, at least—like a man."

"Nancy, no—'tis not—" His words broke on a sob, and at that moment Betty popped a head up from the hatch and said, "Nancy, the mistress calls for you."

She waited one heartbeat for him to reach out his hand, but he did not.

She climbed down the ladder to go below deck and told herself sternly not to look back.

TWENTY-THREE

A Second Encounter Is Postponed

"'TIS RIGHT SORRY I AM THAT I LET THE WENCH CATCH sight of me," Francis said to Ned as he climbed down from the rigging to where Ned stood on deck. "I suppose 'twas too much to hope that on a ship this size we'd go all the way to England without her seeing any of the three of us."

"I never thought to get through the whole voyage. I only wanted to wait until—" Ned found it hard to put into words himself what he meant to do, what he'd had in mind back in James Fort when he had told Peter and Francis that he did not wish to meet Nancy just yet. "I wanted it to be the right time. And I knew if she saw either of you, the first question out of her would be if you'd had word of me. She's not one to hold her tongue, is Nancy."

He gave Francis a grim smile. Memories drifted back of him telling the other lads in Cupids Cove that Nancy would not stand for any light behaviour or foolishness. It was still true, but now he was the butt of her anger—and rightly so.

"Aye well, the cat is out of the bag now, for certes," Francis said. "She's seen you, and you've seen her. What now?"

Ned said nothing. What was there to say? He'd thought that perhaps, if he could plan the time of their meeting, plan what to say, he would get past this odd reluctance. For months after Nancy was taken, he had imagined what their reunion might look like, imagined taking her in his arms, kissing her, telling her he would never let her go. Imagined her thanking him, saying how grateful she was that he had come to find her.

Then he had believed she was dead. And from there things had unravelled, like a ball of yarn unspooling onto the floor so it could only be gathered up into a tangled mess again. He could make no sense of his memories of that time, of his nightmares, of the numb despair he had felt for the past two years believing her dead.

Then she was practically delivered to his doorstep, in her own tidy package, well in command of her life and her plans, bound for England with her new master and mistress. He was not even certain she would still want him, the man he had become in these two years. He had taken the coward's way out and hidden from her, as if in hiding he would somehow find a way forward.

"I know not," he said shortly. "It has been a long time. We are neither of us the same people we once were, is all I know."

Francis laughed. "True enough that you're not. You used to be the starry-eyed lover off on a quest, and now you're a right curst bastard, is the truth of it. But she seems a fine lass, for all she's been through."

"Been through worse than I have, and come out better," Ned said. "I know I'm a fool and a curst bastard—you need not tell me that."

Francis gave him a long look. "'Tis not my place to say, but...."

If 'tis not your place to say, then do not say, Ned thought, but contented himself with a grunt that could have meant anything. Francis went on.

"She seems like a good woman."

"She is."

"But mayhap it eats at your mind—what Elfrith said about her back in James Fort. About how a woman might be used, by those men that took her?"

"And what if it does? Do you think I can put it out of my mind?" Ned rocked back on his heels and fixed Francis with a glare. "Could you, if 'twas a maid you cared for? Would you forget how she'd been used by other men?"

Francis flushed, and looked uneasy. "Well, 'tis not—I have hardly been in the same case, have I? I know enough from hearing men talk, that most men would not be able to put it aside."

"Well, then, you have your answer."

He kept himself apart from Francis and Red Peter over the days that followed, though he could feel their eyes upon him. Neither, fortunately, was the sort to pry into a fellow's innermost thoughts, and after a while Ned realized he could work beside them as before, even talk and share the odd jest, without the need to explain why the woman he loved was aboard the ship and he was doing everything he could to avoid seeing her.

Nancy herself he saw often, from a distance. She was usually tending to her mistress's child, or going about on deck with one of the native women. She seemed very much at ease with the Indians; Ned supposed that must have come with living among them. He would have liked to talk with her about that, if he could have talked with her about anything at all. But the gulf was fixed between them now.

The crossing was an easy one: no storms, no pirates, only the endless monotonous routine of waves and horizon and ship's biscuit and boiled salt pork, one day blending into another. He wondered if Nancy was as she had always been—restless and uneasy when she had no work to occupy her. Like as not she was; caring for her mistress and the infant could not have kept her very busy, especially when the Rolfes had three other maidservants.

His longing for her was as sharp as it had ever been: as it had been when he first asked her to marry him in Cupids Cove, when he set out on the seas searching for her, when he was first told she was dead. Now she was only steps away from him and as untouchable as when he had thought her drowned.

Finally, land was sighted. The end of the journey was near. They would sail into London; from there, Captain Argall had told his men that after a few days' leave they would continue to other English ports around the coast. They would not cross the ocean again until the following spring.

Ned lay on his mat below deck, listening to the snores and grunts of the other men sleeping all around him. If only he'd not been caught off guard, not bungled that first meeting with Nancy so badly! The weeks of the voyage had slipped past while he wrestled with his tangled thoughts and avoided facing her again. Before they made landfall, he would have to say something.

He remembered steeling himself to speak his heart to her before— when he'd first asked for her hand in marriage in Cupids Cove, when she turned him down, and again the second time, walking back from Gilbert Pike's plantation, when she said yes. It had taken some courage, both times, to ask her. But at least in Cupids Cove his heart and mind had been clear and free. He knew what he was asking for, what he wanted.

I know what I want, he told himself now, as the ship rocked back and forth and his bed, his world, rocked with it. *I want her. Still. Always.* But the other thing he wanted, just as fiercely as he wanted to hold Nancy in his arms, was to turn back time. To go back to before the pirates came, before they had been separated. To go back to that clean, innocent, simple love in the heart of the clean, innocent, simple boy he had been.

And if he could not have the second of those wishes, how could he have the first?

The ship rolled on through the grey sea, and the night had no answer for him.

TWENTY-FOUR

A Party Arrives in London

"How many English people are in this London town?" Matachanna asked Nancy. They were standing, as they often did, at the rail of the ship, watching the water slip by. Land was visible now to the west, but it was still far distant.

"I've no idea," Nancy confessed. "I've not been to London, but I remember Bristol as it was when I left it. You'd scarce credit the press of people in the streets and all the buildings crowded round you. And London is bigger still, so they tell me."

"Chief Powhatan gave my husband instructions. He brought along tally sticks, and he is to notch them, to keep count of all the English he sees."

"I doubt he'll be able to keep count. There's a great many people."

Matachanna looked troubled. Since boarding the ship, she and the other Indians had worn English clothes, but she kept her hair in long braids rather than pinned up like an Englishwoman's, so that she looked like a being of two worlds. She had her nephew, little Thomas, up in her arms now; childless herself, she doted on Pocahontas's son. Now, pointing out at the waves, she spoke to him in the language of the Powhatan, and he echoed her: he knew words in both his mother's language and his father's.

To Nancy she said, "Will you go to your home when we are in England?"

"I do not know."

"You said you could find a ship there that will take you to your New Found Land. You are not waiting in Virginia for your...husband, now." Matachanna had learned the English word *husband*, though there were other words in the Powhatans' language, she said, for the promises that could be made between a man and a woman.

"I found him."

Matachanna stared. "In Virginia?"

"No, on this ship. He is in the crew."

"But—no! Why did you not tell me?" She looked around at the sailors on deck—Ned was nowhere in sight.

"He does not want me anymore," Nancy said. Then, as she could see the other woman aboil with questions, "I cannot talk of it. Please—do not ask."

Matachanna nodded, and held her peace. She knew how to keep a still tongue; it was one reason Nancy counted her as a friend. But for the rest of the voyage Nancy saw her looking at the sailors as they passed, trying to judge which was Nancy's Ned.

Nancy was glad to have no questions to answer. The only person she wanted to talk to on this ship was the person causing her so much distress. She wanted to rail at Ned, to weep, to ask him what had happened to make him receive her so coldly. But she had spoken her piece.

Then she found someone who did not know how to hold his tongue. She fairly stumbled across him when she was leaving Mistress Rolfe's cabin—not Ned, but the burly, red-bearded sailor she had spotted first. The less talkative of the Ned's two friends. She caught his eye and then looked away, just as he had done when she had seen him on deck earlier in the voyage.

"Mistress. Nancy. I am sorry for what happened. For us keeping it from you, that Ned was here."

She turned to look at him then. There was something honest in his square face and the crease in his brow. "'Tis no matter. You did only what he asked."

"I think he was—not in his right senses. You must know, he wanted nothing more than to find you, all this time, to know you were safe."

"He has an odd way of showing it."

"I know, Mistress."

"No 'mistress' here, if you please. You might tell me this much, though—has he found another woman?"

"I know not what ails him, i'truth. Men are ever fools where women are concerned. He's said nothing of another woman. And he is a fool, if you ask me, to brood so much on what ill-treatment you might have suffered when you were a captive." The man's face was as brightly coloured as his beard now, and he could not meet her eyes.

"So he thinks to add to that suffering by spurning me himself?"

"I know not what he thinks—only 'tis hard for some men, to think that their woman might have been—" he searched for words. "Used, or abused, by other men. I think 'tis folly, myself, but—not all men are the same."

"Indeed they are not." She turned away, feeling as if she'd been struck a blow in the chest, and stumbled towards the ladder, back below decks.

For the second time in the voyage, she was on the verge of tears. The only way she could fight against the storm of grief was to convert it to rage: how *dare* he? She had loved and trusted Ned, and if this sailor's words were true—and why should he lie?—Ned had proved he was ready to discard her at the mere suggestion that another man had touched her. Never mind that she had been forced: the fact that her body was no longer purely his was enough to make him reject her.

With that thought came others, thoughts she had held back and kept pushed far down for more than two years. Diligence Brown—she had not thought of his ridiculous Puritan name for so long, but she could still feel his fingers on her breasts, smell his breath and the weight of his body as he pressed her against the bed.

No more. She must not think of it. The fire of anger burned inside her, and she concentrated on that, on tending that small but intense flame rather than on dwelling on the things that had caused it. She would need that fire from now on.

On the evening of the sixth of May, the *Treasurer* sailed up the Thames River towards London. Nancy crowded onto the deck with the rest of the passengers. "You are seeing your own country again," Mary said wistfully: she missed Virginia greatly already.

"I have never seen this part of it before," Nancy said. She wondered how far it was from London to Bristol. As a girl she had heard people talk of going to London, but she could not recall how long the journey took.

"The towns look like your towns in our land," said Betty, and Nancy nodded. The English, in Virginia as in the New Found Land, had built their settlements to try to mimic the look of English houses and towns, even though, as Mistress Rolfe and the maids had often pointed out, the homes of the native people were much better suited to Virginia's climate and land.

But Nancy's mind was not truly on her first sight of England in four years. Through the bodies and faces of the passengers gathered on deck she was watching the crew, busy about their work. Looking for Ned, even if she did not want to admit it to herself.

She saw him, finally, as the houses grew closer together and nearer to the riverbank. Saw him standing on the aft deck looking down at the gathered passengers at the rail. He was watching for her, as she was for him. Their eyes met, and this time Nancy did not look away.

When the other passengers went below, Nancy remained on deck. She stayed alone at the rail, watching the lights of London flicker around them. So many lights; so many people. She had not truly understood how big the place was. The ship would dock overnight, and on the morrow the city would swallow them up.

He came. When almost none but the crew were left on the deck, and the night was almost fully dark, Ned stood at the rail beside her, half an arm's length away.

"I am sorry," he said.

"You said that before. 'Tis not much good to me."

He looked out at the busy shoreline slipping past. "I truly am, Nancy. I never thought—I thought if I ever found you, I'd be nothing but glad."

"And instead you are—what? Disgusted? Ashamed?"

"Ashamed—aye, perhaps that's it."

She felt that burning, as real as if the flame were in her hand. "I was a fool to believe you were any different from other men, Ned Perry.

Once a maid is soiled goods, you think she's no better than filth—even if she had no choice in the matter. 'Tis vile, that men use women so, and then other men think we are like clipped coins, or—or meat that's gone spoilt, for something that was no fault of our own!"

"God's teeth, Nancy, I never said such a thing!"

"But can you deny you meant it?" She did not even care, now, who heard her voice raised, what eyes were turned towards them. "For 'tis true, Ned—'tis true, for all I did to make it untrue. I spent months on that ship with those knaves. I barred my door and said my prayers, did their chores and cooked their food, all to keep myself from shame. And in the end, one of them forced himself on me anyway. He'd have taken my maidenhead, save that I'd given it freely to you—thinking, like a fool, that it was a thing you'd treasure always."

"Nancy!" He had closed the little space between them and reached out to take her in his arms, but she twisted, pushing him away.

"You mistake my meaning," he said, stepping back from her, his face grim. "Whatever man hurt you—I'd like to find him and tear his liver out."

"He's long gone—you're left only with me. And well I know that every time you look at me, you'll see his mark upon me. Nothing will ever be right, or simple, or clear between us again—not as it was back in Cupids Cove."

"Nancy, I swear—"

"I do not want your vows, Ned Perry. I'd have been glad if we could have put everything from the past two years behind us, forget it all, and go forward together. And now—"

"Now you no longer want that?"

"Do you?"

"God's wounds, you know I do."

The words sounded as if they were torn from his lips, and in his eyes she read only misery. She had seen Ned before when he told her he wanted her—his bright gaze, his ready smile, his hopeful eyes. There was nothing of that lad in the man who stood before her now. "I do want that, still," he repeated. "But all that's happened—it cannot be wiped away. And I do not know—"

"No. Nor do I."

"Nancy!" It was Betty, poking her head up through the hatch. "Pocahontas—Mistress Rolfe—is calling for you."

She had best get out of the habit of calling the mistress by her Indian name once we are in London, Nancy thought. She felt poised between two lives: the one she had lived these two years in Virginia, serving the Rolfes, and her own, truer life, unfolding here on the ship's deck with Ned. She had never seen him look like this—shorn of all joy, as if whatever had happened to him in the years they were apart had defeated him.

And yet, whatever he had suffered, surely she had suffered more, and was not defeated. What right had he to come to her looking like a cur that had been kicked away from the table? "I must go. Tomorrow we will be off this ship."

"I'd not have us part this way, Nancy."

"I know not what you want from me."

"What do you mean to do? Once we are in London?"

"I mean to serve my mistress as long as she is here in England. Then she has promised to give me a purse and a good character, so I can keep myself till I find another place—either back in Bristol, or mayhap back to the New Found Land, to serve Kathryn." At her old mistress's name she remembered. "You've not spoken of Kathryn—was she well when you left?"

"Well, but heartsick with worry for you. I told her I would bring you back, or bring word."

"I can bring myself back well enough. Perhaps I did not need to be rescued at all, Ned."

"I've bungled this whole business."

She turned towards the ladder. "Aye, that you have."

"I am staying aboard the *Treasurer*, for a time at least. If I were to come looking for you—"

She managed a laugh, albeit one that cost her something. "Lord ha' mercy, Ned, I am serving the Indian princess of Virginia. They say she will be presented to the king at court. D'you think 'twill be hard to find me—if you are looking?"

TWENTY-FIVE

An Adventurer Returns Home

HE WAS LOOKING AT THE SIGHT HE HAD NEVER expected to see again in this lifetime, for all his travels. Sailing up the Avon, seeing the houses and church steeples and finally the docks of Bristol taking shape around him. *Home*.

Six years ago he had left, thinking he would never be back. Thinking he had thrown in his lot with the colonists and would never cross the ocean again.

Now he was home, working alongside the other sailors on the *Treasurer* to secure the ship's lines as she pulled up to the quay. After docking, there was cargo to unload. Finally, near evening, Captain Argall told the men they were free to go into the town.

Ned took leave of his shipmates and walked along the wharves, hungry eyes taking in every sight, trying to remember what had changed and what he had only forgotten. That house there on the corner of Fish Street—had that been there, or was it new? He passed the bakeshop, now shut for the day, where his brother Dickon worked, Dickon who had married the baker's daughter. He might well own the shop now; perhaps the baker was dead.

Ned realized how little he knew of what had befallen his family. When the women came out to Cupids Cove four years ago, Nancy had brought greetings from his parents, both alive and well at the time. But in the years since, anything might have happened. Anything—indeed, everything—had happened to him. It was folly to imagine the world at home going on without any changes.

All the same, he half expected it to be unchanged. Standing in the street before the house he'd grown up in, he thought of the faces he would see behind that door: his father and mother grown older, the younger siblings grown up. And the nieces and nephews, too—they would be older, and more numerous. He squared his shoulders, took a deep breath. Realized he was not fearing what changes he would find behind that door as much as what changes they would see in him.

A stranger answered. Or not quite a stranger. He knew the man, though he could not put a name to him. A neighbour, or—no, it was someone who had worked with his father for years.

"Nay, Perrys have been gone from here this two years—since the old man passed," he said. "The widow Perry lives with her son now, over the bakeshop." He angled his head towards the street Ned had just passed through.

"My—John Perry is dead? Two years since?"

The man in the door looked at him more closely. "Who be you, sailor? Sure you're not—"

"I am Ned Perry. I did not know my father—had died." His voice caught on the last words. Not so strange or terrible that his father would be dead—he had been nigh on sixty. But that Ned had gone about his business for two years knowing nothing of it was hard to bear.

"Young Ned—back from the colonies! Your mother will be glad to see you—oft times she talks of her son over in the New World. I'd not ha' known you, lad, but I suppose you were no more'n a stripling when I saw you last. Go to your brother's house, now, and make them glad." After a pause he added, "I am sorry to be the one to tell you of your father. He were a good carpenter, and a good man too."

"And a good father," Ned said.

Standing outside another door, now. Time had, indeed, not stood still. His father was dead, his mother a widow. Peele the baker must have died too, if Dickon had the bakeshop. It was Dickon's wife who came to the door, and like the man who had lived in their old house, she stood a moment looking without seeing him. Had he changed so much, or was it only that no-one expected a man to return once he'd sailed off the edge of the world?

There was no hesitation in his mother's eyes, when he climbed the stairs to the rooms above the shop. His sister-in-law ran ahead shouting, "Mother Perry! You'll not believe who is at the door!" but no announcement was needed. His mother—a tiny woman, whose fair hair had turned white since he last saw her—rushed into his arms.

"Ned. My boy...my boy. Look at you!" She pulled him close and then held him away, looking him up and down. "Look at you—a man grown. Ah, your poor father—how proud he'd be to see you. Back from the colonies!"

"Back from the colonies, but I've made no fortune, mother dear," he said, pulling her close again. Then the rest all crowded round—his brother Dickon and four—*four!*—little children. Only Dickon's wife had disappeared; she had run straight back down the stairs and out the door to inform the rest of the family.

They all crowded in. His sister Sal was married now, while Betsy and Mary were in service. They all came to see him during the evening, along with Francis and his family. John had married and moved to Gloucester with his wife, but the rest of the family remained in Bristol, in a cluster of streets in St. Nicholas's parish. The children—there seemed to be a dozen of them—paid little attention to the uncle they did not know, and tumbled happily into playing with each other, a tangle of cousins who were growing up together.

Mother and brothers and sisters all wanted to know what had befallen him since he left Bristol. Every detail of the six years of his absence they were eager to know, and Ned told as much of the tale as he could. News of the attack on the Guys' plantation had made its way back to Bristol, but they did not know that Ned had left the colony, gone off to try to find Nancy. By this part of the tale, even the older children were listening with attention.

"Did you fight the pirates?" Francis's little fellow Edward asked.

"Did you save the maid who was captured?" Dickon's daughter Rosie wanted to know.

"Nay, I did none of that," Ned said. They wanted a tale with a hero, but he could not give them one. He met his mother's eyes over the children's heads. "Nancy is alive and well, though 'twas not I who rescued her."

"Oh, I am glad to hear that," his mother said. "She's a good maiden—a level head on her."

"Who rescued her, if you did not?" Rosie again.

"Why, she—I suppose she rescued herself." *Perhaps I did not need to be rescued at all*, he heard her say. "There was a shipwreck, and she got away from the pirates, and got to safety." He realized he had no idea how this had come about. All that time they had spent crossing the ocean, he could have been learning her tale, had he not been so wrapped up in his own folly.

"But did you ever fight any pirates?" Edward was a persistent little fellow.

"No." He could offer no more than that bald denial. Images twisted between memory and nightmare rose up before his mind's eye like a red tide: the Spaniard's plantation, a sword thrust between a man's ribs. A chain around the wrists of a slave woman, the terror and rage in her eyes as she struggled. The screams of the dying and of the captives. The scent of smoke in the air. *No, I never fought the pirates.*

He dodged the questions, talked about the places he had been and seen, how he had fought off seasickness to become a sailor and ship's carpenter. To the children's delight, he did tell about Elfrith's capture of Spanish ships, since there was no shame attached to privateers attacking England's enemies.

"Should have taken a French ship, 'tis the bloody Frenchmen we have to worry about," grumbled Francis.

"What a pity I didn't think to tell the captain that, I'm sure he would ha' listened to his ship's carpenter," Ned said, and they all laughed.

"Ship's carpenter is a grand trade to have, Ned," his mother said, when the laughter died down. "I know you 'prenticed as a mason, but I hear there's always a berth for a carpenter aboard ship, if you've decided to keep going to sea. Or did you think to settle back here in Bristol?"

"Ah. Well. You're asking of the future now, not the past, and that I cannot tell you," Ned admitted. "I'm not settled in my own mind what I want now, save another ale and mayhap a little more of that plum tart, Bess."

It was like that all evening—brushing aside their questions about the future, and about the past, too, when they strayed into uncomfortable territory. But they had plenty to tell him as well, and as much as he could Ned sat quiet and listened—to the happy tales of weddings and births, to the local gossip and scandals, to the tally of friends and neighbours dead of plague or accident or old age.

Late in the evening when he sat alone with his mother and brother, Ned heard about his father's last days, how he had coughed up blood and choked and wheezed his last hours away, dwindling to a slender shadow of the man they had known.

"In the end, 'twas a merciful release," Ned's mother said, dabbing at her eyes with a kerchief. "Six months he was sick, and by the time he was laid in the churchyard I thanked God for taking him, for I could not have seen him suffer so for much longer, Ned, that I could not." She looked up at him through the dim flickering of the rushlights around the chamber. "He spoke of you often, at the last. The others were all round him—even John came from Gloucester to visit—but he'd say, *Oh, if I could see my Ned one more time. But he's gone off to make his fortune.* He was proud of you, you know."

Ned nodded. He knew his father had been proud of him. As for him saying those words—mayhap he had truly said them, or perhaps his mother had constructed them out of oddments of words his father had said, or what she thought he would have liked to say. He guessed that other people's stories were much like his own—bits of the truth, spliced with the things people wanted to hear.

He told more of those stories the next day, when after sleeping on the floor by the bakeshop oven and breakfasting on the morning's fare of bread and cakes, he walked to Master Gale's house.

"Nancy is alive and well. We came over on the same ship," he was able to tell Aunt Tibby. "The truth is she's in England now, and if she gets leave to go, I'm sure she'll come and see you."

"Thank God," Tibby said. She was not a woman given to displays of emotion, but she closed her eyes a moment and clasped her hands at her breast.

"Bless the dear girl, what good news," Mistress Gale said. "And here in England serving an Indian princess! I am sure for all the fine company she keeps, she had rather be serving our Kathryn again."

They had fresher news of Kathryn and the Cupids Cove colony than he did, for letters came across the ocean, albeit rarely. He learned that Nicholas Guy had moved back to his own land and built a new house. He and his family—there was a second child now, a daughter—had been living, fishing and planting there for nearly two years now—"if all still be well," Master Gale added, "for the last word we had was when the fishing fleet came back last autumn."

"Let us pray they all made it through the winter, and we will have more news this year," Mistress Gale said. "Do you mean to go back to the New Found Land, Ned?"

He turned their questions aside as he had done those of his own family, and spent the rest of the day with the Gales. The children had grown up, young John and Phillip working alongside their father in the stoneyard. Lily, who had been a chattering little lass when Ned went away, looked as he remembered Kathryn looking in the years when he had fancied himself in love with her—all dark curls and plump cheeks. She was sixteen; soon she, like her sister, would be the family's stepping stone to a better life, for with a face and nature like hers she could surely marry well. The Gales were prospering. He stored these thoughts away, wondering if he would ever have a chance to tell Kathryn of them.

He went to visit a few other people in Bristol, having the whole day free: Walter, who had been just starting his journeyman's service when Ned was an apprentice, was now a master mason in his own right, but was thinking of leaving Bristol, for there was too little work for too many stonemasons in the city. "What of the colonies, Ned? Should I go out there?"

Ned was happy to talk about the colonies, not only about Cupids Cove but about Virginia and Bermuda, and Walter was amazed to find that the younger man had seen so much. "You can make a life for yourself out there—mayhap not a fortune, as some say, but a life. But 'tis hard—there are hardships men face out there that they never dream of in England."

He met one person that day he'd had no mind to meet, strolling through the streets of Bristol saying hello to this and that familiar face. A young nobleman walked past him near St. John's Gate, the sort of lofty, well-dressed fellow who would never give a labouring man like Ned a glance. But between the high-crowned hat and the white ruff, Ned saw a face he recognized, and in that glance of recognition he saw that the other man knew him also.

"Hail, fellow! Penny, is it not? Or—"

"Perry, sir. Ned Perry."

"Ned Perry!" The young nobleman stopped, his handsome face quirking into half a smile, which was as much as he ever had for anyone. "Ned Perry from Cupids Cove. Back in Bristol! And a sailor, from the looks of you."

"Yes, sir. I've been aboard the *Treasurer* for some time now. Only in port for a day or two, visiting with family and friends."

"Ah, so you've not just come from Cupids Cove?"

"Nay, sir. I left Cupids Cove nigh on three year ago."

"The same as myself, then. But I am thinking of going back."

When Ned had known him in Cupids Cove, Thomas Willoughby had been dressed in breeches and tunic like all the other working men, doing his share—albeit reluctantly—in the labour of the colony. Though everyone knew whose son he was, they had never called him "my lord" or treated him as gentry. But here in Bristol, he wore a fine doublet with points at the waist and roses on his shoes. He looked every inch the nobleman he was.

He looked pleased with himself, too, his hand straying to the sword at his side as he spoke—not as if he intended to use it, but as if he were reassured to know it was there.

"Are you indeed, sir? For the season, or to bide?"

"To bide, for a time at least. My father means to send me back there—not as a punishment this time, but to see to his interests over there, and develop his land for myself."

"I thought you hated the place."

"I hated my position there. But to go back as my own man—'twould have its compensations. There are some attractive things about the land, to be sure." On the word "attractive" he half-smiled again. "You served Nicholas Guy, did you not? Is his pretty wife still well?"

"Mistress Guy was well when I left there, sir. But as I said, that was not long after you left yourself."

"What a fine lass she was—well, mayhap I'll see her again if I go. I've a wife of my own now, but I'll not be taking her out to the colonies—'tis no place for a lady, at present."

"I wish you much happiness, sir." Ned touched his cap, nodded to Willoughby, and walked away. He'd never liked the man much, but this encounter, with Willoughby so clearly preening in his status and making sly comments about Kathryn Guy, left a particularly bad taste in his mouth.

But it was the only ill encounter he had over the two days in Bristol. Everyone else he ran into seemed happily surprised to see him alive and back on English soil. It was hard to shake the feeling that he walked through Bristol's streets as a ghost, but a ghost that, in general, people were glad to see.

The night before the *Treasurer* was due to sail, he sat alone with his mother by the hearth in the bakeshop, struggling to find the words to say goodbye.

"You may come back again," she said. "But even if you do, you might not see me again. I never thought to live long after your father passed. Will you be well, Ned?"

"I...I cannot say, Mother."

"Something is troubling you. I've known it since you talked of your journeys. Is it the lass?"

He had told the family that Nancy had pledged to marry him—he had to, in order to explain him going off in search of her. "I always thought well of her—thought 'twould be a good match," his mother went on. "It put my mind at ease many a time, thinking you and she would come to an understanding out there. She's a good woman."

"Aye, that she is."

"And now you have found her, and all is well. A happy ending?"

"I know not, in truth." He sighed. "So many things happened, Mother. You know I did not tell all my tales."

"No, though the little ones longed to hear them."

"Some of them are—not tales you would tell to children." He looked into the fire, with its banked and smouldering embers. He longed to tell someone, though—to unburden the whole unhappy tale, as papists were said to do to their priests, and be assured that all was washed away, forgiven.

Nancy believed, as Francis and Peter did, that Ned could not bear the thought of the woman he loved being soiled by another man's brutal hands. In truth, that thought did turn his stomach. But no more than the thought of the things his own hands had done. The blood, the chains, the screams, the fire. The horror of becoming the very thing he had set out to defeat. Only now, in the peace of his old home, did he realize that that was the gulf that lay betwixt himself and Nancy—not any guilt of hers, but his own.

No priest could offer him forgiveness; he knew that was papist superstition. And he could no more tell his mother such things than he could tell them to children. Instead, he said, "I am—not the man I thought I would be."

"I doubt many men are, son." She squeezed his hand. "You are not a bad man, whatever you might have had to do to survive."

A stick of wood fell into the fire and flared up for a moment, tracing his mother's lined face with brilliant light as she went on. "The world out there—in the colonies, out on the sea—'tis not like our world here in Bristol. Here a boy grows up, learns his trade, works at it, marries a wife and has children, and in his time, lays down his tools and dies. As your father did. There's not much scope here for a man to be either very great or very wicked—though I suppose a few manage it." She laughed. "You entered a different world when you sailed away from here, Ned. Do not be too hard on yourself for it. I doubt Nancy would be—she's got good sense."

Ned dropped a kiss on his mother's cheek. "I ought to try to sleep— I'm to be at the ship at dawn."

TWENTY-SIX

A Masque Is Attended

THE SEAMSTRESS CAME WITH MISTRESS ROLFE'S NEW gown on the eighth day of Christmas, four days before the Virginia party was to be presented at court to view a Twelfth Night masque. Betty and Sally brought in the packages for Nancy and Mary to unwrap under the watchful eye of the seamstress. "So much cloth for one gown!" she heard Betty whisper to Sally as the heavy garment was opened and shaken out.

It was, indeed—yards and yards of rich, wine-coloured fabric. There was a gold brocade jacket as well, studded with pearls, not to mention the petticoat and the ruff, and, in a separate box sent from the milliner, the high-crowned hat. Only when everything had been opened and laid out in the upper chamber of the inn did Betty go to call their mistress for the final fitting.

Measurings, fittings, visits from the seamstress had been a constant since their arrival in London in the spring. The simple gowns that Mistress Rolfe had worn when she arrived were no more suitable to her status in London than her Powhatan dress of animal skins would have been. For being taken around and presented at the houses of various English lords and ladies, and receiving visitors at the inn, the Virginia Company had decreed that new gowns were needed—and since the Virginia Company was very thrifty but still desired to show their Indian princess off in fine style, most of the sewing had to be done by Nancy and the maids.

An English seamstress had shown them the patterns for the kind of gowns women of quality were wearing in London. It made a change from cleaning house, cooking meals, and curing tobacco, but Nancy was growing weary of hours spent at her needle, making and re-making the gowns her mistress was required to wear for various occasions. Simpler but good-quality English gowns had also been required for Matachanna, who, as Pocahontas's sister and wife of the Indian holy man, was deemed to be of high status and sometimes invited to these grand occasions as well.

Nancy had taught the English style of making garments to the maids—Betty was the only one who took naturally to that kind of work, while the others struggled with it. They had all had to learn to dress Mistress Rolfe's hair in high English styles as well, and to lace her into the complicated gowns required for formal occasions. But nothing in these last months of visiting and sight-seeing could compare to the fuss that was being made over the visit to the royal palace, and for that, only a professional seamstress's work would serve. All the Indian women would have new gowns, for all were going to court, and the three Powhatan men needed breeches, doublets and hose. But Mistress Rolfe's gown was the most lavish by far.

Rebecca Rolfe stood patiently now, as her maids and sister dressed her in layer after layer of the stiff fabric. "It is still very strange to me," Matachanna said, as she fastened the starched white ruff around her sister's neck. "The greater in power an English lady becomes, the more hard to wear the clothes become!"

"That ruff is a foolish thing!" Betty said, clicking her tongue. "And what is the purpose? To make a lord or lady look like a chicken, with a great ruff of feathers around the neck!"

"The purpose," Mistress Rolfe said, "is the same as beads and embroidering on a chief's robe—to show how highly placed a person is and how they are esteemed by others. If the English king is to respect Powhatan as a fellow king, then I must be arrayed as an English princess."

Nancy well knew by now that Mistress Rolfe was not considered royalty by her own people; the mistress herself had told her that, long ago, and since then Matachanna had explained more to her about how rank and status were measured among the Powhatan. Both Matachanna and Pocahontas were Powhatan's daughters, but neither of their mothers came from chiefly lines, so the women themselves were not accorded any special honour because of who their father was. Powhatan had other daughters from loftier matches who might more properly be given an honorific something like the English title of "princess," but to the English settlers of Virginia, Mistress Rolfe was *their* Indian princess. So the Virginia Company styled her here in London, and so she carried herself, determined that her status here might win greater respect for her people among the English settlers.

Nancy knelt at the mistress's feet, where lavish gold embroidery around the skirt of the gown complemented the colour of the jacket. "It could come up an inch or so here," she said to the seamstress, "but I can alter that myself."

"Yes, you do so—the Company'll not pay me for further alterations," said the seamstress, who was already packing up her bag after looking over the whole outfit with a critical eye. "There's a few darts that could be taken here in the waist as well—I swear she's thinner than she was when I took measurements before Christmas. Mind you do it yourself, though—I want none of the savages taking a needle to my work." With that she was gone, leaving a shocked little silence in her wake.

"Never mind her," Nancy said, after a moment. "She's not to know who's been at her precious creation once she's out of the way, and Betty, you're as good as I am at this kind of work. You take up the hem and I will bring in the waist. 'Tis true as she said, Mistress—you have lost flesh these last weeks."

"Even though we have been to so many feasts," Matachanna added. "But the English food is still not pleasant to my tongue."

"Mine as well," said Mistress Rolfe. "I will not be able to eat at all when we go before their king. So much depends upon this meeting."

Through all the long months of making visits and seeing London, Nancy had often heard Mistress Rolfe fretting over her meeting with the king and queen, wondering why it was taking so long to happen. She was frequently closeted with Matachanna and Tomocomo; all three had pressed Master Dale to find out when they would be brought to meet King James. For all the talk of a royal audience, the Virginia party had

been lodged in a middling sort of London inn and brought to a round
of teas and dinners at various fine London houses, but there had been
no hint of being invited to court during the long, hot, stinking summer
months, nor yet in the cooler months of autumn. Finally, just before
Christmas, the summons had come to attend the king and queen at a
masque on Twelfth Night.

"She is so serious now," Matachanna said to Nancy, as the two
women sat sewing the waistline of the new gown later that day. "You
know that the name I call her is a private name, for family—Matoaka—
but she was given the name Pocahontas as a child. It means something
like 'little laughing one' in English. She was daring and bold in all the
games, always ready for fun. Now I never hear her laugh, unless she is
playing with Thomas."

"'Twould be hard not to be changed by all she has been through."

"You would know this yourself, for you also were taken captive from
your home," Matachanna pointed out.

"True enough. But I was never the little laughing one."

"Always so serious, our Nancy," the Indian woman said, with a smile.
"How will we do without you, when you go home at last?"

"Ah, there's time yet to think about that," Nancy said, and proceeded
not to think about it, as she had been not doing for months now.

When Rebecca Rolfe stood before them on the afternoon of the
Twelfth Night masque, arrayed again in her court finery, she looked
every inch the princess. Matachanna and the maids also wore their new
gowns, sober and simple in comparison to Mistress Rolfe's. Nancy, the
only female member of the party not going to court, had had a busy
morning helping everyone dress, and stood back now to enjoy the effect
of the five Powhatan women garbed in English style.

"Will we get to meet the king ourselves?" Betty wondered.

"Belike you will," Nancy said, "though 'twould not be common for
servants to be brought before such great people. But the king and queen
have said they want to see all the natives of Virginia, so at least you will
be expected to kneel down before them."

"If he wants to see what the people of our land are like, he ought to
see us in our own dresses, not the dresses of English ladies," Sally said.

"Imagine if we went before their king wearing our own clothes!" Mary said, laughing.

"They would be greatly shocked," Matachanna said. "For an Englishman, to see a woman's bare skin is a great shame, though we have seen their great ladies show a little of their neck and bosom."

"My husband has told me how much it troubled him to see me dressed in the manner of our people, when first we met," Mistress Rolfe said. She adjusted the high-crowned hat that she alone wore, and looked to Nancy for a nod of approval that it she was wearing it properly.

"I think still that it looks foolish," Betty said, "but you could not go about in a deerskin apron in London in the winter—never mind who might look at your buttocks, for surely they would freeze!"

More laughter; the young maids were in high spirits at the thought of the royal palace. The visit promised such glimpses of dizzying luxury that even Nancy was a bit envious. What a thing it would be, if she ever got back to Cupids Cove, to be able to tell Kathryn that she had been to the palace and seen the king!

The men joined them then: Master Rolfe and Master Dale and the other Englishmen, then Tomocomo and the two manservants. More than any of the other Powhatans, he looked uncomfortable in English dress; he had brought his full native regalia with him, as he would be dressed for his own religious ceremonies, and wore it sometimes for visitors, along with demonstrating some of the Powhatan dances and chants. Now he spoke to the other Indians in their own tongue; it looked as if he intended a longer speech, but Master Dale cut him short, hurrying everyone towards the door of the inn.

Nancy watched them all go, waving at the grand carriage that had been sent for them as all the Virginia entourage piled into it. Even little Thomas, who was usually left behind in the care of Nancy and the maids when his parents went visiting, was being brought along to be shown to the king. His Majesty was said to be very interested in seeing the first child born of a match between an Englishman and a Virginia native.

The inn—the Belle Sauvage, a name that seemed almost too perfect for housing the Indian princess, although Master Dale assured the Rolfes that the choice was a mere coincidence—was quiet with all the party gone. The Virginia Company had booked their rooms for several months, so there were no other guests staying there. In the early weeks of their stay, folk from the neighbourhood would come to eat and drink at the inn so they might gape at the Virginians, but that novelty had worn off by now, and only a few old men sat at a table in the corner drinking ale. Nancy went to the kitchen, where she was friendly with the cook and maids, and got an eel pie to eat by the hearth as she awaited the return of the court party.

As she ate, she pondered her own position. Sometime the Rolfes would return to Virginia, and Nancy's indenture would end. She was unsure what to do next. Go home to Bristol, she supposed. See Aunt Tibby, Master and Mistress Gale. And then? A ship to the New Found Land, to piece together the life she had begun over there. That had always been her intention.

But now that Ned was somewhere in England, and this distance was between them, she was unsure. The thought of seeing him again was like a dull ache in her stomach. She was angry at herself, realizing how much she had believed that foolish dream of romance. She must put it aside before she could decide for certain what to do.

Those thoughts chased themselves endlessly round in her head—truly, 'twas a good thing she had so little time to rest and think, for she would run mad if she had nothing better to do than ponder such things. She fell asleep by the hearth, finally, and only woke up when the inn doors blew open, bringing in a chilly blast of winter air, a few snow-flakes, and the loud, merry, excited voices of Betty, Sally, and Mary.

"Oh Nancy, I wish you had come!" Mary said, rushing to her side. "Such a grand place—none of the houses we have seen were anything like it. So big—and all the lords and ladies—the jewels, the food, the music—"

"There was a sort of—a show, like the players put on," said Sally, who had been quite intrigued by the players in the inn-yard at Christmas. "But very grand, with lords and even ladies playing parts in it..."

"'Tis called a masque, a sort of play they put on at court," said Master Rolfe, who was carrying his sleeping son in his arms as he and his wife entered the inn. He passed the child to Sally as the young women con-tinued to chatter about all they had seen.

"—a masque, yes, and 'twas made up just for tonight, for our party, so they said—"

"—and we said, do you remember Nancy, we said a Powhatan woman could not go into court with her buttocks bare, but the ladies there go about with their breasts almost bared—"

"—oh, the dresses, you should have seen—"

"—there was dancing, and so much wine to drink—"

"I believe you had too much wine yourself! You are so giddy," Betty chided Sally, and again all three of the girls laughed, and Mary said, "Surely no chief in Virginia could ever live in such a great hall, or command such wealth and power!"

For the first time since they had entered, Mistress Rolfe spoke. "No. No chief of the Powhatan, or any other tribe in our land, could have such wealth and power. That was the whole end of the invitation—to show us the greatness of the English king and his power."

She looked across the heads of the rest of the party at Tomocomo, and there was a coldness in her words that stilled the chattering maids, sobered the whole party for a few moments. Then the swirl of activity started again; Sally went upstairs to put little Thomas to bed while Nancy went to the kitchen in search of warming possets for those who wanted a hot drink, and the conversation over what they had seen and heard at the palace continued.

Only Rebecca Rolfe stayed apart from it all; the guest of honour seemed greatly troubled by her court presentation, and sat at a table near the fire lost in thought while her husband, her uncle, and Master Thomas Dale discussed what the king had said. Matachanna came and sat beside Nancy. "I wish you had seen it," she said.

"I'd not have known what to make of it, most like," Nancy said.

"No, as I did not. I think it is as Pocahontas says—the king and queen wanted to show us how rich they are, how powerful. So that we would go home and tell our people that we can never defeat the English. But we have known that a long time. You know my husband threw away his tally sticks."

"Yes, so you told me. Because there's too many people in London to be counted."

The next day, cleaning the chambers, Nancy overheard a conversation between Master and Mistress Rolfe, Tomocomo, and Governor Dale. As grand people always did, in Nancy's experience, they talked as if Nancy were not in the room, ignoring her as she moved around the chamber picking up crockery from the tables.

"I think 'twas a good meeting with the king," Master Rolfe said. "He spoke to us, he said he had great hopes for the peace between our two peoples, for our son to be the first sign of the mingling of our nations— what more could we hope for?"

"Much more!" Mistress Rolfe said. "I thought we would have a private audience with him. Not only to speak to him at a gathering, with many people around."

"It is not how to treat a..." Tomocomo searched for the English word. "One who comes to speak for another king."

"An ambassador," Mistress Rolfe said. "It is not how he should treat the ambassadors of Powhatan."

"That is not what they do, at such a thing as a court masque," Governor Dale said. "It is only intended as a formal presentation. Now that he has met with us, I am sure the summons will come for a private audience. The king will invite us to meet with him privately, and then you can speak on behalf of your chief," he added to Tomocomo.

"I would speak to him also," Mistress Rolfe said. "I am Powhatan's daughter."

She sat proud and straight-backed in her chair before the hearth, now wearing her everyday English clothes. Her hair was dressed not in the elaborate hairstyle she had worn for court but in the simple style Nancy arranged for her most mornings: the long braids common for Powhatan women, coiled and pinned in place atop her head in English fashion. She looked serious, thin-faced, and very much alone, a woman speaking out in the affairs of men, Powhatan's daughter in the land of the invader.

Nancy stared at her for a moment, and Rebecca Rolfe caught her eye. Nancy dropped her gaze, sorry to have been caught staring; she took the tray of used crockery and slipped out of the room.

TWENTY-SEVEN

A Departure Is Planned

GOVERNOR DALE'S CONFIDENCE IN A WELCOME FROM the king was not rewarded. Days passed, a cold, rainy January month rolled on, and no further summons to the palace came. Mistress Rolfe grew more pensive. Though she and her husband continued to be invited to the homes of wealthy Londoners and to entertain visitors at the inn, she was plainly upset not to be granted an audience with the king.

Compounding the gloomy mood of the Rolfe party was Betty's illness; she began to cough and grow feverish two days after their visit to the palace. Mistress Rolfe immediately put Thomas into Nancy's care. "I do not want my sister or the maids to care for him—I fear this is an illness that will strike all our people, and I will not risk my son."

Her fears were justified. Over the next few weeks, several of those staying at the inn fell ill, with the Indians more likely to be afflicted than the English colonists in the party. Betty, Sally, and Mary were all sick, as was Tomocomo, although Matachanna and the two younger Powhatan men were not affected. When baby Thomas woke one morning feverish and coughing, Mistress Rolfe was distracted with worry.

"There is something evil in the air of this country," she told Nancy, who was pacing back and forth across the floor of her chamber with the fussy child on her shoulder, trying to soothe him. "So cold, so much smoke, so many people crowded together. It is not healthy for our people."

"'Tis true, Mistress, there does seem to be more sickness in England than I saw in Virginia," Nancy said. "But bad fortune comes to all men sometimes."

The Indian woman looked down at her son. "He is so small, and babies die so often," she said. "And he is the only hope for our union of England and Powhatan."

"Perhaps he will fare better when you take him back to your own land. Do you know if the company plans to take you home soon?"

"I told them I did not wish to go back—not yet. I thought to stay here until I am properly received by the English king, until Tomocomo and I can treat with him as is due to my father's dignity. But now...I think we might stay in this inn till we die, and never be called for by the king."

The sickness lingered. Some of the Virginians recovered; others remained weak. There was no word from the palace, nor from the Virginia Company about their plans for the travellers. *Perhaps*, Nancy thought, *we truly will stay here until we perish. Perhaps we have been forgotten*. It came to her that her fate was not tied to that of the Virginian party; she could ask for her wages and be free to make her own way. But she stayed; with so many sick, she could not leave now.

A message came to the Belle Sauvage inn: the *Treasurer* was in London again. Captain Argall was coming to meet with Governor Dale, Master Rolfe, and the other members of the Virginia party, to discuss whether his ship or another would take them back across the ocean.

"We cannot go now!" Nancy heard Mistress Rolfe tell her husband. "Some of my people are too sick to travel. And still we have not been called to meet with your king, to speak on my father's behalf."

"That meeting may never come. And if it does not, what is the good of staying here?"

"If it does not, what was the good of coming here at all? That my family and I could be shown around like—like captives taken in battle? For English people to come and stare at us?" The rage in Mistress Rolfe's voice startled little Thomas awake, and his mother handed him off to Nancy.

Nancy put the little boy down in his bed and then made the rounds of the sick, bringing them pottage and watered wine. Sally seemed better, but Mary and Betty were still quite ill. Baby Thomas, when she got back to him, was lively and wanted to play, in spite of the cough that shook his whole body. Nancy sat on the floor and rolled his ball back and forth to him until he tired of that game.

"I want Mama," he said, when Nancy tried to get him to sleep. His mother was in the habit of coming to him every night at bedtime, singing and talking to him in the language of her own people. It was hard to settle him on nights when she was taken up with visitors.

"Hush now. I will go see if Mama can come up."

In the parlour of the inn, Mistress Rolfe sat with the men, debating their departure. "You could not set sail before the end of March," Nancy heard Captain Argall say, as she beckoned her mistress out of the room, and then Master Rolfe began talking about how long the crossing would take and whether he would be back in time to plant this year's tobacco.

Nancy wanted nothing more than to go to the captain, pluck him by the sleeve, and ask, "Is Ned Perry still aboard the *Treasurer*?" Eight months had passed since their arrival in London, and in all that time she had heard nothing from him.

Belike you'll find me still waiting, she had told him, and it must have been truth, for here she was, her very skin turned to goose flesh at the word that the *Treasurer* was back in London.

Mistress Rolfe had gone above-stairs to tend to her child; Nancy could turn and walk out of the inn at any time. Though 'twould be a long walk to the London docks, she knew her way about the city by now.

Even we were right at the river's edge, I'd not go searching for him, she told herself.

In the parlour, Master Rolfe said, "Some of the Indians will have to be left behind if we go in the next few weeks, for they are hardly well enough to travel."

Matachanna said, "What will become of them? We cannot leave our people alone here."

"The company will see they are well cared for," said Governor Dale. "They can be put into homes with some of our folk, where they will be looked after until they recover. After that, they may wish to go into service here. If they want to return home, passage can be arranged."

Nancy moved away from the parlour door, through the main room of the inn, where a few people sat eating, drinking, talking. She went outside, into a chill grey afternoon. The thought of walking to the docks, or for that matter all the way to Bristol, had little appeal on such a day. But she must go somewhere, do something.

"Nancy."

She turned. She knew his voice but did not let herself believe it until she saw him standing there. He was dressed in his sailor's garb, cap in hand. His face looked less browned and burnished now, after these long months in English ports, than it had when she last saw him after his time in the warmer southern seas.

"So you have come after all."

"I have. 'Tis the first time we've been back to London. We went to Plymouth, then we were in Bristol."

"Bristol? Did you—"

"I did. I went home, and saw them all. Aunt Tib is still at the Gales' house, ruling the roost. I told her of all that had befallen you, and that you were safe and well and serving a great lady here in London, and she was fair amazed at my tales. They all send their love, and hope you will come see them."

"I'd thought I might return to Bristol, when I leave Mistress Rolfe's service."

"You are leaving, then?"

"I am. They are going back to Virginia soon, and—'tis a good place, but 'tis not my place. When my service is done, I had thought to find my way to Bristol, then from there take a ship bound for the New Found Land."

"Back to serve Mistress Kathryn?"

"Yes, I suppose so." What a small and simple life it seemed now, the colony that had once been a terrifying adventure. Tending to a plantation house, catching and curing fish, farming the rocky soil. Doing household tasks alongside Kathryn, helping care for her children as they grew. A small and simple life: the most appealing thing Nancy could imagine. "What will you do? Stay aboard the *Treasurer*?"

"No. I have been at sea long enough now. I want solid ground beneath my feet again. But I'll not go back to Cupids Cove without—ah, Nancy, I've not got the words for what I need to say."

"You will have to find some then, for I cannot read your mind."

"You should be able to. There's been but one thing on it all this long time."

"And yet—"

"Can you ever forgive me for what a fool I was aboard the *Treasurer*? See now, this is the part where words fail me." He stopped, looked down at his feet, took a long breath and looked up at her again. "When I thought you were dead—when I heard that the *Happy Adventure* had wrecked, and there was no woman among the survivors—"

"You heard that?"

Ned nodded and went on, his words coming all in a rush. "So I thought you were dead, and I signed on to the service of a man called Daniel Elfrith. He goes by the name of privateer, but in truth, he's a pirate. We did things—I did things—that shame me. That would shame you, if you knew of them. I could not see my way back—back to the man I'd been in Cupids Cove. The man who thought he was fit to be your husband."

"And now? What has changed?"

"I' truth, Nancy, I know not. I cannot change the past. But I've come to think—well, a man must go on living, after all. And the only life I could ever imagine wanting is with you. Back in the New Found Land, if you'll have me there."

"You fool. I would have had you here, there, or anywhere, if you'd not behaved like such an ass."

"Can you forgive me? And, mayhap, marry me after all?"

"This is three times now you've asked me to wed you."

"Third time's a charm, or so they tell me." He grinned, and she saw it: a ghost of the old Ned, the boy he had been.

The man before her now was someone she did not truly know, after all their years apart. And she was not the same young woman who had pledged herself to him on a clifftop overlooking the ocean in the New Found Land. They could never be, either of them, the old Nancy and

Ned, those children who had taunted each other in Master Gale's house in Bristol, those young colonists setting out to conquer a new world. *I am six-and-twenty*, Nancy thought, feeling suddenly old.

He held out his hand, and after a moment she took it. "I cannot have you asking for my hand in marriage every year or two—'twould be tiresome," said Nancy. "Best if I say yes, and whatever happens afterward, we face it together."

TWENTY-EIGHT

An Old Acquaintance Is Renewed

"I MEAN TO GET THAT FENCE REPAIRED TODAY," NICHOLAS said, as they broke their fast that morning, "before Frank and I work on the boat."

"Good, for we need that fence—the goats are already getting at the garden. Without a fence, they'll dig up every blessed turnip we put in the ground," Kathryn said. She was trying to eat her own pottage with one hand and, with the other, hold the baby while he nursed. Jemmy was six months old now and getting too lively to suckle easily; he wanted always to be sitting up and looking around.

The room was fairly a-bubble with children as Daisy served up everyone's breakfast: Kathryn's two older children and Bess's two had been kept at table till they had all eaten something, but now all four of them were playing with a ball, kicking it back and forth in front of the hearth—at least, Will, Jonathan, and Alice were kicking, and Bess's littlest one, Molly, was trying her best to join in the fun. But, still being at the stage of toddling about and falling down frequently, she could not quite manage kicking.

"Get away now, all of ye! If one of you falls into the fire, your mothers will be blaming me!" Daisy shooed them away like chickens and they tumbled towards the door, Bess rising from her own meal to follow them out.

With the distraction of his siblings and their playmates gone, Jemmy settled down to finish his breakfast in more contentment, leaving Kathryn free to discuss the garden fence with her husband. "I've a mind to plant oats this year, but since we had none last year, 'twill mean a trip down to Cupids Cove to trade. Though we may have no more good fortune with it than with the wheat and the rye and the barley."

"If there is a grain that will grow in this land, we've not found it yet," her husband said, "but you may as well try the oats—mayhap our soil here is sweeter than that in Cupids Cove. We can take the pinnace and sail down there in the afternoon, if you care for the trip—a ship came in yesterday, and 'twould be good to see who is aboard, and what news, and what they have to trade."

Spring was always an exciting time as the ships began making the crossing from England again, and Kathryn was more than happy for an opportunity to sail down the shore to Cupids Cove and see what the latest vessel from England carried with it. She left the house and children in Daisy's and Bess's care; she thought Jemmy big enough now to be apart from her for a night, and Bess could feed him on goat's milk and thin pottage. Kathryn relished the thought of a day and a night free from the duties of caring for her children, and now that Jemmy was taking some solid food he nursed less often, so her breasts might not be too tender and full of milk if she stole a day away.

There was a clean, fresh wind in their sails as they made the short journey down to Cupids Cove; the sun danced on the water and although the day was chilly, it truly felt like spring.

The same thought must have been in her husband's mind, for he said, "We have made it through another winter here, little wife."

"Each one feels like a prize. As if we should get a medal, as generals do for battles won."

His tone turned more serious. "I hope it is not always a battle for you, to live here. We could still return to Bristol, you know."

A year had passed since word had come that Nicholas's father was dead. Last summer, he had been unsure whether to sell his house and business there, cut all ties with Bristol, or to return home. Kathryn was pleased that he cared for her opinion, but she had not known what to advise. In most ways, she was well contented with the New Found Land

and the home they were building there, but she knew that if Nicholas sold his Bristol property, they would likely never return to England. That seemed a huge step to take.

Now, on this cold spring day with the fresh salt breeze in her face, she felt surer than she had in a long time. "You must do what you think best, of course," she said, "but I am well content to stay here, even if it means we never see Bristol again. This is our home now—I truly feel it. For all we've suffered here, this is where we belong."

"In truth, Kathryn, 'tis glad I am to hear you say it. The same thought has been in my mind, but I did not want to bind you to this place if you longed to be back in England. If you are as content to stay here as I am, then I will take up Rob's offer to buy the shop. I'll be no more a Bristol cobbler, but a New Found Land planter."

She gave him a brilliant smile: the thought that they were together in this, truly committed to their adventure together, made her heart sing. As did the sight of Cupids Cove in the distance—for all her troubled memories of the place, it was where her life in the New World had begun. She had landed on its shores five years ago full of excitement and hope. Coming back now as a guest, as a planter's wife with her own foothold in this land, she felt, despite everything, like the heroine of a story whose tale was about to reach its happy ending.

Cupids Cove had both grown and shrunk in these past few years. In one way, it had grown larger, flinging out its tentacles along the shore as some of the settlers followed Nicholas Guy's example and cleared land for plantations of their own. But fewer people lived in the settlement itself; between those who had returned to England and those who had started their own plantations, Governor Mason presided over a smaller colony than Governor John Guy had, and the village had not the sense of bustle and growth that it had had in those earliest years.

Kathryn liked the governor's sensible, no-nonsense wife, Mistress Anne Mason, who always welcomed her warmly on her visits. On this occasion, as she had done before, Mistress Mason offered the Guys a bed in the governor's house.

There were people in Cupids Cove that Kathryn was glad to see again, old friends from the time she had lived there. Jem Holworthy and his wife Elsie were still there, as was John Crowder, who had married a girl who came out from Bristol the year before. Holworthy talked of starting his own plantation in a year or so—his father was a well-off Bristol businessman who would no doubt back the venture—and he had invited the Crowders to come work for him when he struck out on his own. While the men talked with Nicholas about clearing and building and fishing, the women wanted Kathryn's opinion on how life on a plantation differed from life in the settlement.

Two people she was not pleased to see were George Whittington and his wife Nell; George had stayed in Cupids Cove and was making himself quite the big man in the colony, and Nell, who had been a humble serving-girl when she first came out from Bristol, put on more airs than the governor's wife did. Sam and Sally Butler had moved on to their own land, which pleased Kathryn; she had no more desire to meet them again than she did the Whittingtons, for she still blamed all of them for accusing Nancy of witchcraft.

But Anne Mason was soothing company. New to Cupids Cove, she knew nothing of the troubles that had happened that first year. Indeed, with folk coming and going these past few years, Kathryn did not find the place as haunted by memories of the past as she had once done. She and Anne Mason went aboard the ship, the *Fair Wind* out of Portsmouth, to see the goods available for sale. Kathryn, Daisy, and Bess had all learned to make homespun, trading for wool with folk here in Cupids Cove who kept sheep. But Kathryn yearned for softer, lighter fabrics that could only be obtained from England. The gowns she had brought out with her five years ago were faded and worn thin now; only her red mockado wedding gown remained whole, while all the others had been cut down and altered to make clothes for the children. When they could be made over no more, garments were cut up to make quilts for the beds or hooked rugs for the chilly floors.

"I would make myself a gown out of this," Kathryn said to Mistress Mason, holding up a length of blue uncut velvet, "but wherever would I wear it? 'Twould make more sense to get more russet to make smocks for the children and a few shirts for the master, for I've no need of pretty gowns."

"Nonsense, you must not think like that—make yourself a lovely gown and wear it on a Sunday or a holiday, in your own household. When we have no society, we must make our own," Mistress Mason said, choosing a similar length of velvet in dark green for herself.

"I might be persuaded to your way of thinking," Kathryn said, "if it would give me an excuse to buy this." She ran her hand over the fabric, soft and warm as a summer's day. What matter if no-one but her husband and servants ever saw her in it? She ought to have one gown finer than Daisy or Bess could wear, if only to remind herself of her station.

"'Tis a strange life," she said to Mistress Mason, as they left the ship with their bags and bundles of goods. "My husband and I are lord and lady of our own estate, yet we work as hard as any peasant farmers! Look at my hands!"

She thrust them out in front of the other woman: they had been pretty hands when she was a stonemason's daughter in Bristol. She had had to do her fair share, then, of the work around the house, but she had been able to keep her hands pretty all the same. Now they were roughened and calloused with the hard labour around the farm and on the fish flake.

"But you have your own land," Mistress Mason said. The implication was unspoken but clear: people of Nicholas and Kathryn's class could not own such a stretch of land in England. Only the gentry could dream of such an estate—but the gentry would have an entire village full of folk to work the land, while Kathryn and Nicholas still had only three men and two women servants, with an additional two men hired on for the fishing season. Perhaps this ship might carry a few young men willing to stay in the colony, who might be persuaded to come and settle and work on the Guys' land.

Mistress Mason had invited the captain and officers of the ship to sup with them, "So," she told Kathryn, "we shall hear all the news from England."

And indeed, as the afternoon's work drew to a close and the Masons' household began to gather for the evening meal, four men joined them—the captain, the bo'sun, the quartermaster, and a fourth man who was not dressed as a sailor. His clothes proclaimed him to be a young man of some rank and status, and Kathryn was idly wondering who he might be when he turned his gaze upon her and her heart turned over in her chest.

"Mistress Guy," he said, cutting through the introductions and crossing the room to take her hand. "What a pleasure! I had heard you were still in this country, but that you no longer dwelt at Cupids Cove." He took her hand and brought it briefly to his lips.

"You heard right, Master Willoughby." She was momentarily so dazzled by his unexpected appearance that she wondered if simple *Master Willoughby* was correct; was he Lord Thomas, or Sir Thomas, or some such thing? But no, his father was only a knight, though still many levels of grandeur above herself or anyone else here at Cupids Cove. She had called him *Tom* and *Oh, Thomas!* once, breathing the words against his naked chest as he held her in his arms—but that was in another life. "My husband and I have our own grant of land up the shore. I am here only to trade."

"I hope you have been well."

"Exceedingly so. I have three children now." As she said the word *children* she felt the soft, lightly painful swelling of milk in her breasts; a little leaked out onto her shift and she felt embarrassed, though he could not have seen it beneath her gown. "Our family thrives."

"Indeed. Quite the colonial matron, are you not?" He turned from her as if there could be nothing more of interest to say to a colonial matron, greeted her husband, and then went to talk to Governor Mason.

"You knew him back in England?" Mistress Mason asked, having seen the little interaction between the two.

"No. He was out here before, in Cupids Cove, the first year I came out. He did not like it very much and returned home at the end of the season. You know who he is? Sir Percival Willoughby's son."

"Ah yes, we all know of Sir Percival's interest in the colony," Mistress Mason said. "No doubt the son has come out to look to his father's investment. Shall we sit and eat?"

When Kathryn thought of the things that had happened during that crowded, confused last summer she spent in Cupids Cove, it all rolled together in her mind—George Whittington's accusation, her own reckless decision to take Thomas Willoughby to bed in hopes he would use his authority to set Nancy free, the sudden removal to the new plantation, the pirate attack. The grief over all that had been lost, especially over Nancy, blotted out so much else in Kathryn's memory. When she remembered Thomas Willoughby in her waking hours, it was as a foolish mistake that she had somehow got away with. *I never think of him*, she would have told herself.

But she did think of him. She thought of him in the darkness of her bed, when her husband reached for her. Not every time: most of the time she was able to think of doing her duty as a good wife, of the children they would have together. Sometimes, though, memories broke through the darkness: memories of being touched not merely with a sense of kindly duty, but with wild passion, with the urgency with which drowning men fight for air. Thomas Willoughby's mouth, his hands, his body—they were still there in her memory, despite all her careful efforts to forget them. She could not quite push aside the memory of how it felt when his fingers awoke her to her own pleasure, and she had thought she might go mad with delight.

She thought of him, too, when she looked at her daughter Alice, her little fair-haired pixie child who looked nothing like Nicholas Guy or Kathryn herself. She had their brown eyes, not Thomas's telltale ice blue. But she was so fair, and there was something in her delicate face that made Kathryn think of Thomas Willoughby.

At any rate, she had told herself, whenever those memories arose, that it did not matter. Thomas Willoughby was back in England, likely married to some young woman of good family. What happened in the Cupids Cove colony concerned him no longer. He was living the life he had been born to live, while Kathryn could keep him tucked safely in memory, like an old brooch pinned to the inside of a gown.

Now he was back.

They had no more conversation that evening; it was all men's talk about the price of fish, the finances of the Newfoundland Company, the quarrels between the Bristol investors and the London men, the possibility of starting a second colony. Thomas, who had once seemed so uninterested in the business of the colony, was in the thick of conversation, plying Governor Mason and Nicholas Guy with questions about Cupids Cove and the handful of plantations that had been started around it. What were the advantages to year-round settlement over the summer fishery? Had there been any more development of the promised mines that would bring great riches from beneath the earth? Had the settlers made further contact with the natives and established trade with them? What did the governor think of bringing Negro servants out to work the fishery? And what of pirates—had there been much trouble with them?

The men's talk washed over the table; Mistress Mason asked Kathryn about the everyday details of life in her household and about her children and servants. Kathryn was always happy for the company of another woman, someone new to talk with besides Bess and Daisy, who were dear but too familiar. But now she was distracted, for every time Willoughby's clear, high-born accents cut across the other men's voices in conversation, her heart skipped a beat.

He did not go back to the ship with the other men, but took up the offer of a bed in the governor's house. Only bed-curtains and other sleeping bodies separated him from where Kathryn lay beside her husband. She lay awake half the night, aware of his nearness.

On the morrow, she thought, they would sail their pinnace back to the plantation, and she need have no further dealings with Thomas Willoughby. But when morning came, Nicholas asked her if she would mind spending another day.

"I know 'tis hard for you to be away from the baby," he said, "but there is further business I want to do here with the governor—some of it concerning this matter of piracy. I have told him all we learned from our dealings with the Pikes, and there is no doubt that this Captain Sly and some other pirates besides have used Harbour Grace as a base for their raids. 'Tis most like, as we suspected, that Master and Mistress Pike are deep into the business, trading with Mistress Pike's people back in Ireland. If Bristol men want to establish a second colony along the shore, this nest of pirates must be rooted out."

Kathryn's breasts were aching, and she wondered if one of the women here had anything she could use to make a poultice for the soreness, since she would not be able to nurse again until the morrow. It was too early, for certain, to wean Jemmy, though the lad would likely thrive well enough without her for another day. "I can manage," she told him. "'Twill give me another day to gossip with Mistress Mason."

It proved to be a busy day in Cupids Cove, for the caplin struck in—the small fish that arrived in the foggy, cool days of early June. The caplin ran for only a few days and were most easy to catch—they could be captured in small nets or buckets, or even in bare hands if you did not mind the cold, wriggling feel of a fish between your palms. In each of the last two springs, Kathryn and her household had had a fine time catching them in the cool June evenings, building a fire to cook and eat some on the beach afterwards. Jonathan and Will would be big enough this year to take their little wooden pails and catch a few for themselves. *Tomorrow evening*, she thought.

She and Anne Mason went down to the beach in late afternoon as the settlers, mostly men but a few of the young women among them, ran about on the beach catching the small silver fish. It was almost a festive time, the incoming waves soaking the hems of the women's kirtles, the men running knee-deep into the freezing water with their shoes and stockings off, everyone laughing and cheering as one bucket or net after another was filled. It was not that they were such a delicacy to eat, though there would be fires on the beach here this evening as well, and some of the caplin could be dried and smoked for later eating. Their best use was as fertilizer for the garden. But they were a sure sign of the coming of the codfish, an important milestone in the turning of the year.

"Ah, how I've missed these rustic frolics," said a voice in her ear. "The peasants on our estate in Nottinghamshire would be much at home here, I do believe."

She did not turn to look at Thomas Willoughby. "Well, we are simple folk here, sir."

"Yes, you are. Well I remember being put to work like a common fisherman, drying and salting the fish on the flakes."

"You hated that work."

"I did. Indeed, there was only one thing I enjoyed in all that summer."

She swallowed hard, still watching the happy tableau of fishers on the beach. "'Twas a long time ago. Years ago."

"And in all those years, Mistress Guy, did you miss me?"

"I have been busy. Keeping house, tending the land, making fish, raising my children. I had little time to think of—mistakes I made in the past."

"Mistakes?"

Now, at last, she turned and looked up at him, meeting his blue eyes defiantly. "No. I spoke wrong—'twas not a mistake. It was a bargain. And you kept your side of it—spoke out to defend my maid. So our bargain was done, with satisfaction on both sides."

Now he laughed softly. "Ah yes, I had forgot you made a bargain with me. What was it—was she accused of adultery, some such thing?"

"Witchcraft. I feared for her life, and you promised to speak in her defence."

"And that was all, was it? A bargain, made and kept? No pleasure in it? I'd have sworn otherwise, at the time."

A little distance away on the strand, Mistress Mason glanced towards them. Kathryn scanned the beach for her husband, but he must still be with the governor, talking of important affairs. Men's affairs.

"Come with me, Kathryn."

"What?"

"When I leave here. I am going to a plot of land I've told my father I'll clear for him, and build on. I mean to be a planter here too—for a time, at least. 'Twould be less lonely if you were to keep me company."

"You are mad. I am a married woman, a mother."

"You were all that before, and still—"

"I told you, 'twas a bargain, and 'tis done."

"Then make another bargain with me. My pleasure in return for yours—a simple exchange."

"Do you think you can come here and claim another man's wife, like plucking an apple from a tree?"

"Would Master Guy want you, if he knew what you had done?" His lazy smile that had once looked like such a promise now seemed like a threat. "I heard you talking of your children to Mistress Mason. Your second-born—'twould be about nine months, would it not, after I left Cupids Cove, that he came along?"

"She," Kathryn said, and could have bitten her tongue. But she went on. "I have a little girl, Alice. But she is my husband's daughter."

"A daughter. Well. Hardly worth making trouble over. If it were a son, that would be a different matter. Does your husband have any doubts? No? How sad 'twould be if anyone planted any doubts in his head."

"I'll not stay to bandy words with you," Kathryn said, and walked away towards Anne Mason and Elsie Holworthy. She did not want to turn back and look, but she did. And he was still looking, still smiling, arms crossed over his chest. Like a young lord who knew he had only to ask and take what he desired.

He spoke no more to her that night, as the colonists ate caplin on the beach. There was singing and dancing. Kathryn stayed close to her husband, or to Mistress Mason, and avoided being alone.

But in the morning, as she and Nicholas loaded the pinnace with their new purchases and her husband bade farewell to the governor and the other men, Thomas Willoughby was there. He shook Nicholas's hand.

"We shall be neighbours, Master Guy, when I go to clear my land. No doubt I will be coming to you for advice on planting and fishing and managing an estate."

"I'd be glad to give you the benefit of my experience, sir, for what it may be worth," Nicholas said, bowing his head a little in respect to the younger man's status. "And I hope we may be good neighbours."

"The very best, I am sure," Willoughby said, and turned to offer his hand to Kathryn. "And to you, Mistress Guy—may we meet again soon."

Her hand, where he had held it, felt as warm as if he had pressed into it a piece of burning coal.

TWENTY-NINE

A Hope Is Extinguished

IN THE END, THEY SAILED NOT ON THE *TREASURER*, BUT ON another ship, the *George*. Ned had arranged for passage as far as Plymouth, where the Virginia-bound ship would stop to take on supplies before crossing the ocean. From Plymouth, he told Nancy, they could either find a ship for the New Found Land or make their way to Bristol.

The mood of the Virginia party was sombre. Most of the Indians, by now, had the coughing sickness, some worse than others. Tomocomo was recovering, and Matachanna and the young men had escaped falling ill at all. But the three young maids were all sick, and worst of all, Rebecca Rolfe herself was now weak with coughing and fever.

There was much debate over whether any of them were well enough to travel. Master Dale and Master Rolfe finally decided that Betty and Sally, the weakest of the party, should be left behind in London in the care of some members of the Virginia Company.

Mistress Rolfe insisted that she and baby Thomas were well enough to make the journey. "What do we gain by staying here longer?" she said to Nancy, who had brought her some broth. "The air of the city is poison to our people. The maids we are leaving behind will not live. I do not think my son and I will live, if we stay longer." She paused for a long, racking series of coughs. "And I must go home with Tomocomo, to tell my father what I know now about the English."

What does she know of us? Nancy wondered. Over the months she had seen the eager curiosity, the interest in her surroundings that Mistress Rolfe had shown upon their arrival, dwindle like a spark in a dying fire. It was not only the illness, though that was surely part of it. Ever since the visit to court, the Indian woman had seemed like a light that was dimmed. She had sat to have her portrait made, and the engraving showed a stern-faced woman older than her years. Captain Smith, the first Englishman she had known long ago when she was a child in Virginia, came at last to visit her, and she refused to speak with him at all for nigh on an hour, then chided him for breaking his vows to her father. She looked, Nancy thought, like a warrior defeated in battle.

But now the Indian princess was going home, and Nancy was parting ways with the Virginians. She had, along with the promised purse of coin for her service, a letter from Master Rolfe giving her a character and commending her services. "For none of us knows what the future may hold, and whether you remain in England or go back to the New Found Land, there may be a time when you need a word of recommendation."

Indeed, Nancy and Ned's future was as uncertain as that of the Virginia party, save that neither of them was ill, and they were together. Mary wept bitterly as their little party boarded this ship; she could not bear the thought of leaving her two kinswomen behind in this land that was as alien to them as it had been when they landed.

"I should have stayed with them," she said to Nancy, who stood at the rail with her and Matachanna as the ship slipped away from the London docks.

"They have each other, and they will be well cared for—I hope," Matachanna said.

"I hope they will."

Mary fell silent, but Matachanna said to Nancy, "I wish you would come back with us."

"You know I never meant to go back to Virginia."

"But Tsenacommacah is—it is the heart of the world." She used the Powhatan name for Virginia, as all her people did when they spoke of it.

"For you, because it is your home."

"And you—will you go to your home?"

Nancy had no answer for that question yet. The New Found Land was full of possibilities, and Ned was eager to begin again over there. They talked of this as the ship sailed down the Thames—how they might go back to working for the Guys, or even see if the colony's masters would grant them a small plot of land of their own. "'Tis a new world, Nancy—we might be lord and lady there ourselves, in time!"

Nancy laughed—her first laughter since boarding this ship of sickness and sorrow. "Not many lords and ladies in the New Found Land, you know that."

He took her hands in his. "Let us find a church that will marry us, as soon as we are off this ship," he said. "Before we go back to Cupids Cove."

"We should go to Bristol," she said. "Be married in St. Stephen's Church, so your family and the Gales and Aunt Tib can be there. Then go...home."

Home. The word did not mean to her what it meant to Pocahontas and Matachanna and the rest. To them, *home* was the place where their ancestors had lived for generations, where the land was as much a part of them as they were of it. There were, she thought suddenly, people in the New Found Land who belonged to the land the way the Powhatan belonged to Virginia. She had never laid eyes on those people.

That thought still troubled her as she stood in the captain's tiny cabin, loaned to the Rolfes for the journey, taking away soiled clothing and linens while Matachanna urged her sister to eat. "Perhaps she can drink the broth, at least," the Powhatan woman said to Nancy, then turned to her ailing sister and spoke quietly in their own tongue, urging her to eat. "Matoaka," she called her: her private name, shared only with those who loved her best.

Rebecca Rolfe coughed a hard, tearing cough, before replying. The Powhatan women always spoke to each other in English when they were around Master Rolfe or other Englishmen, but often used their own language when they were together. Nancy had picked up a good few words of the Indians' tongue, though she could speak it only a little herself. She knew their word for *No*, and for *death*, and for *child*. Even had she not, she would have been able to guess at the meaning of the sisters' hushed conversation: Matachanna telling her sister she must fight to live, for her child's sake.

Nancy could hear the distress in Matachanna's urging and the despair in Mistress Rolfe's replies without needing to know all the words they said. She paused at the door of the cabin, her arms full of linen. This moment between Mistress Rolfe and her sister was too private, she thought, to be shared with an English servant. As she turned to go, she heard the Indian princess say *Powhatan*—did she mean to name her father, or her people, or both? And then, a few more words in the native tongue that Nancy knew—the word for *enemy*; the word for *defeat*. She thought, perhaps, that Pocahontas had said *We are defeated by our enemy*, but she could not be sure she had heard it aright.

Nancy went out, closing the cabin door behind her. In truth, this was not for her to hear.

Tomocomo was waiting on the deck. "How fares she?" he said. The older Indian man spoke the least English of any of the Virginia natives, but even he could make himself well understood by now.

"She is—very weak," Nancy said.

"She is dying. And now she has seen England, her thoughts are the same to my thoughts. If more of your people come over the sea, we will never rule our land again."

He went past her into the cabin, to sit with Pocahontas. Nancy could not think of her as Mistress Rolfe, now; the English name was ebbing from her as the English tongue was, leaving her once again Powhatan's daughter.

Nancy tried to tell Ned something of what the mistress had said. But Ned did not know Mistress Rolfe; he had only seen this weak shadow of a woman that remained of her. "I suppose the natives in the New Found Land would feel the same, if we brought one of them over to England," he said. "Surely they must look at our cities, our castles, our ships, and know that we will rule all the New World someday."

"I've no wish to rule anything. I just want my own little house, my own plot of land, my own quiet life."

"I wonder if the folk in Cupids Cove have seen any more of the natives since we have been away? Perhaps they have made treaties with them. Perhaps..."

Nancy guessed what he was thinking: that having their own little plot of land might well mean taking someone else's, as it did for the Virginia settlers and the Powhatan. But she pushed the thought away. The Indians of the New Found Land never came to the shores near Cupids Cove; the island was big. Surely there was land enough for all? They were not like the Powhatan, in any case, planting crops and building towns; they were hunters, moving through the forest almost like the beasts they hunted. It was not the same thing, she assured herself: not the same thing at all.

Slowly, London slipped away from them. They were still on the river, not yet on the open sea. Master Rolfe went to the captain. "My wife is too sick to go on," Nancy heard him say. "We cannot—she must rest, at least."

"We will make port at Gravesend," the captain said. "You can take her ashore, find a doctor."

Mistress Rolfe had seen a doctor—all the sick people had—in London. The Gravesend doctor could do no more for her than the London man had. Most of the party stayed aboard the ship when they docked there, but the Rolfes were invited to stay in the minister's house.

"You think the Indian princess will die?" said Ned, when Nancy returned to the ship after helping bring Thomas Rolfe and his parents' baggage ashore.

"She cannot eat. She's so thin—'tis as if she's fading away."

"Remember the sickness in Cupids Cove, that winter? When Matt died, and Molly and the rest?"

Nancy nodded. It was not the same sickness, but it stole people in the same way—slipped them out of their lives bit by bit, till they disappeared and only an empty shell remained. She had not watched people die before going to Cupids Cove. Now she had seen it so often, in so many ways.

It was Matachanna who told Nancy, later that night. Just as the sun set, with her English husband and her Powhatan kinsmen around her borrowed bedside, Mistress Rolfe—Rebecca, Matoaka, Pocahontas, that woman of many names—had died.

They buried her in the churchyard in Gravesend. The minister there said the burial service over the grave. When all the English mourners had gone, Nancy saw that Tomocomo, Matachanna, Mary and the two Powhatan young men lingered. Tomocomo's head was bowed in prayer—doubtless a prayer in his own language, to his own gods, over the grave of his niece who had been baptized and buried a Christian.

THIRTY

Two Wanderers Return

T HE SHIP MADE READY TO SAIL ON FROM GRAVESEND.
Little Thomas Rolfe was growing better from the illness that
had taken his mother, but his father was deep in despair.

"You cannot take the boy with you," Master Dale told the grieving
father. "He is too weak still—he would not survive the voyage. Leave
him with your family here in England until he is stronger."

"He should be in his mother's homeland," Matachanna said.
"Tomocomo and I will bring him back to Powhatan land, raise him
among his people."

"No!" Master Rolfe sounded shocked. "Thomas is an English child. If
I cannot care for him myself, he will be cared for here in England until
he is able to join me. I have lost one wife and child, and now a second
wife. I will not lose another child."

Before they left Gravesend, Master Rolfe sent a message to his
brother in Norfolk, explaining his wishes for the child and asking that
he meet their ship in Plymouth. When they came to Plymouth, Master
Rolfe's brother was not there, but a letter was waiting. "My brother says
that Sir Lewis Stuckley will take charge of my son until he can come
to bring Thomas to Norfolk," John Rolfe told Nancy. "But Sir Lewis
will not arrive before our ship sails. Will you keep my boy safe and care
for him until his guardian arrives? I will pay you extra, and pay for your
keep till he comes."

"How can we say no?" Nancy asked Ned.

"Of course we will do it. 'Tis not as if we are in such a great hurry to be anywhere, that we cannot wait awhile here in Plymouth, for the little lad's sake."

Ned found them a room at an inn in Plymouth, where it seemed most natural to present themselves as husband and wife. Together he and Nancy and little Thomas Rolfe bid farewell to John Rolfe, to Tomocomo and Matachanna, to Mary and the other Virginia natives. Mary threw her arms around Nancy and wept. Matachanna, more reserved, took Nancy's hands in hers.

"You have been my friend," the Indian woman said. "I am sorry we must part."

"And you have been mine. I hope all will go well, for you and your people."

Matachanna shook her head. "I do not think so, now that my sister is dead. Perhaps even if she had lived—" She paused, and brought her attention back to Nancy. "Go well and in peace."

Nancy had been embarrassed when Mary had wept, but now she felt tears spring to her own eyes. When all had boarded, she and Ned and Thomas stood on the dock and watched the ship sail for Virginia with the remnants of the party that had sailed west with such high hopes a year before.

Thomas, still crying out for Mama and Papa, slept poorly those first nights after the ship sailed, and threw fits of temper. Ned took to carrying him about the streets and markets of Plymouth on his shoulders, which seemed to be the only thing that soothed and entertained the child, "and 'tis little trouble to me," Ned said, "for he weighs little, and 'tis a mort of pleasure to walk about the streets and see people buying and selling and talking and working, after so many years out of England."

"Do you miss it? Should we settle here, rather than back in the colony?" Nancy asked. They were walking hand in hand through a marketplace, Ned's free hand holding Thomas's legs. The child's hands were knotted in Ned's hair, and he shouted with delight when a juggler passed by, tossing bright-coloured balls in the air.

"Nay, 'tis a grand pageant to see it all about me, but I'd not want to go back to this life. I'll be well pleased to cross the ocean one more time, and then never again."

"At least you no longer get seasick."

He laughed and squeezed her hand. Since they had left the ship, Ned seemed freer, more lighthearted; there was more of his old self in the new man he had become. And she could not help but admire his easy way with Thomas and imagine him with children of his own. *Of our own*, she thought.

After three days, Sir Lewis Stuckley came to take charge of the boy. He was grateful enough to offer them a seat in his carriage as far as Exeter, where he turned off the main road to go to his estate at Affeton. Thomas clung first to Ned, then to Nancy: the last person he would see for a long time who had known his mother, Nancy thought. She kissed his soft brown cheek and thought of Pocahontas, and of Matachanna, and the land they called Tsenacommacah.

From Exeter they walked towards Bristol, sleeping some nights in inns and other times by the roadside or in a copse of trees. The spring weather was clear and fine, and it felt like a carefree adventure, a welcome respite from their real lives. There was time, in those long days and nights, to tell each other the tales of the past years, of the curious things that had happened to them, the places they had been and the people they had known, since they had been apart.

Some of their stories were things to wonder at: the Powhatan town in Virginia, the Lenape town where the Dutch traded, the time they had both spent in the Bermuda Isles. Other things were harder to talk of. When Ned told Nancy the story of the raid on the plantation in the Indies, of the slaves and how he killed a man defending the property, she was silent a long time. She understood, then, a little better why he had seemed so changed, why he talked of not being worthy of her.

When she told him about Diligence Brown on the *Happy Adventure*, it was late at night. That was one night when they slept in an inn, sharing a mattress on the floor with other travellers snoring nearby. Ned was silent then, too, for a long time, but he took Nancy in his arms and kissed her and said, "I wish I could wipe that memory from your mind."

Nancy shook her head. "I have wanted to forget, but now I know I cannot. It happened to me—all of it."

Then, after five long days of walking, Bristol. The place they had always called home. They crossed the bridge into the city and saw it all spread out before them, the familiar streets and churches, the remains of the old city walls.

"Let us go to your brother's house first," Nancy said. She was curiously reluctant, having come so far, to go to the Gales' house. Ned had been here only a few months ago; he had seen and spoken to them. She could wait.

Ned's brother was cleaning up the bakeshop at the end of a day's work when they arrived. His face brightened. "Ah, Ned—you've come back. Mother didn't dare to hope she'd see you again. And—can it be Nancy Ellis?"

Upstairs, Ned's mother greeted them with the same warmth, and she pulled Nancy's face down to kiss her. "I am so glad to see you with my Ned," she said, and then her face grew serious. "You have only just come into town? You've not been to see the Gales yet?"

"No, we had thought to go there tomorrow," Ned said, but his mother shook her head.

"Go tonight," she said. "They'll want to see you. It has been a hard time, since you were here, Ned. We've had plague in Bristol."

Dusk was falling as they reached the little house near St. Stephen's church, where the ring of hammers in John Gale's stoneyard would once have been heard in a long spring evening like this. Ned stopped and gazed around at the empty yard. "Do you remember what you said to me, when I was a boy with a foolish fancy of being in love with Kathryn?"

Nancy nodded. "That John Gale had two sons living, and no need to leave his shop to an apprentice boy who would marry his daughter." That ordered world they had lived in seemed so far away now, as they knocked at the door of the oddly still house.

The young girl who answered was the very image of Kathryn at seventeen, dark curls under her white cap, and shining brown eyes that looked wet with tears. It took Nancy a moment to piece together her image with the little girl who had been running about in short skirts five years ago. "Lily," she said. "Lily—'tis I, Nancy. I have only just come back and heard the news. I am so very sorry."

Lily brought them inside to Tibby, who was mending by the hearth. When she saw Nancy, Tibby sprang up and crossed the room in half a heartbeat, taking Nancy in her arms. "Oh, you dear, dear girl. I never thought—even when I saw our Ned here, I never dreamed to have you back again. Oh, the Lord has not forsaken us after all."

The plague had come swiftly to Bristol, only a few weeks after Ned's visit. Mistress Gale had been the first to fall ill, then John, Phillip, and Lily, all in a row. Lily had recovered as her mother and brothers grew sicker. Tibby and Master Gale, spared the illness, tended to the sick as best they could. Within a fortnight, Lily's mother and two brothers were dead.

"And your father...is he...?" Nancy could not find the words to frame how Master Gale must be.

"He's like the ghost of himself," Lily said. "He goes about his work, and then I'll come out to bring him a bite to eat and there he is with the mallet in his hand, frozen like a statue."

"Does he have any apprentices, anyone to help him?"

Lily nodded. "'Tis Walter does most of the work now—he's a mason in his own right, but he was finding it hard to get work. Papa would be out of business altogether, I'd say, were it not for the guild and for Walter. Come summer, now, Walter and me will marry. Then we can both care for Papa, and for the stoneyard too."

She sounded not lighthearted, as a bride should, but content enough under the terrible circumstances. Unlike her father, she was young, and able to think about new beginnings. If Walter was not, perhaps, her first choice for a bridegroom, she did not speak of the coming marriage with dread.

"Go back to your brother's house," Nancy told Ned. "They will want to see you, and I will stay here with Aunt Tib."

When Nancy had paid her respects to Master Gale, who seemed to have aged twenty years since she had last seen him, she sat by the hearth with her aunt and Lily, telling tales and listening to them. It was, in some ways, like the long hours of tale-telling she and Ned had shared on the road to Bristol, but while she had tried to be truthful and tell Ned everything, even the most painful parts of her story, she shielded Tibby from the worst of it, and told her only the parts of the story that led to the happy ending.

Tibby had but one tale, though they had spent five years apart: the tale of those two weeks in February when, one after another, the Gales had fallen victim to the plague. She wept as she relived those terrible hours and days, and at the end Nancy put her arms around Tibby and said, "How awful. I hardly know how you survived, but I am so glad you did, so that I could see you again."

Tibby dabbed at her eyes with her apron. "Oh, I survived as I always have. Turn your hand—"

"—to the task at hand," Nancy finished. "If only you knew how many times those words have saved me, these past five years."

Lily and Walter might wait till full summer for their wedding, but Ned and Nancy had no mind to delay so long. Ned went the next morning to the minister at St. Stephen's, to have the banns read on Sunday, so that they could be wed in a few weeks. The rest of the day he spent on the Bristol docks talking to sailors, trying to find when a ship might be leaving for the New Found Land.

"Seems a vessel called the *Fair Haven* is sailing for the New Found Land in the middle of May," he announced, returning to the Gale house. "So we will have time for a wedding, and leave-taking, and then be on our way." He hesitated a moment. "If...that is still what you want?"

"What, the wedding, or the ship?"

"Either one."

"Either and both, Ned Perry," she assured him. "You'll not back out of marrying me now, and then we'll set sail for the colonies. I'll stay here with Tibby until we've said our vows—'twill be less of a scandal than if I stay with you."

"You know how little I care for scandal."

"Yes, but your mother and your brother may not feel the same. At any rate—" she glanced over her shoulder at Tibby, who was busy at the table preparing the evening meal—"'tis best for me to spend what time I can here, ere we go."

That night, when the chores were done, Master Gale went up to bed early, as was his wont, and Lily went out walking with Walter. Nancy sat with Tibby at the table in the dying hour of daylight. She told Tibby her plans, and posed a question. "When Ned and I go to the New Found Land, would you not think of coming out with us?"

"What—me? Go out to the colonies? At my time of life?"

Nancy had no idea what Tibby's age was—forty-five, perhaps, or fifty? "Truly, I mean it. What is left for you here? Your job was to care for the house and help raise the children, but there's no-one left save old Master Gale, and he will have Walter and Lily to care for him. You are my only flesh and blood in all the world, and if I am going back to the New Found Land, you should come with me. Mistress Kathryn will gladly take you into her household, and you will help her raise her children—and help me raise mine, when I have them. I—I want you with me."

Tibby shook her head. "You are a dear girl, but 'tis no life for an old woman. All them stories you told me—people dying of the scurvy, and the pirates, and all..."

"While you stayed safe here at home in Bristol, and half the family died of plague? No place on earth is safe, Aunt Tibby. We may as well be with those we love, when we can."

"Ah, well, as to that..." Tibby's voice trailed off, as if she were weighing how much to say. Then she looked up. "You know I'm not one for sentiment or foolishness. You're my own dear girl; I'm proud of you, and gladder to see you again than you'll ever know. But you've shown your strength, and you don't need old Tibby around to care for you. That's all I know of love—caring for them as needs you. And Master John—he needs me, Nancy. Even with Walter and Lily here—he'll still need me."

"He has no need of a maid, Tibby."

"No. Not a maid. He needs me."

Tibby's eyes were dark little beads in her round, work-lined face. "I don't ask you to understand—I've kept secrets from you too long, and I know young folk never like secrets. But Master John was good to me when he didn't have to be. Many a man with a young wife would have put a servant girl in my situation out in the street—never mind 'twas his own doing. But he kept me on, and kept the secret too, so the mistress never knew the rights of it."

"In...your position?" Nancy remembered the day she had left Bristol for Cupids Cove, that long-stifled urge to finally ask Tibby, *Are you my mother?*

She had long suspected there was something too tidy in the story of her parents dying of plague, and the Gales letting their servant take in an orphaned niece. There were threads here she had already begun to unravel, but when Tibby said "He needs me," she saw the one thread she could never have guessed.

Nancy thought of all the times Kathryn had said, "You are like a sister to me." Truer words than Kathryn could have known, though Nancy was not sure she could ever tell her that. Tibby was not one to tell a long tale of—what? A forbidden romance? Or simply a young man taking advantage of his maidservant? Yet there was affection there, it seemed—affection that had lasted through the long years, strong enough still to make Tibby feel she needed, or wanted, to stay with John Galc.

Nancy waited in silence, to see if Tibby wanted to tell the whole tale. But the older woman said nothing, and Nancy did not know what to ask. Instead, she put her own hands over Tibby's knotted, work-roughened ones, and Tibby turned hers so they were clasping hands, and so they sat hand in hand while the light died.

A Disappearance Is Remarked Upon

S EAGULLS SCREECHED OVERHEAD AND A FRESH BREEZE
blew off the water as Daisy More went down the path from the
house to the wharf. The boats were coming in; the men had been
out fishing since before dawn. Outside the house, the laughing, shouting
voices of small children vied with the gulls' cries. The sun shone in a
clear blue sky overhead; it was almost a perfect afternoon.

Almost.

Hurrying along the pebbled beach, Daisy tried to fight back the sick
feeling in her stomach. She often thought terrible things were about
to happen, and she was usually right. She knew there was a curse on
her when it came to men, which is why she could never marry again,
no matter how sweet young Isaac talked to her. But it might be bigger
than that; it might be that everyone she cared about was touched by
the curse. What would she do if...?

Stop your fretting, she told herself sternly. She had news to deliver
to the master, who was bringing his boat into shore laden with that
morning's catch. He would not want to hear about curses and ill luck,
only the simple facts.

Nicholas Guy leapt over the side of the boat into the shallow water
and helped his man Harry haul it in. The second boat, with Frank and
Isaac in it, was still out on the water. "You must be eager to get to the
splitting table today, Daisy," the master said with a laugh. Then he

took a good look at her still, frightened face. "What is it, Daisy? Has something happened to one of the children—or to Kathryn?"

"Yes, sir. 'Tis the mistress."

"Is she sick? Or hurt?" He had left Harry to the business of unloading the fish and was wiping off his hands on his breeches as he spoke, turning towards the path to go up to the house. Daisy scurried to fall into step beside him.

"This morning, sir, just after she nursed Jemmy, she put him down and went off into the woods to gather some berries. She said she'd be back well before noon, so we thought nothing of it. But when I gave the youngsters their dinner there was no sign of her, and Bess and I took turns having a look in the woods, calling for her, thinking she might have been hurt or lost. But she were clean gone, sir, no sign of her. Like she were took by the fairies."

"Lost her way in the woods, more like," Nicholas Guy said, glancing up at the sky as Daisy stumbled along in her master's wake up the path to the house. "Isaac and I will search for her—'tis a fine clear morning, but there's rain coming on later, and if Kathryn has gone astray in the woods we must find her. How long is it since she left?"

"Must be four hours or more now, sir. She'd never be gone so long, only picking berries and the like in the woods by herself. She always stays close to the house. We tried not to let the children know anything's amiss, but Alice is asking for her mama, and—" They were standing before the house now, the children playing with a ball, Bess bouncing the baby in her arms as she came to join Daisy and Master Nicholas.

"We looked all over, Master," Bess said, her voice tight with worry, "and 'tis as if the mistress just vanished. She's gone without a trace."

Afterword

HISTORICAL FICTION BEING A HYBRID OF HISTORY AND FIC-
tion, there are places in this narrative where I have strayed significantly
from known history in order to further the adventures of my fictional
characters. My personal guideline is always to try to stay within the
bounds of what *could have happened*, given the historical events we know.

Readers of *A Roll of the Bones* will know that this whole novel is
built upon a not-quite-historical premise. While pirate activity was fre-
quent and dangerous along the Newfoundland coast during the early
years of permanent English settlement, there is no record of pirates ever
attacking an English plantation, nor of them carrying away an English
serving-maid. That incident is wholly invented to drive the plot and
get my characters off the shores of Newfoundland and out into the rest
of the world.

Sheila NaGeira Pike, the Irish princess captured by pirates who
settled in Carbonear, is a popular figure in Newfoundland folklore, but
there is scant evidence that she and her husband actually existed. If
real people are somewhere behind the story, they could not have been
here as early as legend suggests—there is no evidence of any permanent English settlers in Newfoundland prior to the founding of Cupids.
However, I wanted to honour the legend by including Sheila as a
character, and I felt that *if* such people as she and her pirate husband

really had settled in Conception Bay at that time, they could have been involved in trade with the many pirates who frequented the area in those years.

Many of the people I describe as living at the Cupids colony were real people. (As I noted in *A Roll of the Bones*, I call the colony "Cupids Cove" for the sake of consistency; it was known by several names at this time.) Their personalities and motives are, of course, wholly imagined. These include Nicholas Guy, Philip Guy and his wife, John Mason and his wife Anne, George Whittington, and a few others whose names are drawn from the early accounts of the colony. While we don't know the name of Nicholas Guy's wife, we do know that their family remained in Newfoundland and became prosperous planters in Conception Bay for generations.

Similarly, the people that Ned and Nancy encounter on their travels include some real people, such as Captain Samuel Argall, Captain Daniel Elfrith, Reverend Alexander Whittaker, John Rolfe, and of course Pocahontas/Rebecca Rolfe.

Pocahontas is the most significant real-life person that I have used as a fictional character in this novel. Like most women and most Indigenous people of the Americas—thus, doubly so as an Indigenous woman—she is something of a "blank slate" for those who would imagine her story, as her own words are mostly unrecorded, except as they were filtered through the writing of Englishmen who had their own motives for ascribing certain thoughts and words to her.

Even once you strip away the Disney movie and other inaccurate and romanticized versions of her story, there is much debate about Pocahontas, her motives, her feelings about the English and about her own people. In the course of researching her story, I read works as diverse as *Pocahontas and the Powhatan Dilemma*, by Camilla Townsend; *Pocahontas, Powhatan, Opechancanough*, by Helen C. Rountree; *The True Story of Pocahontas*, by Linwood "Little Bear" Custalow; *Pocahontas: Medicine Woman, Spy, Entrepreneur, Diplomat*, by Paula Gunn Allen, and others books, both scholarly and popular.

The most believable picture that emerged to me is of a lively, intelligent, curious young woman caught up in events beyond her control, who did her best to use the little power available to her to advocate for her people, and who likely knew enough about the English—after marrying an Englishman, living among them, and travelling to London—to know that devastating impacts on the Powhatan and other Indigenous people were an inevitable result of colonization.

Though Pocahontas is the best-known Indigenous woman in American history, much about her life is subject to debate. The status she was accorded in English Virginia and her welcome in London were based on the idea that she was an "Indian princess," but it's likely that, although she was the chief's daughter, she did not hold a particularly elevated status in her own society. Though she certainly married John Rolfe, the tradition that she lived with him at Henrico rather than James Fort may not be historically accurate. During her time in England, she and the rest of the Virginia party stayed in two inns, one of which was named the Belle Sauvage; I have kept the party at one inn throughout their whole stay for simplicity. We know the time and place of Pocahontas's death, but the cause is unknown, as are so many other details about her life.

Bringing Nancy Ellis to Virginia and having her serve in the Rolfe household fulfilled one of my important goals for this story. From the beginning of this series, I wanted to explore the English colonization of Newfoundland as part of the larger context of what was happening all up and down the Atlantic coast in the first two decades of the seventeenth century—the English colonial experiments in Newfoundland, in Virginia, and in Bermuda, the French at Port Royal and Quebec, the Dutch in what became New Netherlands (later New York), the Spanish and Portuguese in the Caribbean, Latin America, and South America.

Along with the "discovery" of these lands by Europeans came the exploitation and mass murder of Indigenous people and the enslavement of Africans. I wanted my Newfoundland characters—and readers—to have some sense of this bigger world, this wider perspective, of which the little colony at Cupids Cove was one small part.

No Englishman in the early seventeenth century saw an American native person as a human being fully equal to himself. However, most did not initially support wiping out the Indigenous population either—they were aware they needed the knowledge of the Indigenous people, and trade with them, in order to survive in these lands. Reading the writing they left behind, it seems that most colonizers saw the ultimate goal as assimilation—convert the natives to Christianity, and eventually they would adapt to European ways. There was also, of course, the suggestion that they could be used as enslaved labour, the way Africans were already being used.

In trying to portray these attitudes, I have wrestled with many aspects of the story, trying to accurately portray the ways in which English settlers viewed the Indigenous people they encountered—as aliens, as exotic, as subhuman—without perpetuating these views in the text itself. The use of the word "savage" at a few points in the text is part of this wrestling: no modern reader should be comfortable with this word and its violent history, but leaving it out altogether seemed to gloss over the harshness of European attitudes towards peoples such as the Beothuk, the Powhatan, the Lenape, all of whom my characters encounter in this trilogy. I have therefore used the word in some places to reflect that harshness. Attitudes among European nations differed, also; the French, for example, were more likely to treat Indigenous people as respected allies in this period than the English were.

These are broad generalizations, and we all know the devastating consequences that unfolded over the next several centuries. What interested me was: how did colonization appear to "ordinary" colonizers—not the leaders or influencers, but working-class people who moved to the colonies to better their own situation? When confronted with the fact that their new home was being built on someone else's land, how did they cope with this knowledge?

Some, of course, believed wholeheartedly in the goal of converting and assimilating the natives; some went further and carried out acts of violence against the Indigenous people they encountered. Most probably dealt with the wrongs of both colonization and slavery the way we deal with injustices in the world today when we know our own actions are complicit—such as buying goods made by people working in unjust conditions. Some of our settler-colonizer ancestors may have felt a little uneasy about the treatment of Indigenous people and enslaved Africans, but found justifications, telling themselves that it wasn't so bad, and that anyway, there was little they could do to change it. Over generations, they would teach their descendants that what happened was not only unavoidable, but the right thing to do.

From those who knowingly participated in genocide to those who just stood by and allowed it to happen, *all* my settler-colonizer ancestors (which is all my ancestors) were complicit in the extinction of the Beothuk and, in a broader sense, in all the devastation wrought by the founding of their "New World." And they stayed here, and taught us, their descendants, that it was "our home and native land." I didn't want to write a novel about settlers without grappling with those realities.

In thinking through these issues, I have been helped greatly not only by the many books I've read about settlement, but by sharing parts of this book with an Indigenous Sociocultural Reader, Leahdawn Helena, a member of Qalipu First Nation, whose insight and suggestions were extremely helpful. As always throughout the process of writing about this time period, I have also leaned heavily on the expertise of people who are more knowledgeable about the early seventeenth century than I could ever be. For this book, those people include especially Dr. Beverly "Bly" Straube, Senior Curator at James Fort-Yorktown Foundation, Virginia; Dr. Neil Kennedy of Memorial University of Newfoundland; and of course the expert on all things Cupids-related, William Gilbert, Chief Archaeologist with the Baccalieu Trail Heritage Corporation and Site Supervisor at the Cupids Cove Plantation Provincial Historic Site. As is always the case, any historical errors that remain in the book after consultation with these wise people are entirely my own.

Thanks to those who read earlier drafts of this book and gave me feedback: Jennifer Morgan, Lori Savory, Christine Hennebury, Michelle Butler Hallett, and my dad, Don Morgan; your input is unfailingly helpful. To the wonderful team at Breakwater Books and my editor Marnie Parsons, infinite thanks. I am grateful as always to the Newfoundland and Labrador Arts Council for Professional Project Grants that helped to support this project. I would be nowhere without the constant love and support of my husband, Jason, and my two young-adult offspring, Emma and Chris, both pursuing their own paths as creative artists.

Much of this book was researched and written after COVID-19 became a reality in our lives in March 2020. Lockdown gave me extra time to write, which was wonderful—but research was made more difficult because of the impossibility of travel, and, for some of the time, even the impossibility of meeting with people face to face or visiting the university library.

I had dreamed that while researching this book I would visit Bermuda, maybe make another trip to Virginia, and spend some time on a sailing ship to literally learn the ropes. 2020–2021 being the year it was, none of those things happened. Perhaps most inconvenient of all, when the coffee shop where I most often went to write reopened after lockdown, I joyfully went back to writing there—until that location closed permanently. Somehow, I still struggled on to finish the book, but I'll always miss the staff at Starbucks in Chapters, who felt like extended family to me for all the time I spent with them.

The final volume of the Cupids Trilogy will be released by Breakwater Books in Fall 2023.

TRUDY J. MORGAN-COLE IS A WRITER AND TEACHER IN ST. John's, Newfoundland. Her historical novels include *A Roll of the Bones*, *By the Rivers of Brooklyn*, *That Forgetful Shore*, *A Sudden Sun*, and *Most Anything You Please*. At her day job, she works with adult learners at The Murphy Centre. She is married and is the mom of two young adults. Trudy's passion is uncovering and reimagining the untold stories of women in history.